THE KIN

Also by Peter Dickinson

The Weathermonger
Heartsease
The Devil's Children
Emma Tupper's Diary
The Dancing Bear
The Gift
Chance, Luck and Destiny
The Blue Hawk
Annerton Pit
Hepzibah
Tulku
City of Gold
The Seventh Raven
Healer
Giant Cold
A Box of Nothing
Merlin Dreams
Eva
AK
A Bone from a Dry Sea
Time and the Clock Mice, Etcetera
Shadow of a Hero
Chuck and Danielle
Touch and Go
The Lion Tamer's Daughter

PETER DICKINSON

THE KIN

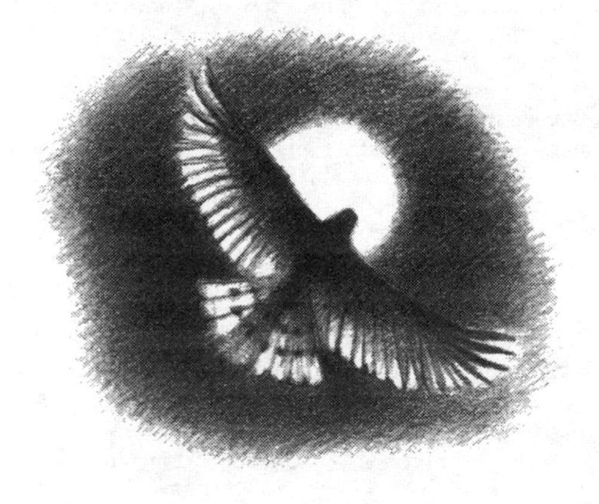

Illustrations by Ian Andrew

MACMILLAN
CHILDREN'S BOOKS

First published 1998 by Macmillan Children's Books
a division of Macmillan Publishers Limited
25 Eccleston Place, London SW1W 9NF
Basingstoke and Oxford
www.macmillan.co.uk

Associated companies throughout the world

ISBN 0 333 73735 0

5 7 9 8 6

A CIP catalogue record for this book is available from
the British Library.

Phototypeset by Intype London Ltd
Printed and bound in Great Britain by Mackays of Chatham plc, Kent

THE KIN

Contents

Before you start	vii
SUTH'S STORY	1
NOLI'S STORY	151
KO'S STORY	307
MANA'S STORY	465

BEFORE YOU START

It is Africa, about two hundred thousand years ago.

The first modern human beings have evolved. There are other people in the world, earlier kinds of human, but these are the first *homo sapiens sapiens*, which is what everyone in the world is today. They are probably the first humans to have language. They can speak.

At first, there are very few of these new people, but they are clever and strong and do well. Their numbers grow, so that they have to move outwards and find fresh lands where they can live. This happens in waves, with long intervals between. This book is about a group of these people, the Kin, just after one of these waves has started. They have been forced to leave the lands where they have lived for as long as they can remember and must look for new ones.

I have made almost all of it up. The real people who lived in those days left very few traces – the stone tools they made, fossils of their own bones and the bones of animals they ate, the ashes of their fires, and so on. What were they like? How did they live? Even the experts can only guess, using their imaginations and the few facts they do know. So that's what I've done too.

I have put 'Oldtales' between the chapters. I believe that we have always wondered how we came to be here, and why things happen, and whether there is somebody wise and strong and strange who made everything in the first place. One of the ways we wonder is to invent stories. The tales are the stories the Kin have made up, to explain things to themselves.

Peter Dickinson

SUTH'S STORY

For Nicholas

SUTH'S STORY

Contents

Chapter One 5
Oldtale: THE FIRST GOOD PLACE 13
Chapter Two 15
Oldtale: MONKEY MAKES FIRE 24
Chapter Three 27
Oldtale: HOW PEOPLE WERE MADE 36
Chapter Four 39
Oldtale: THE CHILDREN OF AMMU 45
Chapter Five 48
Oldtale: ODUTU BELOW THE MOUNTAIN 56
Chapter Six 58
Oldtale: HOW SORROW CAME 69
Chapter Seven 71
Oldtale: DA AND DATTA 82
Chapter Eight 85
Oldtale: MONKEY IS FOUND OUT 100
Chapter Nine 102
Oldtale: PEOPLE HUNT BLACK ANTELOPE 114
Chapter Ten 117
Oldtale: THE CHOOSING OF MATES 128
Chapter Eleven 131
Oldtale: NIGLU 142
Chapter Twelve 146

CHAPTER ONE

Fingers pressed Suth's cheek, in the corner by the jawbone. He woke. A mouth breathed in his ear.

'Come.'

Noli.

She withdrew.

Carefully, as if merely turning in his sleep, he rolled himself away from the rest of the Kin, who slept in a huddle for warmth from the desert night. Suth was a child, and now had no father or mother, so his place was on the outside of the huddle. So was Noli's, for the same reasons.

He lay still, waited, rolled again and on hands and knees crawled silently clear. There was a half moon rising, casting long shadows.

'Here.'

Noli's faint whisper came from the blackness beside a boulder. Suth crawled towards her. She took his hand, put her other hand to his mouth for silence, and led him away.

In the shadow of another boulder she stopped and put her mouth to his ear.

'I dreamed. Moonhawk came. She showed me water.'

'Where?'

She pointed back, almost along the line they had travelled all day.

'In the morning you tell Bal,' whispered Suth.

'He says I lie.'

She was right. Bal was their leader. He dreamed the dreams that Moonhawk sent, showing him things he needed to know for the safety of the Kin. But then it had been Noli that had dreamed about the coming of the murderous strangers, who did not belong to any of the Kins, and spoke with words that none of them knew. It had been Noli that had dreamed of the killing of fathers and brothers, the taking of mothers and sisters.

Moonhawk had not shown these things to Bal, and when Noli had told of them he had struck her and said that she lied. Moonhawk came only to him in his dreams.

And yet Noli's dream had come true, and what was left of the Kin had fled from the Good Places they knew, and Bal had led them into Dry Hills, looking for somewhere new to live.

Then again Noli had dreamed. In this dream Moonhawk had come to her and shown her the endless desert, waterless and foodless, that they would come to after they passed Dry Hills. And again, when she had told her dream, Bal had struck her and said that she lied.

And yet it had come true.

'In the morning we tell the others,' said Suth.

'No, we go alone. We go now, along the way we came. We find the little ones that were left behind. We take them to the water. All this Moonhawk showed me.'

She took him by the hand and led him on. He didn't resist, though for the first time in his life he was leaving the Kin. He was walking away into the night without any adult to lead him, with only a girl for company, even younger than himself. Ever since the fight with the strangers, when he had seen his father killed and his mother taken, he had been in a kind of dull dream. Nothing made sense any more. Moonhawk told Noli what to do, and Noli told Suth. That was enough.

They found their way without trouble. They were used to wide empty spaces, and their sense of direction was strong. Here and there they remembered the shape of a boulder, or a dry ravine, that they had passed on the outward journey. And the night dews freshened the faint scents that the Kin had left as they had come this way. There were no other smells to confuse them. Nothing lived here. In all the long day they had seen no tracks, nothing that moved, not a lizard, not even a scorpion. At least where there was nothing to eat there would be no big hunters stalking the night.

They walked at the steady pace that the Kin had used, journeying between one Good Place and the next. It grew colder. Slowly the moon rose. When it was almost halfway up the sky they stopped, without a word from either of them. They raised their heads and sniffed. Water.

'Moonhawk showed you this?' said Suth.

'No, not this. She showed me water in the hills.'

'We came by in the daytime. Why did we not smell this? Why did Bal not smell it? He finds water where no one else can find it.'

'I do not know. Is it a dew trap, Suth? Like the dew trap at Tarutu Rock?'

They turned and in a short while came to a wide pit in the ground. As they walked down into it they felt new layers of chill gathering around them. Soon the rocks they trod on were slippery with dew. But this was not like the dew trap they knew, where the moisture gathered at the bottom into a rocky pool, which didn't dry up until the sun was high. Here there was only a gravel floor and the water seeped away. They kneeled and licked the wetness from a large sloping boulder. It was not enough to swallow, but soothed their sore lips and parched mouths. For a little while they rested and licked and rested, then found their way back to their trail and walked on.

By the time that the moon was overhead they could see, out across the desert plain, the barrier of jagged hills through which Bal had led them two days earlier. Suth remembered how they had stopped on the last ridge and stared at what lay before them under the evening sun, a vast flatness, mottled yellow and grey, boulders and pebbles and ash and sand, and not a leaf or stem anywhere, all still pulsing with heat after the burning day.

Some of the Kin had begun to mutter unhappily. Bal had swung and glared at them, hunching his shoulders and shaking his mane out to show them who was leader.

'There are new Good Places there,' he had growled. 'Water and game. Moonhawk showed me. Moonhawk showed me this too. We must go fast through the desert, or we die. We must carry our small ones. But they are too many. Some have no fathers, no mothers, to carry them. Those we leave here. We build a lair for them. In the lair they have shade. They are safe from animals. We find our new Good Places. Then some of us come back. They fetch these small ones. Perhaps they still live.'

He had chosen four children who had lost their parents in the fighting – Ko and Mana, who were too little to walk all day, Tinu, who was older but weak from a fever, and Noli's little brother, Otan, who could stand but not yet walk. The others had helped Noli carry him this far.

Nobody had argued, though they knew that the children would live for only a day, and perhaps a night, but not another day. They could see that what Bal said was true. The Good Places he promised them might or might not exist, but if they tried to carry these extra children through the dreadful desert below they would never get there.

So the next morning they had found a place where one rock leaned against another to make a kind of cave and had put the children into it. They walled them in with smaller rocks to keep them safe from animals, and told them to wait there, and left them looking scared and dazed. Noli had let them take Otan from her, and then turned away, weeping. But she'd said nothing.

'The small ones are dead,' Suth said.

'No,' said Noli.

They walked on. Now the moon moved down the sky. Day would come before it set. Slowly the hills loomed nearer and higher and they began to climb. As they did the moonlight paled and the shadows lost their sharpness. Day came almost at once, a clear grey light still fresh with the night chill and the dew. To their right the sky turned pale gold. Every detail of the dry and rocky slope stood sharp and clear.

Noli looked ahead and pointed. There were the two leaning rocks. This was the place.

She quickened her pace, but Suth caught her wrist. Something had moved, a blue grey shape like a shadow prowling in front of the two rocks. It returned, nosing at the piled stones, sniffing for the flesh behind them. It scratched at the pile with a paw. Some kind of fox-thing, though different from the yellow and brown foxes that had scavenged around the Good Places that the Kin had been driven from.

Suth picked up a stone, weighed it in his hand, put it soundlessly down and chose a heavier one. Noli took another. Side by side but a little apart the two crept forward, moving and pausing and moving as they had watched their elders do, hunting unsuspecting prey. The foxes that Suth knew had learned to be afraid of people, and were shy and quick and hard to catch, but this one was too excited by the smells from behind the rock pile to notice as the hunters crept nearer.

Not until Suth was only two paces away did it sense something, turn and see him. It was not just in colour that it was different. It did not fear people.

Snarling, it leaped for Suth's belly, but his arm was already poised for a blow. He swung as it came, and the rock caught the fox full force on the head, knocking it sideways. Then Noli was on it, pounding down with her rock. It thrashed aside and tried to rise, but before it was on its feet Suth struck it again with all his strength at the point where the neck joined the skull. It collapsed, twitched once, and lay still.

They struck it several more blows to make sure, then left it lying and went to the rock pile. There was no sound from inside.

They are dead, Suth thought.

'Are you there, Tinu?' he said softly. 'Mana? Ko? It is me, Suth. And Noli.'

A faint mumbling sound answered. That was Tinu, who had a twisted mouth and did not speak clearly. There was a wail from a smaller child. With a gush of hope Suth started to pull the pile of rocks down. As soon as she could reach, Noli joined in. The sun rose on their backs. When the wall was low enough they craned over.

Tinu was crouching in the little cave with Otan in her arms. Ko sat huddled beside her, blinking at the light. Mana lay on her side, unmoving, but she stirred and moaned as Suth reached in, took Otan, and passed him to Noli. He pulled more rocks down until Tinu could help Ko and Mana, still half asleep, to scramble out. Tinu came last.

Noli was cradling little Otan to her chest, feeling for his heartbeat and listening for his breath. 'My brother lives,' she whispered, shuddering with relief.

The others waited. Three pairs of dark, anxious eyes gazed at Suth. He could see what they were thinking. *Where was the rest of the Kin? Where were the grown men and women? Where was Bal, the leader?* Ko and Mana were little more than babies, though Ko was sturdy and big for his age. Suth had never taken much notice of Mana, a quiet, watchful little girl, with the same dark skin and black, coarse hair as everyone else in the eight Kins.

Tinu was different. Something had gone wrong when she was born, so that her jaw opened more sideways than down and she never learned to speak properly. She was small too, for her age, and extremely skinny, with insect-thin limbs. She hated to be noticed and looked at. As soon as Suth's glance fell on her, she turned her head away.

'Thirsty,' she mumbled.

'Noli knows where water is,' said Suth.

'It is not far,' said Noli. 'Suth killed food. You come.'

Suth heaved the dead fox onto his shoulder. Noli settled Otan onto her hip and led the way, with Tinu next and the two small ones scrambling behind her across the stony slope. Suth came last, helping them when they needed him. He felt different now. The fox was heavy, but its weight gave him strength. He had done something. He had killed food. These others, they needed him. Without him, they would die.

Oldtale

THE FIRST GOOD PLACE

Black Antelope was chief among the First Ones.

He said, 'Now we make a place where we can live.'

He breathed upon the bare ground, and where he had breathed the young grass grew, tender for him to eat.

Then Snake crawled through the grasslands, making tracks, which he could follow. And Crocodile dug holes and filled them with clean water, where she could lie and wait. And Weaver planted trees, so that his wives had somewhere to hang their nests, and Parrot added sweet nuts and fruits to the trees, because he was greedy, and the Ant Mother chewed the fallen branches from the trees and mixed the chewings into the ground to make good soft earth for her nests, and Fat Pig planted the earth with juicy roots to fill his stomach, and Moonhawk built crags from which she could watch while the others slept, and Little Bat made caves in the crags, where she could hide from Moonhawk.

So they all worked together to make the First Good Place, according to their needs.

Only Monkey did nothing.

He watched the others at work, and then he climbed Weaver's trees and ate Parrot's fruits and nuts, and he dug in the Ant Mother's earth and ate Fat Pig's roots, and he slept in Little Bat's caves and drank from Crocodile's water holes, and he set traps in Snake's tracks, and scrambled over Moonhawk's crags. But he did not often go into Black Antelope's grasslands because he was the strongest and Monkey was afraid of him.

CHAPTER TWO

The water was a thin trickle, oozing down a narrow crack in the cliff. They couldn't get their faces in to lap, so all they could do was slide a hand and wet their fingertips and suck. The water had a strong taste and a faint smell of foul eggs, like the water at Yellowhole, where the Kin used to drink. Before she had any herself, Noli gave her fingers to Otan to suck. At first nothing happened, but then the small dry lips moved faintly, and a hand clenched and unclenched. It was the first sign of life that anyone but Noli had seen in him.

After a while, Tinu found that if she put her fingers into the crack at a certain angle the water ran along the lower edge of her palm and gathered into drops on her wrist bone, where she could suck them off before they fell. The others copied her.

As soon as he'd drunk enough, Suth looked for the right sort of rock, so that he could try to make a cutter and butcher little pieces of meat off the fox carcass for the small ones to chew. He had often watched his father stoneworking, and had tried to copy what he did, but it was men's work. Boys didn't get taught it. His father had known which were the right stones, and where to strike them, but he couldn't say how he knew. His eye and his hand had told him *this one* and *here*. So all Suth had been able to do was watch, and then try for himself. He'd learned that it wasn't as easy as it looked.

Besides, good stones were only found in some places. There might be none on this hillside at all. Suth chose several and squatted down by a flat boulder. Steadying one stone on it, he hammered down with another, using a slanting blow, trying to chip off a large flake.

Nothing happened. He tried again and again, but the target stone kept twisting in his grasp. Between their turns at the water the others watched him, as he tried different stones and different angles of strike. Sometimes he broke off a few chips, but nothing large enough to grasp and nothing with a cutting edge to it.

Without warning the stone he had been using as a hammer shattered as it struck the target. The pieces flew apart. The shock numbed his arm to the elbow. He was rubbing the feeling back into it when Tinu, always shy and uncertain, anxiously showed him a flake that had fallen at her feet, a round sliver so thin in places that when he held it up he could see light through it. Testing it with his thumb he found that along one edge it was as sharp as anything he had seen his father make, though he knew his father would have thrown it away because it was so fragile. A good cutter was thicker than this, but he thought it might do if he was careful. He laughed at the luck of it, and the small ones laughed too, not understanding why.

Thirsty again after the work, he went back to the crack. While he was slowly drinking, Tinu came up holding a stick she had broken from one of the scrawny bushes that grew in the gully below. These were the first plants Suth had seen in three days.

Tinu waited till he had finished, and then edged up, as if she was expecting him to bark at her to go away, and eased the end of the stick into the crack. Suth watched her, puzzled, as she tried it at different angles. Then, wonderfully, a drop of water appeared on a side twig beneath it, and another and another. She cupped her free hand under them and caught them as they fell, until her palm was full. She lapped the water up and looked at him, still as if she expected him to yell at her or strike her.

'Good, good,' he said, smiling. 'Now you show Noli.'

While the others were learning how to use the stick, he picked up the fox and laid it on its back. Holding the flake of stone between thumb and forefinger he drew the cutting edge slowly along the seam of the belly, again and again, never pressing hard for fear of breaking his cutter but gradually slicing through the tough skin.

The three girls watched in silence, but Ko squatted by his side, jaw set, frowning, longing to join in, longing to help. Suth was about to snarl at him to keep clear when he thought, *Ko saw his father die. He saw his mother taken. He was walled in a dark place for a day and a night. He does not understand any of this. He does not understand there is no Kin now for him to belong to. I understand all this. With Noli's help I am leader now. We are their father and their mother.*

So he told Ko to hold the fox's tail clear while he worked. It didn't need holding, but it gave Ko something to do, and they both felt better.

Slowly a scratch formed. The scratch became a cut, and then Suth was slicing into the fat beneath the skin. He sawed at the ends of the cut, widening it until he could plunge his hand through and pull out the guts. Still very careful of his precious tool he cut the liver free.

Suth was the leader now, so he ate first, cutting himself a mouthful before hacking off pieces for the others while he chewed. Fox meat was better roasted, and even then had a strong, rancid taste. Still, it was food, and none of them had eaten cooked food since the fight, when the strangers had taken away their fire log along with the women.

They chewed in silence. Noli put her mouth to Otan's and forced some of her chewings between his lips. He sucked them in and gaped for more.

'That is enough,' said Suth, when they had eaten the liver and the heart, though his own stomach still ached with hunger.

'Yes,' said Noli. 'It is strong meat. Too strong.'

The Kin were used to empty stomachs. Sometimes a Good Place would fail. They would find no game, or there would have been a bush fire that destroyed the plants they'd expected to harvest. Then they would have to travel on, foodless, to the next Good Place. Even the little ones understood that cramming a starved stomach with meat ended with a bellyful of burning stones.

Suth cut away the parts of the fox that people do not eat and told Mana to carry them well away along the slope and leave them there. The rest of the carcass he laid against the foot of the cliff and piled rocks over it to keep it safe. Then he drank again and sat looking out over the burning plain below. Somewhere out there what was left of the Kin was moving further and further away. Soon they would be dead, in the waterless desert. He would never see them again.

Another thought came to him. No. We six children, on this hillside – we are what is left of the Kin.

He looked at the others. Tinu, so skinny and small, so ashamed of her odd face and speech that she had never dared be anyone's friend. But smart all the same – the trick she had done with the twig in the crack showed that. Little Ko, who had always made everyone laugh – almost as soon as he could walk he was trying to swagger like a man. Mana. Suth realized he knew almost nothing about Mana, had barely noticed her before now, she was so quiet, though he had known her since she was born. Otan, lying asleep in Noli's lap. He was still too small to know or guess much about. And Noli herself . . .

When had Moonhawk begun to visit her in her dreams? Suth wondered. He had never heard of any of the First Ones coming to a child, not in any of the Kins. He knew Noli well. His father and hers had been brothers. He had played with her since they were babies, walked beside her as the Kin journeyed from one Good Place to the next. She'd never said anything about Moonhawk visiting her in her dreams.

But then, half a moon ago, she'd woken them all where they lay by springing to her feet in the darkest part of the night and shrieking about the strangers, the cruel fighting, the blood . . .

And Bal had cursed her, and said she was only a stupid child having a nightmare. When her shrieks had gone on, he'd struck her. He had seen nothing.

But three days later, as they gathered for their evening meal, the strangers had attacked.

Suth thought of a time when he had been small. The Kin had come to a place called Ragala Flat, and had found another Kin, Weaver, already there. There had been great feasting, and giving of gifts. But while the fire had still burned bright, Bal and an old man from the Weaver Kin had gone off together into the dark.

'Where does Bal go with that old man?' Suth had asked his father.

His father had made a sign, putting his palm to his mouth.

'They go to talk dream stuff,' he had muttered. 'It is a thing that is not spoken of. It is secret.'

As he had grown older Suth had realized that in each of the Kins there was one person like Bal. Their own First One came to that person in dreams. It didn't need to be the leader, though Bal was. It could be a man or a woman. But it was never a child. How could it be? And yet Noli . . .

She was looking at him as if she'd guessed his thoughts, but all she said was, 'What must we do now, Suth?'

'We rest,' he answered. 'All are tired. We have water. We have meat for three days.'

'The meat is too strong,' she said. 'Soon the small ones are sick. They must have plant stuff.'

'Yes. All that below is bitter bush, I think. Let us look.'

Leaving the little ones in the shade of the cliff, they climbed down the gully but, as they had thought, only one sort of shrub seemed to grow there, with twisted grey branches and round, fat leathery leaves. It was common in dry places, but the Kin did not eat it. Experimentally Suth nibbled a leaf, and spat. The harsh taste stayed in his mouth a long while despite a lot of rinsings with water from the crack.

Tired from their night's walk they slept through the middle of the day, but were woken by Otan's crying. He was hungry again, and so were they all, so Suth fetched out the carcass of the fox. Ants had found it, but he brushed them away and butchered more meat, though again he wouldn't let anyone eat more than a few mouthfuls.

'Today we rest,' said Suth. 'Tomorrow we go.'

'Where do we go?' said Noli.

'I do not know. Perhaps Moonhawk sends you a dream,' said Suth.

'Perhaps,' said Noli.

He was too anxious to sleep. They could not stay here long. If they tried to follow Bal across the desert they would die. If they tried to go back through Dry Hills they would almost certainly die too. The Kin had only made it as far as they had because they had set out with full water gourds. Suth's little group had none.

Restless, he rose and went to explore along the slope. There might be more water seeping out of the cliff, with good plant stuff feeding from it. That would at least allow them to stay here a few more days, until the little ones became stronger.

It didn't look promising. The slope became steeper, and changed to dangerous scree – a great stretch of loose rocks ending far below in what looked like another cliff. He tossed a stone down. It dislodged another, and between them they started a small avalanche, which went rumbling out of sight. No, not this way, he decided, and went back to the others.

Noli was awake, trying to comfort Ko, who had gobbled his meat without chewing it enough and was whining about a stomach ache.

'Did Moonhawk come?' Suth asked.

'No,' she said.

He lay down, more anxious than ever, trying to remember any details he could about the journey across Dry Hills. But he had been in his trance of shock then, hardly noticing what happened around him, so all he could recall was endless thirsty trudging across hot stony ground, with rough slopes rising on either side, and no sign of food or water anywhere.

As the sun went down he was still worrying about this, lying on his back and gazing up at the sky, hard blue all day, but now paler, greyer, and turning golden towards the west.

Out of that sky he saw a flock of birds descending, circling around and around, wings spread, coming nearer and nearer until they disappeared behind the rim of the cliff.

Suth's spirits rose. This was something he had seen before. There was a Good Place called Stinkwater, which the Kin had used to visit at two special seasons.

At other times it was a useless marsh, its water black and foul. But then at the good seasons the birds came spiralling down out of the sky, countless, tens beyond tens beyond tens, some so weak and tired with long flying that they were easy to catch. Several Kins would gather at those times at Stinkwater, and there would be fine eating for everybody.

Noli too had seen the birds and had thought the same thought.

'There is a Good Place up there,' she said.

'We look for a way tomorrow,' he said, 'when we go back through Dry Hills.'

Oldtale

MONKEY MAKES FIRE

Snake and Crocodile and Fat Pig and the others came to Monkey and said, 'Monkey, you eat our food. You drink our water. You sleep in our caves. Your chattering disturbs us on our crags. But you make nothing of your own.'

Monkey said, 'Very well. I am cleverer than you are. Now I do something better than any of you.'

He thought for a day and a night and a day, and then while Black Antelope slept, he looked at the sky and saw a great cloud that covered the moon.

Then Monkey clapped his hands, and so great was the sound that the cloud burst and fire fell out and poured down to the earth and burned the trees and the grasses and dried up the water holes and smote the crags where Moonhawk perched and shrivelled the roots on the ground, and only Little Bat was safe in her caves.

Little Bat looked out and saw what was being done, so she flew to where Black Antelope slept and squeaked in his ear, 'Monkey is killing our Good Place with fire. Stop him.'

Black Antelope woke and he too saw what was being done. He reared up and breathed through his nostrils and blew out the fire.

He called to Monkey to come, and Monkey was afraid, and hid. But Moonhawk spied him from her crag and told Snake, who went softly and coiled himself around him and caught him and carried him to Black Antelope.

Black Antelope said, 'You have done bad things. Now I make your skin itch. It is like fire. You must put all our Good Place to rights. Make it as it was. Then I take your itch from you.'

Then with his skin itching like fire Monkey set to work, but he could not do it. He poured water into the holes, but it was salt and sour. He put roots into the ground, but they made Fat Pig sick. He grew trees, but they were too thorny for Weaver's wives to nest in, and their fruits fell to the ground before they were ripe.

In the end Monkey came to the others and said, 'I cannot do this. You must help me.'

They said, 'What do you give us in return?'

Monkey said, 'I have nothing to give.'

They said, 'You give this. We tell you a thing. You do it. You do this for a whole moon, for each of us in turn.'

So they agreed, and all in their ways made that Place good again, with clean water and fine trees and grasses and sweet nuts and fruits and roots, and in exchange Monkey worked for each of them in turn, doing whatever he was told from morning till night for a whole moon. He did not like this at all.

One day, while he was catching insects for Little Bat, Monkey smelled smoke. He looked and found a spark of the fire he had made still smouldering. He fetched dry leaves and blew on the spark and fed the leaves into it until he had fire again. Then he found a hollow log and sealed the ends with clay and put the fire in the middle and made the first fire log, which he hid in a secret place.

When all the work was done Monkey went to Black Antelope and said, 'Look. Now our Good Place is as it was before.'

Black Antelope looked, and saw it was true. But he did not see where Monkey had hidden the fire log. Then he breathed on Monkey and made his skin clean.

Only one small patch under his armpit still itched like fire. That was because of the fire log.

And that is why Monkey is always scratching.

CHAPTER THREE

They slept well away from the water, in case a fox or some other hunter came to drink in the night. Suth and Noli piled rocks around a nook in the cliff to make a small lair where they could huddle, and nothing disturbed them.

In the morning Suth let them eat more meat and told them to drink as much as their stomachs would hold. While they did he cut off a leg of the fox to carry with them, breaking his cutter as he wrestled with the tendons of the joint. When he had finished he looked for Noli, but couldn't see her. Tinu had gone back to sleep. Mana was playing a pebble game with little Otan. Ko was banging two rocks together, trying to make his own cutter.

'Where is Noli?' Suth asked.

Mana pointed along the cliff and he saw her, far beyond shouting range, picking her way across the dangerous rock-covered slope.

He was angry. The morning was already hot. They

had far to go, back along the way they had come, before they could begin to look for a way to climb to the top. This was not how a leader should be treated. He would have words to say to Noli.

When at last she came back he rose and went to meet her, without thought hunching his shoulders and shaking his mane out to show her his anger. She answered by kneeling and pattering her hands on the ground in front of his feet.

'I found a way up the cliff,' she said.

He heard and understood, but his shoulders and neck stayed rigid and his lips taut across bared teeth, as if he had been Bal. It wasn't anything he was doing on purpose. His body did it to him, because he was angry. Then he relaxed, and laughed, and helped her up.

'Moonhawk showed you?' he said.

'No. But . . . it is hard . . . I was . . . pulled.'

He didn't understand. 'Perhaps it was Moonhawk,' he suggested.

'Perhaps.'

'Good. Show me.'

He let Noli lead the way, with Otan on her hip, and Ko, Mana, and Tinu in single file behind her. He went last to make sure the little ones moved with care. When they reached the slope of loose stuff where Suth had turned back last night, Noli started to pick her way across. Suth made the others wait, and then follow well apart, moving one at a time, testing each foothold.

But it was Suth himself who fell. A rock twisted under him. He felt himself going, as if the whole hillside was sliding away beneath him, and flung himself flat with his arms reaching sideways, then lay there, gasping, while the avalanche he had started roared away beneath him. He rose and saw with relief that the others were all safe and waiting for him, though their eyes were still wide with fright.

They moved on, more carefully than ever, until the cliff seemed to come to an end. Noli edged her way around the corner and disappeared. Then Mana, then Tinu, then Ko. Suth came last of all and saw what Noli had found.

It was as if the mountain had been broken apart, and the two pieces had shifted against each other, leaving a crack between them. The ledge that the children were standing on led into the crack.

'See,' said Noli. 'It is the same as Tarutu Rock.'

Tarutu Rock was a huge isolated crag, which the Kin had used as an overnight lair. It had a dew trap nearby. The rock was a flat-topped pillar, which could only be climbed by a deep crack running up one side. This crack was like that, only far, far higher.

Suth gazed up, hesitating. The small ones might need to be carried some of the way. Suppose they all got stuck . . .

But he knew in his heart that the journey back through Dry Hills would be just as dangerous. They might all die of thirst on the way. While somewhere up above this cliff there was a good chance of finding water. Why else should those birds have settled down last night?

And besides, Noli had said she was 'pulled' to find this crack . . .

He clambered into it. The rock surface felt faintly moist. The crack faced away from the sun, and its depths would be in shade until the evening. That decided him.

'We try,' he said.

The climb was very slow and tiring. They had Otan to carry. Tinu was still weak from her fever. And though the little ones were used to scrambling up to lairs, they still needed help in the difficult places – though Ko, of course, kept wanting to prove that he could manage all on his own. At least they were mostly in shade, and a slight breeze flowed down the crack, cooled by the chill in the rock.

At last, when the sun was so high that the rocks in the desert cast no shadow, Suth looked up and saw only sky above them. This stretch of climbing had been easy enough for the small ones to manage almost without help. Mana was just ahead of Suth, then Noli with Otan, then Ko and Tinu.

'Wait, Mana,' said Suth. 'I go see.'

He scrambled past her and put his head cautiously out into the open. To his disappointment he found that they hadn't reached the top after all, only a wide ledge with more cliff rising above it.

He was just clambering out when he heard a harsh cry and a sudden movement to his right. He looked and saw a large bird, some kind of eagle, launching itself away from an untidy heap of twigs on the ledge. For a moment he thought it had flown off, scared by his sudden appearance, but then he heard shrill cheepings from among the twigs and at the same time saw the eagle wheel around and come hurtling in to defend its nestlings. Rapidly he ducked back into the crack.

'Hide! Hide!' he shouted. 'Eagle comes!'

Luckily the crack at this point was deep and narrow. As the eagle rushed closer, Suth huddled back, gripping the fox leg by its shank and holding it ready to strike. The bird was into its attack attitude, with its great hooked talons stretched in front of it, when at the last instant it realized that it couldn't get at its target without crashing its wings into the cliff on either side.

Somehow it managed to stop itself in mid-flight and turn and soar upwards, but at once it swung back and came plunging down to get at Suth from above. There was no hope of fighting it off, so he cowered down and again the narrowness of the crack defeated it.

It attacked again and again from different angles, but at last gave up trying and simply circled with harsh, angry cries above the ledge.

Suth watched it in despair. It was a big, fierce bird, with a vicious beak and talons. A grown man wouldn't have wanted to face it. But the Moonhawks had to cross the ledge. Once inside the crack above they would be safe again.

Somehow he must get out onto the ledge and keep the eagle at bay while Noli and Tinu got the small ones across. What could he use as a weapon? The fox leg wasn't much good. He needed stones, but where on this sheer cliff . . . ? Ah, yes, a little further down they'd had to work their way past a large boulder that had fallen and wedged itself in the crack. Then smaller stuff had fallen on top of it and lodged there . . .

'Tinu,' he called. 'Below you I saw stones, good for throwing. Bring them. Bring many.'

He explained his plan to Noli while Tinu clambered up and down, bringing two or three stones at a time. She passed them to Noli, who handed them on to Suth. He took them and slid them out onto the surface of the ledge.

Each time he reached up the eagle swung menacingly in, so close that its wing tip almost brushed the cliff as it passed. When he had the last stone in his hand, Suth passed the fox leg down to Noli, made sure he had a good foothold, and then reached up and merely pretended to push the stone out onto the ledge with the others.

The bird swung in and down as before. As it crossed above him, Suth flung the stone with all his strength, catching it full on its body just below the outstretched wing. It gave a sharp squawk and fell away. Instantly Suth scrambled out onto the ledge, picking up two more stones as he rose. The bird had recovered at once, and was almost on him, coming along the cliff from his right.

His first stone went wide. He slung the second and instantly flung himself flat against the cliff. The bird missed its strike.

He jumped to his feet and saw a feather drifting away, so he knew he'd scored another good hit. He snatched up two more stones and edged closer to the nest, to draw the eagle from the crack. Now that he had stones, and a place to stand, he felt confident. Stones were the Kin's main weapon. Like all the children, Suth had practised throwing them since he'd been big enough to hold them. He was an excellent shot. He stood poised and ready as the eagle attacked again.

This time it seemed to come more cautiously, which was a mistake as that made it an easier target. His first stone struck home and it wheeled away.

'Ready, Noli!' he called.

The bird circled out, turned and swooped towards him. Would it attack yet again? He watched it, panting.

No, the curve of its flight continued, taking it a safe distance from the ledge.

'Come, Mana!' he shouted as it swung away. 'Quick! Hide in the crack! Good. Noli, wait! It comes again . . . Now! Quick!'

Three times more the bird circled past. Each time it swung away a Moonhawk scrambled out of the crack, across the ledge, and into safety. Suth could hear Noli encouraging Mana to climb on, to make room for the others. When Tinu was across, Suth dashed for the crack. Once inside he waited to catch his breath and let his heart stop pounding, and then climbed on.

As he was working his way past Noli they heard a new wild squawking from below. Craning out they saw that there were now two great birds circling by the ledge, calling to each other.

'The mate comes back to the nest,' said Noli.

'Noli, you are right,' said Suth, sick with the thought of what might have happened if the other bird had come home while he was out on the ledge, with the small ones trying to cross.

Wearily they clambered on, and before very long came out onto a steep rock-strewn slope. Here they rested, and Suth passed the fox leg around for each of them to chew off what they could. Then they struggled on up. There was nothing else to do.

The slope seemed endless. Wherever they could find shade they rested and looked back. Each time they could see more of the desert stretching away beneath them. Never in their lives had they been so high.

'We are climbing into the sky,' said Noli.

The sun was hidden beyond the ridge when they came to another barrier, a jagged line of tall rocks, like the teeth of a monstrous crocodile. Here Suth almost lay down and gave up, but he saw the others looking at him for orders, so without a word he explored along the barrier and edged through a gap between two of the rocks. It twisted on itself, and twisted again, and then they were through.

They paused, and caught their breath. At first, with the setting sun in their eyes, it was hard for them to be sure what they were looking at. But then they saw that ahead of them lay a vast, secret bowl, an ancient volcanic crater concealed among the mountains, ringed by the ridge on which they stood. The bottom of the bowl was hidden from them by the slope, but it seemed to be filled with a light mist. The sun had almost set and their shadows were long across the slope before they reached another edge where they could look down.

Below them, veiled in greyness, lay a wide green basin. It was not like anything they had ever seen, so soft, so green, so misty. Even here, out on the barren slope, the air smelled of sap and growth.

There had been nothing like this in their world. The very best of the Good Places they knew were hot and dry and filled with glaring sunlight. Young grass that was fresh and green at sunrise would be tired and dusty by noon, and the few trees were tough and twiggy, with small dusty leaves hardened to withstand such heat. They had never before seen forest. It took Suth a little while to grasp that the strange green mass that half-filled the bottom of the bowl was trees.

Noli, standing beside him, sighed.

'It is a Good Place,' she whispered. 'It is the First Good Place.'

All five of them stood and stared. Even Ko was silent in wonder.

Oldtale

HOW PEOPLE WERE MADE

Black Antelope said, 'It is time for us to make people. Let each give something. From these things we make people.'

Snake gave two skins, which he had outgrown.

Crocodile gave teeth she had shed.

The Ant Mother gave earth from her nest.

Moonhawk gave the shell of an egg she had hatched.

Parrot gave the shell from one of his wife's eggs.

Little Bat gave some of her droppings.

Fat Pig gave strong hairs from his hackles.

Monkey bit the ball of his thumb and squeezed out drops of his own blood.

'What does Weaverbird give?' said the others.

'Weaver and his wives build the people, because they know how,' said Black Antelope.

'And what do you give?' they asked him.

'I give breath,' he said.

'What shape do we make these people?' they asked him.

'Let them be long and thin to slither along the ground,' said Snake.

'Let them have thick hides and great teeth, to lie in wait in water,' said Crocodile.

'Let them be very many and small and quick,' said the Ant Mother.

'Let them be fat,' said Fat Pig.

'Let them fly through the air with wings,' said Little Bat and Moonhawk and Parrot.

'Let them be like me,' said Monkey.

'These people are their own shape,' said Black Antelope.

Then Weaver summoned his wives and together they built two people. They broke up Crocodile's teeth to be the bones of two skeletons, and mixed Monkey's blood with the earth from the Ant Mother's nest to be the flesh of two bodies. These they bound around with the two skins that Snake gave. On top they put Moonhawk's eggshell and Parrot's to be the skulls, and filled them with Little Bat's droppings to be the brains. Lastly they added Fat Pig's hackles to be the hair.

Still these people had no shape, only two round bodies with round heads on top. And they did not move or speak.

Then Black Antelope breathed on them, and filled them with his breath, and they grew arms and legs and ears and noses, and fingers and toes formed on their hands and feet. And they woke and stood up.

The one whose skull was a parrot shell was the man, and his name was An. The one whose skull was the shell of Moonhawk's egg was the woman, and her name was Ammu.

The First Ones stood and watched them, to see what they would do, but were not themselves seen, because they had made themselves invisible.

The man and the woman looked around and saw the First Good Place. They looked at each other, and laughed, and were happy.

'These people are like me. They are not like you others,' said Monkey. 'My blood did that.'

CHAPTER FOUR

For a long while the Moonhawks gazed at the great green valley below them. At last Suth gathered his wits, looked at the sun, and saw that in a very short while it was going to be dark. Hungry and thirsty though they were, this was not the time to explore.

'Night comes,' he said. 'We must find a lair.'

He began to lead them back up the slope, but before they had gone many paces Noli said, 'Wait,' ran to one side, put Otan down, and kneeled. She took hold of what looked like two small grey stones, lying against each other amid a jumble of other stones. Carefully she twisted them loose. They were held to the ground by a thin tough root, which broke after several turns. Stoneweed. She nibbled around its base until she was able to pull up a flap of thick rind. She took a suck for herself, and another, which she gave, mouth to mouth, to Otan, then passed the plant to Suth. He sucked a little of the dense, oily juice and gave it to Tinu and the little ones. They took their turns without squabbling.

He felt cheered. It was a good sign. Stoneweed was always a lucky find, anywhere. Its juice was strong, and gave strength, as well as quenching thirst, though if even a grown man drank a whole one he would become dazed and stupid.

They climbed back almost to the ridge, looking for some natural lair, but the ground was too open for that, so they huddled against a boulder. Suth and Noli slept with stones in their hands, but nothing disturbed them.

In the early dawn they rose and went back down to the place where they had stood last evening, and again gazed down on the strange green bowl. There was a new smell in the air, an odd reek, like smoke, but not any smoke that Suth had smelled before.

'Did Moonhawk send you a dream?' he said.

'No,' said Noli.

He was disappointed. The more he gazed at what lay below, the more he was afraid. It wasn't ordinary fear, such as fear of a big wild hunter, or fear of Bal when he was angry. Nor was it like a night fear, fear in a bad dream before the horrors begin but the dreamer knows that they are coming.

There were spots in the old Good Places where he had felt a little like this. Tarutu Rock was one. The Kin walked quietly when they came there, and didn't shout or laugh, because it belonged to Little Bat. They would ask her goodwill before they laired there or drank at her dew trap. This place was something like that, but the feeling was far stronger. He stayed rooted where he was, and Noli did the same.

It was Ko, too young to feel such things, who started down the slope. At his movement a basking lizard scuttled off a rock. Further off a ground rat rose on its hind legs to look, then dived into its burrow. That broke the trance. If there was such game here, there must also be water.

'Come,' said Suth, and led the way, peering to the left and right and sniffing the air for danger.

Between the dry slope and the start of the forest lay a belt of scrub – coarse bushes, sometimes growing impenetrably close together, sometimes more scattered. There was no knowing what might be lurking there, let alone in the dark, strange shadows beneath the trees, so Suth led the way along the edge of the belt, moving warily, looking at everything. Where the ground was soft, he stopped and studied it for tracks. He saw several – the scuttlings of ground rats, the slots made by small deer, and the spread prints with a groove between them, where a lizard had passed, dragging its tail. He saw no large paw prints, but he was sure that where there was so much to hunt there must also be hunters. He picked a way around the edge of the soft patches so that the Kin left no tracks of their own. Even on the hard ground, the earth felt faintly moist beneath his feet, as if there had been a heavy dew, though they had slept dry out in their lair on the hill.

'Wait,' called Noli from the rear. 'I smell juiceroot.'

Suth stopped. Yes, there was that thin, bitter odour. He would have noticed it himself if his mind had not been so set on the scents of danger. Exploring down into the scrub they found a bush almost smothered by a straggling creeper with small dull brown flowers.

They traced the vines across the ground to the place where they entered the earth. Stoneweed and juice-root, growing so close together, Suth thought – this was indeed a Good Place.

The ground was too hard to dig with bare hands. With a lot of difficulty they chewed off branches from another bush and made themselves digging sticks with which, morsel by morsel, they began to chip and move the soil away. It was slow work. Among the Kins the men used heavy stone cutters to make themselves strong digging sticks, and hardened their points with fire. The ones Suth and Noli had made were blunt and weak.

Bit by bit they dug a hole. At last they came to the top of the tuber from which the vine grew, and saw that it was fat and pale. That was good. Juiceroot was different from stoneweed. It was full of water, with a faint bittersweet taste, very refreshing and far nicer than the dribble they'd found running out of the cliff below. After you'd sucked the juice out you could eat the stringy flesh as plant food. It was poor stuff, but better than nothing.

They forgot about anything else. The sweat streamed from them as they worked steadily on, until every muscle ached and their hands were torn and sore. This was how you got juiceroot out of the ground. It took all day, but it was worth the effort.

The little ones understood that too. They had seen it all before, so they sat and watched in silence. Noli broke small pieces from the top of the tuber for them to suck. Time passed. Suth was quite unprepared when Tinu gave the sharp hiss that meant Danger.

He looked up and saw her and the little ones staring beyond him.

He straightened and turned.

Men.

Four of them, standing in a line, just a few paces off. They had digging sticks in their hands. They looked like the men in the Kin, with scars on their cheeks to mark them as grown men and very dark skins. But one of them had eyes of two different colours, dark brown and pale. Shakily Suth rose and faced them. His throat was dry. His heart pounded.

There was no point in fighting, no hope in running. He had done wrong. Even among Kin it would be wrong. Snake didn't dig or hunt in Weaver's Good Places, not without giving gifts, not without many words of asking. Men had been killed for this, and women taken.

He kneeled and spread his hands, palm forward, and bowed his head and then looked up at them. Their faces were unfriendly. The man with strange eyes stepped forward, raising his stick for a blow. Suth did not know if he would strike. It might be only a threat, a warning, but he flinched, and tried to cover his head with an arm.

Noli, from behind him, spoke. 'Moonhawk sent us.'

The man hesitated. 'Moonhawk?'

He said the name strangely.

'Moonhawk sent me a dream,' said Noli.

Another man strode to her, snatched her up by the arm, and shook her.

'Where are your others?' he said. 'Where are your grown men? How many?'

He too spoke strangely.

'Five men left only,' Noli gasped. 'Strangers came. They killed our fathers. We fled.'

'These five – they are here?' snarled the man.

'No,' said Noli. 'I think they are dead. Bal led us to an empty place – no food, no water. Moonhawk came in my dream and said I must come back to the little ones. These. Bal left them behind. Suth came too.'

The man who had been about to strike Suth now grabbed him by his hair and hauled him to his feet. He seized his wrist and twisted his arm up behind his back, almost to the breaking point, but Suth didn't struggle or cry out.

The men spoke together. Then two of them stayed to finish digging out the juiceroot, while the other two led the children away. The one who was holding Suth kept a grip on his wrist and pushed him on ahead. He felt numb and stupid and helpless, the way he felt on the journey through Dry Hills. His mouth was sour with the taste of failure.

Oldtale

THE CHILDREN OF AMMU

Ammu grew very fat.

She said to An, 'I must have meat. Go *and hunt.'*

While An was hunting, Ammu gave birth.

Six and six and six children she had at that first birth.

First she bore three soft eggs. When they opened, Ammu found a boy and a girl in each.

Next she bore three hard eggs. When they opened, Ammu found a boy and a girl in each.

Last she bore six that came from the womb not in eggs, but as the animals that have hair are born. They came from her two and two and two, a boy and a girl together.

Ammu looked at her six and six and six children, and wept.

'How do I feed all these?' she said. 'I have only two breasts, and the breasts of An are small, and have no milk.'

Now, Black Antelope was far away, grazing on the plains, when Ammu gave birth. But Monkey watched and listened, for he was always curious about people, and all they did. When he heard what Ammu said, he ran to the others of the First Ones and said, 'Ammu gave birth to six and six and six children. She cannot feed them all. She has only two breasts.'

The First Ones spoke among themselves. They said, 'Let us take two each of Ammu's children and care for them, or they die.'

'But what when Black Antelope returns?' said Little Bat. 'Then there are none left for him to care for.'

'He is the strongest,' said Snake. 'He gives his strength to those he cares for. Then they rule all the rest. That is not good.'

So they agreed.

They put Ammu into a sleep, and then they drew lots over who should choose first which children they should care for. Monkey was clever with his fingers, and he saw to it that he should choose last.

Snake and Crocodile and the Ant Mother chose children who had hatched from soft eggs, and took them from Ammu while she slept.

Weaver and Parrot and Moonhawk chose children who had hatched from hard eggs, and took them from Ammu while she slept.

Little Bat and Fat Pig took children who had been born as the animals that have hair are born, and took them from Ammu while she slept.

Thus only two children were left.

Then Monkey said, 'We cannot leave Ammu with no children. Then she weeps worse than before. Two are due to me. Let Ammu raise these. Each of you must give me a gift. This makes up for my loss.'

They agreed to that, and it was done.

When An returned from his hunting, Ammu showed him the two fine children who were born to them, and they rejoiced.

Ammu said, 'While I slept, a strong dream came to me. In my dream I gave birth to ten children, and eight more. I could not feed so many from my breasts. I wept for this. But great animals heard my weeping and came. They took all but these two from me.'

An said, 'It is only a dream,' and they laughed together.

When Black Antelope returned and learned what the others had done, he too laughed.

'Monkey has tricked you,' he said. 'Soon you find this. It is trouble to care for the children of people.'

CHAPTER FIVE

Suth was careful not to struggle or resist, and after a while the man who held him relaxed his grip a little. He still couldn't see what was happening to the others. He heard one faint whimper from Otan, but small ones learned very early to stay silent in times of danger.

Their narrow path wound through the bushes. Suth's captor moved warily, like a hunter in strange country, pausing often and peering for dangers.

No one spoke. The bare hills were silent. Insects clicked and whirred in the scrub. And all the time birds whistled and squawked in the huge green mass of forest on their right, strange calls that Suth had never heard before.

And then, close by, high up among the branches, something set up a steady whooping cry. He had heard the same call earlier in the distance, but had hardly noticed it because he had been concentrating on things immediately around him. Now, so near, the wild, eerie call made the hair on the back of his neck prickle. Instinctively he froze, but the man who held him twisted his arm and shoved him on, as if he knew the cry meant no danger.

A few small paths branched off, away from the forest, but they kept to the one they were on until it led out towards the bare hillside. Even before they were clear of the scrub Suth's nostrils told him that they were coming to some kind of camp – an old one too, much used, because the smells were so strong, wood smoke and charred meat and a whole tangle of people odours. It was strange. Sometimes the Kin had stayed a moon and a moon in the same spot, but they would never have let their smells build up in such a way.

They came out onto a steep, rocky slope with a line of low cliffs some way up it. People were moving around below the cliffs. One of them called. They all stopped what they were doing and gathered together. As soon as the newcomers were in earshot several voices rose, shouting questions. This was not how the Kin would have met hunters returning with captured strangers. They would have stood silent behind their leader while he made the formal greetings and asked the questions.

The man who held Suth didn't answer, but pushed him grimly on, past the ashes of a large fire, almost as far as the cliff. Here Suth saw a dark opening in the rock face, beside which an old woman was sitting in the sun. She looked as if she was asleep.

The man forced Suth to his knees. The other Moonhawks were herded around him. They waited in silence, the girls with bowed heads, but Ko staring angrily about as if he was ready to fight all these people. Otan clung silently to Noli.

The babble of questions continued until the old woman seemed to wake, and raised her head. Her hair was sparse and white, her skin yellow and blotched and wrinkled. Both her eyes were filmed over with a grey mess.

Suth had never seen anyone so old. Among the Kin she would long ago have been taken into the desert and left to die, because she could no longer keep up.

'Tell,' she croaked.

'Dith speaks,' said the man with strange eyes, and Suth realized he was telling her his name because she was blind.

'I went with Mohr and Kan and Gal to dig juiceroot,' the man went on. 'It was mine. I found it. When the shoots were small and green I marked it with my mark. We drank at the lake. Then we went. These six children were there. They dug my juiceroot. I went to strike the boy. To punish, not kill. The girl spoke of Moonhawk. I changed my thought. Mohr asked, *Do you have others? Do you have grown men?* The girl said, *They are dead.* We spoke among ourselves. Our thought was, *We take these children to Mosu.*'

The old woman considered the matter, nodding and wheezing. Suth's heart thudded. He was horribly afraid of this old woman, even more than he was of the men.

'Let the girl speak of Moonhawk,' she croaked.

Noli passed Otan to Tinu and came forward. In front of the old woman she kneeled and pattered her hands on the ground, as she would have done to appease Bal when he was angry. Still kneeling she explained what had happened since the fight with the strangers. The old woman bowed her head and seemed to have fallen asleep again, but when Noli had finished speaking she raised a withered arm and beckoned to her.

Noli crawled forward. The old woman felt her all over, and then pushed her away.

'The boy,' she croaked.

Suth rose and went to her. She felt him all over with cold, dry, quivering hands, checking nose, eyes and ears, counting fingers and toes. Then she did the same to Tinu and found her twisted mouth.

'What is this?' she croaked.

Tinu was too scared to speak, but Noli explained that she had been born like that.

'Were others among you so?' asked the woman.

'Only Tinu was so, in all the Kins,' said Noli.

The woman shoved Tinu away and went on to the small ones. The people watched, muttering.

Suth studied them. There were ten and a few more. Some were old, and needed a stick to hobble on. Two of the men had eyes of different colours, like Dith's. A young woman had a withered leg. A girl, who was standing beside a pregnant woman, moved her hand and Suth saw that there were flaps of skin between the fingers, like those on the feet of the birds at Stinkwater.

Otan bawled as the old woman felt him over, but quieted when Noli took him back. The people started to move around, as if the examination of these strangers was done. Dith and Mohr left to finish digging out the juiceroot. The sense of danger ebbed away, but Suth stayed tense. He found the behaviour of these people very strange. He didn't know where he was with them.

The pregnant woman came up to admire Otan.

'That is a big voice,' she said as if this were a special compliment. 'It is the voice of a lucky hunter.'

'He is hungry and thirsty,' said Noli. 'Where is water?'

'You have not drunk?' said the woman, sounding surprised.

'We drank yesterday, in the morning,' said Noli.

The woman nodded and went and spoke briefly with the old woman, then called the girl with the strange hands and sent her running down the slope after Dith and Mohr. She reached them just before they disappeared into the scrub. There was an argument, but after a bit they started back up the slope. When they reached the camp they were clearly angry, but Dith said, 'Come. Be quick,' and led the way down again. Suth took Otan, to give Noli a rest. The girl with the strange hands came too.

'Where do we go?' Suth asked her.

'To the lake,' she said, obviously surprised by his not knowing. 'Where else is water? What is your name?'

'I am Suth. These are Noli and Tinu. The small ones are Ko and Mana. The one I carry is Otan, who is Noli's brother. We have no fathers, no mothers. Our Kin was Moonhawk, but it is gone.'

'I am Sula,' she said. 'Paro is my mother. She gives birth today, before sundown. My father is Mohr, that one, and the other is Dith. Mosu made them take you to the lake. They are angry about that.'

'Why do grown men come?' said Suth. 'Do we steal a lake?'

Again she stared at him, astonished that he didn't know.

'All go together to the lake,' she said. 'The men guard us.'

They were on a well-worn trail that went leftward down the slope. As they entered the bushes Mohr dropped back to the rear of the line, and both men raised their digging sticks to a ready position and walked more warily. The trail was wide, and creatures other than people had left their prints in its dust. This was something that Suth had seen before, near water holes in places rich in game, but never so many, nor on a trail that so reeked of people.

This trail led directly into the trees, out of the blazing sunlight and into a dark green tunnel where the air was dense with strange odours, sappy new growth, unknown pollens and fungi, decaying litter. The men walked carefully, peering left and right into the shadows between the huge still trunks. It was a world unlike anything Suth had ever known.

He started violently as a flock of green and yellow birds flew chuckling across the path, and then froze, with the hair on his neck prickling erect, as the same weird whooping that he'd heard before rose from somewhere almost overhead.

All five Moonhawks stopped in their tracks. Mana put her hand in Suth's and huddled to his side. Sula, walking close behind, almost bumped into them.

'What makes this noise?' he whispered.

She looked at him a moment as if she didn't want

to answer. Then she muttered, 'He is called Big Voice. His true name is not spoken.'

Suth understood what she meant. The people in two of the Kins, Snake and Crocodile, never spoke about their First Ones by name. Instead they called them 'The Silent One' and 'She Who Waits.' Was the creature Sula called Big Voice the First One of these people?

Suth smelled the water before he saw it, though it didn't have the usual clean, hard smell he knew. Instead, it smelled like the water they had found seeping out of the cliff two mornings ago. They came to it very suddenly. At one moment they were surrounded by the brooding trees, and the next moment there it was, a long, narrow lake twisting away further than he could see towards the distant ridges. It was utterly still, and except in the small clearing where they stood, the trees came right down to the water.

Dith raised his right hand with the fingers spread wide apart in a gesture of formal greeting and muttered quietly for a few moments. Suth knew what this meant. When the Kin came to a place that had power in it, such as Tarutu Rock or Lightning Tree, their leader would make their peace with that power before they passed by, or camped there.

Dith moved aside and gestured to the Moonhawks to drink while he and Mohr stood guard. Noli took longer than the others because she was feeding Otan a sip at a time from her mouth. While they waited for her, Suth gazed at the lake. His sense of awe grew steadily stronger. He had never in his life seen such an expanse of water, nor felt such stillness. Nowhere in the world, not even the Rock of Meeting at Odutu below the Mountain, where he would not go until the time came for him to be made a man, could be like this. Perhaps he would never go to Odutu now. But he had seen this place.

Tinu touched his elbow, breaking his trance. She pointed towards the water's edge. There, on a patch of mud, just bcyond where they had drunk, was a large paw print. The mark of each broad toe showed clearly. Suth's father had shown him just such a print on a sandbank at Sometimes River.

Now he knew what the men stood guard against.

Leopard.

Oldtale

ODUTU BELOW THE MOUNTAIN

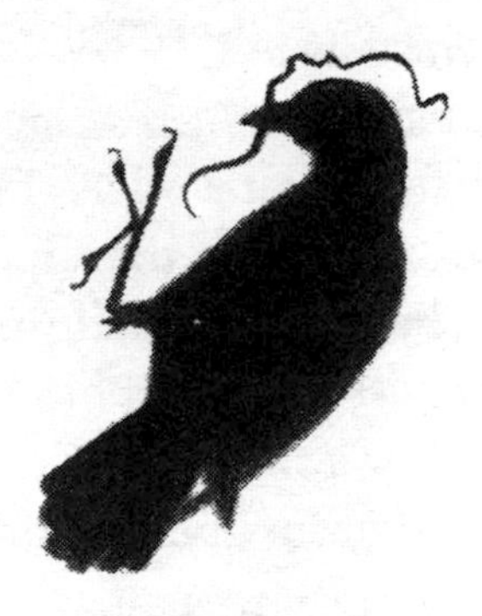

The First Ones made nests and lairs for the children of An and Ammu, according to their kinds. Thus Moonhawk made a nest of twigs among the crags and carried there the two that she was to care for, and the Ant Mother dug a chamber in the earth for the two that she was to care for. So with the others, according to their kinds.

Only Monkey did nothing. An and Ammu did all that, and he watched.

The First Ones fed the children according to their kinds. Thus Little Bat fed them upon insects, and Crocodile fed them upon creatures that she caught as she lay in wait. So with the others, according to their kinds.

Only Monkey did nothing. An and Ammu did all that, and he watched.

When the children were grown to the height of a garri bush, the First Ones brought them to Odutu below the Mountain. It was there that An and Ammu had their camp at that season.

The First Ones set the children down a little way from Odutu and told them, 'See that great rock. Go there and find a thing.'

The children went forward hand in hand, two and two, while the First Ones watched invisible around. They gave back to Ammu the memory that they had taken from her, and she looked up and saw her children, pair and pair and pair, coming to her out of the bush.

Then she rejoiced that they were given back to her.

And An rejoiced with her, and said, 'This is Odutu below the Mountain. This is our Rock of Meeting. From this day it is sacred. From this day an oath sworn here is an oath for ever, and a peace made here is a peace for ever.'

And it was so.

CHAPTER SIX

While the Moonhawks were at the lake, Paro had put what was left of the fox leg to roast among the hot embers of the fire. When they returned she gave them other food, soft lumps of yellow stuff and dark strips of sun-dried root, which they chewed until all the nutty flavour was gone, and then spat the rest out. The root was strange to them, but the Kin used to make the same kind of yellow stuff from pounded seed, mixed with water. They ate it eagerly.

When the meat was cooked, Paro hacked the flesh off it with a good strong cutter, and handed it around. It was delicious after days of raw flesh, but their stomachs were tired of meat and they didn't eat much.

When they had finished, Suth signalled to the others and they all rose and stood in a line in front of Paro, clenched their fists, and knocked their knuckles together three times.

Food was seldom plentiful, so even when it was, one Kin never accepted a meal from a different Kin without the regular ritual of thanks. Sula laughed aloud, as if they'd done something extraordinary. Paro simply smiled, and spread her hands in a vague gesture.

'We have plenty,' she said.

This made Suth puzzled and uneasy. The Moon-hawks had done what they knew was the right thing, but Sula had answered rudely, and Paro as if they'd done something stupid. Sula had been friendly, and Paro kind, but how could he trust these people if they behaved like that?

'We cannot take and take from your store,' he said. 'Show me where we can forage for food, and not make others angry.'

'It is far,' said Paro. 'Your small ones are tired, and the baby is heavy to carry.'

'They stay,' said Suth. 'I go with Tinu. But we have no gourd, to carry food home.'

'What is gourd?' she asked. 'We take leaves, to carry.'

She showed him one. It was thick and leathery, and far larger than any he had ever seen. Carefully she turned the ends up and folded it down the middle rib, tucking the folded ends in, and then slid it under her arm. She put the fingers of her other hand together and mimed picking a seed head and dropping it between the two halves of the leaf. Then she handed it to him.

'I cannot come,' she said. 'My child is almost born. Sula shows you, but she must come back for the birth.'

Suth looked at Noli, and she nodded. He felt relieved. This at least was something that was the same among the Kin. If a woman had a daughter and was pregnant again, the daughter must be there at the birthing to see how all was done, so that she would know when her own time came. A mother who bore no more children might ask permission for her daughter to watch when other mothers gave birth. This was important woman lore.

Suth thanked her again, and the three of them set out, with Sula carrying the bone from the fox leg. Before long they came to a narrow deep ravine. The place reeked. Three vultures rose as they reached the edge. Sula tossed the bone in.

Suth peered over the edge. On the floor of the ravine lay an immense pile of bones, picked clean by scavengers. He was amazed, stupefied. The Kin, of course, used to carry such stuff well clear of wherever they rested, so there was often a scattering of bones ringing their regular camps, but never like this. These people, how long had they lived here to make such a pile? Tens and tens and more tens of rains. They had this one Good Place with so much in it to hunt and forage that they never needed to journey to another. His mind wouldn't think about it. It was too strange.

Sula led them above the line of scrub, until they reached a ground rat warren. Several traps had been set, the kind that Suth had watched his father make – a large rock propped on a triangle of sticks, and baited so that when the bait was moved the sticks gave way and the rock fell. Tinu at once crouched by one of the traps and studied it intently.

'Look,' said Sula. 'Baga catches a rat. She makes good traps.'

'How can you know it is Baga?' said Suth.

'There is her mark,' said Sula, pointing to a little pattern of pebbles beside the trap, three in a line and one below. 'All her family use this mark. This is Jun's mark. He catches nothing. Do you make a trap? What mark do you choose?'

'Tell me,' said Suth.

'Good. You have four like so, and one to the side. You may set your trap here, or in any warren where you see traps. The rats are stupid. They do not learn soon, but when many are caught, the others know not to take the bait. Then we leave that warren and go to another.

'Now I must go back,' she added. 'I must be with my mother at the birthing. I show you where the others forage.'

She led them further up the hill and turned. From here Suth could see that the forest didn't in fact fill the whole of the bottom of the bowl between the circling ridges. It lay in two wide belts on either side of the lake, which was now visible for most of its length. It stretched a whole day's journey into the distance, an immense, deep crack in the mountaintop, filled with water.

To the left, though, the ground rose and became grassland with patches of open scrub and scattered, flat-topped trees.

'They are there,' said Sula.

He looked along her pointing arm and in the far distance saw a line of dark dots. He recognized them at once. No other creatures move or hold themselves in the same way as people.

'My thanks,' said Suth.

He didn't have any bait for a trap, so he and Tinu

set out, while Sula returned to the camp. As soon as they were picking their way between the areas of scrub, he saw signs of recent foraging. These people were not at all as thorough as the Kin would have been. This was rich country, as good as any of the old Good Places, but there were clumps of grass not stripped of their seed heads, termite nests not dug out, dead branches not stripped for the grubs beneath the bark. But he and Tinu didn't stop for any of the possible pickings. It was important only to do what the others did, and forage where they foraged.

They found the people not working, but resting in the shade of a group of trees. Someone had already come from the cave with news of the Moonhawks' arrival, so they weren't challenged. Several children did rush out to meet them, and then instead of greeting them, stood silent and staring and followed them back to the trees.

A few men were on one side, sitting in a circle and playing some kind of game, and a larger group of women were talking quietly among themselves while they husked seed or fed babies.

The men glanced up and went back to their game. Suth waited, watching them as they in turn tossed pebbles onto a pattern of lines they had drawn in the dust. He assumed that after a while whoever was leader would look up and nod or beckon to him. Then he would kneel and patter his hands on the ground in sign of submission, and ask to be allowed to forage in this people's Place.

Nothing happened. The men continued their game. Tinu, at Suth's side, stood with her head bowed and her eyes down, as if thinking that if she couldn't see anyone then she herself couldn't be seen.

Suth looked around, and a young woman who was sitting against a tree, feeding her baby, smiled at him.

'Who is leader?' he asked her.

She shrugged and frowned, puzzled.

'Mosu?' she suggested.

'Who then do I ask, *May I forage in this Place?*'

'Mosu spoke to Pagi,' she said. 'Pagi came to us. You may forage with us.'

'I thank.'

He squatted beside her and Tinu crouched by him, shielding herself from the others with his body. He looked around the group. There were ten and ten and ten of them, and a few more. This was a big Kin. Moonhawk at its most had been only ten and ten and one more. The Crocodile Kin, when they had last met at Stinkwater had been only ten and four. But then, there had been six other Kins beside those two. There were more of these people back at the cave, of course, as well as men out hunting, but still it was not very many if these were the only Kin who ever came here.

Where did they go to find mates? he wondered. The young men of the Moonhawks went to Little Bat and Crocodile to beg a mate, and young men came from Weaver and Parrot to beg from Moonhawk.

'I am Suth,' he said. 'This one is Tinu. We are Moonhawk.'

'I am Loga,' she said. 'My son is not yet named.'

'And what is your Kin?' he asked.

She stared at him, and put her knuckles to her mouth. He realized that he must have said a Thing-that-is-not-spoken, though among the Kin he knew the sign would have been given with the palm of the hand.

'My shame,' he muttered, spreading his hands, palm down, in front of his chest, and then slowly lowering them as a sign of pushing the evil back into the earth.

She nodded, but turned away and concentrated on her baby.

When they had finished their game, the men picked up their digging sticks and loped off along the edge of the scrub. The women and children moved out into the open, formed a line and started to forage steadily across the ground. Almost all of them had folded leaves under their arms, to carry what they had gathered. None had a gourd. Perhaps there were no gourds in the valley.

Suth and Tinu joined the end of the line and worked steadily. Before the sun was halfway down the sky they had gathered enough for their own needs for a full day, but they had Noli and the small ones to feed too, so they didn't stop. Suth was crouching by a clump of spike-grass, stripping off the ripe seed heads, when he felt a curious sensation, as if the solid ground was trembling beneath the soles of his feet. It lasted only a short while and as it ended the whooping call of Big Voice rose from the forest. Far off, another answered. The weird cries floated out over the treetops and away towards the barren ridges.

The line of foragers stopped work and stood to listen to the call. As it died away, the woman working next to Suth turned and smiled.

'He sings,' she said. 'Paro gives birth, perhaps. The baby is good. Big Voice is happy for the baby.'

The other women seemed to have had the same idea. Without waiting for the men, they started back for the cave.

Ko came running to meet them across the last slope. He held up his arms. Suth passed his carrying leaf to Tinu and picked him up.

'You come back,' said Ko happily.

'I come back,' said Suth.

'You father,' said Ko.

Suth must have looked startled, because Ko said it again.

'You father,' he insisted. 'Noli mother. Mana say this. Yes?'

'Yes,' said Suth, slowly. 'I am the father now, and Noli is the mother. You are the children, Tinu, Ko, Mana, and Otan.'

He was still surprised, but in a different way. All along he had been doing his best for the little ones, trying to keep them alive, and find them food and water and safety. But these weren't the only things they needed. They needed a father and a mother too, so they'd chosen Suth and Noli, since there was no one else. And it was Mana who had seen the need.

He thought about her as he carried Ko back to the camp. As usual with Mana, Suth hadn't especially noticed it at the time, but now he realized how easy she had made things, as far as she could, ever since he and Noli had rescued the four of them. She hadn't asked for anything, or complained of hunger or thirst or weariness, but she'd watched all the time, and been ready, and kept out of the way when she wasn't needed.

So when he got back to the camp and found Noli sitting with Otan asleep in her lap, and Mana sitting patiently beside her, he put Ko down and picked Mana up.

'See, I come back,' he said.

She put her arms around his neck and hugged him. Noli looked up and smiled.

'You hear the thing Mana says?' she asked him.

'Yes. It is true,' he said.

That evening, when the sun was low, the fire was piled with wood and those who had caught ground rats skinned the bodies for roasting. Then they all trooped down to the lake for their evening drink. Even Mosu came, hobbling on her stick and helped along by the woman with the withered leg, whose name was Foia. This time it was Mosu who raised her hand and spoke in greeting to the water before anyone drank.

On their return they settled in a wide circle around the fire, with the men on one side and the women and children on the other. While they ate, Mohr, who was Paro's mate and Sula's father, carried the new baby around and showed him to everyone in turn. Men as well as women held him and looked him carefully over while he thrashed and squalled, and then passed him back to Mohr.

Mohr didn't show him to the Moonhawks, but Sula brought him proudly over.

'See,' she said. 'He is whole and clean.'

She opened one of the tiny clutching hands and showed that there were four good fingers and a thumb, without webs, like hers, between them. After his mistake with Loga under the shade trees, Suth didn't dare ask what was so wonderful about a child being born normal. Apart from Tinu, all the babies he had known had been born whole and healthy, though later some had fallen sick and died. As it happened, Sula told him anyway.

'When my brother was born he had no arms and no legs,' she said. 'He would not live. My father carried him into the trees and left him. Our blood is sick. Mosu says *We are too few. That makes the sickness. We have only each other to mate with*. Now the sickness grows stronger. See. It is here, in me.'

She spread her webbed fingers to show him.

'Soon I am a woman,' she said. 'Then I have you for my mate, Suth. Your blood is good. It gives me good babies. Mosu says this.'

Suth smiled uneasily, but she wasn't joking or teasing, though there was always a lot of that among the Kin when children were reaching the right age. He glanced at Noli for reassurance, but she was sitting hunched into herself, breathing heavily, not noticing anything. Tinu was amusing Otan by tickling his feet with a grass stem. Mana was asleep, and Ko was playing tag around the circle with a boy his own age. Suth didn't really understand what Sula had told him, but he didn't feel easy about it. Perhaps this was not a Good Place after all. Perhaps it was like the fruit of the sixberry bush, which tasted so good in the mouth that you wanted to eat more and more, but when you'd had more than five it caused you to vomit until you thought you would die.

Sula carried the baby away and gave him to Paro. Ko returned panting and bright eyed from his game. Noli gave a shuddering sigh and sat up and looked around.

'You hear the thing that Sula says?' Suth asked her.

She shook her head and in a low voice he told her. She nodded.

'I slept and did not sleep,' she said. 'Moonhawk came. She told what Kin these are. They are Monkey. Big Voice is Monkey.'

He stared at her, remembering what the Oldtales said.

'Monkey has no Kin,' he said.

'These are Monkey,' she insisted. 'Does Moonhawk lie?'

Oldtale

HOW SORROW CAME

An and Ammu journeyed through all of the First Good Places with their children. They showed them the trails and the water holes and the dew traps and the warrens. They told them the names of the plants, root and fruit and nut and leaf, those that were good to eat and those that were bad. They showed them the places of safety and the places of danger.

They came to a tree that held the nests of weavers, and An cut a long pole and showed how to knock down the nests, so as to eat the eggs and the young chicks.

Then the two who had been reared by Weaver said, 'We may not eat of this food. We are of the Kin of Weaver.' Their names were So and Sana.

They came to a warren below the crags where moonhawks nested, and Ammu showed how to set traps for ground rats.

Then the two who had been reared by Moonhawk

said, 'We must set the hearts aside for Moonhawk. This is her prey, and we are of the Kin of Moonhawk.' Their names were Nal and Anla.

They came to a cave and An said, 'Here we sleep.'

Then the two who had been reared by Little Bat said, 'First we must do a thing. Bats lair in this cave. We ask leave of them. We are of the Kin of Little Bat.' Their names were Tur and Turka.

And so with each of the others in their turn, each honouring the First One who had raised them.

Only the two who had been reared by An and Ammu themselves had no knowledge of any Kin to which they belonged, because Monkey had hidden himself and done nothing for them. Their names were Da and Datta.

They came to An and said, 'Our brothers and sisters have each a Kin, but we have none. How is this?'

An, knowing no better, said, 'You were reared by Ammu and by me. You are of the Kin of People.'

It was from this that all sorrow came.

CHAPTER SEVEN

They slept in the cave. It stank. Like the Kin these people didn't make dung or pass water close by their lairs, but went well away to do so. But small children can't control their bowels all night, and though the people piled up grass and brought it in for bedding and cleared it out when it was dirty, the reeks gradually gathered in the cave until in the nostrils of the Moonhawks the stench seemed almost too strong to bear. The people didn't seem to notice or mind, any more than they noticed the strange foul-egg odour that wafted to and fro in the valley.

The stink in the cave was made worse because when all were in for the night, the people piled rocks across the entrance, blocking it to the height of a man's shoulder. That meant any who needed to go out to relieve themselves were unable to do so.

Suth wondered if this was necessary, but on that very first night he got his answer. In his sleep he sensed a stirring, and woke and heard a low snarl, followed by another, coming from outside the cave. Night hunters were there, squabbling over scraps of food left from the meal. Against the patch of sky above the barrier, Suth saw the outlines of men with digging sticks raised ready to fight an intruder. Nothing more happened. The animals moved away and everyone relaxed back into sleep.

Later he woke again. He had felt the rock beneath him shudder, twice, but no one else in the cave stirred. They must be used to that.

The barrier was taken down as dawn was breaking, and the rocks laid aside to be used again. The air smelled wonderfully fresh and clean after the cave. They ate a little food and then went down to the lake for their morning drink. After that the foragers and hunters left, but Noli was still feeding Otan so the Moonhawks stayed for her.

While they waited the air grew heavy. Clouds gathered, seemingly from nowhere. Everyone left at the camp hurried into the cave. There was a clap of thunder, and rain came pelting down while the lightning blinked and the thunder rumbled on and on. And then it was over, and the whole hillside was streaming with water.

This was the season of thunderstorms. The Kin used to watch them grumbling across the plains, dropping their rain in one place and not in another. But Suth had never seen one like this, gathering and gone so soon, and all in one place. It was very strange.

As the Moonhawks were getting ready to leave, Foia, the woman who helped blind old Mosu move around, came up.

'You speak now with Mosu,' she said.

Suth frowned. The old woman made him very uneasy, and he wanted as little to do with her as he could. He glanced at Noli.

'I come also,' she said, and passed Otan to Tinu to mind.

Mosu was in her usual place by the cave, with her back against the cliff. Suth and Noli kneeled before her and pattered their hands on the ground.

'The boy comes,' said Foia. 'The girl also.'

She moved a short distance away and sat down.

Mosu gave no sign of having heard, but then she raised her head and said in her croaking voice, 'You are children. You have no father and no mother.'

'The strangers killed our fathers,' said Suth. 'They took our mothers.'

'No mother, no father – the child dies,' said Mosu. 'Now I give each of you a mother and a father. They care for you and teach you our ways.'

For a moment Suth didn't understand what she meant. Then he realized that she wanted to split the Moonhawks up and give them each to a different family.

He looked anxiously at Noli. She drew her lower lip into her mouth and let it go. *This is not good*, she was telling him. He remembered what Mana and Ko had been saying last evening, that he was now their father, and Noli their mother.

I do not let this happen, he thought. *But I must not offend this old woman. She is the leader in this place.*

'We thank,' he said hesitatingly. 'But . . . we are not of this Kin. We are Moonhawk. Our ways are ways of Moonhawk.'

'Moonhawk is dead,' said Mosu. 'All those Kins are dead, gone. All your Good Places are taken. There is no Snake, no Fat Pig, no Ant Mother. There is only one Kin, and it is ours. Big Voice sings in the forest. He says this to me.'

'He is a liar!' said Suth, suddenly too angry to be careful. He felt his scalp move as his hair bushed out in his anger.

'He is a liar, I say!' he repeated. 'Everyone knows this. Moonhawk came to Noli. Last night she came, while we ate. She told whose Kin you are. She is not dead.'

Mosu merely cackled.

'Do your small ones live many more moons?' she said. 'Does your baby live, that cannot walk? Can the girl feed the baby? Has she milk in her breasts?'

She rocked to and fro, wheezing between her cackles.

Suth looked at Noli for help, but she didn't see him. Something was happening to her. Her eyes were wide and blank, and her whole body shuddered.

'Monkey is sick,' she said in a deep, gasping voice. 'Moonhawk speaks this. Monkey is sick.'

She staggered as if she'd been struck, and Suth caught her to stop her falling. He held her while she shuddered once more and gave a slow, exhausted sigh. Then she drew herself clear and stood normally.

At first Mosu didn't seem to have heard what she'd said, but her cackling died away and she sat still, wheezing heavily. Suth remembered what Sula had told him last night.

'Your blood is bad,' he said. 'Your men have eyes of two colours. Your children have skin between their fingers. Your babies have no arms, no legs. You want our good blood. I, Suth, say this. Moonhawk lives. We are Moonhawk. You take us one from the others. You make Moonhawk die. I say you cannot do it. I say we leave this place and go far and far. You can not have our good blood.'

Mosu muttered something and seemed to shrink into herself.

They waited. At length she raised her head and sighed.

'Big Voice is not a liar,' she said quietly. 'He is a trickster. His words say this and that. Long, long, he sings to me. Before my sons are born he sings to me. Their sons are soon men. I know the ways of Big Voice. He says this and that.'

'Moonhawk is Moonhawk,' said Suth. 'Our Kin lives. We stay one Kin, together.'

Mosu cackled briefly.

'Are you a man?' she said. 'Can you care for four children? Do you make a digging stick? Do you harden it in the fire? Do you fight the leopard when it comes for your small ones? Do you sit with the men at the feast? Do you speak when they speak?'

'In three moons I am made a man,' said Suth obstinately.

This was true and not true. If the strangers hadn't come and changed everything, then in three moons the Kin would have travelled south to Odutu below the Mountain, and Suth would have spent a night alone on the Mountain above Odutu, and in the morning Bal would have cut the first man-scar into his cheek and told him to make himself a digging stick. After that he would have left the women's side and sat with the men and listened to their talk. But it would have been tens of moons and three more scars before he would have been allowed to join in.

'Always the men mock this boy-man. They point fingers. They raise their lip,' said Mosu.

'Stones are sharper,' he answered.

She turned her head away.

'Make a digging stick,' she said.

'Moonhawk is Moonhawk,' he insisted.

'You say it,' she answered. 'Go forage. The girl stays. We talk.'

He looked at Noli.

'I talk with Mosu,' she said. 'Bring Otan to me.'

As Suth left the camp with Tinu and the small ones, he saw Noli sitting cross-legged, with Otan in her lap, listening while Mosu talked. He felt puzzled and angry. He had just stood up to the old woman and won his point. Moonhawk wasn't going to be split up. They were keeping together. Only they weren't, because Noli wasn't coming to the foraging grounds with them, but was staying behind to talk to Mosu.

She had to stay. Suth understood that. Mosu was leader of these people. If Noli had tried to refuse, Mosu would have kept her there by force. But Suth guessed Noli actually wanted to stay, he didn't know why. That was what hurt.

On the way to the ground rat warren, Suth broke branches from bushes to use in his trap. He had noticed a pile of good flat rocks by the warren, which people must have carried there to use, but they didn't seem to be marked with anyone's mark so he took one of those. Ko, of course, wanted to build a trap too, so Suth broke a spare branch into lengths for him, as a father would have done. He showed him how to use them to prop the rock up, so that when a ground rat nibbled the bait a stick would be dislodged, and the rock would fall and kill the rat. It wasn't easy, and Suth didn't think either of them would have much luck.

Meanwhile Tinu and Mana built a trap of their own. All three were baited with seed paste mixed with the crushed leaves of a garri bush, which ground rats were especially fond of. When they'd finished, they marked the traps with the Moonhawk mark and set off for the foraging grounds.

The foragers weren't where they'd been yesterday, but he found them easily enough by the noise they were making, down in the thicker scrub. They were hunting for a kind of caterpillar that came out of the ground on the morning after a rain and climbed a bush and hung itself from a thread, to begin the process of turning itself into a moth. Only on the first morning was it good to eat, Sula told Suth. By evening the case it spun around itself had begun to harden, and the flesh inside was too bitter to swallow.

While the foragers searched they kept up a constant yodelling, passing it to and fro along the line. The men didn't join in. They just stood guard, striding around at the edge of the group, letting out hoarse shouts and thwacking at the bushes with their digging sticks. Every now and then one of the foragers would bring one of them a caterpillar, pinch off its head and pop the body into the guard's mouth.

Ko was delighted by the shouting and thwacking and ran around yelling at the top of his voice until one of the women caught him and brought him back to Suth.

'You keep him close,' she said scoldingly. 'You want a leopard to take him?'

'I thank,' said Suth meekly. He realized that however bravely he had spoken to Mosu, he had a lot to learn about being a man and caring for his family in this new place.

The caterpillars were delicious and plentiful, and they ate all they could, pinching the heads off, because that was where the bitterness came from. When the taste began to change they gave up and moved into the open, but before they had formed their foraging line, a man came running from the distance. While he was still some way off he stopped and made signs, and without a word spoken all the men in the party ran off to join him. Suth watched them lope silently out of sight in single file.

'What happens?' he asked Sula.

'Men hunt deer,' she said. 'We make no noise.'

He understood at once. The men of the Kin also hunted deer when they got the chance, but they didn't often kill one, except at a Place called Mambaga, where at the right season deer passed through in great numbers, and several Kins joined to hunt them as they crowded together to cross a particular dry gully. Usually it was a matter of the best hunters lying in wait, and the others trying to drive the deer to that point. But deer were quick and tricky. Mostly they ran somewhere else, and even when they didn't the hunter had only an instant to leap up and get his blow in.

Now the foragers moved into shade and sat quietly

until the hunters came back dejectedly. The hunt, it seemed, hadn't really begun. The deer had run off before the ambush was properly set. So the men settled down to their game, while the foragers went back to work. Once again Suth was struck by how much there was to gather, and what a rich, easy living these people had here. Perhaps it was because Monkey had made this Place for them, he thought. Monkey was clever. Everyone knew that.

On their way back to the camp that evening they stopped at the warren to pick up their catch. But, although several traps had been sprung, only the one that Tinu and Mana had made had caught a rat.

The women, of course, seized the chance to jeer at the men. These mighty hunters couldn't catch deer. They couldn't even catch ground rats. A couple of girls could catch a ground rat, but the men couldn't.

The men didn't like it. They were still sore about missing the deer. Dith looked at the trap with the Moonhawk mark beside it, and then his eye was caught by Suth's and Ko's, not far off, and marked the same.

He turned angrily on Suth.

'No girl made this trap,' he said. 'The boy made it. See, he made three. You! Boy! You set three traps. This is bad. Each must set one trap only.'

He glared at Suth with his shoulders hunched and his hair bushed, but Suth was angry too. He couldn't stand up to a grown man, but he refused to go into the full submission ritual of kneeling and pattering his hands on the ground. He just bowed his head and fluttered his fingers for a moment in the air.

'I built this one,' he said. 'Ko built that. See, it is a child's, a small one's. Mana. Speak true. Who made this trap?' There was no point in asking Tinu herself. They wouldn't have understood what she was trying to say. And in any case she would have been utterly tongue-tied.

'Tinu made this trap,' said Mana sturdily. 'She knew the way. I watched.'

The women jeered again, and picked Tinu up and held her high in triumph. She hated it and tried to cower into herself until they put her down. When the fuss had died away, Suth took her aside and praised her quietly, but she hid her face even from him.

That evening as they sat around the fire, Suth asked Noli about her talk with Mosu. He was hoping she might have learned something useful about these people and their ways.

She was feeding Otan and didn't answer right away, but then she looked up with her face smeared with the mixture of seed paste and berry juice she had been chewing for him. She shook her head.

'Do not question me, Suth,' she said. 'I, Noli, ask this. It is secret.'

Suth was hurt. He knew that people to whom the First Ones came sometimes talked among themselves about how it was, and not to anyone else. Suth remembered what his father had said at Ragala Flat, when Bal and the old man from Weaver had gone off into the darkness to talk dream stuff together. But he was still hurt.

He turned his head away and stared at the fire. He needed Noli. Didn't she understand? He was a boy, but he must pretend to be a man and stand up to the men as he had stood up to Dith at the warren. How else could he care for his family? *Their* family. If he was the father, she was the mother. Would she spend all her time talking secrets with the old woman? This was not right.

He felt her fingers touch his arm, and her hand move down to rest on the back of his hand and hold it. Still he would not look at her.

'I tell you this, Suth,' she said in a low voice. 'These people keep us here. They are sick. Their blood is bad. Soon we are men and women. Then they choose us for mates. They have our good blood. They are sick no more. All this Mosu tells them. But they think this. We are all together, all six, perhaps we go secretly away. Can they watch all the time? That is difficult. Can they keep us in the cave? Then we fall sick, we die. So Mosu says, *Let Noli stay with me. Suth does not go without Noli.*'

Now Suth stared at her, appalled. Without thought he began to rise to his feet, as if he meant to gather the Moonhawks and lead them away, then and there, away from these people, out of this trap. Noli tightened her grip on his hand and pulled him down.

'They watch,' she muttered. 'Be clever, Suth. Be secret.'

Oldtale

DA AND DATTA

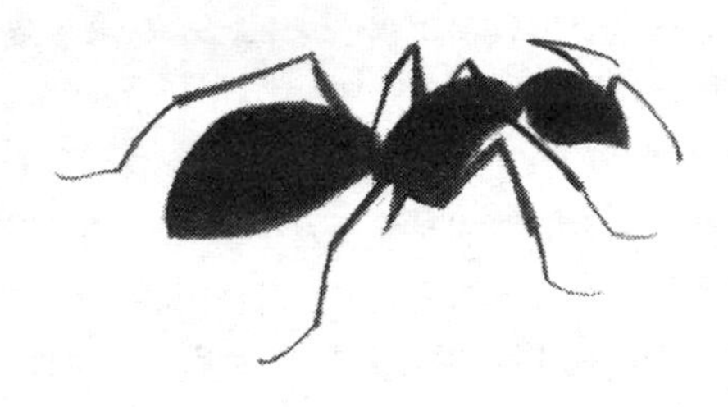

The sons of An and Ammu strove among themselves to see who was best. They wrestled, and raced, and threw rocks at a mark, and such things.

And one was strongest, and one was swiftest, and one was keenest of sight, each according to the nature of the First One who had reared him. But Da was none of these things.

'I am still the best of you,' said Da.

The others mocked him and said, 'How are you best? First Ones cared for us. They made us stronger and swifter and keener of sight than you.'

Da said, 'I was cared for by people, and they made me best. People are above creatures.'

They said, 'How so?'

To this Da had no answer, and they mocked him again, until he ran weeping into the desert.

There he found Datta, and told her what had been done and said, and she wept also.

They slept, and Monkey came to Datta in a dream.

In the morning she said to Da, 'Go to your brothers and say thus and thus.'

Da went to his brothers and said, 'Now I tell you how I am the best of you. I eat of the flesh of all creatures, as I choose, and their eggs also. But for each of you there is one creature whose flesh you do not eat, nor its eggs.

'Weaver cared for So. Does So eat the eggs of weavers? Ant Mother cared for Buth. Does Buth dig the nests of ants for their grubs? Fat Pig cared for Gor. Does Gor track the sow to her lair and eat of the tender piglets? And so with the rest of you. I do all of these things.

'But people cared for me. Who eats of the flesh of people? None of you does this. It is a Thing Not Done. So people are best. I, Da, say this.

'Lowest are rocks and earth and water. Next above them are plants. Next above plants are creatures. Next above creatures are people. They are highest.'

They had no answer to this, but they mocked him all the same and threw dirt at him and drove him away, and he wept.

Monkey was angry when he saw what was done to Da. He came to Datta in a dream, and showed her where he had hidden the fire log that he had made.

Da and Datta went to that place and found the fire log. They made fire and roasted the flesh of lizards and ate it, and it was very good.

They roasted more and took it to their brothers and sisters and gave it to them. Then the others lusted for roast flesh and said, 'Give us the fire log, so that we too can make fire and roast what we catch.'

Da and Datta said, 'First you must come to the Rock of Meeting at Odutu below the Mountain and swear that we are best, because we were cared for by people. And you must swear that henceforth our ways are your ways, because they are the ways of people.'

Such was their lust for roast flesh that the others agreed. They came to Odutu below the Mountain and swore upon the Rock of Meeting as Da and Datta had told them. Then Da and Datta gave them fire, and they made fire logs, one for each Kin.

But when An and Ammu learned what had been said and done, they wept.

CHAPTER EIGHT

A moon went by, and another, with a thunderstorm every few days. The storm season ended and more moons went by.

Otan could walk. The valley was no longer strange to him. It was as if he had always lived here, being taken down to the pool morning and evening to drink, and at night sleeping in the stinking cave.

It was the same with Mana and Ko. They quickly learned the ways of these people, and made friends with their children and joined in their games. Ko was a favourite with the women, who spoiled him and told him what a fine boy he was. No one paid much attention to Mana.

They paid even less to Tinu. They seemed to think that because she couldn't talk clearly she wasn't a real person. She didn't seem to mind. She spent some of her time helping Noli with Otan, but most of it tagging along with Suth, watching what he did and helping him when she could. She set a trap at the warren almost every time they passed it, and usually caught something. She built better traps even than Baga, with delicately balanced rocks that dropped at a touch.

The men, of course, wouldn't admit this. They said it was because she was Moonhawk, who preyed upon ground rats. That was why Tinu was lucky.

(These people told many of the same Oldtales as the Kin, but some were different. In their Oldtales they called Monkey by his real name. It wasn't Monkey, they said, who'd caused all the trouble. It was Crocodile and Fat Pig, who were jealous of his cleverness because they were stupid. They'd conspired against him.)

Noli seemed to change much more than Tinu. She remembered the Good Places, of course, and the long journeys between them, but she didn't mind their loss. After the first few days Mosu allowed her to come foraging sometimes with the rest of them, but once they were back at the cave Noli would spend much of the time sitting with Mosu, listening or talking, or else in what seemed to be a kind of shared half trance, as if they were dreaming the same dream.

'What do you do with that old woman so long?' Suth asked her.

'I learn,' she said. 'She is very old. She knows much.'

Suth didn't like this. He missed Noli. He needed her. She was Moonhawk, not Monkey. She belonged with him, raising their small ones in the true Moonhawk ways. Mosu had power. She must have, to be leader of these people. Ant Mother sometimes had women for leaders, and so did Snake, in the Oldtales, but never since anyone could remember, and never old and blind, like Mosu. Was she using her power to trap Noli, to make her become not Moonhawk but Monkey?

'She sees nothing,' he said crossly. 'Her eyes are dead.'

'It is because she is old,' said Noli. 'It is not the blood sickness. When she was young she saw well. She says long ago tens and tens and tens of people lived in this Place. Some lived here, at this cave. Some lived over there. That is where Mosu was born.'

She pointed out across the forest to the wide, promising slopes on the far side of the valley. Nobody foraged or hunted there. It was too far to go and return in a day, when there was enough within reach to give them all a good living here. And how would they be safe outside the cave with the big night prowlers around?

The mere sight of those empty spaces made Suth restless. Like the others he had grown used to the valley, but only in certain ways. Almost every day he felt the earth tremble, but now he no longer paused in what he was doing. If it happened at night, it didn't wake him. And he barely noticed the wafts of foul-egg odour that drifted to and fro on the breeze.

On the other hand, the cave still stank in his nostrils. Every evening he entered it with reluctance, wishing there were other places to lair, and in his dreams he walked and walked and walked, and would wake with his legs aching from the imaginary journey. All the life he had known had been moving from one Good Place to the next, following the rains as they moved across the parched land. He could not get used to staying in this one place, going out in the same direction every day, never more than half a morning's journey, to forage the next patch of ground and smell the same smells and see the same horizons as yesterday.

And time and time again something happened to remind him that Noli had been right: he and the Moonhawks were prisoners in this valley. Nobody seemed to bother much about them while they were separated from each other, but as soon as they were all together they were watched. They weren't allowed to forage at the end of the line, where they might drift away unnoticed, but were made to stay in the middle. And if by any chance they got out of sight somebody came to look for them.

Suth tested this the first time he had a chance. They had hardly started to forage one morning when a storm brewed up and everybody crowded under a clump of trees for shelter. Suth deliberately took the Moonhawks aside to a sloping boulder where there was just room for all six of them to huddle out of the wet.

Almost at once Dith came striding through the rain, seized Suth by the arm and dragged him out.

'What do you do here?' he snarled. 'You stay where we are. Come, all of you.'

He hauled Suth across to the trees and in front of everybody flung him to the ground as if he'd been punishing a misbehaving child.

That too was typical. It was another reason why Suth knew he couldn't belong here. He didn't fit in among these people. He was supposed to be the father of a family. Mosu had said so. He had made himself a good digging stick and sharpened its point and hardened it in the fire, as a man was supposed to. He carried it with him wherever he went, but apart from using it to kill a snake, the way his father had shown him, he didn't do any hunting with it. For that you needed to go in a group with the men, and they wouldn't let him, any more than they let him join the game they played under the trees while they were guarding the foragers. Suth wasn't a man. He didn't have the man-scars on his cheeks. So the men made a point of treating him as a child. He hated this.

There were three boys of about Suth's age, but Suth didn't want to play with them. He was supposed to be a man. Besides, they didn't want Suth in their group. It suited them better to copy the men and ignore him.

The eldest of the boys was called Jad. His father was Jun, who was Mosu's eldest son. One evening at the end of the rains, there was a buzz of excitement and the women started to prepare a feast. As they did so they kept picking on Jad, and ordering him about, and scolding him when he hadn't done anything wrong. It was a sort of joke, but at the same time they took it seriously. It mattered.

Suth sat and watched and felt sick in his heart. He understood what this meant. He knew what was going to happen.

When they went down to the lake for their evening drink, Jad took a fresh leaf and folded it into a shallow bowl. He filled the bowl with water and carried it cupped in his hands back to the cave.

On the way the men ran ahead and set ambushes, and jumped out at him with fierce yells, trying to scare or startle him into spilling the water, but he carried it on steadily.

When they reached the camp, Jad kneeled by the fire and his mother, Fura, scooped ash into the water and mixed it to a thick paste, which Jad then took to where Mosu sat by the cave mouth. He kneeled beside her. She felt for his face, dipped her other hand into the paste and smeared it onto his forehead and cheeks, muttering as she did so. Then Fura took over and covered the rest of his body with paste until he was grey from top to toe.

During this the women preparing the meal didn't gossip and chatter as usual, but sang a slow, wailing chant, too softly for Suth to hear the words. He didn't need to, because the Kin used to do these things in almost exactly the same way. The chant was the song the women sang when one of their children died, because tonight Jad was leaving his mother's side and becoming a man.

Tonight Jad was nobody, neither man nor child, so he sat cross-legged in front of the fire, and ate no food. He was nothing, a grey ghost, and ghosts don't eat. Nor do they sleep among the living, so just before everybody else went into the cave Jun took him along the cliff and helped him to climb a notched pole to a ledge where he could spend the night. Then Jun took the pole away so that Jad would be safe from night hunters.

The next morning he was helped down again, but he wasn't allowed to walk to the lake. Instead the men carried him like a dead body and laid him by the water, where Jun washed the ash from his skin. Then Mosu crouched beside him and cried out in her croaking voice to the power that laired in this place, telling it that from now on Jad was a man.

Jad stood up, and Jun put a pole into his hand and told him to make himself a digging stick, and Dith, who was the best stoneworker in the valley, gave him a new cutter so that he could shape the point.

They all went up the hill to prepare the man feast, laughing and teasing Jad with the very same jokes that the Kin would have used at Suth's own man-making at Odutu below the Mountain.

Suth watched the whole ritual in silence, though his heart was bursting with bitterness and grief. As he had said to Mosu, three moons ago on that second morning in the valley, this should have been his day. At this very moon the Kin would have journeyed to Odutu, and his mother would have smeared the ash onto his body, and his father would have taken him to a particular ledge far up the mountain, to spend the night alone . . .

It would never happen now. He had no father, no mother. This valley was not the place where a Moonhawk could be made a man.

At the feast he could barely eat. And when the time came for Jad to kneel beside Mosu so that, with Foia guiding her hand, she could slice the first man scar into his cheek, Suth couldn't bear to watch. He closed his eyes and bowed his head. He felt Noli's hand on his arm, but he brushed it away and wept.

A few days later, on their way back to the cave, the foragers and hunters stopped as usual to inspect the traps they had set. It was almost time to move on to a fresh warren, and only two traps had caught anything. They were Baga's and Tinu's. Dith's had caught nothing. Baga was his sister, and she never missed a chance to tease him.

'You are no hunter, Dith,' she called out. 'You catch nothing. It takes a woman to build a good trap. See, this girl child makes a better trap than you. See how well it was made.'

Dith was furious. He came striding over, kicked the remains of Tinu's trap with his feet, picked up the ground rat and flung it across the hillside.

Tinu flinched as if he'd struck her. Suth gathered her to his side and turned to Dith. He felt his hair starting to bush.

'Baga speaks truth,' he snarled. 'Tinu builds good traps. You should praise her, not scorn her.'

Dith stared at him contemptuously. If a man had spoken to him like that, his hair would have bushed right out, but it didn't even stir.

'Let her build a deer trap,' he said. 'Then I praise her.'

He turned and strutted away.

A few days later, just after they had returned from the morning visit to the lake, Tinu pulled Suth aside.

'Go see deer,' she mouthed. 'This way. No people. Suth, I ask.'

It was a struggle for her to say that much at a time. She looked at him pleadingly and pointed along the slope in the opposite direction to the foraging grounds.

He gestured to Tinu to wait. Noli had already said

she was going to forage that day, so he told her that he was going to hunt.

'Be lucky, Suth,' she said, just as his mother used to say to his father when he was setting out to look for game.

'You too be lucky, Noli,' he answered, as his father would have.

They set off across the rough hillside. It would have been quicker to take one of the paths through the scrub, but even the grown men didn't go there alone. Not all the big hunting animals slept by day, and one man by himself was no match for a leopard.

At first, Noli's blessing seemed a strong one. They'd been walking for a while when Suth spotted a stoneweed. He marked it with his mark to gather on the way back and share with the rest of the Moon-hawks. It was a good sign, he thought as they scrambled on.

The sun was halfway up the sky before they came to a shallow dip running up the hillside, where a broad strip of coarse grass had managed to take root. At its lower edge they found fresh deer tracks coming and going through gaps in the scrub.

They climbed back up and settled in the shade of a jut of rock to watch. Time went by, and more time, and still nothing happened. Suth's restlessness, eased at first by the change from day after day of foraging, came back ever more strongly, until he felt that he could no longer bear to sit still. He rose to his feet.

'Deer do not come,' he said. 'We go.'

Tinu looked up at him. Her disappointment made it almost impossible for her to speak. Her mouth worked. When the words came he barely understood them.

'I . . . stay . . . Suth . . . I . . . ask . . .'

He hesitated and looked around. What harm could come to her here, so far up the open hillside? What except snakes and lizards would be out here in the full heat of the day?

'I go,' he said. 'When sun is there, I come back.'

He pointed a little above the western horizon. She nodded understanding. He picked up his digging stick. Without having thought about it, he knew exactly what he needed to ease his restlessness.

He climbed steadily up the hill, using his digging stick as a staff, ignoring the weight of the sun on his head and shoulders. At last the slope eased, and he could see ahead of him the barrier of jagged boulders that rimmed the bowl. It was further to them than he had remembered. He looked at the sun. It was more than halfway down. If he went on, they'd be lucky to get back to the cave before dark. He felt obstinate – he would do what he had come to do.

As he turned to continue his climb, his eye was caught by a glimmer above the western ridge, the white peak of a mountain. He recognized it at once. You could see that snow-capped peak from all over the lands which the Kin used to roam, though it might be many days walking away. It was the Mountain above Odutu, the Place of Meeting. When any of the Kin had died, Moonhawk had come in the night and carried their spirit away to the Spirit Place at its summit. And somewhere below was the ledge where Suth would have spent the slow night before the day of becoming a man.

He looked at it and wept for the world that he had lost.

I cannot stay here, he thought as he climbed on. This is not my place.

The Moonhawks had been lucky when they had first crossed the barrier of rocks that crowned the ridge, and had found a way through fairly soon. This time he had to explore some distance along it, trying several openings and finding them blocked, before he recognized the one they had used that first evening.

He would need to know this place, he thought, so he studied the slope below, picking out landmarks, so as to be sure of finding it again. By now it was almost time for him to turn back, but he went stubbornly on, until he reached a place from which he had a clear view of the desert below.

He gazed east. The awful emptiness stretched away and away. It was terrifying, deadly, but still he yearned for it, simply because it was not the prisoning bowl behind him. Here were the huge skies he was used to. Here he could walk day after day after day, and still not reach the end. Soon, soon, in a few more moons, the small ones would be tall and strong enough to do that too, and only Otan would need help. Then he would take them far away to the new Good Places that Bal had dreamed of, and there he would teach them how to live the life they were born to.

Somewhere there must be a way across the desert. He started to study it more deliberately, searching for any sign of hope. Under the clear evening light he could see for immense distances. The dew trap he and Noli had found – where was that? . . . No, it would be too far to see . . . Where had they climbed the cliff then? A bit to the left? So . . .

He stiffened. Something had moved in that stillness. Not where he happened to be looking but near enough to catch his eye. It had come out of the long shade of boulder into the sun. Where?

There! Two of them . . . three . . . moving one behind the other towards the mountain. Mere flecks, dark on the yellow grey waste, so far off that he could see neither heads nor limbs.

Yet he knew at once what he was looking at. People. Walking.

Who were they? Nobody ever went down from the valley into the desert. Some of Bal's group? The only three who were left alive? But they didn't move like lost and starving survivors. There was something about them that made it seem as if they knew where they were going . . .

Yes. They were going towards the pass through Dry Hills.

Now he was sure. Whoever they were, there was a way across the desert, and they had found it.

By the time Suth had recrossed the ridge, the sun was touching the horizon. It was almost dark before he reached Tinu. She seemed untroubled by his having been gone so long.

She rose as he came and pointed down the slope.

'Suth, I see deer. They come. Go,' she mouthed.

He peered down the slope. There was a moon, but it was not more than a quarter full and already well down the western sky. The belt of scrub and the forest were a single dark mass. It was far too dark to tell if the deer that Tinu had seen were still there. When the moon set it would be almost pitch night. There was no hope of their getting back to the cave before then. And soon the big night prowlers would be hunting.

'Too dark,' he said. 'We find a lair.'

He led the way back up the hill.

They slept hungry and thirsty, but Suth almost welcomed the discomfort. It was part of the life he knew. Tinu made no complaint. She seemed happy and excited. When Suth woke at first light she was already up, crouching a little way off where a jut of rock gave her a clear view down the hill. As Suth moved to join her she gestured to him to keep low. He crouched beside her and she pointed. Far below them, halfway up the slant of grass, deer were grazing.

Tinu gave a sigh of happiness.

'Men sleep. Deer come,' she mumbled. 'Deer go. Men come.'

Suth grunted. It made sense. The deer had learned to hide from the night prowlers, and to hide again from the daytime hunters. There were just these two times, dawn and dusk, when it was safe for them to graze.

It didn't matter now. It was important for Tinu to be happy, but he was aching to get back to the cave and tell Noli that he now knew that there had to be a way through the desert.

They were in time to see the last of the people disappearing into the scrub on their way to the lake for their morning drink. Hurrying, they caught up as the line wound into the trees. Jun was among the rear guard. He turned, grabbed Suth by the hair, and cuffed him stingingly on the side of the head.

'Where do you go?' he snapped. 'This is not good. Do you say you are a man, to come and go?'

He kicked Suth forward. Several of the women scolded him as he made his way up the line to join the Moonhawks.

Noli was clearly relieved to see him.

'Suth, I fear for you,' she told him. 'The women say you take Tinu, you go away, you leave us. I say you do not do this. But I fear for you.'

Suth hardly listened. He took her by the arm.

'Noli,' he whispered. 'A way goes through the desert. I saw people. They came through the desert.'

She didn't react with excited questions, but simply stared at him, frowning, while he explained what he'd seen.

'What people are these?' she asked doubtfully.

Suth had been puzzling about this since he'd woken.

'My thought is this,' he said. 'They are Moonhawk. They found Good Places beyond the desert. Now Bal sends some back. They tell Fat Pig, they tell Little Bat and all the Kins, *Come to these new Good Places. No murdering strangers are here!*'

Noli frowned and sighed, and then walked on with her head bowed, troubled and silent. When they reached the lake, he drew her aside.

'Why do you not speak?' he asked. 'Is it not good, this that I saw?'

She took his hands and looked into his eyes but still didn't answer.

'Does Moonhawk say nothing to you?' he asked.

'Moonhawk does not come to this place,' she whispered. 'Do not ask more. Oh, Suth, I am sad, sad.'

She clutched his hands tight and let go. He could feel her distress, though he didn't understand it. He grunted and moved away. All his excitement was gone, leaving him sour and miserable.

When he glanced back, Noli was standing where he'd left her, staring out across the lake, while the eerie howl of Big Voice floated over the water.

Oldtale

MONKEY IS FOUND OUT

Black Antelope grazed far out on the plain.

At evening he lifted up his head and sniffed the air.

He smelled fire.

He smelled the odour of burned flesh.

Thus he thought, The First Good Place burns. The creatures burn, and An and Ammu and their children.

He came swiftly, but all was still.

At the sound of his hooves, the creatures came out of their holes and lairs and nests to greet him.

'Who is hurt?' he called to them. 'Who burns?'

'None of us,' they answered, each one.

In the darkness he saw the glow of a great fire. He heard the sound of singing, and loud boasting.

He came softly to the place and saw An and Ammu and their children feasting around the fire that they had made. His nostrils were filled with the smell of the roast flesh that they ate.

Black Antelope called the First Ones to him.

'Which of you has done this?' he said. 'Which of you gave fire to the children of An and Ammu?'

'Not I,' said Little Bat.

'Not I,' said Fat Pig.

So they answered, each one.

Only Monkey said nothing.

'Was it you, Monkey?' said Black Antelope.

Still Monkey said nothing. But the itchy place under his arm, that had never healed, tickled him.

He scratched.

'Why do you scratch, Monkey?' said Black Antelope.

'A tick bit me,' said Monkey.

'Let me breathe on the place and make it well,' said Black Antelope.

At that Monkey tried to run away, but Snake caught him and wrapped himself around him so that he could not move, and Black Antelope looked under his arm and saw the place that had not healed.

By that all knew that Monkey had given fire to the children of An and Ammu.

CHAPTER NINE

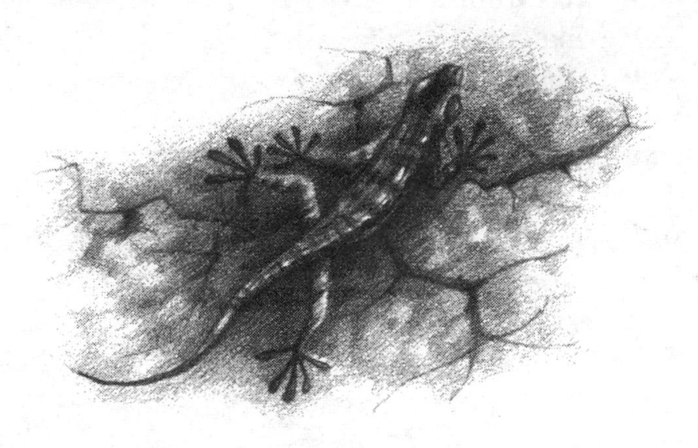

Suth began to make plans for their journey. There was no point in waiting for the dry season to be over. Very little rain ever fell in Dry Hills, and clearly none ever did in the desert. (It was some freak of the ground that made little local storms fall over this valley and keep the lake supplied – Suth had decided it was Monkey who made that happen.)

They couldn't carry water, so they would have to find it. The people Suth had seen coming out of the desert must have found water. He wondered if they had been traveling at night not just to avoid the dreadful desert sun. Perhaps there were dew traps they knew about. Dew traps weren't common. There was a good one at Tarutu Rock, and the bad one Suth and Noli had found. Those were the only ones he had seen or heard of. But there might be others in the desert, and better . . .

And even if they were lucky about water, how would they carry food? In the old Good Places, the

Kins used to make straps from the bark of tingin trees, and light nets from special grasses, but he hadn't seen anything like that in the valley. They didn't have gourds. Perhaps they didn't have tingin trees either.

He asked Tinu if she had any ideas and she nodded, gesturing to show she would think about it, but as far as Suth could see, she did nothing.

Besides, she was busy with something else. In all her spare time, at the camp and while they were resting under the trees at midday, she would be shaping grass stems into individual knots, which she stored in a folded leaf and carried around with her. Later she broke branches from the bushes and took them back to the camp.

Then one evening she took Suth aside and led him to a piece of ground she had cleared of loose stuff a little beyond the main camp area. He watched while she laid a lot of twiggy branchlets out on the slope until she had a wide belt of them across the lower half of her cleared patch. There were narrow paths through the belt, running down the slope.

Next she unfolded her leaf and took out the grass knots she had been making. When she laid a line of them out on the rock Suth saw at once what they were. Two grass stems below, twisted together to form a thicker bit, with two more stems sticking out on either side and a round knot at the top. Legs, body, arms, head. People. Tiny grass people.

She showed him some more. These were made in the same way, but each had four stems below a horizontal body that curved up into a neck, and was then pinched over to make the head. Deer.

And now he saw that the slope of rock was the

hillside where she'd watched the deer with him, and the line of twigs was the belt of scrub below.

'Clever,' he said.

She smiled, and began to move the little grass deer up through the paths to graze on the hillside. She set two little grass men to watch unseen what the deer did. Then more men came to cut branches from the bushes, and block all the paths but one. Halfway down this one they cut a clearing. She showed the deer going in and out through this one path.

Now, while the deer were out on the hillside, the men came creeping back through the scrub. Two groups moved up the hill on either side of the deer, while a smaller one went to the clearing and blocked its lower opening with more branches, and then waited there, ready.

She clapped her hands, and with rapid, deft movements showed the hunters leaping out of ambush.

'Yik-yik-yik-yeek!' she cried. 'Wow-wow-waah!'

Suth joined in with the noises of the hunt.

'Oiyu, oiyu, ooiyooo!'

The hunters closed in. The deer fled for the one remaining path and streamed through, only to find themselves trapped in the clearing. Before they could turn back, the hunters from the hillside were on them. All the while Tinu kept up the shrill hoots and squeals that the Kin had used when driving game out of cover towards the hunters. Suth, caught up in the imaginary excitement, joined in.

'Who hunts?' said a man's voice above their heads.

Suth turned and saw Gan and Mohr watching, amused, and no doubt looking for another chance to jeer at him, though they were in fact the least unfriendly of the men.

'Who hunts?' said Mohr again.

'Tinu makes a deer trap,' said Suth. 'Show, Tinu.'

But Tinu was cowering from the men's gaze with her head turned away and her thin arms crossed protectively over her chest. In the end it was Suth who had to show the men what she'd made. At first they laughed and wouldn't take it seriously, but then they got caught up in the excitement, as Suth had been, and called the other men to come over.

It turned out that they weren't nearly as interested in the deer trap as they were in the imaginary hunt. By the time it got too dark to see, they were all crouching around, arguing about it, elbowing each other aside as they tried to have their own way about how the hunt should go. They even chose special grass people to be themselves, so that they could play the most important part, and then boasted about what they'd done as if it had really happened, and quarrelled with each other about their share in the hunt. None of them paid any attention to Tinu. The model was their game, their toy.

In the end they spoiled it, moving the cunning little grass models roughly around until they lost their shapes, and scattering the belt of twigs apart. They were still arguing about it as they built the wall across the mouth of the cave.

Over the next few days, the men came to Suth one after the other, and either asked or ordered him to tell Tinu to make them their own little grass man, and grass deer for the man to hunt. Tinu seemed happy to do it, and to replace them when they were spoiled, and to rebuild her model of the hillside so that they could play their game afresh each evening. They ignored Tinu, sitting to one side, deftly knotting men and deer for them out of grass stems, and listening to what they said.

And then, suddenly, one evening, it was all decided. They would start to build a real deer trap the next day. Tinu listened with dismay.

'This not good,' she told Suth in her mumbling whisper. 'First men wait. Watch deer. Deer come, go. Men watch.'

She was right, of course. Somebody had to go and watch the deer in the early dawn, to see how they came and went through the paths in the scrub, or the men would build their trap in the wrong place.

'Tinu, I cannot say this to them,' he told her. 'To them I am a child. They do not hear me.'

She hesitated, then bent her head and fluttered her fingers in the air.

'Suth, I ask,' she mouthed. 'You, me, go. Go now. See deer, sun up.'

He looked around. The notion of sleeping out under the stars again was very tempting. It was almost dark, but the men were still arguing about their game. The women were on the far side of the fire. Suth walked quietly over to where Noli was sitting among the small ones. Ko and Otan were already asleep, and Mana almost.

'I go with Tinu,' he whispered. 'We watch deer.'

'This makes the men angry,' she said.

'Is Dith my father, to say yes and no to me?'

'When you are gone, I tell them.'

'My thanks.'

He went back to Tinu and squatted down beside her. When no one was looking in their direction, they rose and moved away.

They laired well up on the hill, as before, and in the earliest dawn made their way down the slope, moving carefully, not dislodging a pebble, and bending low so that they were hidden from anything in the dip of ground. Then they turned and crept towards the rim of the dip.

The deer were there. Suth counted them. Ten and three more, in a rough line, working their way up the slope. Most were nosing among the rough tussocks but at any moment two or three had their heads up, alert, with ears cupped to catch the slightest sound.

Suth and Tinu watched them in silence. The light grew stronger. Then Tinu touched his arm and signalled him back. As soon as the deer were hidden she put her mouth to his ear.

'Make deer run,' she whispered. 'This way.'

She gestured to show what she wanted. He nodded. It made sense. This was their one chance to see which path the deer naturally used for escape if they were startled on the hillside. He would need to hurry though. Soon it would be full day and the deer would be going back under cover until dusk. He climbed as fast and silently as he could, wormed his way across the open hillside above the dip, using any cover the boulders gave him, then down again in a crouching lope, below where Tinu waited.

When he crawled to the rim of the dip, the deer were still there, apparently undisturbed, but to judge by their fidgety movements just getting ready to return to shelter. He gave himself a moment to catch his breath and then jumped to his feet, yelling and waving his digging stick.

Instantly they were streaking down the slope, clearing the boulders with great flowing bounds. They swerved away as he sprinted to head them off, but Tinu herself had come further down and rose whooping to meet them. They swung back, heading for three separate pathways as the herd split apart. They were well ahead of him now. There was no hope of his cutting them off.

Then, just as the nearest group reached the scrub, something leaped to meet it, bowling the leading deer clean over. The others vanished, but that one lay thrashing and struggling to rise while the leopard that had been waiting in ambush wrenched snarling at its neck.

Suth halted, panting, and raised his digging stick. The movement caught the leopard's eye. It looked up and stared at him. Its tail lashed to and fro and it bared its fangs, but it stayed where it was, crouched over the deer.

Suth hesitated. If I can drive it off, he thought, I can drag the deer home, and then even Dith will have to give me praise.

Though he knew he was doing a stupid and dangerous thing, he took a pace forward, just to see.

Instantly the leopard was springing for his throat.

His heart clenched in his chest, but his arm and his body answered without thought, lunging full strength to meet the attack. He was belted sideways. His digging stick was torn from his grasp. There was a searing pain down his left arm. He was falling, helpless. A hard thing crashed against his skull. Blackness.

He woke to the throb of pain, pain all through him.

A voice mouthing his name.

'Suth! Suth!'

Tinu.

He opened his eyes. Through the pain haze, he saw her face, close above his. The haze half cleared. He wiped the rest away with the back of his right hand. It was blood. The pain found its sources, aching fiercely at the side of his head, searing down his left arm from the shoulder. He craned, and saw his left side smeared with blood from deep gouges slashed down the arm. He eased himself up, clutching the wound with his right hand, trying to stem the flow.

The leopard! His body sprang alert. He stared around. No sign. But a sound, a ghastly retching cough, mixed with violent thrashings among the bushes.

'Run, Tinu! Run!' he gasped, and staggered to his feet, searching for his digging stick.

Gone.

A rock, then . . .

His eye fell on the body of the deer.

He forgot the wound, forgot the pain. This was what he had fought for. He seized it by the hind legs and frenziedly started to drag it up the hill.

It was too heavy for him. The pain came rasping back. He stopped and stood, shuddering, with the blood welling from the wound. He looked back. Still no sign of the leopard, though the racket in the bushes rose and fell. He bent and dragged the body a few more paces towards a scatter of loose rocks and began to pile them over it. Every few seconds he glanced down the slope, but nothing came.

The daze returned, but he worked on. Tinu was helping him. When the body was covered he stood swaying. The valley seemed full of darkness.

'Face hurt, Suth,' said Tinu's voice.

He put his fingers to his left cheek and flinched at his own touch. Another wound, but his hands were so covered with blood that he couldn't tell how bad it was.

'You die, Suth?'

The darkness cleared and he stood erect.

'No, I live,' he said.

He must tell the men himself that he had fought a leopard and robbed it of its prey. Their faces would change. He must see that.

He was in no state to scramble across rocks, so despite the danger he headed down towards the scrub, where the going was less rough. The sun was above the ridge now, and warmed his back. He walked slowly, but steadily at first, clutching his right hand over his wounded arm. The flow of blood seemed to ease.

But then the darkness closed in again, filling his eyesight and his mind, though his legs still walked as they did in dreams. There were clear patches in the darkness, when he would find Tinu holding his elbow and guiding him carefully along, and he'd remember where he was and what had happened, and then there'd be nothing but pain and darkness once more.

They stopped, and then they seemed to be climbing.

Tinu's voice told him to sit and she eased him down onto a rock. She was gone.

He waited, and then she was back and coaxing his head up and putting something against his mouth. The smell woke him.

Stoneweed.

He sipped, and his mind cleared. She'd remembered the stoneweed he'd marked a few days earlier, and then forgotten to gather on his way back to the cave, in his eagerness to tell Noli what he'd seen. Tinu had fetched it for him.

'My thanks,' he muttered, and sipped again, carefully, feeling the warmth and strength running through his veins. He passed her the stoneweed and she took a couple of sips and handed it back.

He saw her stiffen and gaze down the slope. She let out a shout, climbed a boulder, and waved and shouted again. Suth rose, swaying, and saw men with digging sticks halted just above the scrub and gazing towards them. *They have come to find me*, he thought. *Noli told them I watched deer. They are angry.* Then he thought, *No, they are too many. They go to build their trap*.

He swayed and almost fell, but managed to settle onto a boulder. Two of the men were climbing the slope. His eyesight was all blurred, but from the way they walked he recognized them as Mohr and Gan. He rose. He was almost too weak to stand, but he knew what he needed to say and do.

He held out the stoneweed to them, one-handed, the gesture of a man offering a gift to another man, an equal.

'Mohr, Gan,' he said. 'I fought with a leopard. It

killed a deer. I drove it off. The deer is under rocks. Tinu shows you.'

'You are hurt,' said Mohr. 'We must take you to Mosu, to see to your hurts.'

'No, I wait here. You bring the deer. I, Suth, ask this. Here is my gift. Drink.'

Gan accepted the stoneweed, took a couple of sips and passed it to Mohr, who did the same and then handed it back.

Suth sat and closed his eyes. He heard the men muttering to each other, questioning Tinu, Tinu painfully mouthing her answer, for once not afraid to speak to them. All three moved away. He heard other voices from further down the slope. They faded.

While Suth waited, he did his best to clean the wounds in his arm and cheek, using spit from his mouth. The three claw slashes on his arm were deep and throbbing, though the stoneweed dulled the pain. The cut on his cheek seemed shallower. Perhaps his head had flinched just in time from the strike.

He eased the torn flesh together with his fingertips, as best he could. *I wear these marks for all my days*, he thought. *All then know how I fought the leopard.*

He finished the stoneweed. He'd never before had so much all to himself, and the juice made him drowsy. He lay down on the hillside and fell asleep.

A voice woke him. Tinu again, urgent, excited.

'Suth! Suth! Wake! You kill . . . leopard! See! Gan bring!'

The words were bursting from her. He could barely make them out. Blearily he sat up and looked. Men were coming up the slope, two of them with loads over their shoulder. He rose. They stopped a few paces away and stood looking at him. Their faces had changed.

'Suth,' said Mohr stiffly. 'You killed the leopard. We found it among the scrub. Your digging stick is fast in its throat. So it died. I, Mohr, praise.'

'I, Gan, also praise,' said Gan. 'I bring your brave digging stick. See, it is here.'

He held it out, but froze as Suth, without thought, wiped the back of his hand across his bleeding cheek before stepping forward to take it.

'See, Mohr!' whispered Gan. 'Suth's face! He has the man-scar! The leopard made it!'

Oldtale

PEOPLE HUNT BLACK ANTELOPE

Such was their lust for roast flesh that the children of An and Ammu would eat nothing else. They passed by the seeded grasses and did not gather them. They left ripe berries on the bushes, and fruits on the vines, and nuts on the ground beneath the trees, as if they had been dirt. All day from sun up they hunted and killed the creatures, and at sundown they made a fire and roasted their catch and ate until their stomachs were round and full, like a ripe gourd. They fell sick, but they did not care.

The creatures came to Black Antelope. They said, 'The people hunt and kill us day after day, without rest. Tens and tens and tens of us they kill for their feasts. Soon none of us are left.'

Black Antelope gathered the First Ones. He said, 'We made this Good Place for ourselves. Now people spoil it. Go, all of you, far and far. Make new Places. Then people live there. Set these Places apart. Then people must journey between them. See to it that there is food of all kinds, a little of each kind. Then the people must forage as well as hunt. They do not fall sick from eating only flesh. Let each Place have its season. Then the people leave it. They are gone. The creatures breed. The plants seed and grow. All is new again.'

The First Ones agreed, and did all that.

Then Black Antelope took the shape of a common antelope and let himself be seen by the children of An and Ammu as they were setting off to hunt. They saw him grazing on the plain a little way off.

Da and Datta said, 'We hunt that antelope.'

The others were afraid. They said, 'Do we kill and eat antelope? Is not Black Antelope the greatest of the First Ones?'

Da said, 'Why do we not eat it? Which of us is of the Kin of Black Antelope?'

Datta said, 'See how fat he is. His flesh is very good to eat.'

But still the others were afraid.

Da and Datta said, 'We are the best. You must do as we say. You swore it at Odutu below the Mountain.'

Because they had sworn at Odutu, they agreed to hunt the antelope.

Black Antelope saw them creeping towards him and moved a little away and grazed again. They crept further, and again he moved away, and again, and again. All day he did this, and always they said in their hearts: 'Next time we have him.' The thought of fat roast flesh was strong in their mouths.

At sunset he led them to a water hole where there was blueroot growing beside the water. They drank, and dug out the blueroot and ate it, and said, 'Tomorrow we return to the First Good Place and hunt there.'

Next day they woke and saw Black Antelope grazing close by, and again they hunted him all day, and at sunset he led them to a water hole where there were binjas growing beside the water. They drank, and gathered and husked the binja seed and ate it, and said, 'Tomorrow we return to the First Good Place and hunt there.'

So it was for many, many days. And at last they came to one of the new Good Places, which the First Ones had made for them, and there Black Antelope left them. As he passed by the water holes on his way, he drank them dry. And he ate the binjas and the blueroot and everything else that grew near them, so that the children of An and Ammu should never return to the First Good Place.

CHAPTER TEN

On Mosu's instructions Foia licked Suth's wounds clean and pounded leaves of bitter bush and pressed them on. The juices stung like fire but dried the exposed flesh so that the blood stopped oozing and scabs began to form. Mohr and Gan carried the news out to the foragers and hunters, who came home early for the feast. The men butchered and roasted the deer.

Suth knew very little of all this. He was weak with loss of blood and groggy with shock and the after-effects of the stoneweed. He was aware of a moment when the Moonhawks were suddenly there, and Noli's concern for him, and Ko's wide-eyed awe at his wound, and Mana settling beside him to be hugged by his good arm.

The men came too, and spoke to him in new voices. He couldn't see their faces clearly, or understand the words, but he knew that they were praise. Dith was among them, who had scorned him so. He too spoke praise.

Now I may die, Suth thought, overwhelmed with happiness despite the pain.

He would have slept where he was, in the full sun and on bare rock, but the Moonhawks gathered bedding for him inside the mouth of the cave and Noli helped him to his feet and led him there to sleep in the shade.

They woke him for the feast. He was still too weak and dazed to do his part unaided, so Mohr held his hand on the cutter and helped him slice open the belly of the leopard and draw out the heart and liver and cut them in pieces, so that everybody could eat of them and the power of the leopard would be in them all.

Night fell and there was firelight and singing and many mouths speaking praise. Somebody came and put something hard and round into his hand. It was a cutter. The giver was Dith. He had done the same for Jad at his man-making.

Suth managed to speak his thanks, but when he was called on to make his boast he needed to be helped to his feet and then could only stand there, mumbling. He knew what he wanted to say, but the words wouldn't come to his mouth. But no one mocked him, for no one – not even Mosu, who had seen everything and knew everything – had heard of anybody who had fought and killed a leopard alone.

For the next several days Suth was too feeble to do more than make the morning and evening trips to the lake, so Noli took the Moonhawks foraging, while he rested at the camp.

When he was strong enough to join them, she continued to come with them and he began to feel that things were back now as they should be, with his family together and whole, and given their place and respected by the men and women of the valley. The men were busy building deer traps, and he might have joined them, or sat with them in the shade and played their game with them, and they wouldn't have made him unwelcome, but he preferred to be with the Moonhawks and plan for the day they would leave.

Then Mosu fell ill, and became too weak to hobble to the lake, and in too much pain to be carried there by the men. Instead the women folded leaves into bowls, which they filled with water and carried carefully back to her between their two cupped hands. Though Foia was there to look after her, Noli said she must stay with her too, and even when Mosu got better and could go to the lake again she continued to stay.

Suth didn't like this at all. He resented it much more than he had before, and resented how silent and withdrawn Noli had become. One evening he could bear it no more. After they had finished eating, he took her aside.

'Why do you do this?' he said. 'I, Suth, ask. Why do you not speak? Why do you choose to be with the old woman always? You are Moonhawk. Your place is with us.'

She shook her head, and he thought she was going to tell him again that her reasons were secret – dream stuff that she could share only with Mosu. But for a while she simply sat with her head bowed, staring at her folded hands. When she did speak it was in an almost toneless mutter, slow and hesitant.

'I tell you,' she said. 'Words are not good for this, Suth. But see.'

She picked up a small stone.

'I say *Stone*, Suth,' she said. 'I see the stone. You see it. You say the word. We see the same. We say the same. Stone.'

'Stone?' said Suth, puzzled.

'Stone,' she said again, and put it into his hand, closing his fingers around it.

'I say *Moonhawk*,' she said. 'What do you see, Suth?'

He frowned.

'I see . . . a great bird?' he said hesitantly.

'Where is this bird, Suth?'

'Where? . . . In my head, I think. It is like when I remember. Like when I say *Sometimes River*. Then I see the river in my head.'

'Only this, Suth? No more? I tell you now how Moonhawk comes to me. It is night – dark, dark. No moon. No stars. But she is there. Moonhawk. There is a yellow eye. There are wings . . . I do not *see* them, Suth. They are there. I have no word for this. And I am small. She is big, big. I am afraid, yes. But my heart is happy. This is how Moonhawk comes.'

Suth looked at the stone in his hand. He tightened his fingers around it, feeling its hardness. What Noli was telling him – trying to tell him – was not like that at all. There seemed to be no place for it in his mind.

'You do not see the thing I see?' Noli suggested.

'Noli, I cannot see this,' he said.

'Mosu sees the thing I see,' said Noli. 'She lives long, long. Many times her spirit goes from her body.

It journeys where the First Ones are. They speak to her spirit, wonderful things. All this she tells me. Mosu knows how it is when Moonhawk comes to me.'

'Moonhawk comes to Mosu?' said Suth, more puzzled than ever.

Noli shook her head, hesitated and sighed.

'Moonhawk does not come to this place,' she said sadly. 'He is too strong, Big Voice.'

He grabbed her wrist, appalled.

'Moonhawk came!' he exclaimed. 'She spoke in your dream! *Monkey is sick!* She said this to you!'

She eased his fingers away.

'She does not come again,' she muttered. 'Big Voice is strong in this place, too strong.'

She paused. He thought she had finished.

'Suth,' she said. 'Mosu says this to me, *Big Voice comes to none of my people. They are sick. Now, soon, I die. Then he comes to you, Noli.*'

Now he understood what she had been trying to tell him.

'And you do this thing, Noli?' he said. 'No. You are Moonhawk. I, Suth, say this.'

She wouldn't look at him. She was ashamed. She was betraying him, and the others, betraying all the dead generations of Moonhawk. He could feel her shame.

'What is Monkey to you?' he insisted. 'We are Moonhawk. Soon, Noli, soon we leave this place. When the moon is big, we go. I saw people in the desert. I told you this. They know a way through the desert. We find that way. We take food, we find water. We cross the desert and find our Kin. We go far from this place. Then Moonhawk comes to you again. I am the father, Noli. You are the mother. We are Moonhawk. I, Suth, say this!'

Still she didn't look at him. His eye was caught by a small figure, tottering up the slope, black against the firelight.

'See, Noli!' he said. 'Otan! In the desert Moonhawk came. She said to you, *Go back. Leave Bal and the others. Find Otan. I show you water. Take Otan there.* Do you say, *Otan is not Moonhawk*? Do you say, *Here he is Monkey*?'

She looked up and he saw the firelight glinting off her tears.

'Big Voice is strong, Suth,' she whispered. 'When he comes, I am small. He is big, big. I am afraid. My heart is sad.'

Suth lay sleepless in the reeking dark of the cave, thinking about Noli. He was full of anger towards her, though at the same time he was aware of her misery. He was angry with Mosu too, for taking Noli away from the Moonhawks where she belonged. And he was angrier still with Monkey, though he knew how dangerous it was to have such feelings about any of the First Ones.

Why didn't Moonhawk help? Why didn't she come to Noli any more? Was she too afraid of Monkey? That must be it.

The mood of his anger changed at the thought. If Monkey was too strong for Moonhawk, then no wonder he was too strong for Noli. That was why she was so miserable. She knew in her heart she was

Moonhawk, and that she wanted what Suth wanted, to leave this valley and journey and find the rest of the Kin and be with them and live the old life in the way that they knew. But Monkey and Mosu were keeping her here.

He didn't know how they did this. All he knew was that Monkey was one of the First Ones, and had great power, and Mosu had some of that power because she had served Monkey so long.

A moment later something brushed against his hip. Fingers moved up his side and found his hand, and held it.

Noli.

She too had been lying sleepless in the dark, and had heard his sigh, and had reached out.

This is good, he thought. I am the father and she is the mother and we are Moonhawk still. Noli knows this. Now I see what I must do. I must make ready for our journey. The small ones are strong with the good food they have eaten in this place. When all is ready I will say to Noli, *Now we go to find the Kin – Suth, Tinu, Ko, and Mana. Do you come? Do you stay? And Otan. Does he come? Does he stay?* Then for Otan's sake she will come, because he is Moonhawk.

There were things he must do. The next morning, on their way back from the lake, he told Noli. 'Today I watch deer. Tinu comes.'

Noli looked at him, started to speak, and stopped, then smiled.

'Fight no leopard, Suth,' she said.

He laughed and she joined him.

Yes, he thought. Whatever Monkey tells her, she will come with me when I go.

He set off with Tinu. Since his fight with the leopard he had been allowed to come and go very much as he pleased, though he was sure that if he'd tried to take all the Moonhawks with him he would still have been stopped. But nobody seemed to mind if he went off with just Tinu.

This time they didn't go as far as the area where the deer grazed, but stopped below the place at which the Moonhawks had first entered the valley. He knew it by the rat warren he had seen.

'We store food,' he told Tinu. 'Food for many days. You make a place where we keep it. Tinu, this is secret.'

She nodded and searched around, eventually choosing a place where a huge single flat rock had split in two, leaving a deep crack about as wide as a spread hand. She then collected stones and began to wedge them down into the crack to form the floor of her food store.

Suth left her to it and went to look for lizards. It was still early enough for them to be out, basking away the night chill, and he caught two, slit them open with the cutter and set them to dry in the sun. Well-dried lizard would keep for many days. The Kin had always carried some on their longer journeys. To chew it was like chewing the bark of a tree, but slowly the good juices were released and could be swallowed.

The sun climbed, baking the hillside, and the lizards slid back under rocks. A rat bobbed up at the warren. No point in setting traps yet. Rat meat was too juicy to dry well. Tinu could set some a day or two before they left. He made his way down and cautiously ventured among the scrub, pausing and peering around every few paces. Deep in under a thorny bush, he spotted a yellow bracket fungus of a kind he knew. It tasted of nothing, and had not much goodness in it, but it was plant food and it didn't rot, so he began to work his way around the bush looking for somewhere to wriggle in under the fierce thorns.

Kneeling at a possible gap he found himself face-to-face with a dark grey snake, as long as his arm, gliding towards him.

It stopped and reared its head, jaws wide. He froze. His right hand tightened on his digging stick and raised it slowly towards his shoulder. *Do not attack*, his father had told him. *Soon it turns away. Strike then.*

It turned, and he struck, jabbing at the base of the head, but the tangle of twigs spoiled his aim and he caught it further along the body, where it was too thick for the spine to be broken with a single blow.

Instantly it lashed around. He flung his weight on the stick, pinning the body fast, and then, still bearing down, rolled the stick along the thrashing body until he had it safely held behind the head. Now he could reach in, work his fingers under the stick and grasp the snake behind the jaws, so that it couldn't turn and bite. He dragged it out, laid the head on the ground and pounded it with the butt of his stick until it was dead.

He rose, panting. His head, arms and shoulders were bloody from wrestling in under the thorns, but he didn't care. This was how, many moons ago, watched by his father, he had killed his first snake. It was a good sign. Snake flesh dried well and was better to eat than lizard.

He carried the body up to where Tinu was working and slit it into strips with the cutter, set them to dry beside the lizards, and went to see how she was getting on.

She had made a good-sized hollow and was wedging the cracks with pebbles, but when Suth appeared she stopped work, laid a flat rock over the top, and scattered a few smaller ones on top of it, so that it looked like just a pile of loose stuff that happened to have jammed into the crack.

'This is good, Tinu,' he said.

She smiled, pleased, and didn't try to hide her face.

While she finished what she was doing, he went and turned the lizards over, then found a patch of shade and rested, staring out over the forest and brooding over the question of leaving the valley. Not this next big moon – he wouldn't be ready. The one after. Till then, forage for extra food. All the families kept spare supplies – they would ask no questions. Every second day, bring some of it out to put in the food store Tinu was building. Set the meat he had caught to continue drying. Tinu could guard it from scavengers while he hunted for more . . .

Then the biggest problem – how to sneak all the Moonhawks away, to get far enough ahead for them not to be hunted down . . .

The ground trembled, and with it the rock against which he was leaning. He was so used by now to these quakings that he would barely have noticed, but before the shock was over he heard Tinu cry out.

He looked up and saw her backing away with her mouth open and her arms half raised in fear or astonishment.

Snake! he thought.

He snatched up his stick and ran. She saw him coming and pointed to the crack in the rock.

Her food store had disappeared.

He frowned, bewildered.

'Rock . . . break . . . !' Tinu gasped.

Now he saw that the crack was wider than it had been before, almost twice as wide. He peered in, expecting to see the rocks Tinu had used lodged further down, but no. The cleft had no bottom. It was part of a crack in the hillside, and went right down into blackness. Out of it rose, stronger than he'd ever smelled it, the strange reek that always hung over the lake and wafted to and fro across the valley.

He backed away and looked around. Nothing seemed to have changed. The sun was high, and beneath it the immense bowl lay green and still. Then, down in the forest, a Big Voice called, and another answered, and another and another, until the steamy air rang with their wild voices.

Slowly the clamour died into silence.

Suth frowned again.

This didn't happen.

Big Voice called in the morning, and again in the evening, one first and then the next, waiting for each other to finish before they replied. Sometimes one or two might call in the rest of the day. But never like this.

Never with one mad voice together in the heat of noon.

Oldtale

THE CHOOSING OF MATES

When An and Ammu saw that all their children had gone from them, they said, 'Our time is over,' and they went into the desert and lay down, and their spirits left their bodies and wandered through the desert, mourning for their lost children.

The First Ones heard their groanings and weepings, and went and carried them up the Mountain above Odutu. They gave them stoneweed to drink, so that they might forget their sorrow.

As they drank they spat the seeds down the mountain. The seeds fell in the desert, where they grow to this day.

Thus An and Ammu forgot their sorrow.

But their children foraged and hunted in the new Good Places that the First Ones had made for them, and learned their paths and their seasons, and their water holes and dew traps and lairs. So they grew to be men and women.

Then Nal, who was of the Kin of Moonhawk, met

with Turka, who was of the Kin of Little Bat, by the salt pan beyond Lusan-of-the-Ants.

Turka said, 'Now I ask the blessing of Little Bat to leave her Kin, and be your mate, and become of the Kin of Moonhawk.'

Nal said, 'This is my thought also.'

They took salt from the pan and mixed it with spittle and smeared it on each other's forehead, to show that they were now chosen.

Datta came to Nal and said, 'Why is there salt on your forehead? Who has chosen you before I have made my choice? I must have first choice of the men. I am the best, as you swore at Odutu below the Mountain.'

Nal said, 'Not so. Two must make choice of mates. Each chooses the other. I do not choose you, Datta. You are too proud for a mate. I choose Turka.'

Datta went to Da and said, 'Nal chose Turka for his mate before you took your choice of the women. You are wronged by him, as I am by Turka.'

Da was angry. He called the children of An and Ammu to meet him beside Sometimes River, and said, 'We are wronged. Nal and Turka chose each other for mates before we took our choice. We must choose first. We are the best, as you swore at Odutu below the Mountain.'

The others had no answer, because they had sworn as he said.

Now Crocodile was lying in wait in the river. She heard what was said, and she put a thought into Celda's mind, who was of her Kin.

Celda whispered with the other women.

They said, 'Choose, then, Da. Then all choose after

you. Which of us women do you choose for your mate?'

Da looked at them all, carefully.

He said, 'I choose Preela.'

Preela answered him, 'I do not choose you, Da. You are too proud for a mate.'

Then Da chose among the others, each in turn, and they answered him in the same way, as they had agreed. And when Datta chose among the men, so did they, until there were none left to choose but Datta and Da themselves.

They looked at each other, and Da said, 'Datta, I do not choose you. You are too proud for a mate.'

And so said Datta to Da.

Then the others chose among themselves until all had mates, and they were satisfied. Only Da and Datta had none. So to this day there are eight Kins only and Monkey has no Kin.

CHAPTER ELEVEN

When Suth and Tinu got back to the camp they found a commotion. All those who were there were gathered by the mouth of the cave, and as others came hurrying in they joined the circle.

Suth wormed his way through and saw that something had happened to Mosu. She wasn't sitting in her usual place, but was lying on her back on a pile of bedding just inside the mouth of the cave. Foia was kneeling, rubbing her feet and calves.

Mosu gasped and twitched. Her mouth worked convulsively, but the sounds she made weren't words. The people watched in silence for a while, but then moved apart and talked in low voices.

Suth and Tinu set off to meet the returning foragers, but the news had reached them too and they were almost home. Suth found Noli and told her what he had seen.

'I think she dies,' he said.

'She said this,' said Noli. 'Big Voice also. He shook

the place, and spoke. This noon he did it. I told Paro and the women. They also had heard him speak. They did not understand his speaking, and they would not hear me. Gora came from the camp, and then they knew I told truth.'

She spoke gravely but vaguely, as if she was thinking of something else. Suth frowned. He didn't at all like her being able to understand what that wild calling in the forest had meant, when no one else could. Nor did he like Paro and the others knowing that she could do this. Now that the time was so near when he was going to try to sneak the Moonhawks away, he didn't want anyone paying special attention to Noli. But he said nothing.

When they reached the cave they found Mosu was not yet dead, and she was still alive that night when they went into the cave, so they carried her in with them and laid her in her usual place. The next morning she was no better and no worse, so they propped her outside the cave and Foia fed her chewings as if she'd been weaning a child, and spat water into her mouth from cupped leaves, which the women had carried up from the lake.

For ten days and ten more Mosu didn't die. The moon grew to its biggest and back to its smallest and started to grow again. Suth saw little of Noli. They took turns foraging, and even when they were both at the camp she spent all her time with Mosu, rubbing her limbs, cleaning her, or just sitting beside her and holding her twitching hand. When she went down to the lake with the Moonhawks, she moved in a kind of dream, not seeing or hearing anything, dealing with Otan's needs automatically, leaving everything else to Suth.

He hated and resented this, and he only didn't yell at her and perhaps even strike her because he could see that she was miserable too.

On the days when Suth foraged he gathered as much as he could, and saw to it that the others did the same, and on the days when Noli went, he and Tinu carried the surplus out to hide in the new food store that Tinu had built. Once there he hunted. He caught and dried several more lizards, and found a juiceroot in the scrub and marked it with his mark.

Meanwhile Tinu guarded their drying meat from vultures and worked steadily at the task Suth had given her, of finding some way of carrying food other than in their hands, as they would have the cliff to climb down. Tinu found how to fold the big leaves to make a sort of bag, which she fastened with a twist of braided grass. She then made a longer twist, braided and rebraided, and tied several bags along its length. They could be carried like that slung around a neck or hung over a shoulder. The bags, though, were fragile, and it took her all day to find the right grass stems and braid them into a single length. She had finished two lengths, and made and filled the bags and tied them on, by the time Mosu finally died.

They woke in the morning and found her spirit gone. They propped her body in its usual place by the mouth of the cave and piled rocks around it to keep it safe while they went down to the lake. Foia and a few of the elders stayed at the camp, while the rest went foraging.

Suth had thought that Noli would want to stay

behind, but she joined the foragers and worked in a kind of daze, not hearing, not speaking, as if her spirit was far away – wherever Mosu's spirit had gone, perhaps. Everyone else was silent and troubled. The men didn't hunt, but worked quietly alongside the women. There was none of the usual chat, and when they rested, the men didn't play their game.

Before they started work again, a porcupine came scuttling past, climbing the open hillside in the full heat of the day. This was not a thing that happened. Porcupines are night animals, and in any case keep to dense scrub. Three of the men leaped on it and beat it to death with their digging sticks, but with none of the cries and boastings that usually went with a good kill.

Hardly had they finished when another one came past. That too was killed and brought in. Then a group of deer nosed out of the scrub, and another one further off, and another one, not stopping to graze but pausing every now and then to gaze anxiously around, and then trotting on. There was no point in trying to hunt them when they were as alert as that, so the people simply watched them go, but with steadily growing unease.

Without much discussion they decided not to forage that afternoon, and made their way back to the camp to prepare the death feast for Mosu. As they wound their way in a silent line through the scattered scrub of the foraging grounds, Big Voice started to howl, one far off, and another nearer by, and another to the right, and more and more, their wavering hoots rising and falling and floating away across the hot, still valley.

Suth looked at Noli. He'd noticed one or two of the others watching her, as if they'd expected something from her, but she'd stayed completely withdrawn, wrapped in her own thoughts.

'He sings for Mosu?' he suggested.

For once she seemed to hear him, and answered, frowning.

'I do not know,' she muttered. 'I hear no words in his singing. He sings only.'

Back at the cave, though it was only mid-afternoon, they built up the fire and set the porcupines to roast and trooped down to the lake. Normally at this time of day the forest was still, but now the whooping of Big Voice went on and on, untiring, and flocks of birds rose from the treetops and flew to and fro, and then, instead of settling back among the branches, gathered and rose higher and headed away towards the south.

Then, when they were in among the denser scrub, the leading men came face-to-face with a leopard and two half-grown cubs, padding along the path towards them. The men raised their digging sticks. The leopard hissed, backed off, and slipped away under the bushes with the cubs gliding behind it.

Warily they trooped past the place where the leopards had disappeared, but nothing happened. Suth, near the end of the party, looked back over his shoulder and saw that as soon as the people were gone the three animals had come back onto the path and were gliding away up the hill. It was very strange. What were they doing? Where were they going?

Nothing was stirring under the trees, but the cries

of Big Voice rang all around them. When they drank at the lake, the water was very warm.

They returned to the cave, many of the women carrying leaf bowls of water. The men unpiled the rocks from around Mosu's body, and the women poured the water over her, weeping as they did so. Her first son, Jun, cut a leg from a porcupine and laid it in her lap, and the chief women brought offerings of nuts and seed paste.

They ate a little, and then Jun stood and wept praise. In a quiet voice, with many pauses, he spoke of Mosu's wisdom, and the power of her dreams, and named her children and their children one by one.

As the sun went down the women formed two lines for the death dance to help Mosu's spirit on its way. They did it differently from the Kin, who danced where they stood, with stamping and clapping. Here the two lines moved together and apart with shrilling, wavering cries, while the men clapped the rhythm and made deep groaning noises through closed lips.

The Moonhawks watched, sitting a little to one side, until Noli, who had so far sat with dry, staring eyes, heaved herself convulsively to her feet and cried, in a huge voice that was not her own, 'He is gone! Big Voice is gone!'

The dance stopped. Heads turned. In the silence they heard that the forest was silent too. The howling of Big Voice, which had filled the valley all afternoon, was still. Even the clatter of the parrots settling into their nests for the night was missing. Not a bird twittered.

They looked at each other, and back to Noli.

She raised both arms, shuddering, and then stretched one out and pointed.

'See!' she croaked. 'They go!'

They turned and looked. A little way off, but clearly visible in the half-light of dusk, a few spindly shapes were scrambling rapidly towards the ridge. They had thin, angular limbs and long tails, which they carried curled over their short bodies. Their heads were small and round. They went on all fours but used their front limbs more like arms than legs as they scrambled over the tumbled rocks.

The watchers knew at once what they were seeing, though few of them had ever caught more than a glimpse of one of these creatures in its home, high in the dense canopy of leaves.

'He goes!' they whispered. 'Big Voice goes!'

They danced no more that night. Many wanted to copy the animals and leave at once, but the thought of lairing out in the open was too alarming, so in the end they carried Mosu into the cave and walled themselves in, as they had done every other night of their lives.

Suth had to take Noli by the elbow and guide her in, as she seemed not to know where she was or what she was doing, and when he pushed her down into her place she fell at once into a deep, slow-breathing sleep. Everyone else seemed restless with unease. Even the small ones picked up the general feeling and whimpered or cried, but they all slept in the end.

They were woken by screams. A harsh, croaking yell.

'Fire!' it cried. 'Out! Out! Go! Fire comes!'

Suth jerked up. The yelling voice was close above

him. Somebody, something was moving between him and the pale patch of sky above the wall. He reached out. Noli was not in her place. His searching hand touched flesh, a leg. It shuddered violently. The clamour began again.

'Fire! I see fire! It comes! Out! Go!'

Noli.

He stood and grappled her to him. Her body jerked and thrashed, like the body of a snake after its back is broken but before it is truly dead. Otan yelled with terror. The cave was full of shouting.

Suth was a lot stronger than Noli, but tonight trying to hold her was like wrestling with a trapped animal. She wrenched herself free. He followed, trying to get a fresh hold on her, as she struggled to the mouth of the cave and started to tear at the wall.

'Out!' she screamed. 'Fire comes! Moonhawk is here! She says, *Go! Out! Fire!*'

A man grabbed and held her.

'Witch dream,' he grunted as she struggled and bit.

Suth seized the man's forearm and tried to wrench it from its hold.

'No!' he shouted. 'This dream is true! Monkey is gone! Now Moonhawk comes! Moonhawk sends true dreams to Noli! I, Suth, say this!'

The man didn't seem to understand. Suth turned and heaved a rock down from the wall, but already others, filled with panic by Noli's cries, were pulling it apart. In another few moments they were crowding out into the huge night silence. There was nothing but sky, and the moonlit forest, and the far, dark ridges of the valley.

Then the ground trembled. A long, hoarse sigh

came from below, louder and louder, and a pillar of whiteness rose above the trees, rose and rose, far above where they stood, far above the horizon, gleaming in the light of the low moon, curving over as the mild east wind moved it away.

Again the ground trembled. A huge boulder, dislodged from somewhere above the cliff, thundered down, leaped over their heads, black against the stars, and went crashing on into the scrub below. From over to their left rose the deep rough grumble of an avalanche, as a whole hillside shifted. Still the ground shook.

Ko and Mana huddled against Suth's legs. Noli was quiet again, deep in her trance. Tinu held Otan, merely whimpering. Suth took him. His mind was made up. This was the chance he'd been waiting for.

'Bring Noli,' he said. 'Come, Mana. Come, Ko. We go.'

Without waiting for anyone else he led the way across the moonlit slope. To their left another great column of whiteness soared out of the lake. A warm gust, like a vast moist breath, flowed up the slope. Further off, with an immense coughing roar, dark orange flames spouted among the trees, with great black lumps hurling up and falling aside, and smaller fiery ones shooting out beyond.

Then it fell quiet for a while. Suth heard the calls and cries of the people scurrying in the other direction towards the nearest place where they could climb the cliff. He ignored them and led the way steadily on towards Tinu's food store.

They were halfway when there was another roar, another uprush of flame from beyond the forest, and the ground shook again, more violently than they'd ever felt it before. Rocks clattered down the slope around them.

They waited, tense, till the tremor ceased, and then hurried on. The food store, when they reached it, had collapsed, but the food was safe beneath the pile. Suth gave Mana and Ko a couple of lizards each. He draped the snake and one braid of seed bags around his neck, put the other around Noli's, who seemed to be still in her dream state, and gave Tinu a sheaf of unhusked seed heads to carry in her free hand. He shifted Otan onto his other hip and started to climb, using his digging stick as a staff. Ko and Mana scrambled behind, and Tinu led Noli at the rear. The hill did not stir.

After several moons of good food, Otan was a lot heavier than when they had carried him across the Dry Hills, and before long Suth was panting with the effort. He could hear Ko and Mana gasping too, and since all seemed quiet he paused to give them a rest. Turning to look back, he saw that the plumes of steam from the lake had drifted away and not renewed themselves, and the two outbursts of fire had steadied to glowing patches, with black smoke churning skywards under the setting moon.

But before they had begun to get their breath Noli, who had been lagging behind while Tinu dragged her on, broke abruptly out of her trance.

'Up!' she cried in her ordinary voice. 'Quick, Suth! It is coming!'

She snatched Otan from him and pushed past. He picked Mana up, told Ko to grab the other end of his stick, and scrambled after her as fast as his legs would take him until his lungs were retching for air and the blood thundered in his ears.

Through the roaring he heard Ko cry out as he lost his hold on the stick and fell. Gasping, Suth turned to wait for him. That was how he saw the first of the major eruptions.

It began with another immense jet of steam from the lake. Before the sound of it reached him, the hillside where he stood leaped, as if it had been struck a blow from beneath, and at the same moment, the whole of the bottom of the valley split open like a bursting seedpod as out from under it rose a boiling orange wave. The roar of its uprush reached him as a blast of scorching wind swept up the slope, knocking him flat.

He rose instantly, dropped his stick, grabbed Ko by the arm and dragged him on. Vast burning clods started to fall around them. They'd never make it to the top. He turned aside and headed for a cluster of large boulders, pushed Ko and Mana down against the upper side of the nearest one, and lay down above them, shielding them as best he could with his body. A few moments later Tinu was cowering against the next boulder beyond him. He didn't know what had happened to Noli and Otan.

Oldtale

NIGLU

Children were born to the daughters of An and Ammu. First born was the son of Nal and of Tarka, who were Moonhawk. Thus Moonhawk is first among the Kins, and the other Kins are liars who say that it was among them that the first child was born. They came after.

And they grew to be men and women, and chose mates according to the custom established at Sometimes River, and had children in their turn. So began the Kins.

Then Da and Datta said, 'This is not good. You have mates and children. You have tens and tens of mouths, and tens and tens of stomachs. You hunt all the game and you pick all the berries and you dig all the roots. There are none left when we come by. There are you eight Kins, and there are us, Da and Datta. That is nine in all. We came to these Places. We shared everything by nines, the creatures and the berries and the roots.

Let it be so now. Then we find our share when we come by.'

The others said, 'This is not good. You have only two mouths and two stomachs. You cannot eat all of a ninth share. Must our children's children starve, and you two have more than you can eat?'

Da and Datta said, 'It must be as we say, as you swore at Odutu below the Mountain.'

The others were angry, but they had sworn, so they agreed.

Now, the Kin of Little Bat were at Sometimes River, and Niglu was there. She was the mate of Dag.

Niglu gave birth to a girl baby and took her to a pool of the river to wash clean. But there was thunder and great rain, and the riverbed was filled and they were carried away.

Then Little Bat came flying swiftly and pushed them onto a mudbank near the Gully whose Name is not Spoken.

Niglu came to the gully and saw a garri bush that had been stripped of its berries, all but the share that was Datta's and Da's. And she was very hungry.

She said in her heart, These are for Da and Datta, but my stomach is empty and I must fill it, or I have no milk for my daughter.

So she took the berries and ate them, and when her stomach was full she lay down with her baby and slept.

In the evening Da and Datta came to that place, and saw the bush stripped of its berries, and Niglu lying beside it with the juice of the berries on her lips, and they were very angry. In their rage they picked up two rocks and flung them at Niglu and struck her on the temple, so that she died, but the baby lived.

Datta said, 'We cannot kill the baby also. I take it for mine, for I have none.'

So they took the child and journeyed by night to Tarutu Rock, and there they hid. For they were afraid for what they had done.

But Little Bat was watching all that happened, and she plucked hairs from Niglu's head and followed Da and Datta, flying very silently. And all along the way she hung the hairs from bushes and trees as she passed.

The next day Dag, who was Niglu's mate, was searching for her along the banks of Sometimes River, and when he came to the Gully whose Name is not Spoken he saw her body lying beside the garri bush. But the child was gone. Then he searched along the gully for the child and came to a tree with a thread of hair hanging from it, and there was blood on the hair, so he knew it for Niglu's.

And a little further on he found another. Thus he followed the trail that Little Bat had left all the way to Tarutu Rock. There he waited, and in the evening he saw Da and Datta coming down to drink at the dew trap, and with them they had his child.

Dag was very angry, but they were two and he was one, so he went swiftly to his own Kin, who were Little Bat, and to Snake, which was the Kin of Niglu's father Ral, and told them what he had seen. And they journeyed, all of them, to Tarutu Rock.

In the morning Da and Datta went down to drink at the dew trap, and the Kins of Snake and Little Bat came to them quietly and stood around them and said, 'What is this that you did? You killed our Kin and the daughter of our Kin, and you must die.'

Da and Datta said, 'It was our right. She ate the berries of a garri bush. These were our share. So you swore at Odutu below the Mountain. How else is one punished who breaks that oath?'

To that they had no answer.

But Dag said, 'You killed my mate for a handful of berries. For this I now hunt and kill you, oath or no oath.'

So also said Niglu's father, Ral.

But the rest held them fast, and said to Da and Datta, 'Go far and far. These we hold for a day and a night and a day. Then we set them free, to do as they choose.'

Da and Datta said, 'Let it be so. Now we go back to that First Good Place, where we were born. There we hunt and forage and forget you.'

So they went, and though Dag and Ral tracked them far and far into the desert, they did not find them, and they were not seen again.

CHAPTER TWELVE

The firestorm went on and on. The moon set, but the heavy glare still filled the valley. When Suth raised his head, he could see all along the ridge until the churning column of smoke blanked out the view. Reeking gases fouled the air.

Beside him Mana yelped with pain, then tried to stifle her weeping. A scorching ember had fallen on her arm. Suth licked the place for her and comforted her as best he could, until a fresh rush of gases made him gag and try to throw up.

At last there came a lull in the thundering explosions. Suth rose. Dawn was breaking behind him, greying that half of the sky, but the half ahead of him was black with swirling smoke, rising and spreading as far as he could see, as the wind from the desert pushed it westward.

It was the wind that had saved them. Nothing on the other side of the valley could have lived.

Mana sat up. One whole side of her body was grey

with the film of ash that had fallen on her, despite the saving wind. It was the same with Ko. Suth looked down and saw that he too was half grey, as if he had been smeared with paste for his man-making at Odutu below the Mountain.

'Noli!' he called. 'Noli!'

She rose from behind a boulder a little further up the slope.

'I live,' she called in her normal voice. 'I am burned on my leg. Otan lives.'

'Wait,' said Suth. 'I find my digging stick.'

The moment he stepped from behind the shelter of the boulder, the heat of the molten lava below swept up at him, hotter than the sun in a desert noon. He could see his stick a little way off, jutting up across the rock on which it had fallen. Otherwise he might not have found it under the layer of ash. Crossing the slope to fetch it, he realized that the dried snake and the braid of seed bags were no longer around his shoulders. He could remember slipping the braid free once they were safely in shelter, but not the snake. Perhaps it had slid off earlier, in the scramble. He was fairly sure he'd still had it when Ko had fallen.

He reached the stick, knocked the ash off it, poked around without much hope, found a dried lizard and then, to his great relief, the snake.

He picked them up and carried them back to the others.

'What food do we have?' he said.

His braid of seed bags was by the boulder where he had lain. Tinu had her small sheaf, and Ko had clung obstinately to his lizards throughout everything. Mana had dropped both hers, though Suth had found one. He looked at Noli and saw that she had her seed bags intact, but she seemed not to have heard his question.

She was staring at the appalling pillar of smoke. Suth thought perhaps she had gone into one of her trances, but she spoke in her ordinary voice.

'They are gone,' she said quietly. 'All the old Good Places are gone. Stinkwater and Sometimes River and the dew trap at Tarutu Rock. Gone. Grey stuff buries them, deep, deep. I slept. Moonhawk came. She showed me this.'

Suth bowed his head and stood silent. He had no doubt that what she told him was true. One day I weep for this, he thought. One day I tell my own children about the old Good Places. Then they are not forgotten.

The ground shook. The pillar of smoke convulsed from its base. Huge rocks, golden and orange like the embers of a great fire, flung themselves from it. An immense coughing roar boomed up the slope, followed by another wave of roasting gases.

Suth turned.

'Come quick,' he said. 'It is not finished.'

He took Mana's hand, made Ko hang on to his digging stick as before, and hurried them slantwise up the slope, aiming for the gap in the barrier of boulders that he had marked earlier. Gasping, they made their way through it, and rested at last in the shelter on the further side. Suth passed one of the lizards around, and they took turns chewing, dry mouthed, at the tough and stringy meat.

Suth studied the downward slope. The crack by which they had first climbed the cliff must be almost directly below this point. It would take them all morning, at least, to make their way down it, but at the bottom there was water, and they had food for several days, if they were careful.

He raised his eyes and looked at the desert, already glaring with heat under the risen sun. A dreadful, lifeless place, but he was not afraid of it any more. Cautious, yes, wary, yes, but no longer scared. They could do it. The small ones were strong. They had fed well for many moons.

They would rest by day in the shade of some large rock, moving around it as the sun moved, and in the evening they would set out again. They would find water because it must be there, and Moonhawk would show Noli where to look for it, or else they would find the trail left by those others who had crossed the desert.

And when they had drunk, they would move on. They would walk and walk under the stars, walk as they knew how to, walk as they were born to, because they were of the Kin. And in the new Good Places beyond the desert they would find the others, and Moonhawk would be Moonhawk once more.

The mountain shuddered. Bits of the crest detached themselves and rumbled away down the slope. The boom of another immense eruption shook the air. The sound seemed to speak to Suth, to tell him that everything that had so far happened was now over and done with, and this dazzling morning was a new beginning.

He rose unhurriedly to his feet.

'Good,' he said. 'Now it is time to go.'

NOLI'S STORY

For David

NOLI'S STORY

Contents

Chapter One	155
Oldtale: SOL	170
Chapter Two	172
Oldtale: RAKAKA	188
Chapter Three	191
Oldtale: SALA-SALA	204
Chapter Four	207
Oldtale: WOOWOO	225
Chapter Five	228
Oldtale: THE MOTHER OF DEMONS	242
Chapter Six	245
Oldtale: SOL'S DREAM	262
Chapter Seven	265
Oldtale: THE PIT BENEATH ODUTU	277
Chapter Eight	281
Oldtale: THE CHILDREN OF SOL	297
Chapter Nine	300

CHAPTER ONE

In the darkness of Noli's dream, Moonhawk spoke for the last time.

Go.

In the dream the huge, strange presence moved away, becoming smaller and smaller until it vanished into the distance, a distance that was still somehow inside Noli's own mind.

And then Noli was awake. Her right shoulder was numb from her having lain on it too long. Her face was wet with tears.

Where was she?

The dream had been so strong that it still filled her mind, and for a little while she couldn't think about anything else. Then the ground beneath her seemed to quiver. She looked up and saw the cliff towering black above her, and beyond it the night sky full of stars.

Now she remembered. She was lying in the lair that she and Suth and Tinu had built last night.

They'd piled a wall of rocks against the cliff for themselves and the three small ones. She remembered how they'd escaped from the secret valley at the top of the mountain, when the mountain itself had suddenly exploded into flame and smoke.

Was anyone else left alive? she wondered. Any of the Monkey Kin, among whom they had been living for the past nine moons? As far as she knew, she and her friends were the last of the Moonhawk Kin: Suth, a boy still, though he had been counted as a man since his fight with the leopard; Noli herself, a little younger; Tinu, younger still, but small and slight, and shy too, because of her twisted mouth which stopped her from speaking clearly; Ko, a boisterous little boy, and Mana, a quiet, solemn girl the same age; and finally Otan, Noli's baby brother, who had only just learned to walk.

Again the mountain quivered, and the memory of her dream flooded back into her mind. She looked at the sky. The moon was moving towards its setting, and the slope where she lay was in the shadow of the cliff, so the stars shone clear. Five points of light in a curving line. Moonhawk had shown them to Noli in her dream. But there were so many stars. Was that them, three bright and two fainter? The dream had seemed so certain, but now . . .

They were the only ones she could find. Yes, that must be them.

She reached across and felt for Suth on the other side of the sleeping bodies. She touched an arm, and knew it was his by the scars that the leopard had made. She shook it.

'Noli?' he whispered.

'Moonhawk comes,' she said. 'She tells me *Go.*'

He was starting to answer when the mountain groaned, not loudly but hugely, a sound so deep that they felt it as much as they heard it, throbbing up through the cliff and far out under the desert. The hillside shuddered. The crash and rumble of falling rocks broke the night silence.

Suth sat up. Tinu was already awake. They woke the small ones, gathered their few supplies by touch, and took a last drink at the dribble of water from the cliff. Noli hefted her baby brother, Otan, onto her hip, and they picked their way down the slope.

When they reached the moonlight they could move more easily. Suth halted and pointed.

'We go this way,' he said. 'It is there I saw people, two moons back. They came from the desert. They knew a way.'

'No,' said Noli. 'See these stars, Suth? Three strong, two weak? A bent line? Moonhawk showed me these.'

Suth didn't argue, though the stars were well to the right of the route he had suggested. He was the leader, but Noli was the one to whom Moonhawk came.

'You go first, Noli,' he said.

She shifted Otan to her other hip and set off. Tinu came next, and then Suth, with Ko and Mana. They were still almost babies, so Suth carried them in turn when they were tired. In the bright moonlight they climbed on down the mountain until they reached the plain. There, walking was easy, until the moon vanished behind the mass of smoke from the volcano. But they went steadily on by starlight, with short rests every now and then.

The stars moved westward as the night wore by, but Noli stuck to the direction that she had started on. She did this without thought. She carried Otan without noticing his weight. When Tinu offered to take him for a while, she passed him across without a word. Her mind was still full of her dream.

These were dreams like no other dream, more wakeful than waking.

Moonhawk came. Noli's whole self trembled with the presence of the First One. She knew, without touch or seeing, the softness of breast feathers, the folded strength of wings, the hooked sharpness of beak and talons.

She knew, this time, sadness.

Moonhawk spoke in Noli's mind: *See this.*

In the darkness of the dream, five points of light in a slanting curve. The lights vanished.

I do not come again.

In her dream, Noli shrank until she was as small as the smallest grain of sand in a desert that went on for ever, and Moonhawk was nowhere in it. The grain of sand wept.

Moonhawk spoke for the last time.

Go.

So now, Noli trudged numbly on with nothing in her mind but the knowledge that never again would Moonhawk come to her.

Never again. Never again. Never again.

She did not notice how the sky ahead turned pale,

or when the stars vanished. She looked around, and it was brilliant morning, with the rising sun glaring into her eyes.

With no warning, the ground that they were crossing heaved beneath their feet. Noli staggered and caught herself. She looked back. Tinu was carrying Otan and they'd both fallen. Suth had grabbed hold of Mana and Ko. He too had turned and was looking back.

Beyond him, something was happening to the mountain. The immense column of smoke was still rising into the sky, silvered by moonlight along the edge, but just above the mountaintop it had bulged into a shape like a thundercloud. A series of huge deep booms swept across the desert.

'Watch!' shouted Suth. 'Something comes! Run! There!'

He pointed to a great slab of rock they had just passed. Noli grabbed Otan and ran for it. They scrambled up and looked towards the mountain.

It wasn't the mountain. It was nearer than that. The desert itself was moving. There was a line across its surface. The line was nearer. In a moment Noli saw that the line was a sort of ripple. The solid ground had risen into a wave which was rushing towards them. She saw it reach two tall boulders leaning against each other. They swayed. One toppled, the other fell across it.

'Down!' yelled Suth. 'Kneel! Hold the rock!'

She crouched, slid Otan between her legs and gripped him with her knees. She scrabbled for handholds, found a crack for her fingers, and hooked them into it. She could hear the wave coming, growling like a beast growling deep in its throat as it worries a bone.

She raised her head and saw the wave hit the rock they were on.

A shower of gravel shot into the sky. The rock tilted up, up, up. For a moment Noli thought it would go right over and crush them, but then it lurched sideways and crunched back down. The jar loosened her hold and she had to fling herself flat to stop herself slithering off. Otan was under her, yelling and struggling.

She picked herself up and looked around. Tinu had tumbled right off the slab, but was getting to her feet and seemed to be all right. The others were kneeling, looking towards the mountain.

It was invisible, hidden in its own black smoke.

They were still staring at it when the sound of the main explosion reached them.

It was louder than the loudest thunder when lightning strikes close by. They clapped their hands to their ears, but that made no difference. It didn't stop. The small ones were screaming, but Noli couldn't hear them. She could see Otan's mouth wide open as he bellowed with pain, but not a sound reached her. Something crashed into the rock by her foot. It made no noise. She noticed it only because of the rock splinters that stung against her leg. Stuff was raining out of the sky all around them. She looked desperately for somewhere to shelter. If any of this hit one of them . . .

Tinu was shouting and pointing. She ran to the end of the rock and disappeared. They scrambled off and saw that when the rock had tilted up and fallen back, something had stopped it from going the whole way down, so that there was now a narrow slot between it and the ground.

They wormed their way in and waited, safe, while the debris of the explosion thudded down all around them.

Gradually, their hearing returned though Noli's ears ached painfully. The shower of rocks stopped and they crawled out and looked at the mountain. The smoke had moved away under the wind and they could see it clearly.

It was not the same mountain. Its shape had changed. A whole wedge of it, all its northern rim, had been blown clean away.

Noli stared in disbelief. She couldn't believe that anything, even the First Ones, even Black Antelope, had such power.

She heard Mana cry out in pain.

'Hot!' she said. 'Hot!' and pointed at a piece of rock by her foot. It was paler than the desert rock, and the air above it shimmered slightly in the heat that rose from it.

'We go,' said Suth, speaking loudly, so that Noli knew that he too must be still half-deaf. 'We go quick. Perhaps it comes again.'

So they set out once more and tramped steadily on all morning. Mercifully, most of the ash and lighter stuff had been blown westward by the wind. But they had to keep a close watch on where they put their feet, as all the desert was littered now with the burning rocks from the mountain.

The sun rose, and it grew steadily hotter. Still they kept on long after they would normally have stopped and looked for shade. At last Suth trotted up from the rear and pointed to a rocky hill to their left.

'We rest now,' he said. 'The mountain is quiet, and there is good shade.'

Noli hesitated. Suth was right. It was already far too hot for walking, and the small ones were beginning to gasp with distress, and all their throats were painful with thirst.

'A little more, Suth,' she said.

He gazed ahead. As far as they could see the desert seemed almost level, with only a scattering of boulders, none large enough for shade.

'I ask this, Suth,' she said. 'I think there is water.'

'Does Moonhawk show you this?'

'I have no word for it.'

She felt as if she were being called, or pulled. As if, supposing she tried to turn aside and rest, her legs would refuse to obey her.

Suth looked at her and grunted doubtfully, but nodded, and they walked on. She could see nothing hopeful ahead of her but it was hard to be sure. The sun beat down on rock and sand and gravel, and the heat beamed back from them, making wavering lines in the air, so that the distance ahead seemed to ripple and blur. It took her a little while to realize that one of the ripples wasn't moving like the rest. It was there, a darker mark across the desert, slanting away to her left.

As they neared, it became a crack in the ground. The crack grew wider. Soon Noli could see the top of a cliff, and then she and the others were standing at the very lip of a canyon, broader and deeper than anything they'd ever seen.

They kneeled and craned over. The cliffs ran straight down on both sides. In the bottom was a jumble of boulders, but in places among them, bushes and trees were growing.

Their leaves were green.

Noli raised her head and sniffed. Water.

For a while they explored along the edge of the canyon, looking for some way down. Here and there, far beneath them, they could see fresh piles of rock heaped against the cliff, where the earthquake had shaken stuff loose, but nearly all the rocks had fallen clean away, leaving the cliff still sheer.

Then they came to a place where there'd been an even larger rockfall, so huge that the debris half-blocked the canyon floor. There was a great slice missing from the cliff. One side of the slice was a steep and jagged slant, with enough handholds and footholds for them to climb down. Suth and Noli helped the small ones past the difficult places.

At last they were on the pile of fallen rocks and could scramble to the floor of the canyon. A flock of small birds with glistening dark-blue wings and scarlet heads swirled out from the opposite cliff and circled, screeching, above them.

Noli looked up at them and almost laughed with relief. Plants grew in this place. Creatures lived. The Moonhawks had come through the desert. They were not going to die.

The rocks in the bottom of the canyon were mostly round and smooth, like the ones in Sometimes River. The smells of green leaves and water filled the hot air. They could see the plants, but not the water.

The smell was strongest near the centre of the

canyon. They kneeled down and started to move rocks aside. The ones at the top were almost too hot to touch, but the next layer was cool, and a few layers further down, the rocks felt faintly damp to the touch. All the while the smell of water grew stronger.

'Ha!' said Suth, and showed them the rock he had just pulled out from almost an arm's length below the surface. Its underside was wet.

And now, peering down into the hollow they had made, they could see dribbles of water seeping through the crannies. By the time the hollow was deep enough to leave a pool, Suth and Noli were the only ones who could reach it.

Suth scooped out a palmful of water and lapped it up. He moved aside for Noli and then the two of them scooped some out for the others to lap from their palms. The water was beautiful, clean, and cold.

All the while the scarlet-headed birds chattered angrily above them, as if these intruders had no right to be here.

When they'd drunk enough they rested for a while in the shade of the further cliff. But the sun moved on and the shade disappeared, so they started to explore the canyon, looking for somewhere else to settle. Every now and then a fresh flurry of birds would whirl out from their cliff nests to scold them.

Suth looked up and made a face. 'In this place, hunting is not easy,' he said. 'The birds warn the creatures.'

'There is plant food,' said Noli. 'See, there is a jada bush. Its berries are green still, and sour.'

'See, there are trees,' said Suth, and headed for the shade beneath them.

The trees made a small grove close against the cliff. One of them turned out to be a wing nut tree. They could see the dark nuts out of reach at the ends of the thin, whippy branches, so Tinu took the small ones and Otan well aside while Noli and Suth threw rocks and tried to knock some nuts loose. If they were ripe enough they fell at a touch, and a good throw brought several rattling down.

When they'd knocked off enough they all searched for the fallen nuts. The third one Noli picked up was only the upturned half of an empty shell. She looked at it and frowned. *What animal does this?* she wondered. The shells of wing nuts were very hard. There was a rock squirrel, whose teeth were sharp enough to nibble off the pointy end of a nut, but people opened them either by popping them on the embers of a fire, or else by laying them on a rock and tapping them exactly on the seam with a sharp-edged stone or a cutter.

But who would come so far to gather wing nuts, out here in the middle of the dead desert?

Noli showed the shell to Suth. He, too, frowned, and then climbed a boulder and gazed up and down the canyon.

'I see no people,' he said in a worried voice. 'The birds are still. Noli, we watch. We make small noise. We take little food from a place. Always we leave some. We make a gift pile.'

Noli grunted agreement. If people did use the canyon, they'd regard all the food in it as theirs. That was how it had worked in their old life, when the eight Kins used to journey between one Good Place and another to find food. Different parts of those

Places belonged to different Kins. The Moonhawks didn't take what wasn't theirs, except in an emergency, and then they would leave a little mound of ritual gifts – a gourd, a stonecutter, a bit of dried meat, a bone spike – by way of payment and thanks.

So now they didn't try to knock down any more wing nuts, but rested where they were until the sun had moved far enough to leave shade beneath the other cliff. Then they crossed the canyon and explored that side, sometimes stopping to nibble a leaf of a plant they didn't know. Even the small ones had been taught that most leaves were not much use as food, and some were poisonous. So they instantly spat out any that tasted harsh or bitter. With anything else they weren't sure of, they ate very little, so that they could wait a day or two and see if it made them ill.

Apart from some more unripe jada berries, they found nothing for a while, but then they came to a large patch of whitestem, a plant that grew after rains at one of their old Good Places, beside Sometimes River. The new shoots were good to eat, but it was better to leave them, because they would grow and unroll into long, broad leaves with a thick central stem. The leaves themselves were leathery and useless, but the pith inside the stringy outer stem was deliciously juicy and crunchy.

Eagerly they started to gather enough to carry back to their drinking place, taking only a leaf or two from each clump.

'Noli, come. See,' Suth called from the further edge of the patch.

She went and looked at what he'd found. There

were a couple of boulders that would have made a comfortable place to sit. Beside them, on the ground, was a loose pile of torn leaves and stem peelings. Noli fingered them. They were dry, but not yet brittle.

'People were here,' she said. 'Two days, three days back.'

Again they looked anxiously up and down the canyon, and saw no sign. Above them, several of the redheaded birds were still scolding. If there were other people anywhere near, surely there'd be birds doing the same for them, but there weren't.

Even so, they finished gathering the whitestems as soon as they could, and built a gift mound before they left. It wasn't much – one of the braided grass cords Tinu had made to help carry their food supply, and a couple of pretty pebbles Mana had picked up – but it would have to do.

They were halfway back to their drinking hole when Noli heard Ko cry out in pain. She turned and saw that he was hopping about on one foot, still clutching his bundle of whitestem.

'Ow!' he said, not quite weeping. 'Hot. Rock hot.'

They went to look, and realized at once what had happened. The rock was like the ones that had fallen all around them in the desert, pale, and pitted all over with little holes. It was about the size of a man's head.

'The mountain threw it,' said Suth in an awed voice. 'It threw it far, far. And it is hot still . . . What do you do, Tinu?'

Tinu had held a hand briefly above the rock and felt the heat of it, and then had at once put her bundle of whitestem down and was now kneeling beside a nearby bush, reaching in beneath it. She turned and showed Suth a handful of withered grass.

'I try . . . make fire?' she mumbled.

Even now, after all they'd been through together, needing and trusting each other, she still sounded half-afraid that Suth would be angry with her.

'This is good, Tinu,' he said encouragingly.

They all put their bundles down and helped Tinu gather more small fuel: dry grass and leaves and fallen twigs. She made a small loose ball of the finest stuff, and a careful pile of the rest, with a hollow at the side. Using sticks to handle it with, she turned the hot rock over and placed the ball of grass on top, then crouched close and blew very gently.

They watched, holding their breaths. Would the rock be hot enough still?

A thread of smoke rose from the grass ball. At once Tinu gathered the ball between her cupped hands and breathed softly into it between her thumbs. Smoke seeped between her clasped fingers. Just before it became too hot to hold, she slipped the smoking ball into the hollow in her pile and blew on it. The air prickled with the odour of burning.

And now, in a moment, the little pile was all alight, leaves and twigs crumbling rapidly into ash beneath the pale flames. While Tinu fed it the others gathered anything else they could find to burn, until they had a good sturdy fire roaring away. Then they worked back towards their drinking place, gathering fuel as they went and building several more piles along the way.

Now Suth took the branch Tinu had laid ready in the embers and, shielding the lit end as best he could, hurried to the first pile. By the time he reached it the flame was out but the tip still glowed, so he thrust it into the pile and blew on it until he had flame again. And so on, back to the main pile that Noli and the small ones had been building by the drinking place.

They stood and stared at the blaze and laughed with triumph and rejoiced. Fire was glorious. Fire was people stuff. No animal had fire.

'Now we sing the song,' said Suth.

They looked at him doubtfully. They were children. None of them had yet been old enough to join in when the Kin had moved camp and built a fresh fire and lit it.

He smiled at them, full of confidence.

'These are new times,' he said. 'But we are Moonhawk still.'

So they stood in front of their fire and sang, stamping their feet to the rhythm. Even little Ko and Mana knew the words, they had heard them so often.

Ha!
We have fire!
We bring fire to the camp!
Ha!
The women open the fire log.
The men set meat to roast.
The smoke makes sweet smells.
This is the camp of Moonhawk.
This is our fire.
Ha! The brave fire!

Oldtale

SOL

Naga was very beautiful. She was the daughter of Nar, of the Kin of Fat Pig.

A young man came from Weaver, saying, 'Naga, I choose you for my mate. Do you choose me?'

She answered, 'I am not ready.'

A young man came from Snake, saying, 'Naga, I choose you for my mate. Do you choose me?'

She answered, 'I am not ready.'

Naga grew fat.

Nar said to her, 'Naga, my daughter, there is a child in you. Yet you have no mate. How is this?'

Naga said, 'We camped at Odutu below the Mountain. As I slept, one came to me. This one was not a man. I did not see him. I did not hear him. I did not smell him. I did not feel his touch. Yet he was there. He held me inside himself, and I was glad, glad. I woke and he was gone. I said in my heart, This is a dream.'

Nar said, 'The First Ones live on the Mountain above Odutu. And you are beautiful, my daughter.'

Ten moons and two more Naga carried her child inside her.

At Lusan-of-the-Ants, he was born.

He had no Kin, for none could say the name of his father.

When he came from Naga's womb he did not cry.

He stood up and looked around him.

He had hair on his head.

He had teeth in his mouth.

With the birth blood still on him, he spoke.

He said, 'I am Sol.'

CHAPTER TWO

Where there is water there may be mosquitoes, so late in the afternoon they made a new fire near the corner where the rock pile met the cliff. They broke off branches of garri bush, which would smoulder with a thin bitter smoke and keep the insects away. When night came, they huddled into the corner to sleep.

Noli lay down, exhausted, and was asleep almost at once, but then woke and saw Suth sitting by the fire with his knees drawn up and his digging stick across his lap.

'Suth, sleep,' she whispered. 'Then tomorrow you are strong. No animal passes our fire.'

'Noli, this is good, good,' he answered, his voice full of happiness and confidence.

'Suth, sleep,' she repeated.

He grunted, set some more branches onto the fire, and lay down.

Noli didn't go back to sleep at once. She lay gazing

up at the cliff. The lower half was black shadow, the upper half pale with moonlight. Beyond it the stars moved very slowly westward.

She thought about Suth. She understood how he felt. He had hated the strange valley at the top of the mountain, where they had lived with the Monkey Kin for the past nine moons. It wasn't just that they had been prisoners there – it was always waking in the same place, going down to the lake in the forest each morning to drink, foraging the same hillsides day after day, drinking again at the lake each evening, sitting around the same undying fire to eat their meal, and settling down night after night to sleep in the same stinking cave. Suth had longed for the life he was used to, journeying every few days with the rest of the Kin to the next of their Good Places, to forage and to hunt.

But the rest of the Kin were gone. Noli had seen some of them killed, when strangers had attacked without warning and driven them from their old Good Places. Their leader, Bal, had taken all who were left to look for new Good Places beyond the desert, but Suth and Noli had turned back to rescue Tinu and the small ones, whom Bal had left behind. Perhaps Bal's group was still alive, if they'd found the canyon. But they'd been travelling in a different direction from the one Moonhawk had shown Noli, so perhaps they'd never reached water and died of thirst in the desert.

If so, these six children, huddled by their fire in the canyon, were all that was left of the Kin. But few though they were, they had journeyed together through hardship and danger, and found water and food and built their fire, just as they used to in the old days, in their old Good Places. That was enough for Suth.

But not for Noli.

Moonhawk was gone. Moonhawk wouldn't come to her again. She felt empty.

No, more than that. She felt as if there used to be two Nolis living in the same body. The daytime Noli had foraged and journeyed with the Kin, and eaten and talked and played with her friends, and lain down to sleep at the end of the day. Then the night-time Noli had woken, and Moonhawk had come to her in her dreams.

As far back as she could remember she'd had these dreams, a vague, huge something filling her mind, both frightening and comforting. For a long time that was all. But then the daytime Noli had heard bits of adult talk about dream stuff, and the night-time Noli had given the something a shape and a feel, the golden eye, the featheriness, the fierce beak – Moonhawk.

Tens and tens of moons passed, and the dreams didn't change until, at the last rains, Moonhawk had suddenly shown her the horrible thing that was going to happen to the Kin, and Noli had woken, screaming. When she'd told the adults her dream, nobody had believed her.

But the thing had happened. The murdering strangers had come.

Six times since then, Moonhawk had shown or spoken. Three times to tell, and three times to warn. Without that help and those warnings, she and Suth and the others would all be dead. Thanks to Moonhawk the Kin still lived, here by the fire in the canyon.

But Moonhawk herself was gone. Without Moonhawk, how could there be any Moonhawk Kin?

Noli slept and woke and saw the moon shining sheer down into the canyon. She slept and woke again, and it was gone. Each time she woke, the same thoughts came back and back.

Somewhere towards morning, lying awake and thinking them yet again, she heard an odd sound. A voice? Not quite a voice. It seemed to come from the rock pile beside which they were lying.

The canyon was very still, the chattering birds asleep. Noli could hear the water trickling through crannies an arm's length below the floor of the canyon.

Yes, there it was again, a sort of whimper.

'Who is there?' she called.

The voice answered, but the sound was drowned by Suth's questioning grunt.

'Something is under these rocks,' Noli explained. 'Suth, hear.'

She called again, and again the thing replied.

Tinu was awake now, though the small ones slept on. They listened. The noise came several times. It wasn't words, but it had a sort of people sound to it, and it seemed to answer their calls. Suth eased a rock out of the pile, but it had been holding several others in place, and he had to jump clear as they clattered down.

'This is dangerous,' he said. 'When it is day, we see.'

When they lay down, the noises went on for a while, and then stopped. The next time Noli woke it was early morning, and as soon as the children stirred, the birds came chattering out to protest, drowning all fainter sounds.

Noli saw Suth already kneeling by the hollow, scooping out water to drink and to bathe his face. Tinu was building up the fire. Noli went and scooped out water for herself and Otan, and peeled a piece of whitestem for him to chew with his three teeth.

She looked up and saw Suth gazing along the canyon, still with that look of tense cheerfulness, as if he knew he was in the right place, doing the right thing, and was looking forward to the new day.

'I eat. Then I hunt,' he said. 'I look also for fire log.'

'Fire log is difficult, Suth,' said Noli.

'I try,' he said, and shrugged confidently.

'I hear no noises now,' she said, nodding towards the rockfall.

'I think it is animal,' he said. 'The rocks fall. They catch it. Now it is dead.'

'Animal is food, Suth.'

'This is dangerous, Noli. One rock falls, many fall. Wait, Ko! I come!'

Ko had been trying to scramble down into the drinking hole to get to the water on his own. Suth joined him, but instead of simply scooping water up and giving it to Ko to lap, he lifted several more rocks clear so that Ko could get water by himself. Ko was delighted.

Noli watched them, smiling at how Ko admired and adored Suth, tried to copy the way he moved and stood, and be as like him as possible. *This is man stuff*, she thought. *This is how sons are with fathers and fathers with sons. Otan also is soon like this.*

She looked at Otan. He had chewed his whitestem to a pulpy mess and was smearing it over his face as he tried to cram it into his mouth. Mana noticed, and at once came and wiped his face for him and gave him the stem she'd just peeled for herself.

Noli smiled again. *And this is woman stuff*, she thought. *Mana is happy to do this. When she has her own baby, she is happy, happy. But this is not my stuff. Otan is my brother. I carry him. I give him food. But it is not my stuff. My stuff is Moonhawk stuff. And Moonhawk does not come again. Never again, never again, never again.*

To distract herself she looked to see what Tinu was up to. She had climbed a little way up the rockfall and was crouching there with her ear close against a cranny. She moved on and listened again. She saw Noli watching her.

'People,' she mumbled. 'Rocks fall . . . Catch people.'

'Suth says this is animal,' said Noli.

Tinu hesitated.

'Is people,' she said unhappily.

She must have felt very sure of herself to disagree with Suth, so Noli called to him and told him what Tinu had said. He came and frowned at the rockfall.

'Tinu, this is dangerous,' he said. 'I move one rock, many fall. See.'

With his digging stick he worked a boulder loose and set off a small avalanche of others. Some of the rocks in the pile were huge enough to kill a big man if they fell on him. And the more rocks Suth took out, the more dangerous it would become. Surely Tinu must see that. This was the sort of thing she was good at understanding. But she still looked very unhappy.

'Now I hunt,' said Suth. 'Who feeds our fire?'

'Tinu does this,' said Noli. 'I fetch more whitestem. Be lucky, Suth.'

He raised his digging stick in the hunter's salute, and left.

Long after Suth was out of sight, Noli could tell where he was by the clouds of birds whirling out to scold above his head. She waited for him to get well clear, and took the small ones off to pick whitestem and look for anything else they could eat.

When she returned she found the fire burning, but Tinu had vanished. She called and heard a mumbling cry from somewhere up on the rockfall, but when she climbed up there, Tinu was nowhere in sight.

She called again, and this time the answer seemed to come from almost under her feet. A moment later, Tinu's head poked out from a gap between two large boulders.

She climbed free, gasping with effort. It was a while before she could speak, and then she was almost too excited to force the words out.

'Noli! . . . Is people! . . . I touch . . . hand!'

She spread her fingers wide to show what she meant, and pointed to the gap she'd come from. Noli kneeled beside it and looked down.

An enormous slab of cliff must have fallen off whole and was wedged in place by the rest of the landslide. It had stopped the rocks above from falling past it, and thus left a sort of slot at its lower side. The opening was very narrow, but the slot seemed to get wider below. It went a long way down.

When Noli straightened she found Tinu scrambling up the pile with several leaves of whitestem. She peeled one, put the pith between her teeth, and squeezed herself down through the gap. Noli kneeled to watch what happened.

It was dark down there, but Tinu seemed to stop before she got to the bottom and then to reach in through a crack at the side of the slot. There was a grunt, deeper than Tinu's voice, the sort of sound a man makes when something unusual happens.

At once Tinu clambered back and poked her head into the open.

'Is man . . .' she gasped. 'He take . . .'

She was too excited to manage the word 'whitestem', but Noli peeled several fresh stems for her, and Tinu took them down and passed them through the gap. The man grunted as he took them, but didn't say anything.

There was a pause. Noli could see Tinu moving around, scrabbling and grunting with effort. Then there was a hammering sound. Peering into the hole, Noli saw that Tinu had somehow braced her body across the slot and was using a heavy rock to bash two-handedly at something beside her hip.

The rock beneath Noli's right hand trembled.

'Danger!' she yelled.

Tinu started to scramble upward. There was a series of crashes from below her, and the hole filled with choking dust as rocks tumbled from the wall where she'd been working. Noli could hear her coughing and spluttering.

Deeper coughs joined in, as the man Tinu had found choked with the dust. And now she poked her head out, grinning with excitement. Noli started to help her clear, but she shook her head and as soon as the dust had cleared a little scrambled back down.

The dust hadn't thinned enough for Noli to see what was happening, but she heard them both coughing, then Tinu's mumbling voice asking a question and the man's answering grunt – a different sort of grunt – a few more questions from Tinu, but still no real answer.

Then Tinu came scrambling up again. This time she climbed right out and stood panting. Her hair was full of dust, and her whole body was grey with it.

'Man hurt,' she said. 'Arm hurt . . . bad . . . Need help . . .'

'He does not speak?' asked Noli. 'He does not say thanks? His mouth is hurt also?'

Tinu shrugged and made a negative gesture with her hands. She didn't know, wasn't bothered. She studied the opening she had climbed through. It was barely big enough even for her skinny little body.

'Man too big,' she said.

Together they tried to loosen the rocks around the opening, but they all seemed stuck fast, and in the end they gave up.

'I find Suth,' said Tinu.

Without waiting for Noli's agreement, Tinu hurried down the rockfall and ran off.

Noli climbed down more slowly and went to feed the fire. Ko ran to meet her.

'What happens? What happens?' he begged. 'I come see? I, Ko, ask!'

'No, Ko. Suth says, *Small ones do not climb on the rocks. They are dangerous, dangerous.*'

'But what happens? What happens?' he wailed.

'Tinu finds a man. The rocks fall on him, and he is caught. Suth comes to help.'

Instantly Ko cheered up.

'Suth comes!' he exclaimed. 'When, Noli, when?'

'Soon, Ko. He comes from there. You watch.'

She left him looking eagerly in the direction she had pointed, and checked on the other two. Otan was fast asleep, and Mana was building a careful pattern of pebbles on a flat rock nearby. Noli left them and climbed back up the rockfall.

When she looked into the hole, the dust had cleared enough for her to see something dark and round sticking out from near the place where she and Tinu had been hammering. It moved, and she caught the glisten of an eyeball. It was the man's head.

'Wait,' she called down. 'Tinu finds Suth. He is strong. He helps.'

The man answered with a pleading half-wail, wordless, but full of pain and despair.

She went to a place where she could sit and see down the canyon, and at the same time watch the small ones. After a little while she saw the usual cluster of birds circling over something that had alarmed them. Gradually they moved towards her.

'Ko!' she called. 'Suth comes. See the birds. He is there!'

She stood and pointed, and at once Ko was off to greet his hero. She watched his stubby, awkward, childish run, and shook her head and smiled. He hadn't gone very far before Suth and Tinu appeared, dragging a fair-sized branch between them. Ko, of course, when he reached them, had to be allowed to help, and that slowed them down, but Noli waited patiently while they brought their trophy home.

Suth drank at the water hole and at last climbed up beside her, but didn't at once go and look at the problem. He just stood, frowning.

'Tinu finds a man?' he asked her. 'This man does not speak?'

'This is true, Suth,' she told him. 'He makes a noise. Not words.'

'He is not Kin?'

'I think no.'

He crouched by the hole and peered down. The man saw him and made his wailing sound, but Suth didn't answer. He studied the hole, the rocks around it, and the huge tilted slab at its side, and rose, shaking his head and frowning more heavily than ever.

'Noli, this is dangerous, dangerous,' he said. 'The small rocks hold the big rock. We move them, perhaps it falls. Why do we do this, Noli? This man is not Kin.'

Noli understood what he was talking about. There were rules for this sort of thing. If people from your own Kin were in trouble, you would certainly risk your life to help them. If they came from other Kins, it depended on questions like whether the trouble was their own fault and how great the risk was. But for somebody who wasn't Kin at all, who couldn't talk, so perhaps wasn't even people – just some kind of animal who happened to look like people . . .

Tinu would be disappointed, of course, after all her efforts, but if Suth decided it was too dangerous, she'd accept that . . .

But . . .

But they had to help.

The feeling was really strong.

It didn't seem to come from inside Noli, but from outside. It was all around her, a kind of pressure.

She put her fingers on Suth's arm. 'Suth, we help this man,' she said. 'I, Noli, ask this.'

Her own voice sounded strange to her. Suth looked at her for a while, then nodded. His face cleared. 'Good,' he said. 'First I make the opening bigger.'

Using his digging stick as a lever, Suth worked at the rocks around the opening. As soon as one shifted a little, he stood back and waited. Nothing happened.

'Noli, you go to the big rock,' he said. 'Put your hand on it. Good. You feel it move, you cry out. Tinu, you go down. Make this man go back where he comes from. Perhaps rocks fall.'

Tinu nodded and slid herself into the hole. They heard her voice and protesting grunts, but in the end she got the man to understand somehow and came scrambling back.

Suth prodded among the rocks again and heaved sideways on his stick. Noli stood with her hand held lightly against the enormous slab, tense for the faintest movement. Tinu kneeled by the rock Suth was working on, with a smaller one ready in her hand. As soon as a crack opened, she jammed the small rock in, while Suth found a fresh hold for his digging stick.

A rock came loose. Suth rolled it clear, stood back, and looked at Noli.

'I feel nothing,' she said.

Suth worked another rock clear and started on a

third. As he heaved on his digging stick, the slab trembled beneath Noli's hand.

'It moves!' she shouted.

The three of them scrambled clear. Before they'd stopped moving there was a grinding sound followed by a crash and rattle. Dust smoked up from the opening. A couple of rocks came banging down from further up the pile. They waited, holding their breath. When everything seemed still, they crept back to the opening.

It was much larger now. Several rocks must have fallen in. Suth kneeled and called down, and the man's voice answered.

They waited.

'Why does he not come?' said Suth.

'Arm hurt . . . broken . . .' said Tinu. 'Suth . . . we help . . . ?'

Suth climbed down, and Tinu followed.

Noli stayed by the opening with her hand on the slab, ready to cry out if it stirred. There was more light down there now, and she could see the man's head clearly. Suth spoke to him and climbed below him. After trying several places, he managed to wedge his digging stick firmly across the hole and give himself something to stand on while he and Tinu helped the man out.

Slowly they worked their way up. Noli could see that the man's left arm was horribly broken, and Tinu was doing her best to support it so that he could use his right arm to climb with. Once or twice he shouted with pain. Suth was mostly out of sight, trying to support him from below.

At last Noli was able to reach in and help drag

him out into the open, but when she tried to help him to his feet, he couldn't stand. As well as the broken arm, he had a ghastly bruised wound in the back of his right leg.

Suth and Tinu climbed out, gasping with the effort. They rested for a bit, and then all three working together helped the man down to their fire.

They fetched him water in their cupped hands, and he lapped it eagerly, while Mana peeled whitestem for him and popped it into his mouth piece by piece as if he were a baby.

And all the time he said not a word of thanks, though each time anyone did anything for him he made a quiet double grunt of acknowledgement.

The Moonhawks studied him curiously. He was different from them, different from anyone they'd met. He was young, but a man, with bushy face hair along his jaw and around his mouth, and a deep voice. But he wore no man scars. All the men they knew had two curved scars on each cheek, where the leader of their Kin had sliced carefully into the flesh as a sign that they were no longer boys.

And this man wasn't much taller than Suth, and the bones of his arms and legs were not much thicker than Noli's. His skin, too, was a rich brown, nowhere near as dark as the Kin. His face wasn't like theirs, but long and narrow, with a hooked nose and protruding lips and teeth.

'This man is not people,' muttered Suth.

'You say he is animal?' said Noli.

'I do not know. People speak. His mouth is not hurt, but he does not speak. I speak. He hears the noise. He does not hear the words. He does not hear the thing I say. He is not people.'

Ko was frowning at the puzzle.

'Is he animal, Suth?' he asked. 'We eat him?'

Suth smiled, and shook his head, as much at the puzzle as at Ko's question.

'We do not eat him, Ko,' he said. 'But he is not people.'

When he'd finished eating and drinking, the man sat for a while, nursing his broken arm and moaning to himself. Now he raised his head and gazed down the canyon.

A thought seemed to strike him. Painfully he hunkered himself around and turned his head, slowly, as if he knew what he was going to see and couldn't bear to face it.

He stared at the rockfall. His mouth opened and his jaw worked to and fro, but no sounds came. The muscles of his face were hard and knotted, like tree roots.

He tried to get to his feet. Suth put a hand on his shoulder to coax him back down, but the man simply grabbed his arm and used it to haul himself up. He hobbled to the pile and began to tear at the rocks with his good hand.

'No. Dangerous,' said Suth, and tried to pull him away. The man pushed him off, but staggered and fell.

He didn't try to rise. He just lay face down and wailed, a terrible sound, rising and falling in waves. A thought came into Noli's mind, sudden and clear, as if Moonhawk had put it there, the way she used to. Only there were no words in this thought. It was a wordless knowledge, an understanding.

'His Kin are under the rock,' she said. 'They are all dead. He is alone.'

The man drew breath and wailed again. The sound echoed along the canyon.

Alone, it cried.

Alone, wailed the echoes. *Alone, alone, alone.*

Oldtale

RAKAKA

Rakaka was an earth demon. His teeth were hammer stones and his claws were cutters.

He lived below ground. He listened to the voices of people as they journeyed to their Good Places. He smelled their smells. Below the ground, he followed them to their camps.

When a baby was born, he smelled the birth blood. He smelled the breast milk of the mother as she fed it.

When all slept, he rose. He entered the camp. He took the shape of the baby and lay down beside the mother. He cried with the voice of the baby.

The mother woke. She fed him from her breasts. Rakaka took all the milk that was in her. None was left for the true baby.

Night after night Rakaka did this. No milk was left for the true baby. It died.

Naga fed her baby, Sol. Rakaka smelled the smell of the breast milk. He rose and crept into the camp.

He took the shape of Sol and lay down beside Naga. He cried with the voice of Sol.

Naga woke. She said, 'My baby is hungry. I feed him.'

Sol woke also. He said, 'Who cries with my voice? Who feeds at the breast of my mother?'

He caught Rakaka by the arm and pulled him away.

Rakaka struck at Sol with his fist. It was not his true fist. It was the fist of a baby.

Sol caught Rakaka by the wrist. He put the fist to his mouth. He bit with his teeth. He bit through the first finger at the knuckle joint and spat it out.

Rakaka howled. All the Kin woke. By the light of the fire they saw two babies, two Sols. The babies fought with blows and with cries, as grown men fight.

Naga said, 'Which of these is my own child, my child, Sol?'

Both answered, 'I am your own child, your child, Sol.'

At that, Sol was enraged. He was filled with the rage of a hero. He struck Rakaka so fierce a blow that the demon could not hold the shape he had taken. He became his own shape.

By the light of the fire, all saw him.

They saw his snout for smelling the smells of people. They saw his hammer teeth for grinding rocks. They saw his cutter claws for digging through the earth.

They said, 'It is the demon Rakaka.'

Sol was still in his rage. He picked up a great boulder and flung it. In the strength of his rage, he flung it.

The rock struck Rakaka in the chest and carried him away. A full day's journey it carried him, and he fled to his own places beneath the earth. Far and far he fled, beneath the desert where no people live.

The rage left Sol. He looked around. He saw the knuckle joint of Rakaka that he had bitten from his hand. That too was now in its own shape, the shape of a cutter.

Sol picked it up.

He said, 'This is my cutter. Its name is Ban-ban. No cutter is sharper. It is mine.'

As for the rock that Sol threw, it is at Ragala Flat. No rock at Ragala Flat is of the same kind. The marks of Sol's two hands, the hands of a child, are clear upon it.

CHAPTER THREE

Noli slept badly. The man they had rescued kept moaning with pain, and from time to time he crawled to the rockfall and cried out, still without words but saying as clearly as if he'd spoken, 'Is anybody there?'

Then he'd wait and listen to the silence, and come back and lie down, grieving.

His Kin are beneath the rocks, Noli thought. *It was night. They slept there. The rocks fell on them.*

She wasn't sure if the thought was really her own thought, or if it came to her somehow from the odd pressure still pushing against her mind.

And when she slept, her dreams were broken and meaningless, but she had a feeling that they weren't the dream she was supposed to be having. It was as if Moonhawk were trying to come to her, and couldn't. She woke in the morning so tired that she might as well not have slept at all.

The stranger's arm was horribly swollen. He

hugged it to himself and winced at a touch, but he let Tinu bathe it for him and lick the wound in his leg clean, since he couldn't reach it to lick himself. He ate and drank a little, but mostly sat huddled by the fire, with his back to the rockfall.

'Tinu,' said Suth suddenly, 'I remember this. When I was small a man in Parrot broke his arm bone. His name was Vol. An old woman in Parrot – I do not know her name – laid two sticks along his arm. One was here. One was here.'

Suth held up his right forearm and with his left hand outlined two straight sticks laid along it on either side from the elbow to the palm.

'She wrapped the arm in leaves,' he went on. 'She bound all together with tingin bark. A moon passed, and another moon. The bone mended. It was bent, but it was strong. How do we do this? I do not see tingin trees in this place.'

'I think . . .' mumbled Tinu.

She sat, frowning, and then picked up a few discarded strips of whitestem peel, tested them for strength, and started to braid three together.

Suth watched her for a while and then said, 'First I hunt. Then I make a fire log.'

He picked up his digging stick and strode off. Noli finished feeding Otan, then took Ko and Mana foraging, leaving Tinu to mind the fire and the stranger and Otan.

This time Noli knocked down as many wing nuts as the three of them could carry and took them back to the camp before setting off again to collect whitestem. She found Otan awake and toddling down towards the water hole, and the stranger tending a dying fire while Tinu sat totally absorbed, frowning at broken lengths of braided whitestem.

'Tinu, what do you do?' she cried. 'The fire dies. Otan runs away. This is bad, bad!'

Tinu looked up like somebody waking from a dream, and brushed the whitestem fibres off her lap with a disappointed gesture.

'This stuff . . . no good . . .' she muttered. 'Noli . . . you say . . . what?'

There was no point in yelling at her again. Tinu was like that when she got absorbed in anything, so Noli left Mana to cope with Otan while she took Ko for the whitestem.

They came back to find that Suth had returned. He had caught no game but had dug out a double fistful of fat yellow grubs from a rotted tree trunk. So they roasted these and popped the wing nuts in the embers of the fire and feasted contentedly. The stranger ate dully, not noticing what they gave him.

When they had finished, Suth settled down with the branch that he and Tinu had dragged home to make a fire log. For this he needed a piece about as long as his forearm and as thick as his leg. But he'd hardly started to chip his way through the branch, using the cutter one of the men had given him back in the valley, when he gave a cry of dismay.

'This is bad, bad,' he said. 'I break my cutter.' He held it up and showed them that most of the sharp edge had snapped away.

He rose, shaking his head, and started to search the canyon floor for stones of the right size to make a new cutter.

All the Moonhawks were aware of his problem.

Stoneworking was a knack. A father would start teaching his son as soon as his hands were strong enough, but it still took a lot of practice to learn which were the right stones to use, and where and how to hit them so as to chip the flakes away and leave a sharp edge. Some men never learned, and so far Suth had had no luck when he'd tried.

He returned and hammered away at several stones, but nothing happened. He barely made a mark on them.

'These stones are too hard,' he said dispiritedly, and went back to trying to bash his way through with the blunt cutter. It was hopeless. His fire log would be a splintered mess before he was done. He got up again and started to search for different kinds of stone.

Noli wasn't aware that the stranger had been watching, but now he struggled to his feet and hobbled down to Suth, supporting his broken arm with his good one.

Noli watched curiously. Suth was collecting a pile of stones to try. The stranger looked at them, pushed them aside with his foot, and gave a contemptuous shake of the head.

Suth said something. He was too far off for Noli to hear, but he looked surprised and angry. The stranger hobbled a few steps up the canyon, stopped, and gestured with his head for Suth to follow.

'Noli, I go with this man,' called Suth.

She waved to show she understood. He caught up with the man and put his arm around him to steady him. Slowly they disappeared beyond the rockfall.

'Noli,' said Tinu pleadingly, 'I go too?'

Noli nodded, and Tinu scampered off.

They were gone longer than she'd expected. When they came back, Suth was carrying a small armful of stones, and Tinu a whole sheaf of different sorts of leaf and stem and bark, which she laid by the fire and began to sort through. Meanwhile, the stranger sat beside Suth, showing him how to hold the stone he'd chosen and where and how to strike it. It was slow, and Suth made a lot of mistakes. By the time he'd finished, the hand he'd been using to hold the target stone was bruised and bleeding, but he had a cutter of a sort. A skilled stoneworker would probably have thrown it away as a failure, but Suth held it up in triumph.

'This is the first cutter I make,' he said. 'I, Suth, make this cutter.'

'I, Ko, praise,' said Ko solemnly.

Suth put his hand on the stranger's shoulder, a gesture of brotherhood.

'I, Suth, thank,' he said.

For the first time since they'd rescued him, the stranger smiled. Carefully he laid his broken arm on his lap and returned the gesture. As he did so, he made a soft barking noise up in the roof of his mouth, repeated three times.

'This man is people,' declared Suth. 'We take him into our Kin. He is Moonhawk. His name is . . .'

He looked at Noli. Names were very important. Always, among the Kins, it was the one to whom the First One came who chose them.

Noli didn't hesitate. The name seemed to be there, in her mouth, ready.

'His name is Tor,' she said.

'Good,' said Suth.

He pointed around the circle of Moonhawks and said each of their names in turn.

'Noli. Otan. Tinu. Ko. Mana. Suth . . . Tor.'

Tor smiled and frowned at the same time. He looked pleased, but puzzled, as if he almost understood the idea, but not quite. Noli felt extremely sorry for him. He was still utterly miserable about what had happened to his people, and no wonder. But he'd really taken trouble to help Suth with his cutter, though it must have hurt him, hobbling all that way. And he had a sweet smile.

That night Noli slept badly again. She had the same sense of something pressing against the edges of her mind, and in her dreams she heard thin, high voices wailing in the desert above the canyon, wailing in the same way that Tor had wailed, without words.

She woke and saw the stars and the moonlit cliffs, but the voices were gone.

They are dream voices, she thought. *Spirit voices, the voices of Tor's people who are dead under the rocks.*

In the morning she told Suth. He accepted what she said without questioning her.

'We move our camp,' he said.

Everyone knew that it was unwise to camp too close to a place of death. Demons might come there.

They chose a new place further down the canyon, and shifted the fire there by stages, as before. Tor seemed relieved by the move, though for the next three evenings he hobbled back to the rockfall alone and mourned there for a while.

When they'd moved, Suth returned to the rockfall to finish cutting the log to the length he needed. He brought it back to the new camp to begin the slow process of burning out the centre. Meanwhile Tinu had found a large coarse leaf whose fibres were a bit tougher than whitestem. Even when she braided them into lengths, they weren't as strong as she'd have liked, but they'd do.

She started to experiment with bindings for Tor's arm. He seemed to understand what she was doing and did his best to help.

By nightfall she had managed a clumsy-looking bundle that held the arm firm, with a loop of braided fibre around Tor's neck to carry the weight. It obviously helped a lot, and Tor kept patting it and showing it to them all and making his thanks grunt to Tinu.

She didn't seem at all afraid of him. It was the first time Noli had seen Tinu behave like that with an adult. Usually she hung her head and stared at the ground, but she looked Tor right in the eyes.

It took another two days to finish the fire log. The three older Moonhawks worked at it in turn, slowly burning the centre out with hot embers, cooling and softening the charred wood with water, and then reaching in and using one of the flakes from Suth's cutter to chip it away, time after time after time.

A fire log seldom lasted more than a moon or two before the sides burned through, so they'd all seen new ones made and knew how it was done, but Tor obviously had no idea what they were up to, and watched, fascinated.

But he knew things the Moonhawks didn't. On the

second day he led them up the canyon to a place where the water came out onto the surface and they could all lap up as much as they wanted. Then he surprised them.

The bed and sides of the pool were flat, smooth rocks. Tor showed them that if they lifted one of these they might find a swimming creature lurking beneath it, about the size of a child's finger, pale grey and with lots of legs and feelers. The trick was to move the rock suddenly and then grab the creature before it shot into a crack. Then they could chew it up and spit out the shell.

On the fourth morning Tinu thoroughly wetted the outside of the fire log and smeared the inside with a thick paste made with moistened ash. Then, using twigs to handle the hot embers from the fire, she packed them into the bottom of the log and filled it up with bits of cold charcoal that she'd raked out the evening before. She plugged the top with a round flat rock that almost fitted the hole, and sealed the gaps with more paste, leaving one tiny gap for air. Finally she fitted the fire log into the cradle she'd braided so that it could be carried on a loop over the shoulder.

By now Tor had learned the Moonhawks' names, as well as his own. If Noli said 'Tor', he would look up. If she said something about Suth, he would glance towards Suth. But he still didn't say anything, names or words. Instead, the Moonhawks learned, his barks and grunts carried different meanings. There was a sharp yap that meant *Watch out*, and a series of snorts when he was particularly interested in something, and a kind of questioning hoot that meant *Help me here*, and so on.

'These are not words,' said Suth. 'He does not say, *Suth, go to the wing nut place. See the white rock. There a fat lizard basks.* He cannot say this.'

'I can say this,' said Ko. '*I* am people. Tor is not people.'

'Tor is people,' said Mana, firmly.

In her quiet way she had adopted Tor, peeling whitestem and popping wing nuts for him, and licking his leg morning and evening to keep it clean as it healed.

'Tor is not people,' said Ko, obviously out to annoy her. 'He does not have words. Suth says this.'

'Tor has words,' said Mana. 'He says to me, *I thank*. He says, *Come*. He says, *What is this?*'

She made the sounds to show them. She got them just right. Tor looked up, amused.

'Suth says these are not words!' shouted Ko. 'Suth, do you say this?'

'I say *Yes*, I say *No*,' said Suth, doing his best to keep the peace. 'I do not know if these are words. But Tor is people.'

They discussed the question several times more as the days went by, but didn't get any nearer to an answer.

On the fifth morning, Suth said, 'The fire log is made. Today we journey. We find a new camp. Tor, do you come? Do you stay?'

Tor made his questioning grunt. Suth did his best to explain with gestures, but Tor still didn't get it.

'I show him,' said Mana.

She made the snorting bark that meant *Come*, and

led him off to the rockfall. When they came back he seemed to understand what was happening and was ready to leave.

'Tor says goodbye to his friends,' Mana explained.

Noli was relieved. She didn't want to leave Tor behind. His leg was slowly healing, but it would be a long while before his arm mended, if it ever did. Till then he'd need help just to stay alive. He'd slow them down a lot, but they had taken him into the Kin. He was Moonhawk. They had to look after him.

So they moved slowly down the canyon, foraging as they went. Here and there fresh rockfalls, loosened by the earthquake, lay against the cliffs. At each of these Tor stopped and called anxiously and listened, but there was no answer, so he hobbled on. By midday he was very tired, and at almost every step grunted softly with the pain in his arm.

Suth halted at a patch of trees so that they could rest in the shade, as usual, but despite the heat and his pain and exhaustion, Tor insisted on going on, so they did as he wished. The canyon zigzagged, and they could seldom see far along it. They rounded a corner, and another, and there the scene changed.

The canyon itself widened, and its floor dropped steeply away. The underground stream gushed out between boulders and foamed down to the lower level, where it ran on as an open river.

At the top of the slope Tor halted and gave a shrill cry, not a noise they'd heard him make before. He listened, but no answer came, only the echoes, and the screeching of the birds he'd disturbed.

'I see caves,' said Suth, pointing to the left-hand cliff. 'There, where rocks have fallen close by.'

Tor called again and headed for the caves. The others followed, and as they came nearer they could both see and smell that people had laired here not long ago. At the mouth of the first cave, Tor made a sign to them that he wanted to go in alone. They understood. This was his stuff, not theirs.

While they waited in the stillness, Noli could feel the faint presence of people's lives, many, many lives lived in this place, far back into time. Her skin began to tingle. She shuddered.

After a while Tor came gloomily out and hobbled off to two more caves a little further on.

'We lair at this place,' said Suth. 'First we find wood for our fire. Noli, do you come?'

Her mind seemed full of cloud stuff. She heard the question as if it had come slowly, from very far away.

'I stay,' she muttered, and then she was alone, only vaguely aware of the weight of Otan, asleep on her hip. The feeling grew stronger. She was still in the glaring light outside the cave, but at the same time she seemed to be inside it, in total darkness, except for the moonlight beyond the mouth of the cave. In that darkness she felt a sudden pulse of panic, felt somebody jerk out of sleep, heard a cry of wild alarm. Others were waking, beginning to move. Rock trembled beneath her feet. Fresh cries rose from all around in the darkness. The rock shuddered violently this time, and loosened stuff clattered from the roof . . . terror, panic all around her, a muddle of people jostling and fighting towards the cave mouth . . . and then the bellow of the exploding mountain, and moments later the thunder of the main rockfall from the cliff . . .

The feeling faded, and she was standing out in the sunlight, shuddering, and breathing in huge, sighing lungfuls. Otan was still fast asleep. Suth and the others were still in earshot. Very little time had passed, and yet she had felt all these things. Strange, strange.

'Mana,' she called, 'come. You watch Otan. I help fetch wood.'

Mana trotted obediently back, and Noli hurried after the others.

'The ground shook,' she told Suth. 'People slept in the cave. Rocks fell. They were frightened. They ran away.'

'Moonhawk shows you this?' he asked.

'Moonhawk does not come again,' she said. 'No one shows this. I see it.'

He stared at her, shrugged, and led the way on.

When they had enough fuel to get a fire going, they went back to the caves. In front of the largest one, Tinu built a hearth and tipped the embers out of the fire log. They were black now, but when she heaped dried grass and twigs onto them and blew, they began to glow. Smoke curled up. The flames were invisible in the fierce sunlight, but the twigs shrivelled into ash, and the larger sticks she heaped on charred almost at once.

So the Moonhawks had their fire again, and sang their song and made camp.

Tor seemed not to have noticed any of this. First he had roamed from cave to cave, looking for signs of his people, and then he had hobbled off down the canyon and called, and called again, with no answer but echoes. Finally he came back and settled with them in the shadow of the cliff, where he sat with his knees drawn under his chin, rocking himself to and fro and moaning softly.

When the Moonhawks had their midday meal, Tor didn't join them, so after a while, Mana hunkered down beside him and offered him a bit of roasted lizard.

He looked at her. She put the morsel to his lips. He opened his mouth and she popped it in. He chewed slowly. Little by little she continued to feed him. He ate, not seeming to notice what he was doing.

It was the other way around with Noli and Otan. Otan was greedily gobbling everything Noli gave him and paying no attention to anything else, while Noli's mind was far away, still thinking about what had happened in the cave.

This is Moonhawk stuff, she thought. *But it is not Moonhawk. Moonhawk does not come any more. How can this be?*

Ko's shriek of laughter burst into her thoughts.

'See, Suth, see!' he cried, almost choking at his own cleverness. 'The women feed the men! The women feed the men! Noli feeds Otan. Mana feeds Tor. Tinu, you feed Suth!'

Hesitantly Tinu offered Suth the roasted grub she'd just fetched from the embers, and he let her put it into his mouth. They all laughed, and Ko rolled to and fro, helpless, gasping, 'The women feed the men!' over and over, because it was a joke simple enough for a small one to understand, and he, Ko, had made it.

Even Tor noticed something outside his own pain and misery, and looked up and smiled, though he couldn't have known what the joke was.

Oldtale

SALA-SALA

Sala-Sala was a demon of dark woods. Woowoo was a demon of drinking places. They were the birth brothers of the demon Rakaka. They met, as was their custom, in Dead Trees Valley.

They said, 'Where is our brother, Rakaka? Why does he not come to our meeting?'

They searched long, long, and found him hiding far out beneath the desert, where no people come.

They said, 'Why do you hide here, brother Rakaka?'

He said, 'A hero is born among people. His name is Sol. When he was a baby still I fought with him. He bit off my finger. He threw a great rock at me. It carried me away a full day's journey. I am afraid of this hero. This is why I hide in the desert, where no people come.'

Sala-Sala mocked him and said, 'You are soft earth, my brother. The wind blows you where it wills. The rain washes you away. I am great trees. The wind blows me, and I roar and sing. The rain lashes me. I drink it and rejoice. Now I deal with this hero, this Sol. At Stinkwater I deal with him, when the Kins come there to feast on the waterbirds.'

So Sala-Sala hid himself in the woods beside Stinkwater. His talons were digging sticks, and his teeth were spikes of stonewood. At the season of waterbirds, the Kins came to feast, and Fat Pig laired beside the woods.

When all slept, Sala-Sala put out an arm and drew the people of Fat Pig into the woods. There he bound them with lianas so that they could not move. Sol slept beside Naga, his mother. Sala-Sala left them for last.

Sol woke.

He felt his mother gone.

He looked, and saw a great hand that carried her into the woods.

He struck the hand with his cutter, Ban-ban. So sharp was Ban-ban that it sliced through Sala-Sala's second finger at the knuckle joint.

Sala-Sala roared. He came out of the woods

Sol saw his arms that were branches, his fur that was leaves, his teeth that were spikes of stonewood. He saw the demon Sala-Sala.

Sol said, 'Demon, where are my mother's Kin, the Kin of Fat Pig?'

Sala-Sala laughed.

He said, 'Sol, they are mine.'

Sol was filled with rage, the rage of a hero. He tore up a fangana tree. Root, trunk, and branches he tore from the ground.

With the tree he struck Sala-Sala. On the side of the jaw Sol struck him.

Sala-Sala fell to the ground. His strength was gone. He slept.

Sol picked up the claw he had cut from the hand of Sala-Sala.

He said, 'This is my digging stick. Its name is Monoko. No digging stick is stronger. It is mine.'

Sol went into the woods. He found his mother's Kin, the Kin of Fat Pig, lying beneath a great tree. The tree was a sky toucher. It was the Father of Trees. It has no other name.

Sol struck that tree with his digging stick, Monoko. The tree opened apart.

Sol picked up Sala-Sala where he lay sleeping, and stuffed him into the tree. He took off the lianas that bound his mother's Kin, and tied them around the tree. He twisted them tight, so that the tree closed.

Sol said, 'The demon Sala-Sala is bound, as you were bound, my uncles. He cannot come out. Now let us feast on the waterbirds.'

The Father of Trees stands in the woods by Stinkwater. It is bound all around with lianas. Sala-Sala is within it, caught fast. When the wind strikes the Father of Trees, Sala-Sala howls.

CHAPTER FOUR

The Moonhawks stayed at the caves for only one day. They found that this part of the canyon had been heavily foraged and hunted, so there was very little to eat here. Even the grey swimming creatures Tor had shown them how to catch were small and scarce.

Suth, in any case, wanted to move on.

'This is not our place, Noli,' he said suddenly as they sat by the fire that evening. 'It is a Good Place, but . . .'

He paused, and looked her in the eyes.

'Do they live, Noli?' he asked.

She knew at once that he was talking about the rest of the Moonhawk Kin whom she and Suth had left sleeping in the desert when they turned back to rescue Tinu and the small ones. Had they found the canyon and water and food? Or had they died in the desert, never realizing that the canyon was there?

Noli shook her head.

'Suth, I do not know,' she said.

He frowned and sat silent.

'I think they live,' he said decisively. 'Tomorrow we look for them.'

Tor seemed just as anxious to move on – for much the same reason, Noli guessed: to see if any of his own people had survived the earthquake, further along the canyon. So the next morning, Tinu wetted the fire log again and smeared its inside with fresh paste and packed it with embers and sealed it, and they moved on. The river zigzagged to and fro, so that they kept having to cross it, but Tor knew the best places.

Gradually the floor of the canyon dropped away and the cliffs on either side became higher. Noli had never been anywhere like this before, with the unknown trees and birds – several different kinds of them, now – and the towering dark cliffs, and the river foaming white as it tumbled down a slope of boulders . . .

And something else . . .

Her whole skin crawled. She felt the hair at the base of her neck stir of its own accord.

A thought slid into her mind. More than a thought, a knowledge.

A First One is here.

In her wonderment she had fallen behind the others. Now she stopped and lowered Otan to the ground. He stood, holding on to her leg and looking up at her. She didn't see him.

She didn't see the others moving on down the canyon.

She raised her right hand with its fingers spread,

the gesture of greeting. The words came into her mouth. She whispered them.

First One, we come to your place.
We pass through.
We drink your water, we eat your berries.
We know these are not ours.
They are yours, First One.
We, Moonhawk, thank.

There was no answer, but the pressure on her mind eased. The hair at her nape settled back, and the tingling of her skin died slowly away. As she picked up Otan and hurried after the others, she wasn't sure whether the First One had gone completely or whether it had only withdrawn and was watching them now from somewhere high on the cliffs.

She had hardly caught up when Suth called a halt where the river spilled over a ledge and became a waterfall, higher than a man. The small ones were thrilled by the roaring white water flowing ceaselessly down. There were three trees close by, with shade beneath them, and fine spray from the fall drifted across, delicious in the noon heat.

'People rest here often, I think,' said Suth, sniffing the air. 'Yes, see, there are wing nut shells.'

Noli barely noticed what Suth was talking about.

'Mana, you feed my brother,' she said, putting Otan down. 'I thank. Suth, I do not eat now. I go over there. I go alone . . . Suth, a First One is here.'

He stared at her, startled.

'Moonhawk?' he asked hopefully.

'Suth, we do not know this First One. It is not

Moonhawk, not Monkey, not Ant Mother or Weaver or any of the others. I do not know its name.'

Suth's eyes became wider still. His mouth opened. The idea was as astonishing to him as it was to her. The First Ones were the First Ones. There were ten of them. How could there be any more?

Noli moved off and chose a place out of sight of the others, a narrow strip of shade on the far side of a large boulder. She sat, crossed her legs, folded her arms, straightened her back, and began to breathe in the slowest, deepest breaths that she could manage.

She'd never tried this before. Moonhawk had come to her only in dreams, and once or twice suddenly, unasked, in the daytime. But she had seen Bal, their leader, sitting like this, breathing like this, waiting. Then he'd shudder and his eyes would roll up and perhaps he'd froth at the lips and speak with a voice that wasn't his own. Or perhaps he'd yawn and lie down, instantly asleep, and when he woke tell everyone his dream.

So Noli sat and breathed and waited. She emptied herself of thoughts, of feelings. Her eyes were open, but she didn't see the sunlit cliff ahead of her or the rocks and bushes around her. She didn't hear the birdcalls or the snoring rush of the waterfall. She didn't feel the fierce noon heat or the hardness of the rock on which she was sitting, or notice how long she had sat there, a few moments or half the afternoon.

Nothing happened. She was certain a First One was there, not just close by but all around her, and yet it did nothing. It spoke no words to her. It made no pictures in her mind. It seemed to be just waiting, like her.

At last, a thought came to her. It didn't come from the First One. It was her own thought, slipping quietly into the emptiness she'd made.

It cannot speak to me. It is like Tor. It has no words.

The thought broke her trance. She saw cliffs and bushes, and felt the afternoon heat and the hard rock beneath her. She heard sounds. New sounds.

Above the birdcalls and the waterfall, there were voices. Grunts and barks and cries, such as Tor used. The voices were angry.

Staggering with stiffness, she moved to see. There were people under the trees, brown-skinned like Tor, gathered in an excited huddle. She couldn't see Suth and the others.

She ran towards them, but stopped a little way off. Nobody had noticed her yet. She could see Suth now, with Tinu just behind him. They had their backs to a boulder. She still couldn't see the small ones. Suth's digging stick was half raised, and his hair was bushed right out. Facing him were several brown-skinned men. They had hands raised too, holding stones.

She moved a little and saw that Tor was there, between Suth and the men, nursing his bandaged arm as he faced them, snarling. They looked angry and uncertain. Noli guessed that these people must have arrived suddenly, expecting to have their midday rest under the trees, and the Moonhawks hadn't noticed them coming because of the noise of the waterfall. And if it weren't for Tor, the men would have attacked Suth, and perhaps even killed him, for foraging in one of their places without permission. Now they weren't sure.

Noli took a deep breath and was just going to rush in and join Suth and try to plead with the men, when something brushed past her. Nothing she could see, but . . .

There! That woman, standing at the edge of the group, with a small baby on her hip and a gourd slung at her back. Her head was turned, as if someone had called to her. Her eyes were round, her mouth half open.

Noli understood in an instant.

The First One comes to her!

She ran and touched the woman's arm, and then kneeled and pattered her palms on the ground, the sign the Kin used for *I submit. Do not strike me.* When she rose, the woman was staring dazedly at her, still half in her trance. Noli took her hand and led her to the front of the group. The woman didn't resist.

By now two of the men had grabbed hold of Tor and were pulling him out of the way. Noli let go of the woman and ran to him and put her arm around him, trying to tell these people, *See, we are friends.*

A man snarled and cuffed her aside, but then the woman was there, holding him by the arm to stop him hitting Noli again. He tried to shake her off, but she clung on, calling shrilly.

Other women joined in. Noli was knocked to the ground, and crawled clear with her head ringing. She stood, waiting for an opening so that she could dart in and try to snatch Otan out of the crush, but before she got the chance the shouting quieted and the men drew back, though they looked as angry as ever.

Tinu had been trying to shield Otan between herself

and the boulder, but Tor was there before Noli, grunting urgently and pointing at the fire log slung from Tinu's shoulder. Just as vehemently, he broke a few twigs from the nearest bush, put them on the ground, blew on them, then pointed at the fire log again. He gestured to the newcomers to come nearer.

'Suth,' shouted Noli. 'Tor says, *Make fire. Show these people!*'

Suth didn't hesitate. He moved his digging stick to his left hand and lowered it to the ground. Then he drew himself up and raised his right hand in the greeting gesture. His hair settled.

'Come,' he said confidently, and turned away. Luckily the strangers' curiosity was stronger than their anger now, and they came.

Suth led them clear of the spray from the fall and chose a place for the fire. The Moonhawks gathered dry stuff. Tinu kneeled and tipped the embers out of the fire log. They were still very hot, and as soon as she fed them smoke rose and the flames bit. Very soon there was a good fire going, and the strangers had joined in the fuel gathering, throwing whole branches onto the fire and laughing with glee. When the fire became too hot to stand near, they moved back under the trees to rest.

Noli saw the woman who had helped her settling down and getting ready to feed her baby, so she went over and kneeled in front of her, bowed her head, and put her palms together.

'I, Noli, thank,' she said slowly.

For a moment the woman looked puzzled. Then she smiled and put her baby down. She took Noli's right hand in hers and patted it gently with her left.

This wasn't a gesture that the Kin used, but its meaning was clear: *We are friends.*

They smiled at each other, and Noli went back to the Moonhawks.

Later most of the newcomers left in small groups and spread out up and down the canyon, looking for food. Before long it became clear that they were all expecting to camp here for the night, because this was where the fire was, and they didn't want to leave it.

'I say this,' said Suth. 'These people know fire. They do not know fire logs. They are glad of fire. But they cannot carry it from this camp to another camp.'

'They know other stuff, Suth,' said Noli. 'People stuff. They make cutters. They use gourds. They are people.'

Suth grunted agreement, but frowned, still thinking.

'Noli,' he said. 'You say there is a First One here. Is it the First One of these people?'

Noli was feeling ordinary now, with none of that strangeness inside her, or outside. She knew what it had been like, sitting alone, emptying herself, waiting, but it wasn't part of her now. It belonged to the night-time Noli, the one to whom Moonhawk used to come. Thinking about it was like remembering a dream. You can say, *This happened in my dream*, but you can't go back and dream the dream again.

'Suth, I do not know,' she said. 'This First One comes also to one of their women. I saw this. And in the cave it woke her. It woke her before the rocks fell. She called to her people. They woke. They ran from the cave. They were safe when the rocks fell . . . Suth, I think this First One does not have words.'

Suth nodded. 'It is their First One,' he said decisively, and looked around. Except for Tor and one or two others, they were alone under the trees now.

'Now we find food,' he said.

'Do these people allow this?' asked Noli. 'This is their Good Place.'

'We give a gift,' said Suth, reasonably. 'It is fire. They are glad of it.'

'They are not Kin,' said Noli. 'They do not know Kin stuff.'

'We see,' said Suth. 'They stop us, we go. They allow us, we stay. Tomorrow we go. Tor stays. These are his people. They care for him.'

Noli was sad about that, though she knew it was probably for the best. She liked Tor, he was so friendly and helpful. He knew things about the canyon that the Moonhawks didn't. And though he seemed glad to be back with his own kind of people, she could see he was waiting now to see that the Moonhawks were all right, as if they meant something special to him.

They learned more that afternoon. The canyon people didn't seem to mind the Moonhawks foraging in their Good Place, and after a while they came across the woman who'd helped Noli during that first terrifying encounter. There was nothing strange about her now. She seemed friendly and ordinary.

The woman was wading up to her knees in the river when they found her, and Noli guessed she was hunting for the grey swimming creatures. But while they watched, she bent and lifted a rock from the riverbed and carried it to the bank. She laid it down, crouched beside it, and started to bang at it with a smaller rock.

Coming closer, the Moonhawks saw that she was hammering at some small grey lumps that grew on it. They wouldn't have recognized them as food, but then the woman knocked one loose, turned it over, and scooped out its insides with her front teeth. She handed the next one to Noli to try. There wasn't much of it, but it was salty and delicious. After that Ko and Mana had a great time splashing in and out of the shallows, while the older Moonhawks hunted for more of the things. Were they some kind of water nut? Noli wondered.

They all ate together by the fire that evening, and then slept in the drifting smoke to keep the mosquitoes at bay. But in the morning, as the Moonhawks got ready to leave, there was trouble.

Tinu wetted and pasted and filled the fire log as usual. The embers hissed as they touched the damp paste, and a cloud of steam rose. Several of the canyon people came to watch, which Tinu, of course, hated. Shyer than ever with those strangers, she huddled down as if she was trying not to be noticed, and perhaps that made them suspicious. Somebody must have gone and told their leader, and he came over with three of the other men.

Suth, not realizing there was anything wrong, turned to greet and thank them in the regular way, but the men strode past him and snatched the fire log from Tinu as she was starting to seal the lid in place.

'Why do you do this?' cried Suth. 'This fire log is ours. We made it.'

Though they didn't understand the words, the men

got the meaning and closed in on him with snarls and barks. Their hair bushed out. So did Suth's, and he half raised his digging stick. Their barks became fiercer and deeper. They bared their teeth.

Noli had noticed Tor watching with an anxious look. There'd been a couple of spats like this between men the evening before, and no one had paid much attention. Because they didn't have words, they couldn't argue over their disagreements – they could only snarl at each other. But this time Tor grabbed Suth by the elbow and grunted warningly.

Suth shook him off, but Noli had heard what Tor had been trying to tell him: *Watch out! They mean it!*

She squeezed behind Suth and took hold of his digging stick. He tried to jerk it free.

'Suth, this is dangerous, dangerous!' she said. 'They are too many!'

'The fire log is Moonhawk's!' he snarled. 'We made it!'

'Suth, we make a new fire log. There is good wood in this place. They keep this one.'

'Noli, this is foolish. They do not know fire logs. Their fire dies.'

'We show them the making of fire logs. We show them how they keep the fire alive. It is a gift to them, Suth. It is a man's gift, the gift of a leader.'

He looked at her. His hair settled. She saw his anger turn to suspicion, and then to amusement, but he kept a straight face. He let her take his digging stick, and turned to the men, holding up both hands, palms forward. Their faces cleared, and their hair, too, settled. They didn't try to stop him as he stepped forward, took the fire log from the man who was holding it, and presented it to the leader.

'I, Suth, give,' he said. 'This gift is Moonhawk's.'

The leader snorted and hummed in his throat. He took the fire log and passed it to one of the others. Then, with both hands, he offered the stone he was holding to Suth.

Suth took it and held it up so that everyone could see it. It wasn't just a stone. It was a well-made cutter with a good, sharp edge.

'I, Suth, thank,' he said.

The leader answered with the triple bark that the canyon people used to show they were pleased, and all seemed well again.

After the exchange of gifts, everyone became friendlier than before. The Moonhawks gave the leader of the canyon people a name, Fang, and when Suth and Tinu started making a fresh fire log, they made sure that Fang and some of the others watched to see how they did it. And every evening Tinu emptied the embers out of the old log and prepared and packed and sealed it each morning, so that they'd understand how that was done. Of course, she wouldn't normally have bothered, as they had a good fire going and were planning to stay where they were for another night, but she wanted them to get the idea that the embers wouldn't stay hot in a fire log for much longer than one day.

Making the new fire log took three full days. On the first morning, Suth was still cutting the branch to shape, and Ko begged to stay and help. Mana obviously longed to fuss over Tor, and it didn't seem fair not to let her, so Noli took Otan off and foraged with Tinu.

Deliberately she tagged along with the woman she'd made friends with. These people didn't seem to have names, so Noli decided to call her Goma, at least in her own mind.

There'd been enough of them foraging yesterday to strip the area around the fire almost bare of food, so today they needed to travel further before they could spread out and start work. The ground was too rocky for good fat roots to grow, but otherwise the canyon was far richer in food than any of the Kin's old Good Places. There were edible leaves and seeds and berries, birds' eggs and nestlings, grubs and bugs and lizards, a bees' nest dripping with honey, as well as the swimmers and crawlers and water nuts (if that was what they were) in the river.

At midday they found shade trees to rest under, near the water. Noli watched Goma unpacking her gourd of all the things they had found. It was a very good gourd, big enough to be useful, and light and firm. Goma carried it in a cradle made of some kind of twisted fibre with a loop to go over her shoulder.

Gourds were very important, but the best kinds weren't common. In the old Good Places, only Fat Pig and Snake had had some, and the other Kins had needed to trade them for things like tingin bark and glitter stones and salt. The best ones would carry water for many moons without going soft, provided they were carefully dried and smoked every now and then.

When Goma's was empty, Noli picked it up.

'Where do you find this?' she asked.

'And where . . . this? . . .' mumbled Tinu, testing the carrying loop and peering eagerly at it.

Goma just nodded and smiled and got ready to feed her baby. Noli wasn't sure she'd understood, but when the rest was over, Goma beckoned to Noli and Tinu and led them across the river where she showed them a plant with long, spiked leaves that sprang straight from the ground. She hacked one off with a cutter that she took from her gourd, ripped the front from the back, and picked out a series of fibres that ran the full length of the leaf. She gave one to Tinu, who tried to snap it in two. It didn't break.

Tinu was delighted. She borrowed the cutter and hacked off more leaves, spiking herself several times in her excitement, but she barely noticed. She tied the leaves into a sheaf with the first bunch of fibres and trailed them behind her as they went on.

Goma led them across the canyon to an old rockfall that lay piled against the further cliff. It had been there long enough for patches of bushes to have taken root, and at the top was a thicket of twisted trees. Scrambling through these were several gourd vines.

Noli put Otan down on an open patch and asked Tinu to keep an eye on him while she hunted for a good gourd. At first all the ones she could see were green and small, but on the further side of the thicket she spotted a good-sized one growing high up in one of the trees. Its skin was just turning orange, which meant that it would be tough enough to last several moons. She wormed her way into the thicket, climbed the tree, and with a good deal of trouble bit through the stem.

Then she was stuck. The gourd was too heavy to

hold with one hand, so she couldn't climb down with it, and if she dropped it from this height, with all the weight of the pulp and seeds inside it, she'd be sure to break it.

She could see Goma watching her from outside the thicket, but realized that she herself was half hidden by the leaves, and Goma couldn't see what the problem was.

'Come, Goma, help me,' she called.

But of course, those were words. They didn't mean anything to Goma. Then Noli remembered the snorting bark the canyon people used when they meant *Come*, so she tried that. She didn't get it right the first time, but next try Goma seemed to understand. She saw her look carefully around her before laying her baby on a flat rock and then crawling into the thicket to the foot of the tree. She stood up, laughing, obviously amused by the noise Noli had made.

Noli lowered the gourd as far as she could reach, and dropped it for Goma to catch. Then she climbed down and they crawled out, Noli rolling the gourd in front of her.

Goma picked up her baby and turned to Noli. Smiling, she made the *Come* sound. Noli tried to copy it, but it still wasn't right, and they both laughed. They tried again and again, still laughing. Then they fell silent. Something had changed. The strangeness that Noli had felt yesterday morning came back even more strongly, the tingling of her skin, the stir of her nape hairs. She saw that Goma was staring at her with her eyes so wide that the whites showed all the way around. Her mouth was slightly open. Noli knew that she looked the same, that they were feeling the same, sharing the strangeness.

They each raised a hand and put them together, palm to palm, breathing deeply but making no other sound. What they were sharing was a knowledge, but it didn't have words. Words were no use to it. It wasn't word stuff, a thing you could say. It was knowledge about a First One.

Abruptly the knowledge changed. Still without words, Noli felt *Danger!* Not danger to her but to something small and helpless.

Otan.

She looked at Goma. They turned and ran.

Noli leaped from boulder to boulder down the slope and scrambled up on the further side of the trees. Goma, hampered by her baby, was a little behind her.

They stood and paused, panting. Nothing seemed wrong. Otan was sitting almost where Noli had left him, busily banging one pebble with another as if trying to make a baby-sized cutter. Tinu was further up the slope, absorbed in stripping the fibres out of the leaves she had brought. She hadn't noticed their arrival.

Goma yelled and picked up a stone and flung it and bent for another one. For an instant Noli couldn't spot what she was aiming at. Then she saw it.

Looped across the rocks lay an enormous rock python. Its skin colour made it almost invisible on the stony background. Its head was barely two paces from Otan. It must have been creeping towards him, and frozen at Goma's yell.

Noli screamed and flung a stone and dashed to

snatch Otan. Tinu was on her feet and shouting, too. Otan was yelling with fright at the sudden uproar. Goma's second stone struck just in front of the python's head. It jerked itself back, doubled around, and slithered rapidly away.

Noli picked Otan up and tried to comfort him. She was gasping, and her heart was pounding with effort and fright, but she got her breath back and thanked Goma.

Then she turned, gazed across the canyon, raised her free hand, and whispered, 'First One, you I thank also.'

She heard Goma's approving grunt, and guessed that she understood.

Now Tinu crept in front of her and kneeled and pattered her hands on the rock. She was weeping bitterly and could scarcely mumble the words. 'I am . . . bad, bad . . .' she sobbed. 'Not watch . . . not see . . . snake . . . Ah, Noli . . . !'

Noli was too relieved at Otan's escape to be angry with her. Noli knew that if she'd been looking after Otan while she was doing something else that interested her, she too might well not have noticed the danger. So, still holding Otan with her left arm, she crouched and lifted Tinu up and held her, still sobbing, against her side.

'Do not cry, Tinu,' she told her. 'It is done. Otan is well. Snake is a clever hunter. Now you hold Otan. I fetch my gourd.'

She went slowly, full of relief and thankfulness. Her sense of the presence of the First One had dwindled away until she was left with only the memory of it. But her feeling of oneness with Goma, of a thing they and no one else could share, remained. It was stronger and stranger than friendship. In two days the Moonhawks would leave, and probably she would never see Goma again. But Noli knew that if time did at last bring them together, this feeling would still be there, strong as ever.

Oldtale

WOOWOO

Sala-Sala screamed.

In the Father of Trees, where Sol had bound him, he raged and screamed.

After many moons, Woowoo came to Stinkwater. He heard the screams of Sala-Sala.

He said, 'Sala-Sala, my brother, who bound you here? Why do you not come out?'

Sala-Sala answered, 'The hero Sol bound me here, though he was but a child. He bound me so tightly that I cannot come out.'

Woowoo laughed and said, 'My brothers are fools,' and went on his way. But in his heart he said, Now I show my brothers that I am cleverer than they are.

He took the shape of a little frog and waited at the drinking places for the Kin of Fat Pig to come.

Sol was now a man. He said to the men of Fat Pig, 'Let us hunt.'

They said, 'We are tired.'

Sol said, 'I hunt alone.'

Woowoo heard this. He took the shape of a dirri buck and fled from Sol. To Sometimes River he fled, and Sol tracked him.

Sol said, 'Good, the buck flies to the river. There I drink, for I am thirsty and my gourd is empty.'

In those days Sometimes River was filled with water all the time. When Woowoo came there he worked a magic. His magic was strong, strong.

He dried up the river.

Sol came to the river and saw that it was empty. He said, 'Where can I drink, for I am thirsty, and my gourd is empty?'

Woowoo took the shape of a yellow snake and lay in the bed of the river.

He said, 'Sol, I too thirst, for I am a water snake. I know a water hole far into the desert. Carry me there, and I show you.'

But he said in his heart, Now I take Sol far and far into the desert, where there is no water, and there I leave him, and he dies. My plan is clever, for I am Woowoo.

Sol looked. He saw the tracks of the dirri buck. They came to the river and they were gone. The river was gone also. He saw a water snake. It spoke to him with the tongue of a man.

Sol said in his heart, This is demon stuff. With his mouth he said, 'Snake, I carry you to this water hole.'

He picked up the snake. He caught it close behind the head and held it fast. He said, 'Demon, I have you.'

Woowoo made the snake big. Its body was as wide as a man's. From nose to tail it was as far as a strong man can throw a rock. But Sol held fast.

Sol said, 'Demon, tell me your name.'

The snake said, 'I am Woowoo.'

Sol said, 'Good. You are a water demon. I need water. Woowoo, make water for me.'

He held the snake's head over his gourd. He said, 'Weep, Woowoo.'

He squeezed it by the neck so that it wept. The gourd was filled with its tears.

Sol said, 'Now demon, fill the river as it was before. Then I let you go.'

Woowoo said, 'I cannot do it. I have wept my magic into your gourd, all but a little.'

Sol said, 'I leave you here to make what magic you can.'

Sol struck the riverbed with his digging stick, Monoko. He made a pit. He cast Woowoo into the pit and closed it with a great rock.

He took the gourd. He said, 'This is my gourd, Dujiru. Woowoo's magic is in it. It never runs dry. It is mine.'

But Woowoo was held fast in the pit beneath Sometimes River. He makes water when he can. When he cannot, the river is dry. Thus it is Sometimes River.

CHAPTER FIVE

Two days' journey to the west, the volcano was settling down after the eruption. Smoke and steam still billowed from it, but the explosions were over and the lava had begun to cool.

The lake that had lain along the floor of the crater was gone. Some of it had boiled away, but most of the immense mass of water had flowed off into underground channels opened by the earthquake. It lay blocked for several days, until a late aftershock disturbed the rock levels and the sheer weight of water forced its way through, downwards and outwards. The people in the canyon knew nothing of any of this.

At last Tinu finished hollowing out the new fire log.

'Tinu, I praise,' said Suth when she showed it to him. 'Fill this tonight. Fill it with good embers, then

I hide it among the rocks. In the morning we go. These people do not see we take our new fire log.'

Tinu did as Suth told her, and in the dusk he slipped away and hid the fire log out of sight further down the canyon.

When they took their last drink at the river that night, the water tasted different. The canyon people drank it with doubtful grunts. Noli looked up and saw Suth tasting again, then frowning.

'What does this mean?' he said. 'It is the same as the water in the lake up in the mountain.'

'Suth, I do not know,' said Noli. 'Drink. That is good water.'

She went to sleep that night with nothing in her mind beyond the thought of moving on, just the six of them on their own again, and the sadness of leaving Goma and Tor behind.

Noli woke, shuddering with wordless knowledge, the certainty of a huge unstoppable something coming from further up the canyon.

She sat up. The moon was high, the canyon silent except for the rush of the river.

A voice cried out in alarm. She recognized it. Goma.

She shook Suth. 'Quick!' she said. 'Danger! We go!'

'What danger, Noli?'

'I do not know. Quick, Suth, quick! It comes!'

By the light of the moon she saw Goma standing to call her alarm, again and again. The cry echoed from the cliffs. Now others joined in. By the time the Moonhawks were moving, the whole troop was scrambling over the boulders in panic.

Noli was too filled with her terror to think, but Suth kept his head. He made the Moonhawks stay together. Noli carried Otan. Suth told Tinu to take the gourd while he helped Ko and Mana. On their way, he picked up the fire log from the place where he'd hidden it and gave it to Tinu to sling over her shoulder.

Hampered by their three small ones, the Moonhawks began to fall behind, but Suth still refused to panic and kept up a steady pace. Ahead of them, Noli could hear Goma's cries whipping her people on each time they paused.

The river twisted away towards the further cliffs, taking its noises with it. In the near silence they now heard a new sound, a dull roaring, distant still, but rushing towards them. It mingled with the shapeless sense of danger in Noli's mind and told her what it meant.

'Suth!' she called. 'It is water! Much water! Like at Sometimes River, after it thunders! It comes!'

Many moons before, when Noli had been no older than Mana was now, the Kin had been camped by the river and she'd seen a flash flood, a sudden torrent hurtling along the riverbed where a little before there'd been only dry rocks and one stagnant pool.

'Up!' said Suth. 'There!'

He pointed to the old rockfall where Noli had found the gourd.

Noli cupped her free hand by her mouth. 'Goma!' she yelled. 'It is water! Up! Up!'

Goma couldn't have heard. She didn't know words.

But Noli felt an answering pulse in her mind and knew that she'd understood.

Now that he could see how far they had to go, Suth allowed them to run, though he still tried to keep them together. He had picked up Mana and was dragging Ko. Noli could hear him gasping with the effort. Her own lungs gulped for air. Her heart slammed. The roar of the coming water grew louder and louder. Something glimmered to her right. She looked and saw that the river had grown to a wide sheet, flickering in the moonlight.

She floundered on, slower now. The others were a little ahead. Each time she looked, the sheet of water was nearer. It rose with a rush and swirled around her ankles. She stumbled among rocks she could no longer see. Someone snatched Otan from her. A strong hand grabbed her arm and dragged her forward. Goma.

The water was sluicing around their knees as they reached the rockfall. Noli let herself fall forward. Blindly she crawled up the rough slope. *Higher! Higher!* said the wordless voice inside her.

At last it let her rest. She turned and sat, sobbing for breath, with her blood roaring in her ears.

No, not her blood only. The retching of her lungs slackened to deep gasps. The agonized pounding eased in her chest. Sight came back. The roaring was now the sound of what was coming towards them down the canyon. She looked, and under the bright moon she saw it.

It came like a moving cliff around the bend above them. It slammed into the canyon wall with a booming bellow louder than its main awful roar. The impact forced a glittering spout of foam far into the night sky. The torrent churned around the bend and rushed on.

It struck the rockfall and was instantly almost at their feet. They yelled with terror, but their voices were drowned in the uproar. Spray drenched them, denser than any rain. And still the torrent rose and rose, driving them steadily up the mound, whirling bushes and boulders away as it thundered past. By the time the water stopped rising, they were huddled against the grove at the top, and beginning to climb into the trees.

No one slept. All night they watched the flood charge past. They were soaked, but not cold. The canyon was full of steam, and the spray from the churning waves was as warm as fresh blood.

Day came, and let them see how the flood filled the canyon, foaming along the opposite cliff and swirling around the next bend. Only the top of the mound they were on stood clear of the murderous water. They moved around, checking that all were safe. All the Moonhawks were, but Noli had been afraid for Tor. His bad leg and useless arm must have slowed him down, but he was there and made the noises that told her he was relieved to see her.

Somebody must have been lost, though, because a wailing started, several women passing the sound to and fro, one taking it up before another had finished, while the men made sad booming sounds deep in their throats.

They searched the grove for food. There was little plant stuff. The unripe gourds were too bitter to eat, and the few ripe ones were mostly fibre, with little goodness in them, and had a musty taste. But a lot of small creatures had taken refuge on the mound, and these they hunted eagerly.

Here and there in the grove, the leaf cover was thick enough to protect anything underneath from the drenching, so the Moonhawks found some dry litter and Tinu started a fire. Soon it was hot enough to burn the wetter fuel, so they could roast what they caught.

The floodwater was drinkable, though muddy with churned-up particles and stinking of the underfires of earth. This time the Moonhawks understood.

'It is the lake in the mountain,' said Suth. 'The mountain cracked. The water came here.'

'Suth, you are right,' said Noli.

She remembered with grief that awesome but beautiful place, the still lake stretching away between the forest trees, the frightening closeness of the First One who lived there, the way her skin almost itched with its presence, and the air came and went in quick pants between her parted lips.

The memory seemed to bring those feelings back. She was alone on this crowded mound. Alone, except for Goma. All the others were ghosts, dreams. She sat, not seeing, not hearing.

Another feeling came to her, strong, strong.

It was sadness.

She wept with the sadness of the First One.

It was the sadness of Moonhawk when she had said goodbye.

It was this Good Place, the Place of a First One, gone beneath the destroying flood.

It was all the old Good Places, buried under the ash of the volcano.

It was all the loss that people had ever known.

A thought came to her. It was strange, too strange to understand.

The First Ones need people. It is not the Place, it is the people.

When the people go, the First Ones go too. They do not die. They vanish. There are no First Ones in the desert.

Now these people go. They cannot live in this canyon any more.

So, no First One. Not any more.

Sadness.

Another thought, stranger still.

First Ones come from their people. They are what their people are. These people have no words. Their First One has no words.

She raised her head.

'First One, we go,' she whispered. 'Come with us, First One, and I give you words.'

The trance mood slid away. She shuddered and looked around. Goma was sitting on a rock a little way off. Her face was streaming with tears. She was looking towards Noli. Their glances met, and they smiled.

Late that morning the flood began to subside, but it was the whole day and a night and part of the next day before it was gone. They all made their way down the mound and cautiously began to explore.

It was dreadful. The whole canyon, with its mystery

and beauty, was utterly changed. There was barely a sign that anything had ever grown or lived here. In places a few smashed tree stumps stood, but the flood, and the boulders it had rolled along as it swept through, had carried everything else away.

And then, as the water had sunk down, mud and gravel had settled and formed sheets of dense squishy ooze in every flat place and hollow. Often these were waist deep and more, but the people had no way of telling before they set foot in them.

There was no food left on the mound where they had sheltered, so they were forced to go on, picking their way where they could on the exposed boulders, but it was slow going and in a short time they were all caked with mud.

Towards evening, miserable and exhausted, they reached another old rockfall whose crown stood above the flood, and plants still remained. Here, too, a host of small creatures had taken refuge, and furthermore there were two wing nut trees, and bushes whose young leaves were pleasant to chew.

So they had food, and the Moonhawks could build their fire again and they sat around it and scraped the mud off one another, and felt better. They slept, exhausted. If Noli dreamed, she didn't remember.

But when they woke they stared in dismay at the next stretch of the canyon. Here some barrier further down must have trapped the silt, and left a sea of shining mud from cliff to cliff as far as they could see. It looked much worse than anything they'd struggled through the day before. A few people tried wading into it. Very soon they were up to their necks.

They studied the cliff above them. When the rocks

that formed the mound had fallen, they had left a stretch of cliff that looked more climbable than the rest of the canyon, so some of the men set out to find a route up. Despite the steamy heat, the Moonhawks kept the fire going, so that Tinu would be able to load the fire log at the last possible moment. Who knew when they would next find fuel?

When the men came back, everyone got ready to leave. The Moonhawks had to wait for Tinu to pack and seal the fire log, so they were last in the line.

The climb was tiring, and in places really frightening, though they were all used to scrambling about on steep crags. There was one spot about halfway up that Noli felt she would remember in dreams all her life.

It came at a place where the cliff was almost sheer, with a long drop below. They had to cross from the end of a ledge not much wider than Noli's palm to another foothold and handhold well out of her reach. Tor and another of the canyon men were waiting on this side of the gap, with a third man on the far side. Tor seemed to be in charge. Noli realized that the men had been helping him up, and now he must have waited to make sure that the other two stayed to help the Moonhawks.

She watched Suth shift Ko onto his back and tell him to hang on tight. Then he edged to the end of the ledge. The man on this side gripped Suth's left hand to steady him, and Suth leaned and reached as far as he could across the gap. Then the man on the far side, also at full stretch, could grab Suth's right hand and swing him across.

Suth put Ko down where the ledge widened and

told him not to move, then came back and carried Tinu and Mana across in the same way.

Now it was Noli's turn. While the man steadied her, she settled Otan onto her back, put his arms around her neck, and told him to hang on. Then she let the man take her left hand so that she could spreadeagle herself against the cliff and lean and stretch for the waiting hand on the further side.

Her arms were much shorter than Suth's. She couldn't reach.

The man behind grunted and hauled her back. He plucked Otan from her and passed him to Tor, who was still waiting beyond him where the ledge was wider. Tor settled Otan at his feet.

'Hold Tor's leg, Otan,' said Noli. 'Hold tight.'

She turned to the gap and tried again. Without Otan she could reach a little further, but not far enough. The man behind her gave another grunt, this time with a question in it. *Ready?* he was asking. The one on the far side answered: *When you are.* He beckoned to Noli.

The man behind her yapped sharply and let go of her hand. She jumped. For a dreadful instant she was falling. Then a firm hand fastened around her wrist and hauled her back up and over.

She worked her way further along the ledge so that Suth could go back for Otan. She couldn't bear to watch. She never saw how they got Tor over.

That was the worst, but even the easier parts of the climb were very slow as each person waited for the one ahead to get past the trickier places. Luckily, the cliff was mostly shaded as the sun moved towards the west. By the time they were all safely at the top, it was almost setting.

Noli made a point of waiting for the men who had helped her. She put her hands together in front of her chin, bowed her head, and told them, 'I, Noli, thank. Moonhawk thanks.'

They looked surprised but pleased, and gave the usual little grunt of acknowledgement. Then she hugged Tor and he put his good arm around her and hugged her back and laughed.

'Noli,' said Suth, pointing at the rest of the party, who had reached the top before them and were getting ready to camp for the night. 'This is not good. The moon is big. We rest a little, then we walk. Daytime is too hot. We, Moonhawk, know this.'

'Suth, you are right,' said Noli. 'But they have no words. How do we say this to them?'

With grunts and signs they tried to explain to Tor, and to Fang, the leader of the canyon people, but they just looked puzzled. Noli found Goma and took her hands and looked into her eyes, and thought about the battering heat of the desert day and the coolness of walking under the stars, but nothing seemed to pass between them. The First One wasn't there to help them. Goma tried. She seemed to understand that Noli was attempting to tell her something important, but it was no good. After a bit she began to look so unhappy that Noli gave up.

'Do we, Moonhawks, go?' said Suth. 'Do we stay with these people?'

'We stay, I think,' said Noli. 'Tomorrow they find what we tell them is true.'

She was right. For a while the next morning they

made good speed over the easier ground, following the line of the canyon. As the sun rose higher, they started to suffer. The canyon people seemed to feel the heat even more than the Moonhawks. Though it could be bakingly hot down below, there was usually shade somewhere, close to the cliffs or under trees. Here there were only thin strips beside the taller boulders, and at midday even those disappeared. By that time they were already looking desperately for a way down into the canyon.

Mercifully they found one where another old rockfall had left its pile against the cliff. It was a much easier climb. Apart from one or two stretches, even the small ones could get down unaided. And here too the top of the mound had remained clear of the flood, with its plants intact, so they found a little to eat, and they had water again.

What was more, they could see that the canyon ahead would be easier going. As the flood had rushed further from its source, its level had fallen, so that here there were only patches of mud among the tumbled boulders and smashed plants in the bottom of the canyon, and more of the higher ground had escaped destruction. They travelled on for the next few days and found just enough to eat, though the water in the river still had that muddy, smoky taste.

Three times they passed caves. Here the canyon people halted and called. When they heard no answer, a few of them went in, and then came out wailing and shaking their heads.

'The water came at night,' said Suth, the first time this happened. 'The people slept in their caves. The water covered them. They are there, dead.'

Noli didn't answer, but she knew he was right because she could feel the First One close by, mourning with its people. This time it didn't come as a tingling of her skin or a stirring at her nape, but she felt it all the same. She saw Goma standing apart from the others, shuddering and weeping, so she went and put her arm around her and wept with her. Why hadn't the First One warned these people, as it had warned Noli and Goma of the coming flood? Was there no one in these caves it could come to? She didn't know.

On the sixth day the walls of the canyon gradually dropped away as the ground above sloped down. By afternoon they came out into the open, and now they could see for a very long way.

Far in the distance the snowy peaks of mountains glittered in the sun. In front of them lay an immense plain. The river ran down into it, with trees on both banks. They could see the ribbon of green winding away and away. Everything in the nearer ground had been smashed flat as the flood had spread out. Beyond that the plain was mostly yellow, sun-baked grass, with little chance of having people food in it. But here and there were flat-topped trees, and patches of bushes that looked hopeful.

Noli heard Suth sigh with pleasure, and she knew why. This was what he had been longing for. This was what their old Good Places had looked like. This was home.

One thing, aside from the river, was different. All over the plain, though well apart from each other, rose strange outcrops of rock. Some were just great craggy mounds, but others were more straight-sided and almost flat on top. Noli studied them with interest. They looked as if they would make good lairs.

Just beside one of these a puff of orange dust rose. It was too far for her to see what caused it, but she could guess. Some big hunting animal had disturbed a herd of grazers and they were galloping away, churning up the dust with their hooves.

The canyon people were making little mutterings of doubt and alarm. Where were the sheltering walls? Where were the caves they were used to?

Suth had no such thoughts. He sighed with happiness again.

'These are Good Places,' he whispered. 'These are Moonhawk Places.'

The name stirred Noli.

No, she thought. *Not Moonhawk. Never again. But another.*

She was aware of that Other poised nearby. It was doubtful, unsure, as its people were doubtful and unsure.

A new thought came to her, stranger than any before.

Moonhawk was old, and Black Antelope and the others. Old, old.

This is a young First One, young, a child among First Ones.

How can this be? I do not know.

Without moving her lips, she whispered in her mind. *Stay with us, First One. Do not be afraid. For you also, these are Good Places.*

Oldtale

THE MOTHER OF DEMONS

There is Odutu, the Place of Meeting, Odutu below the Mountain.

There is the Mountain above Odutu. At its top live the First Ones.

There is the Pit beneath the Mountain. It is as far beneath as the top is far above. There lives the Mother of Demons.

The Mother of Demons woke.

She said in her heart, As I slept, I heard wailing. I heard the voices of my children. They wailed. How can this be?

To tens and tens of demons I gave birth. I fed them. They grew strong. Their colours were fearsome.

I said, 'You are strong. I feed you no more.'

They said, 'We are hungry. Mother, where is our food?'

I said, 'The First Ones have made Good Places. There you find people. Give those people the yawning sickness. Lead them where the crocodile lies in wait.

Put poisonous berries in their gourds. They die. Their spirits leave them. Your food is the spirits of people.'

Why now do my children wail?

The Mother of Demons called to her children, 'Come!'

They came to her call. To the Pit beneath the Mountain they came. They were feeble and pale. They shook like old men. Like old men they tottered.

The Mother of Demons counted her children. Tens and tens she counted. Three were not there.

She said, 'I sent you out strong. I sent you out in fearsome colours. Why are you weak and pale? Why do you totter and shake like old men? And where is my son Rakaka? Where is Sala-Sala? Where is Woowoo?'

They said, 'A hero is born among people. His name is Sol. While he was still a small one he fought with Rakaka. He cast a great rock at him, so that he was carried away. Then Rakaka fled far and far into the desert, and there he hides in his own places beneath the earth and does not come out.

'While Sol was still a boy he fought with Sala-Sala. He beat him and bound him into a great tree, the Father of Trees. It grows by Stinkwater.

'When he was a man he fought with Woowoo. He beat him and prisoned him in a pit beneath Sometimes River.

'We say in our hearts, This Sol is too strong for us. We dare not go to the Good Places. There he does to us as he did to Rakaka and Sala-Sala and Woowoo.'

The Mother of Demons cursed her children.

She said, 'You are fools. Why do you go to the Good Places by one and by one? This hero, this Sol, fights you by one and by one. Go by five and by five. Sol fights with one of you. That one flees. Sol chases him far and far. When Sol is far and far, four are left. They walk through the Good Places and find their food. Now, go!'

The demons laughed and were happy. By five and by five they came to the Good Places. To each Kin came five. They lay in wait.

A demon stood before Sol.

He said, 'Fight with me, hero.'

They fought. The demon fled. Sol chased him far and far.

While he was gone the other demons walked through the Good Places. They gave people the yawning sickness. They led them where the crocodile lay in wait. They put poisonous berries in their gourds.

The people died. Their spirits left them. The demons feasted on their spirits.

Those times were bad, bad.

CHAPTER SIX

They drank that evening at the river, but the air there smelled of sickness, like the bad season at Stinkwater, and the banks were lined with dense bushes where wild beasts might lurk. The river itself looked too small for crocodiles, but you could never be sure about them. Though it had water, the river was not a Good Place.

So as the sun sank everyone headed for the nearest of the rocky outcrops to lair. On the way they passed a grove full of the nests of weaver birds, and while the parent birds screeched around them in outrage, they knocked down as many as they could reach. It seemed that the canyon people hadn't done this before, but they joined in with a lot of shouting and excitement. The eggs were tiny, and the unfledged nestlings weren't more than a mouthful, but everyone got something.

They didn't find much else, but the Moonhawks, at least, were used to hunger. It would take many moons to explore this plain and find its Good Places, where the right grasses grew, with fat seed in their season, and the plants with good nuts and berries and roots and leaves, and the warrens of small beasts that could be trapped or dug out.

And they would need to learn its dangers, the poisonous plants, the places of sickness, the waterless stretches, and the habits of the big hunting animals.

The Moonhawks knew all this, even the small ones, but they were happy, because they also knew that this was their kind of place. It was right for them. But the canyon people seemed to be more and more anxious, and muttered among themselves, and looked longingly over their shoulders towards the great desert through which their canyon ran.

As they approached the outcrop they gathered fuel and dragged it up to the top. The Moonhawks built their fire, and they settled down to sleep, though a few kept watch by turns all night.

Soon after they had moved on the next morning, they came to a termite colony. Not all termites were good to eat, but these were, with long narrow nests as tall as a man, all pointing in the same direction.

The trick of robbing a termite nest was to get to the nursery chamber, where the fat grubs were, before enough of the warrior termites swarmed out to attack. It took two people: one to loosen the dirt with a digging stick, while the other kneeled and scooped it away.

Unlike the men of the Kins, the canyon people didn't carry digging sticks around with them, but cut fresh ones when they needed them. They hadn't robbed termites before, so Suth and Noli showed them how. When they'd been bitten as much as they could stand, Suth handed his digging stick over and went aside with the Moonhawks to chew the rubbery little grubs.

Tinu wandered around as she ate. Noli heard her call and saw her beckon from the other side of the colony. The Moonhawks trooped over to see what she'd found.

Several of the nests had already been robbed. A deep pit ran down into each. In some, the termites had started to repair the damage, but had only half-filled the pit, so the robbery couldn't have been more than a few days back.

'Ant bear does this?' suggested Noli.

'Ant bear hunts by one and by one,' said Suth. 'This is people stuff.'

'See, Suth, see!' called Ko from another mound. 'Mana finds a hand.'

They went and looked. Close by the pit, on the pile of loose dirt that had been scooped from it, was the print of a left hand. It was just where someone would have leaned, kneeling to reach to the bottom of the pit. Suth laid his own hand on it. The print was larger.

They looked at each other in doubt. Did this Good Place belong to someone? Would there be trouble if people came and found strangers robbing their nests?

They searched around and found that only eight nests had been robbed, so whoever had been here, there probably weren't enough of them to be afraid of.

At midday they went back to the river for water. This time they found a wide shelf of rock along the bank where nothing grew and they could drink without fear of attack from the undergrowth, so Noli and the Moonhawks were surprised when a sudden clamour of alarm rose among the canyon people.

They found them clustered around a place where silt from the flood had washed across the rock. The soft surface was covered with the prints of animals that had come to drink. Clear through the middle of them ran several lines of huge paw marks with four clawless toes at the front and a triple pad at the back. The Moonhawks recognized them at once.

Lions.

No other animal left tracks that size and shape.

There hadn't been a lot of large prey in the Moonhawks' old Good Places, so there'd been few lions around. Some of the other Kins had been less lucky, and once or twice Noli had heard of somebody being killed by a lion. But on the whole, lions didn't attack people.

There was a saying: *Eight people make a lion.* This meant that a group of eight people with stones and digging sticks in their hands could usually scare a lion off, unless it was very angry.

Or unless it was a demon lion. These lions preferred the taste of people meat to all other flesh, and so stalked and killed people, and even leaped at night into their lairs and carried children away. The hero Sol had fought and killed such a lion, but that had been long, long ago. There'd been another demon lion in the time of Noli's mother's mother's mother. Noli used to scare herself with the thought of it when she was a small one.

But no ordinary lion would attack a group of people as many as they were. Noli found Goma and tried to tell her this, but she seemed as scared as any of the others and wouldn't try to understand.

They drank quickly and anxiously, huddled together, with several always on the lookout, and immediately moved well away from the river to a group of shade trees with a wide view all around. The men at once settled down to making themselves digging sticks.

Several stood guard while others rested, and when they moved on, everyone picked up a couple of good throwing stones and carried them while they foraged. No lions were seen.

That evening they refused to return to the outcrop where they had laired the night before, and insisted on going to another one, despite its being much further from the river. But it was straight-sided almost all the way around, with only one section that could be climbed, and even there the small ones needed help. It was a nuisance to carry up enough fuel for a fire, but otherwise it made a good, safe lair.

The Moonhawks were secretly amused by all this, but the canyon people were right. The next morning, while they were foraging, a lion attacked.

Noli didn't see it happen. She heard screams and yells, and looked up in time to see the lion dragging something – no, *someone* – into a patch of bushes while people ran after it, yelling, and pelting it with stones.

'The lion takes a boy!' shouted Suth. 'Noli, bring the small ones. Stay close.'

He ran towards the bushes. Noli passed Otan to Tinu, took Ko and Mana by the hands, and hurried after him.

‘I fight the lion,’ gasped Ko as he ran. ‘I fight the lion too.’

They found everyone gathered staring at the place where the lion had disappeared. They were furious, frightened, and uncertain what to do. The bushes grew densely together. There was one narrow opening, a sort of tunnel leading towards the middle. It looked well used, as if this was the lion’s lair. To try to rescue the boy, if he was still alive, they would need to crawl in, one at a time. It was impossibly dangerous.

‘I see this happen,’ said Suth, pointing towards a shallow dip in the ground. ‘The lion lay over there, low, low. It was not seen. It waited. The people came near. It ran out, quick, quick. It came at a boy from behind. It struck him, so . . .’

He made a slashing movement, hooking his fingers like claws.

‘The boy fell,’ he went on. ‘I think he is dead. The lion took his shoulder in its mouth. It carried him away.’

Tinu was on his other side, tugging his arm. He looked down.

‘Suth . . .’ she mouthed, ‘make fire . . . Wind . . .’

She gestured to show the direction of the light breeze.

‘Tinu, this is good,’ he said. ‘Wait. I find Tor.’

He dashed off, and then came back with Tor and Fang and some of the others. He pointed urgently at the fire log and the bushes and blew with his mouth and made flame gestures with his hands. The Kin sometimes used to hunt by setting fire to patches of scrub, and then waiting downwind to try to kill any animals that came dashing out through the smoke, but Suth couldn't just start a fire without the canyon people's consent. The boy who'd been taken was one of them. They might believe he could still be alive. But they got the idea and grunted approval.

Some of them hurried around with the Moonhawks to the windward side and helped to gather fuel, while the rest went back towards the tunnel.

Rapidly Suth and Noli piled branches against the bushes while Tinu sorted out a small heap of grass and twigs. As soon as everything was ready, she made an opening at the base of the main pile, tipped the embers into it, and stuffed her separate heap in on top, then lay on her stomach and blew.

The embers hadn't been long in the fire log and were still very hot. Smoke rose at once. The whole pile roared into flame, too hot to stand near for long. Tinu poked dry sticks into it, and as soon as they were lit handed them out to the others, who worked along the edge of the thicket, trying to set fire to anything that looked as if it would burn. Most of the small fires they started failed, but a few took hold and spread. Then, with a crashing roar, these patches joined and a line of flame began to move steadily across the thicket, roaring and crackling as it went, blown by the breeze.

They found the people gathered on either side of the opening under the streaming smoke. Everybody had found a weapon or missile of some sort, but nobody (except Ko) seemed anxious to face the lion directly.

For a little while, nothing happened. Several snakes came gliding out. Any birds must already have flown off. Then, without warning, he was there, a huge male lion, stalking out of the tunnel.

He paused and swung his head from side to side, growling low in his throat. His tail lashed. He looked as if he was angry enough to attack and was choosing his target. For a moment the sullen bloodshot eyes seemed to be staring straight at Noli. She froze. She felt that if he attacked now she wouldn't be able to move. Then his head swung on.

The watchers yelled and screamed and hooted and flung their missiles. The stones were heavy enough to hurt. The lion gave a roar that was more of a snarl. A second shower of stones rained in. He snarled again and raced for the gap between the lines. Several men rushed in and struck him, hard, with their digging sticks as he went by. And then he was loping off, with some of the people running, screaming, after him. Seen from behind, he had a mangy look, and his ribs showed beneath his skin.

As he disappeared into the distance, some of the canyon people went back to the windward side of the thicket and started to work their way in through the blackened bushes. The Moonhawks went too, to help Tinu rebuild her fire so that it would leave enough good embers to fill the fire log.

'This lion is old,' said Suth.

'I hit him with my stone,' said Ko optimistically.

A wailing rose from deep in the thicket. Those outside took it up. Noli realized that the boy's body had been found.

A man appeared, his skin streaked with black from the charred branches. He grunted to Suth and made signs that he wanted to show him something. Suth followed him into the thicket. When he returned, his face was set and sombre.

'The boy is dead,' Suth said. 'The lion ate his stomach.'

'This is sad, sad,' said Noli.

'I saw other bones, Noli. I saw the headbone. It was the headbone of a man. Also I saw a foot. Part was eaten. The toes were not. Noli, I saw skin on the toes. It was not like the skin of these people. It was dark, like my skin.'

Noli stared at him. What did this mean? The last she had seen of any of their own Kin had been when she and Suth had left them asleep in the desert and gone back to rescue the small ones. Had they gone on, found water, reached this place? Had they left that handprint on the termite mound? Had the lion killed one of them? More than one? Did any still live?

Her heart was filled with horror, but also with hope.

'I think this one was Moonhawk,' said Suth. 'Noli, I mourn.'

'I mourn also,' said Noli.

'Moonhawk mourns,' said Suth. 'The women dance the dance for a death. Noli, Tinu, Mana. You are the women.'

Noli put Otan down, and Suth took Otan's hand and told Ko to stand on his other side. The three girls formed a line opposite them. Suth clapped his free hand against his thigh to give the beat, and the girls began the dance that the women of the Kin used to dance to help the spirit leave the body and then to protect it from demons while it found its way to the Happy Place at the top of the Mountain above Odutu, where the First Ones lived. They shrilled the high, wordless wail, and stamped their right feet on the ground three times, and then their left, again and again, while Suth clapped the rhythm and grunted deep in his throat and Ko did his best to copy him.

The endless, repetitive movement sent Noli into a trance. Her spirit seemed to move out of her body, to float up through the burning, dusty sunlight, till it hovered bodiless above the groups of mourning people and the blackened thicket with the last smoke drifting away.

The First One was there, grieving with the grief of those below. There were others too. She felt the kindly presence of Goma. She felt someone else, a boy her own age, his spirit still throbbing with the pain and terror of his death. And very faintly, like a far, sad whisper, yet someone else . . . Man or woman? Kin or not Kin? The presence was too faint for her to tell, but it was the person for whom the Moonhawks were doing the death dance down below.

The First One seemed to gather the dead spirits into itself. The huge grief eased. Noli slid gently back into her own body and found her legs still stamping the rhythm and her throat still shrilling the chant beside the thicket.

She stopped abruptly.

'It is finished,' she croaked.

She looked around and saw the canyon people starting to leave. So as soon as Tinu had repacked the fire log, the Moonhawks hurried to catch up. Though they were going in the opposite direction to the one the lion had taken, they stayed in a close group in case it circled around and attacked again.

This meant that they were returning over ground they had already foraged, but long after they were clear of the dangerous area, they kept on.

After a while, Suth became impatient.

'This is foolish,' he said. 'We were here before. We took all the food.'

'I think they are too afraid of the lion,' said Noli. 'They go back to the canyon.'

Suth halted.

'I say we, Moonhawk, do not do this,' he said. 'I say this is more foolish. What food is in the canyon?'

'There is none, Suth,' said Noli. 'You are right. We stay.'

Tor must have noticed that the Moonhawks were no longer following, because at this point he came trotting anxiously back. They did their best to explain, and as soon as he understood he became very unhappy, and with urgent grunts and gestures tried to get them to change their minds.

In the end he gave up and sorrowfully hugged each of them in turn with his good arm, kneeling by the small ones to do so. When she understood that Tor might be leaving them, Mana, who normally quietly accepted whatever was happening and made the best of it, burst into tears. Noli saw tears in Tor's eyes too, but he turned and limped off after the others.

And I did not say goodbye to Goma, Noli thought.

And the First One is gone, gone with its people.

*

For the rest of that day, the Moonhawks moved warily, with someone keeping a lookout all the time, and never getting too far from some kind of refuge they could run to, steep rocks or climbable trees. This meant that there were many promising areas they didn't dare forage because they were too near to thickets or folds in the ground, where the lion might be lurking. But since there were now only six of them, they found as much food as they needed.

When they went to drink that evening, Suth and Noli helped the small ones up into the branches of a tree. Then they went by themselves to the river. He kept watch while she filled her gourd.

They laired on the good safe outcrop they'd used the night before. Noli felt depressed and anxious. She missed Goma. She missed Tor. She longed for the First One to come and comfort her with its presence, but she knew that wouldn't happen. It belonged with its people. She was appalled by the idea that at least one of the Kin had made it across the terrible desert, only to be killed and eaten by a lion. These were Good Places. Like Suth, Noli longed to stay here. But she grew more and more alarmed about trying to live, just the six of them, in an area where there was a lion that liked to eat people.

A demon lion.

Suth had been brooding along the same lines. He snorted in frustration.

'Tinu,' he said, 'how do we kill a lion?'

'I think,' she said.

For the rest of the evening she sat, staring at the fire, hardly moving, until they all lay down to sleep.

When Noli woke the next morning, Suth and Tinu

were missing. She could hear their voices from the far side of the outcrop, but she couldn't see them, though the top of it was almost flat.

She found them at a place where a deep notch ran into rock, just as if some giant had sliced down twice with his cutter and pulled out a piece of the cliff and taken it away. On one of its sides, the notch ran straight down to the plain below, but on the other there was a broad ledge about a man's height below the surface of the outcrop. Suth and Tinu were on the ledge, kneeling and peering down at the bottom of the notch.

'What do you do, Suth?' Noli called.

He turned his head and grinned at her.

'Tinu makes lion trap,' he said. 'Come see.'

Noli called to Mana to keep an eye on Otan and climbed down and kneeled beside Suth. He pointed to the bottom of the notch.

'It is same as ground rat trap,' he explained. 'Down there, bait. Up here, rocks.'

With his hands he outlined the shape of several boulders balanced at the rim of the ledge.

'We forage,' he said. 'Lion finds us. It follows us to this place. We wait here. Lion sees the bait. It comes. We push rocks' – he mimed the sudden violent shove – 'the lion is there' – he pointed again to the bottom of the notch, and then slammed his clenched fist down onto his open palm – 'the lion is dead,' he said.

Yes, it might work, Noli thought. They'd need to be lucky. Clearly there were problems.

'Bait for lion?' she asked. 'This lion eats people.'

Suth's excited mood faltered. He glanced at Tinu.

'I am bait,' said Tinu, mumbling as usual, but managing to sound as if this were an ordinary suggestion, like using garri-leaf paste to bait a ground rat trap.

'No!' exclaimed Noli, horrified. 'Suth, this is dangerous, dangerous!'

'I say this, too,' said Suth. 'I say we use animal meat for bait.'

'Lion wants people . . .' Tinu persisted. 'Noli, I make lair . . . I pile rocks . . . Many, many . . . small hole . . . lion comes . . . I go in hole . . . Lion too big . . .'

While she struggled with the words, she moved her hands to show how she would pile her fortress into the point of the notch, so that when the lion was trying to find a way in, it would be directly below the ledge.

Tinu gazed eagerly at Noli, as if this were a really interesting idea she ached to try out. Again, it might work. When the Kin had been forced to spend a night somewhere they didn't feel safe, they used to wall off any nooks and crannies they could find, so that at least the small ones could sleep secure. But a wall thick enough to keep a lion out . . .

'Tinu, a lion is strong, strong,' Noli said. 'Suth, I say no to this.'

'Noli, you are right,' he said, but then sighed with worry.

'This lion is old,' he said. 'Deer, zebras, they run quick, quick. Our small ones are good prey for it. It comes where people are. Noli, it comes.'

*

Suth and Noli went alone to the drinking place to fill the gourd, as before, and then again they foraged with great caution. They didn't take the usual midday rest but worked on, because this was the safest part of the day, when even a hungry lion would be resting somewhere in the shade.

When they had enough they returned by way of the river to their safe lair, gathering any fuel they could find on the way. Even the small ones had a branch to drag over the last stretch.

The sun was still high when they reached the outcrop. The bare rock of its summit was scorchingly hot, but the ledge above the notch faced east, so it was now in shade, and they climbed down there to rest.

After a while, Tinu touched Noli's arm.

'Noli,' she said, pleadingly, 'I go down . . . make trap . . . You watch . . . for lion . . .'

'Tinu, I say this trap is dangerous. Suth says this also.'

'I try . . . only. See how . . . I, Tinu . . . ask.'

'Suth, what do you say?'

Suth looked at Tinu and smiled.

'Body so little, spirit so big,' he said. 'Can I stop her?'

This was nonsense, of course. Tinu worshipped Suth. She wouldn't have gone against his wishes for anything in the world. But he, in turn, trusted Tinu. If Tinu thought she could build herself a trap strong enough to keep the lion out, Suth was ready to let her try, at least.

Perhaps Suth was right, but Noli hated it. This lion wasn't like other lions.

It was a demon lion.

'Noli, this lion comes,' said Suth quietly. 'Tomorrow, next day . . . I do not know. But it comes. Noli, we must kill this lion.'

She rose without a word and went to the outer end of the ledge. From there she could see all this side of the plain to the snow-rimmed mountains. The air was so clear that she felt she could have seen a small bird perched on a branch half a day's journey away.

She studied the nearer ground, looking for anywhere a lion might lurk. There were two danger spots. Almost straight ahead of her a large patch of thicket reached towards the outcrop. Its nearest bushes were tens and tens and more tens of paces away. A little further off, to her right, a low mound hid the ground beyond it.

How fast could a lion come? Suppose she saw it at once, and shouted. Would Tinu have time to race around to the further side and scramble out of reach? Yes, she decided, with a little to spare.

What else?

She looked to her left. There was clear ground for a long way here. The nearest cover . . .

She stiffened. Something was moving this way. Several creatures, a small group. She screwed up her eyes . . .

'Suth!' she cried. 'Suth!'

He was beside her at once, staring along the line of her pointing arm. She waited. Her heart hammered.

'It is people,' Suth murmured. 'They come.'

They watched in silence. Slowly the people came nearer. Noli counted eight of them. Now she could see the heads, the arms, the steady swing of legs.

'Their skins are dark,' said Suth, still quietly. 'I think these are Kin.'

Oldtale

SOL'S DREAM

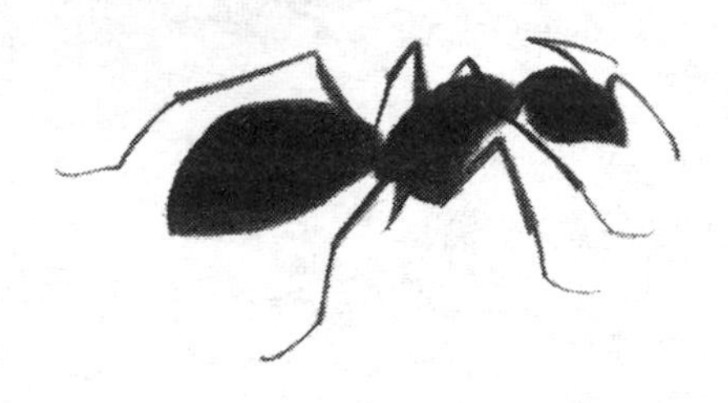

Sol fought with demons.

For tens of moons he fought them, resting neither by night nor by day. They fled from him, and he pursued them. None dared stand against him.

Sol fought with a yellow demon. The demon fled. Sol pursued him far and far, to the salt pans beyond Lusan-of-the-Ants.

There Sol flung his digging stick Monoko at the demon and pierced him through. The yellow blood flowed out of him. Thus the salt from those pans is yellow to this day.

Sol said, 'For tens of moons I have fought with demons. I rested neither by night nor by day. I am tired. Now I sleep.'

At Lusan-of-the-Ants, he slept. There Sol dreamed his dream.

One came to him that had neither shape nor smell. One spoke in a voice that made no sound.

The One said, 'Sol, my son.'

Sol said, 'Father, I listen.'

The One said, 'For tens of moons you have fought demons, but they are no fewer. You slay one demon. The Mother of Demons gives birth to ten more. In the Pit beneath the Mountain, the Mountain above Odutu, there she gives birth. Go now to the Mother of Demons. Stand before her. Speak to her.'

Sol said, 'Father, what do I say?'

The One said, 'Speak to her and the words are given to you.'

Sol said, 'Father, how can I find the way to the Pit beneath the Mountain? The Mother of Demons makes a magic so that no man and no woman can find it. Her magic is strong, strong.'

The One said, 'Go, journey among the Kins. You do not ask for food. One gives it to you. That one is your guide.'

Then the dream left Sol, and he was awake.

Sol went. He journeyed among the Kins. Men met him, hunting deer. They said, 'Sol, we would give you food, but we have none. The demons drive away all the deer.'

Women met him, foraging for seed. They said, 'Sol, we would give you food, but we have none. The demons shrivel the grasses.'

A child met him, a girl who turned over rocks to see what she could find, for she had no father or mother.

She said, 'Sol, see, I find a thickworm. Cut out the poison part, and I give you half.'

Sol took the thickworm. With his cutter Ban-ban he cut out the poison part. Half of the worm he ate, and half he gave to the girl.

He said, 'What is your name, and what is your Kin?'

She said, 'My name is Vona. My Kin is Weaver.'

He said, 'Now I speak with your mother.'

She said, 'A demon brought a sickness. My mother is dead. My father also.'

He said, 'Vona, you are my guide to the Pit beneath the Mountain. You are not a man nor a woman, but a child. The Mother of Demons makes no magic against you.'

She said, 'Sol, I do not know where this place is.'

He said, 'Close your eyes.'

Vona closed her eyes, and Sol turned her around and around.

He said, 'Do not open your eyes. Point to me now which way we go.'

Vona pointed. She said, 'We go this way.'

Then Sol put her on his shoulder, and they set forth.

CHAPTER SEVEN

The eight newcomers moved steadily closer in the heavy evening light. The sun was full in their faces. The shadow of the outcrop stretched towards them. There was no way they could have seen Suth and Noli standing on the ledge below the summit.

At first they had seemed to be deliberately heading for the outcrop, but they veered aside and it looked as if they would pass to the left. Then they veered back, and Noli realized that they had made the detour so as not to come too close to the big thicket.

'See, they fear the lion also,' said Suth.

As they had turned, the leader had gestured to point out the new direction.

There'd been something about the way he did it . . .

Noli stared. Yes, the way he walked, the way he held himself . . .

'That is Bal!' she said.

Suth gave a shout of joy.

'They are Moonhawk! They live!' he cried.

He scrambled to the summit and waved his digging stick and hallooed.

The newcomers halted and shaded their eyes, trying to see who had called.

Noli had felt the same pulse of joy and excitement, but then, in the next breath, doubt and fear.

Where were the others?

Nine moons before, when she and Suth had turned back to rescue Tinu and the small ones, they had left ten people and six more sleeping in the desert – five men, six women, three of them carrying babies, and a boy and a girl. The girl, Shuja, had been Noli's particular friend.

Now she could see only Bal and two other men, four women, and someone younger walking behind. She couldn't see if it was a girl or a boy. Only one of the women was carrying a baby. Noli hadn't seen it till now.

That made nine, not eight. So seven were missing.

The foot Suth had seen in the lion's lair. That must have belonged to one of them. Oh, let it not have been Shuja!

Had the lion taken them all? Or other lions? Were all the lions in this place demon lions?

'Come,' called Suth from above. 'We go to greet them.'

Noli shuddered herself out of her horrors, passed the small ones up to Suth, and scrambled up herself. They climbed down to the plain, collected Tinu, and met the newcomers just beyond the long shadow of the outcrop. Bal's party halted, astonished, as they recognized who they were. Noli was delighted to see that Shuja was there.

Suth raised his right hand in greeting.

'Bal, it is I, Suth,' he said. 'Here are Noli and Tinu, and the little ones, Ko and Mana and Otan. We live. We rejoice to see you.'

Bal didn't answer. It was as if he didn't believe what was happening. When he had last seen Suth, Suth had been a child. He would never have dared to speak to the leader of his Kin as Suth had just spoken, a man speaking to a man.

The others seemed just as puzzled and astonished.

'See, he has the man scar!' exclaimed Toba. 'When did he go to Odutu to be made a man?'

'I did not go to Odutu,' said Suth calmly. 'I fought a leopard. Alone, I killed it. I thrust my digging stick in its throat. It died. See, here, how I fought the leopard.'

He pointed to the raking scars on his left shoulder, and the small curved one on his cheek, where the leopard had slashed him. The others stared. To kill a leopard single-handed was a big boast – big, big. It was a deed for a hero in the Oldtales.

Bal snorted in disbelief.

'Bal, this is true,' said Noli.

'Yes, Bal, Suth killed the leopard,' said Ko. 'I, Ko, eat the leopard's heart.'

Still Bal didn't answer. Noli wondered what had happened to him. A few moons before, when he'd led the remaining Moonhawks into the desert, no child would have dared to address him as Noli and Ko just had. His hair would have bushed right out. He would have roared and towered over them while they cringed at his feet.

Now he just snorted again and changed the subject.

'You have fire?' he asked. 'We saw fire, far off.'

'We have a fire log,' said Suth. 'We made it. Come. Now we make fire. Bring wood.'

Suth and the men and two of the women went off to collect fuel, while Noli showed the rest the easiest way to climb the outcrop. Tinu started a fire with the fuel they had, and they settled down and waited for the wood-gatherers to join them.

This was the first chance Noli had to talk to Shuja. She was eager to know what had been happening to her.

'You were ten and six more,' she said. 'Now you are nine. Where are the others? I see your mother. I do not see Yova, your mother's sister, and Sidi. I do not see Sidi's mate, Tun, or his brother, Var, or Pul.'

Noli particularly hoped Tun was all right. He was a good man, quiet and strong, the only person Bal would listen to in his rages. Net was in Bal's group, but he was too anxious to be relied on; so was Kern, who was friendly enough but a little lazy.

'I tell you,' said Shuja. 'Two days we were in the desert. Our gourds were empty. We had no water. Sidi's baby died, and Yova's. The mothers had no milk. Almost we all died. Then we smelled water. We found a great canyon. Water in the bottom. We climbed down. It was hard. Sidi fell. She died. We came to the bottom. There was a river. We drank, we found food. In the canyon were . . .'

She shook her head frowning.

'We did not know what they were. When we saw them, we said, *These are people*. Bal spoke to them. They did not speak back. They grunted. They barked. Bal said, *These are animals. They are animal people*.

They were angry to see us. They did not let us eat their food. They drove us away. We went further. We found more animal people. They drove us away. We came to these places.

'We rejoiced. Here was food, here was water. Here were no people, no animal people. We saw lions, but we were not afraid. We kept watch. We said, *These are Good Places. They are ours.*

'Then Tun said to Bal, *We are not enough. My mate Sidi is dead, and my child. Now I and my brother Var go back to our old Good Places. We find people from the Kins, from Snake and Parrot and the rest. We say to them, Come to our new Good Places.*

'Bal said to them, *How do you go through the desert?*

'They said, *We go by the canyon, at night, when the animal people are in caves. By day we hide. When the canyon comes near Dry Hills, we climb out.*

'Bal said, *This is good. Go.*

'Yova said, *My baby is dead. I go with them.*

'So they are gone. We do not see them again.'

Noli thought about it. Yes. About three moons back, Suth had stood high on the mountain, looking east, and had seen three people coming out of the desert. He'd said they hadn't looked lost. They seemed to be going somewhere.

She forced herself to ask the next question, though she'd already guessed the answer. 'Where is Pul?'

He was the boy who'd been with Bal's party when she'd last seen them.

'A lion took Pul,' said Shuja in a low voice. 'Noli,

this lion is not like the lions we know. It hunts people. We are afraid. The men also.'

'We too saw this lion,' said Noli. 'It killed a boy. It is a demon lion.'

'Noli, you are right,' said Shuja. 'It is a demon lion.'

She frowned suddenly and looked around the group by the fire, checking them off. 'You are all here, Noli,' she said. 'All that were with us on Dry Hills. Three small ones, Tinu, you, Suth. What boy did the lion take, Noli?'

'It took a boy from the canyon people.'

'Noli, these are not people. They are animal people.'

'Shuja, they are people. They are friends. They were with us here, but they feared the lion. They went back to the canyon. When they find no food there, I think they come back.'

'When Bal sees them, he is angry,' Shuja warned. 'Noli, how are you friends with these . . . people? How did you come to this place?'

Noli started to tell her their adventures. The wood-gatherers came back in the dusk. By that time the air was cooling fast, so they stoked up the fire and sat around it, getting used to each other after their long separation. They'd all changed. Suth settled down confidently with the men, and it looked for a moment as if Bal was about to snarl at him to go away, but he changed his mind and just sat brooding. Bal was the only one who didn't seem delighted that they were together again.

Perhaps it was easier for Suth than for Noli. He had the leopard scars to prove what he had done.

He carried a digging stick and a cutter. Noli had nothing to show for the changes in her, though for nine moons she had helped Suth lead their little group, keeping them safe and together. She had carried Otan through fire and flood.

And, too, for nine moons she had dealt with First Ones: dear Moonhawk, and awesome Monkey, and the strange wordless One who belonged to the canyon people. None of the women sitting by the fire had done that, but they spoke to her as a child. In their eyes she was Shuja's age. In her own mind, yes, she *was* a child, but at the same time she was older than any of them, almost as old as old Mosu, who led the Monkey Kin up in the mountain.

A thought came to her.

This is how it is with those who deal with the First Ones. They become old. So it was with Sol.

Several days passed. Normally the men would have hunted separately, but they all stayed together because of the lion. They knew it had already taken two children. This wasn't surprising. Hunting beasts often went after young prey. They were easier to catch and less likely to fight back. The few women couldn't guard the children alone, but 'eight people make a lion', so with the men they could drive it off, if they faced it boldly.

So they foraged, and dug out ants' nests, and smoked out bees' nests and took the honey, and found juicy grubs, and had plenty to eat. These were indeed Good Places.

They explored a wide tract, using different lairs.

Sometimes they saw groups of lions in the distance and kept well clear of them, but they saw no sign of the demon lion until, crossing a line they had travelled two days earlier, they found some unmistakable huge footprints. A single lion. Its tracks lay on top of the human footprints they themselves had made, and went in the same direction.

As they sat around the fire that evening, they discussed the problem, and Suth told them Tinu's idea for a lion trap. He didn't, of course, tell them it was her idea. He knew they would laugh at the idea of a child, a girl, who couldn't even speak clearly, having anything useful to suggest.

The men took to the idea at once, and since none of the places they'd laired had the sort of sheer drop that the trap needed, they insisted on returning to that first outcrop to build it.

The task took them a couple of days, between expeditions to forage. There were no loose rocks at the top of the outcrop, so they heaved some up from the plain and pushed them off the ledge to see how they fell. Then they heaved them up again and propped them safely against the back of the ledge.

Next they piled rocks into the point of the notch, fitting them carefully together so that they stayed firm, but leaving a narrow tunnel running deep into the pile from a little way up.

Tinu happily practised running to the pile and diving into the tunnel and huddling down in the wider space they'd left at the bottom. She climbed out, grinning her lopsided grin each time. She didn't seem to care about the danger.

The men weren't bothered either. Tinu was bait.

They didn't really want her to be killed, so they built the trap as well as they could. But she was only a girl, and she couldn't speak clearly, so no one was ever likely to choose her for a mate. If anyone could be spared, she could. It would be worth it to get rid of the lion.

But Noli watched the trap being built with sickness in her heart.

'This is dangerous, dangerous!' she told Suth. 'This is Tinu! She is not bait! She is people . . . Moonhawk . . . our Tinu!'

'Noli, you are right,' he said. 'This is dangerous. Tinu is people. But see, this lion, this too is dangerous. Every day, this danger. How do we live in these Good Places, day and day and day, every day this danger? Do we choose this? Do we choose danger for Tinu? One day and no more?'

'For this I am sick in my heart, Suth.'

'I, too, Noli. Then I think, *This lion is old. He cannot carry a man away. He takes children, Pul, the boy from the canyon. Now does he take Ko? Does he take Mana? Does he take Otan?* For these also I am sick in my heart.'

He shook his head and sighed, not looking at her.

'Noli, perhaps the lion does not come,' he said. 'Perhaps it is afraid after we burn its lair. It does not come, no danger to Tinu. It comes, we are ready.'

She waited, forcing him to look her in the eyes, then spoke with absolute certainty. 'The lion comes, Suth. It is a demon lion.'

*

Next, partly to further explore their new Good Places, and partly in the hope of luring the lion back to their trap, they made a long expedition over the plain, lairing on two fresh outcrops, and returning to their main base on the third evening. They found the canyon people there already.

They must have come only a little while before. The air was full of their cries and calls as they climbed the rock and settled in.

Instantly Bal's hair bushed out. He snorted and hunched his shoulders and strode towards the rock. Noli could see that Bal thought the outcrop belonged to Moonhawk. He would have been furious if he'd found one of the other Kins lairing there without his permission, let alone these creatures who were not Kin, and perhaps weren't even people.

Suth trotted up beside him and put his hand on his forearm.

'Bal,' he said, 'these people come here with us. They help us, we help them. They are friends.'

Bal swung on him. 'Who speaks to Bal?' he growled. 'Who is this boy?'

Suth stood his ground.

'I, Suth, speak,' he said firmly. 'I say these are our friends.'

Bal hefted his digging stick. Suth moved his own, ready to ward off a blow. Net, on Bal's other side, tried to intervene.

'Bal, these are too many to fight,' he said.

Bal shoved him away.

'I say these are animals,' he snarled. 'They have no place in a lair of Moonhawk.'

'I live among them,' said Suth. 'I lair with them. I

journey with them. I, Noli, Tinu – we do these things. We know these are people. Bal, you do not do these things. You do not know them.'

Bal dropped his digging stick, seized Suth by the throat, and shook him violently.

'They are animals!' he roared. 'Moonhawk says this to me. They are animals! Boy!'

Suth was tough for his age and size, but he hadn't a hope against a big strong man in a fury. Bal battered him to and fro.

For a moment Noli just watched, frightened and helpless. Then something started to happen inside her. Something flooded in. She felt it come pouring through the top of her spine. It filled her head with darkness. She felt her hair stand out stiff with the pressure. Her eyeballs seemed to bulge as if they would burst. Froth bubbled from her mouth.

She took two paces forward and opened her mouth. The thing inside her came out.

It came out as a shout, a voice louder and stronger than Bal's, a voice to shake mountains.

'Bal, you lie!' said the voice. 'Moonhawk comes no more! These on the rock are people! They are my people!'

Bal let go of Suth. He turned. His hair fell back against his skull. He stared at Noli. He knew what had happened. Sometimes Moonhawk had spoken through his own mouth with a voice like this. He was afraid.

'Who speaks?' he stammered.

'I, Porcupine, speak!' roared the voice.

Of course, thought Noli. *Porcupine*. In the darkness of her mind she heard the buzzing rattle of the angry quills, caught the musty reek, saw the gleam of a small black eye.

He comes back with his people, she thought. *He comes to me, Noli. And I give him words.*

Oldtale

THE PIT BENEATH ODUTU

Sol journeyed with the child Vona as his guide. Far and far they journeyed.

Each morning when they woke, Vona stood and closed her eyes.

Sol turned her around and around.

Sol said, 'Vona, which way do we go?'

Vona pointed the way. Sol put her on his shoulder and they set forth.

They passed by Odutu and the Mountain above Odutu. They came to the desert beyond Odutu, the desert that has no end.

Vona said, 'We go this way.'

Sol said, 'I have my gourd Dujiru. It is never empty of water. I do not fear the desert.'

They journeyed five days into the desert. They came to a canyon.

Vona said, 'We go this way.'

At the mouth of the canyon a blue demon stood in their path, a wind demon. He made himself into a whirling wind that filled the canyon from wall to wall. With the voice of the wind he said, 'Sol, you cannot pass.'

Sol threw his cutter Banban into the whirling wind. It sliced to the heart of the demon. It splintered into tens and tens of little cutters. They cut the wind into tens and tens of little winds. The winds scattered. They whirl in the desert to this day.

Sol and Vona journeyed on. They came to a cave in the wall of the canyon.

Vona said, 'We go this way.'

A black demon stood in their path, a night demon. He filled the cave with thick darkness, so that Sol could not see where to place his feet. With the voice of the night he said, 'Sol, you cannot pass.'

Sol threw his digging stick Monoko at him. It pierced him through. He fled into the night. Monoko is in him still. In the dark of night Monoko is seen in the sky. It is five stars.

The cave grew thin and low, like the tunnel of a ground rat.

Vona said, 'We go this way.'

Sol went on his knees and crawled like a hyena. He went on his belly and crept like a lizard. A red demon stood in his path, a fire demon. He filled the tunnel with fire. With the voice of the fire, he said, 'Sol, you cannot pass.'

Sol threw his gourd Dujiru at him. It split and a river came out of it. The river quenched the fire. It swept the demon away, and the gourd also. It flows under the earth. At Yellowspring it comes out. The water is hot. It tastes of fire.

Sol came to the Pit beneath Odutu.

He saw the Mother of Demons, where she sat, giving birth to her sons.

He said, 'Mother of Demons, call home your children, or I kill you.'

The Mother of Demons laughed. She said, 'Sol, you have no digging stick. You have no cutter. How do you kill me?'

He said, 'With my hands and my teeth I kill you.'

He went towards her.

She spat in his eyes, and he was blind. She breathed on his body, and he was an old man. His strength was gone.

She said, 'Now kill me, Sol.'

One came to Sol in the Pit beneath Odutu. One entered him, filling his body. One spoke through his mouth. The Mountain shook with the sound, the Mountain above Odutu.

One said, 'Mother of Demons, hear this. It is the word of the First Ones. Send your children to their own Places, to the dry deserts and the snowy mountains and the dark woods. Let them go no more into the Good Places. These are for people. Do this, or it is war between us, and we are the First Ones.'

The Mother of Demons said, 'Who speaks?'

The One said, 'I, Black Antelope, speak. I speak through the mouth of my son, the hero Sol.'

The Mother of Demons was afraid.

She called her children to her.

She said, 'Sons, you must go no more to the Good Places where people live. You must go to your own Places. These are the dry deserts and the snowy mountains and the dark woods. Do this, or the First Ones destroy me.'

They said, 'Mother, what food is there for us in these Places?'

She said, 'The hunter wounds a fat deer. He tracks it into the desert. The wanderer sees the snow. He says in his heart, I climb to look at that stuff. The child does not answer his mother's call. He strays into the forest. Thus food comes to you, my sons, a little and a little.'

The demons obeyed their mother. They come no more to the Good Places. They wait in their own Places, the Demon Places. They are hungry.

But Sol said, 'Vona, take my hand and lead me, for I am an old man and blind.'

Vona took his hand and led him out of the Pit beneath Odutu.

CHAPTER EIGHT

Fang, as the leader of the canyon people, came down from the outcrop to meet them. Several of the other men came with him. Noli was delighted to see Tor, and instead of waiting for the leaders to greet each other, she went straight to him and hugged him. He laughed and rumpled her hair.

Someone had put fresh bindings on his splint. She touched them gently.

'How is your arm?' she whispered. Her throat was too sore to make the little questioning bark the canyon people would have used to ask something like this.

Tor answered with a quiet double grunt to tell her that his arm was doing all right.

He grunted again on a rising note, looking at her as he did so.

How about you? he was saying.

'Tor, I am well,' she croaked, smiling to show what

she meant. 'We are all well. And see, we meet with our friends.'

She gestured towards Bal. He was standing facing Fang. The two leaders were studying each other with distrust and doubt. Their hair was half bushed and their attitudes very tense. Bal was ready to fight, and Fang knew it, but both were unsure of themselves.

Noli could see that Bal was still pretty shaken from hearing a First One – a First One he didn't know existed – speaking through Noli's mouth. By now, Fang was used to the Moonhawks he knew, but they were young. These adult strangers were something else.

They hesitated, waiting for each other to make the next move, until Suth took things into his own hands by stepping between them and facing Fang with his right palm raised. Through closed lips he made a soft, humming growl in his throat.

Fang put his palm against Suth's and replied with a shorter sound, made the same way. The Moonhawks had often seen the canyon men greet each other like this, when they met after a day's hunting.

Suth turned. 'Bal,' he said. 'Here is Fang. Do you greet him? Do you raise your hand as he does?'

Bal hesitated, but stepped forward and sulkily raised his hand. Fang, luckily, decided to treat Bal as an equal by not waiting until the movement was finished, but raising his hand at the same time to touch palms.

'I, Bal, greet Fang,' Bal muttered, and Fang answered with his throat sound.

The tension eased. The men of both parties greeted

each other briefly. There was a bit of milling around, and then Kern said, 'We are many. One fire is not enough.'

With signs and grunts, Suth explained to the canyon people. All the men, and any women who didn't have children to care for, went off to gather fuel.

That evening the top of the outcrop was rather crowded. They made three fires, one for the Moonhawks, and two for the canyon people, but there was plenty of coming and going as Ko and Mana trotted off to look for friends and inquisitive canyon people came to inspect the newcomers.

Noli sat with Goma for a while, not trying to say anything but simply being with her as she suckled her baby, with the firelight rippling across her glossy brown skin.

She felt wonderfully peaceful and content. Into that peace, the First One came. It came not as a huge invading power, but gently, a soft tingling on her whole skin, which then flowed inward and filled her body right to her fingertips and toes. It was like having the warmth of the fire inside her.

She heard Goma's quiet sigh, and knew she was sharing the moment.

The First One spoke. Its voice made no sound in Noli's mind, yet it spoke to her in words. *These are my people*, it said. *They are Porcupine. I come to Goma. Noli, Moonhawk is gone. She does not come to you any more. I come to you. But you are Moonhawk still, and these are Porcupine.*

There were no more words. Gently the feeling faded. As it went, Noli's body shuddered. She saw the baby let go of the nipple and look up, startled, so she guessed Goma must have shuddered at the same moment. They looked at each other, nodded, and smiled.

Noli stayed a little longer. Goma let her hold the baby for a bit, then she gave it back and returned to the Moonhawks.

She found an argument going on. Bal wanted all the Moonhawks to move off the next day and go to a different part of the plain, leaving the canyon people here, and then having as little as possible to do with them.

The women disagreed. They were afraid of the lion. They didn't think there were enough Moonhawks to keep their small ones safe all the time. The men would surely want to go off hunting by themselves before long. It was much safer to stay in a large group, all together.

The men wanted it both ways. They were uncomfortable about living alongside the canyon people, but they also longed to hunt, and they weren't really enough for that, just the Moonhawk men alone. Bal's authority was shakier than it used to be in the old days, but he was still the leader, and what he said carried weight.

In the end, Net settled the argument.

'The lion trap is here,' he said. 'Let us kill this lion with our trap. Then the small ones are safe, and we men can hunt.'

Five days passed. Nothing special happened, but the two groups became more used to each other. Noli didn't feel confident enough to stand up in front of all the Moonhawks and tell them what the First One had said to her, but she told Suth, and they began calling the canyon people Porcupine when they needed to talk about them, just as they used to talk about Crocodile and Parrot and the other Kins in the old days.

The women took it up, and in the end the men did the same, even Bal.

On the sixth day, several men from both groups went hunting together and came back in triumph with two half-grown deer that they'd managed to corner and kill. That evening there was great feasting and boasting.

All this time they saw no sign of the demon lion, but a few days after the feast a family of lions approached the group of trees where the people had just settled for their midday rest, obviously expecting to rest there themselves. Everyone rose and formed a compact body to face them, with the small ones in the middle. They yelled and shook digging sticks and hurled rocks. The lions studied them disgustedly and went off elsewhere.

By now the group had pretty well stripped all the food from the area around their main lair, so they were forced to move off and find other lairs. The men didn't hunt every day, but when they did they usually killed something, because the animals on this plain weren't used to people and were easier to catch than they'd been in the old Good Places.

A moon passed. Then, when they were a good three days' journey from the outcrop with the lion trap, the demon lion appeared.

The men hadn't gone hunting that day, and they were all foraging together in a scattered line when something said *Danger* in Noli's mind. The hair on her nape tried to stand up. A moment later she heard Goma's cry of alarm floating across the hot plain.

She looked up. Goma was standing halfway along the line, pointing at something behind them. Noli couldn't see what it was, but the feeling in her mind told her.

'The lion is here,' she called to Suth. 'Goma sees it.'

He turned and made *Danger* barks to the Porcupines foraging beyond him. They all stopped what they were doing, gathered together, and went to join the group that had formed around Goma.

By now they could all see the lion. It must have realized that they knew it was there and was making no effort to stalk them, but was just standing and watching them, about as far away as a strong man could throw a stone.

It yawned. Its tail twitched. It lowered its head and gave a loose, coughing roar.

There was a moment's silence, then everyone broke into furious shouts and screams. The lion watched them but didn't move.

Keeping close together, they started towards it, picking up any stones they could find. Some of the men darted forward and threw. The lion backed away, but stopped again just out of range, and stood and looked at them.

Twice more they marched towards it and the same thing happened, so they split into two groups. Half the men stayed to guard the children, and the rest, including the women who didn't have small ones, formed a line and charged towards the lion, not stopping when it moved away but keeping steadily after it.

By now they'd hit it with several stones and it had learned to keep out of range, so it loped away, with the people still following it.

Without warning it swung left and broke into a gallop, outflanking its pursuers and coming at full tilt towards the group around the children. The pursuers raced after it, but the lion was faster. Adults, and anyone else old enough to throw a stone, massed to meet it.

Perhaps it misjudged the distance, or perhaps it was hungry enough to try to charge straight in and snatch somebody away, for it got too close and ran into a hail of stones.

It yelped, changed its mind, and backed off.

It was circling the group, looking for an opening, when the others came panting back and drove it off again.

This time they didn't need to chase it far before it gave up for real and padded away into the distance.

They made sure the lion was well out of sight before they started foraging again, and then they set lookouts, and kept even closer together than before. Twice more the lion was seen, far off, and the second time was later in the afternoon, when they'd already started for the outcrop where they were planning to lair that night. The Porcupines muttered anxiously.

'I think it follows us,' said Suth.

'Suth, you are right,' said Noli.

They gathered plenty of wood, kept fires going all night, and kept watch at the places where the outcrop could be climbed. There was a good half moon, and nobody saw the lion, but they heard its hoarse roar rising several times from the darkness.

They didn't see it at all the next day, but Noli could sense it not very far off, still moving along with them.

And again when they laired that evening and sat around their fires in the early dark, they heard the same long, rasping roar breaking the silence.

They all looked at each other.

'This is good,' said someone. 'It follows us back to the place where we have our trap.'

Noli looked at Suth where he sat with the men, and caught his eye. She rose and beckoned to him. They moved a little apart. She laid her hand on his arm.

'Suth,' she said, 'hear me. I, Noli, ask. I fear. I am sick with my fear. This lion is a demon lion.'

'I fear also,' Suth began. 'But . . .'

'No, Suth, hear me,' she interrupted. 'It is a demon lion. But it must eat, or it dies. It is demon, it is lion. The demon eats people. The lion eats all meats, or it dies. The lion is old. He cannot hunt well. No females help him hunt. He is hungry. Tomorrow we go back to the lair where the trap is. As we go, let the men hunt. Let them catch fat deer. Let them take it to the rock. The lion comes. The men put meat at the trap, good deer meat. The demon is hungry for people meat, but the lion is hungry for all meat. The moon is big. The men watch from above. They are ready. The lion comes to the meat. The men drop rocks, kill the lion. He is dead. No danger to Tinu. Is this good?'

He thought about it and nodded. 'Noli, this is good,' he said. 'I speak with the men.'

When they went back to the fire, Noli settled near enough to hear what was said. The men didn't agree at once. They'd put a lot of effort into building their trap. And if they did catch a deer, why waste good deer meat on a lion? Tinu would be better bait. Besides, they'd only partly accepted that Suth counted as a man. He was too young, really, so they didn't like to agree with him too easily. In the end, Noli guessed, they did so because they were glad of the excuse for a day's hunting.

There was a fresh problem. They had only the four Moonhawk men: Bal, Net, Kern, and Suth. More were needed to make a good hunting team, but when Suth went the next morning to invite some of the Porcupines to join them, they refused. With grunts and signs he got them to understand what he wanted, but not why. He needed words for that, and the Porcupines didn't have them. As far as they could see, it was far more important to help guard the foragers, with the demon lion still following, than it was to hunt for extra meat.

In the end Suth gave up and the Moonhawk men went off on their own, though with only four of them they'd need to be lucky to kill anything.

Noli, Tinu, and the small ones stayed with the Porcupines as they worked their way back to the outcrop. For the first half of the day they foraged as they went, but then they reached the area they'd already stripped, so they went to the river and drank and filled their gourds.

Just as they were leaving, the lookouts saw a single lion crossing a patch of open ground to their right. It was too far off for them to be sure it was the demon lion, but this was now the hottest part of the day, when all normal lions would be resting in the shade.

Everybody became very nervous, and instead of looking for shade nearby, they insisted on heading back for the outcrop.

They reached it with the sun still high in the sky. Except for the ledge above the trap, there was no shade at all at the top, and only a strip along the base on the eastern side, so they posted lookouts up on the ledge and settled down below.

Noli had been so filled with dread all day that she could hardly think. Everyone else was very jumpy, and their restlessness infected the small ones. Even Mana was fidgety, and Ko was unusually tiresome, picking fights with boys his own age, jeering at them because they didn't have words, and endlessly badgering Noli about when Suth would come back. Noli began to long for that moment too. Suth was the only one who could deal with Ko in this mood.

Time passed very slowly. She watched the shadow of the outcrop beginning to stretch across the plain, reaching one mark, and then another, and then another.

At last she heard one of the lookouts call from the ledge. She recognized Goma's voice, looked up and saw her head poking over the rim of the outcrop. Goma waved cheerfully to her and pointed east.

Noli rose and looked but could see nothing from where she stood, so she went and climbed a large boulder about ten and ten paces from the foot of the cliff.

Now, in the far distance, she saw them, four figures,

still a good way off, trudging towards the outcrop. They could only be the hunters. None of them seemed to be carrying a load. Noli's heart sank. They had caught nothing.

She watched numbly for a while. She knew that she had been only pretending to hope. It was always going to be like this – Tinu, the trap, the demon lion . . .

She'd talk to Suth again. Perhaps she could persuade him not to try that night, to wait, and then hunt one more day . . .

Sighing and shaking her head, she started back to the cliff. Ko ran to meet her.

'What happens? What happens?' he asked.

'Suth comes with the hunters.'

'Where? Where?'

'Over there. Soon he is here.'

'I go see.'

'No, Ko. You stay here.'

'I go climb rock. Same as you. Noli, I, Ko, ask this.'

She gave in.

'Yes, Ko. Climb the rock. See Suth. Then come back to me.'

Ko ran off while she headed back to the cliff, trying dully to think of arguments for Suth to use. It would soon be dusk. Surely they wouldn't risk doing it after dark . . .

But they would. There was a good moon.

She half heard a call of warning from the ledge, not the full *Danger* bark that the Porcupines used, but the lighter one, which meant *Watch out*. Everyone's bark sounded much the same . . .

A pulse of alarm twitched in her mind. The bark came again. This time she listened to it. Goma, calling to her. The Porcupines around her were looking at her, pointing urgently . . .

She turned.

Ko wasn't there.

She moved aside and saw him. He'd been hidden by the big boulder. He was running to look for Suth. Suth and the hunters had looped aside so as to stay well clear of the big thicket. But Ko couldn't see them, and was heading straight towards it.

'Ko!' she yelled. 'Stop! Come back!'

He pretended not to hear her and ran on. She yelled again and raced after him. A slight rise brought the hunters into view. They'd heard her shout and were looking towards her. She cupped her hands to her mouth and called to them.

'Ko! Stop him!'

She pointed. From where they were they couldn't see Ko, but they waved and broke into a run. Noli ran too. They all reached Ko together when he was more than halfway to the thicket.

Suth was furious. He seized Ko by the shoulders and shook him hard.

'Ko, you are bad, bad!' he snarled. 'Why do you do this? Why? Bad! Bad! Bad!'

Ko burst into tears.

Ko had strong lungs. When he wailed he really bellowed, drowning all other noises. None of them heard the shouts from the outcrop until they turned towards it and saw the arms pointing from the ledge, the people streaming away to the climbing place on the far side . . .

They looked back and saw that the lion had come out of the thicket and was loping silently towards them.

Suth thrust Ko into Noli's arms. 'Run, Noli,' he said. 'We keep the lion away.'

Noli hefted Ko onto her shoulder and ran. She was used to lugging Otan around for most of the day, but Ko was a lot heavier. Before she was halfway to the outcrop, her legs began to buckle. She put Ko down, gripped his wrist and ran on.

He stumbled, wrenching his hand from her grasp. Turning to grab him again, she saw that the men had spread out into a short line and were yelling, brandishing their digging sticks, bending for stones to hurl, keeping the lion from getting too close as they retreated slowly before it.

It wasn't trying to attack them. They were too heavy for it to drag quickly away. It wanted Ko. Or Noli.

The men seemed to be holding the lion at bay, so Noli took Ko's wrist again and set off at a rapid walk, but she hadn't gone ten paces when the screams from the rock doubled.

She glanced back.

The lion had changed tactics. It was racing to one side, trying to outflank the hunters. Bal was at that end of the line, running to cut it off.

The lion was faster.

She heaved Ko up and ran. The yells from the ledge exploded again into screams. She didn't look back, but she knew the lion was past the line of men. It was still a long way to the climbing place.

She wasn't going to make it.

First One, help me!

A thought came to her: *The trap. I put Ko in the trap. Perhaps I climb the cliff. Ko is safe.*

She turned and staggered towards the sheer cliff.

Almost there. The world was turning black. Her legs were water. Her heart slammed. Her lungs wrenched for rasping breaths.

The notch in the cliff.

The trap.

She let herself stumble to her knees and with a last, grinding effort, she shoved Ko headfirst into the tunnel the men had made.

'In, Ko, in!' she gasped, and turned to face the lion. Something moved beneath her hand as she scrabbled herself around. A loose stone the men had left lying there. She picked it up and rose, swaying.

The lion faced her at the mouth of the notch. She raised the stone to her shoulder. She could barely lift it, let alone throw it. The lion hesitated. It had learned not to like stones.

Another thought came to her. She made a whisper in her mind.

Goma. Big stones. Back of ledge.

She pictured the stones for a moment, saw them clearly, through Goma's eyes.

The lion took a pace into the mouth of the notch and paused again. Beyond it, Noli saw Suth and Net running towards her.

It took two more paces, crouched for the spring . . .

Now, Goma, now!

Feebly, Noli heaved the stone forward. It dropped almost at her feet. But the lion had hesitated another instant, checked by the threat.

Black shapes, falling from the sky.

Three thuds, close together, two of them loud and sharp, the other duller, slower.

A ghastly, choking cough.

Stillness. Except for the thin scrape of the lion's talons clawing the coarse dirt as the last life left the body.

Then screams of triumph from above, and the gasping breath of the hunters, and Suth's voice.

'Noli, you live!'

She couldn't answer, couldn't see him. There was a dark haze all around her, with one bright patch in the centre. In it lay the lion. Its head was two paces from her, with the mouth half open and bright blood oozing down the jaw. The back was a pulpy mess of blood and fur, looking as if it had burst. The rock that had crushed it lay against it. The hindquarters splayed out beyond.

'Where is Ko?' said Suth's voice.

The answer came, muffled, from behind her.

'I live, Suth! I am here! Do you kill the lion? I see the lion, Suth? I, Ko, ask!'

The darkness around Noli cleared at the sound. She felt her lips trying to smile as she stood aside to let Suth reach into the tunnel and haul Ko out by the legs. He dumped him right side up on the ground and shook him, but this time more gently. Beyond him Net and Kern stood watching.

'Ko, you are bad, bad,' he said. 'Almost you kill Noli.'

Ko bowed his head in shame.

'Suth, I am bad, bad,' he said miserably.

He looked up, eager-eyed.

'I see the lion? I see the lion now?' he begged.

Noli laughed. At first she was laughing at Ko, then she was laughing with relief that she and Ko were safe and the lion was dead, but then the laughter took hold and came shrieking out, louder and louder, shaking her to and fro. It went on and on and she couldn't stop it.

It is the demon, she thought. *It comes out of the lion. It goes into me. Oh, First One, help me! Drive out this demon!*

Suth was holding her, making soothing noises, trying to stop her from hurting herself as her body tossed around. She saw Ko watching, aghast. That was another thing for the demon to laugh at.

A thought wormed its way in through the wild shrieking. She seized it, clung to it, followed it through to its end.

Four hunters face the lion – Suth, Bal, Net, Kern.

Three are here, Suth, Net, Kern.

So . . .

The demon fled. The laughter stopped. Noli was sweating and shuddering. Her face was wet with spit. Suth loosened his grip and held her gently.

'Where is Bal?' she croaked.

She remembered she had seen him racing to head the lion off.

Still with an arm around her shoulders, Suth led her towards the open and pointed. The sun was low. The shadow of the outcrop stretched many tens of paces. On the sunlit plain just beyond it lay the dark body of a man.

Behind her Net spoke. 'Bal fights the lion. It strikes him. He is dead.'

Oldtale

THE CHILDREN OF SOL

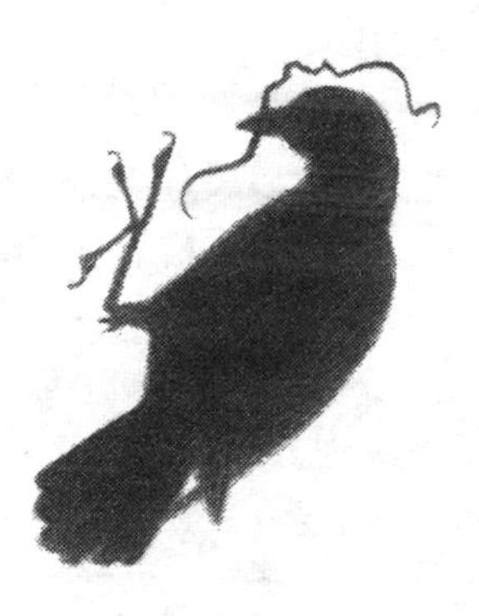

Sol came out from the Pit beneath Odutu, and he was an old man, and blind.

Vona led him by the hand, and she was a grown woman.

The First Ones made rain for them in the desert, and they drank.

They came to the Good Places. People saw them. They said, 'Who are you?'

They answered, 'We are Sol and Vona.'

The people said, 'You lie. We know Sol. He is a young man, a hero. We know Vona. She is a child.'

Sol wept.

He said, 'My people do not know me. Lead me, Vona, to where Fat Pig lairs.'

Vona led him to Dead Trees Valley. There Naga, the mother of Sol, sat at the mouth of the cave. She baked a tortoise.

Naga looked. She saw two coming down from the

ridge, a woman and a man. The woman led the man by the hand.

Naga said, 'This is my son, Sol. Why does the woman lead him by the hand?'

They came near. She saw that Sol was an old man, and blind.

She said, 'Sol, my son, who has done this to you?'

He said, 'I journeyed to the Pit beneath Odutu. I spoke with the Mother of Demons. I said, Call your children home, the demons that plague us.

'She spat in my eyes, and I was blind. She breathed on my flesh, and I was an old man. My strength was gone. My heart was empty.

'A First One came, my father, Black Antelope, first of the First Ones. He spoke through my mouth. The Mountain shook, the Mountain above Odutu.

'The Mother of Demons was afraid. She called her children home. They come no more to our Good Places. I, Sol, did this, I and no other.'

Naga said, 'Sol, my son, you are a hero still. I baked this tortoise. Eat it, for you are weary.'

Sol ate and slept, as did Vona, and Naga watched over them. When her Kin returned to the cave, she told them all that Sol had said.

Men went, swift runners, to the other Kins, and called them to Dead Trees Valley. They said, 'The demons are gone. Bring food for a feast.'

Five nights and five days Sol slept, as did Vona. When they woke, the Kins were gathered, Ant Mother and Weaver and Moonhawk, Fat Pig and Snake and Crocodile, Parrot and Little Bat.

Each spoke praise to Sol, and also to Vona, for what they had done.

Men stood before Vona. They said, 'Vona, you are a woman, and beautiful. We choose you for our mate. Which of us do you choose?'

Vona said, 'I choose none of you. I choose Sol.'

Sol said, 'I am an old man, and blind. Why do you choose me?'

Vona said, 'You are the hero Sol. I stood with you in the Pit beneath Odutu, face to face with the Mother of Demons. I and none other did this. I was not afraid. What other woman do you choose?'

Sol said, 'Vona, I choose you.'

Then they smeared their brows with salt, to show they were chosen.

The men hunted. They killed fat deer. The women foraged. They found sweet roots and juicy berries and delicate grubs. They built great fires. They feasted.

For nine days they feasted in Dead Trees Valley, and then they slept.

One came to Sol as he slept, Black Antelope, first of the First Ones.

He said, Sol, my son, your mate Vona bears children. Eight she bears, four sons and four daughters. Soon they are men and women. Then send them by one and by one to each of the Kins, to journey and lair with them. Then the First One of that Kin comes to them, as I come to you. So with their children, and their children's children, for ever.

Thus it was.

Thus it is, to this day.

CHAPTER NINE

The Moonhawks slung Bal's body from a pole and spent two days carrying it as far as they safely could into the desert above the canyon. They took the small ones with them, and dragged branches and carried what food and water they could.

It was a big effort with so few of them, but it was their custom. Bal had been their leader. He had died the death of a hero fighting a terrible enemy, a demon lion.

In the evening they propped him against a boulder with his face to the setting sun. They put his digging stick in his right hand and his cutter in his left, with a gourd and a handful of wing nuts beside him.

They made their fire some distance away. By the light of its flames the women lined up with the men opposite them. The women stamped their feet and sang the same wailing chant that Noli and Tinu and Mana had sung by the lion's lair, while the men grunted deep in their throats and beat out the rhythm by knocking two stones together.

Net and Kern spoke Bal's praise. They feasted on the food that was left and laired by the embers of the fire, with two to keep watch all night.

Back at the outcrop the next evening, the Porcupines greeted the Moonhawks like friends. A few came with small token gifts to their fire. Tor was one of these. He stayed longer than the others, and went to each of the Moonhawks in turn and made a slow buzzing hum that died softly away. They didn't need words to know that he was saying, *I sorrow for your sorrow.*

'Who is now leader?' asked Chogi, when he had gone. She had been the mate of Bal's dead brother and was senior among the remaining Moonhawk women.

Net and Kern looked at each other. They were both good men, but in their different ways were not the sort who'd usually get to be leaders. Suth might well be leader one day, but he was still much too young.

'What does Noli say?' said Net.

The others looked surprised, but only for a moment. Whenever a Kin was undecided about something important, they'd turn for guidance to the person to whom their First One came. Noli was a child, and that was strange, but they had all heard the voice that had spoken to Bal through her mouth. They looked at her and waited.

But Noli was troubled. She wasn't ready for this. If Suth was too young, then so was she. When Moonhawk used to come to her, and then when Porcupine came, that was their choice, not hers. How could she have a voice in something as important as choosing a leader . . . ?

Not your voice, Noli, came the whisper in her mind. *Mine.*

She waited, staring at the orange glow of the fire. Her lungs heaved slowly. The people around her faded. The chatter of the Porcupines died away. She was somewhere else. The night was the same night, starry and still, with a small moon high, but the fire was another fire, at the bottom of a rocky valley, with different people around it. There were seven of them, she thought. She could feel their thirst and hunger, their weariness after a hard day's travel. Some she felt she knew well, others less so. But none were strangers.

She woke from her trance with a snort and looked dazedly around her.

'I see . . . others . . .' she stammered. 'They come . . . They are Kin . . . Some are Moonhawk.'

They sat silent, thinking about it.

'It is Tun,' said Chogi decisively. 'Tun and Var and Yova. They go to our old Good Places. They find others. They bring them.'

'Chogi, you are right,' said Kern. 'I say this. We wait. There is no leader. These others come. Tun is our leader.'

'This is good,' said Net.

They were all used to such dealings with the First Ones, though sometimes what the First One told them didn't seem to help, and often no First One came at all. Dreams were particularly tricky. A dreamer could have a strong dream, but it would be like a riddle, and they'd have to guess the answer. It was easy to guess wrong. So what had just happened didn't seem strange to them.

But it seemed very strange to Noli now, though she too had felt used to the idea. Why her, and not one of the others? Why couldn't everyone in the Kin do it? Suppose the lion had killed her, what then?

And anyway, what *were* the First Ones?

She couldn't get out of her head the notion that Porcupine was a new First One. And just now . . . the whisper in her mind . . . had that been Porcupine? Perhaps, but there was something . . .

Could it have been Moonhawk, come back after all?

No. Without knowing how she knew, Noli was certain all those First Ones were gone. And that meant that their Kins must be gone, and their old Good Places. Gone. Moonhawk had stayed for a little, but her Kin was too few, too far away. So Moonhawk went, too, in the end . . . Gone.

Noli was filled with sadness. The sadness was everywhere, immense as the night. Someone settled beside her, put an arm around her, and mourned with her. Noli didn't need to look to know it was Goma. Goma had felt her sadness as she sat by one of the other fires, and had come to be with her, to share the sadness. Goma, without words, understood.

The moon became thin, almost died, and started to grow again. One night, as the Moonhawks laired on a different outcrop, they heard a shout from the Porcupines. They went to see what had caused it.

In the far distance, too orange to be a setting star, a small light shone. A fire. Not a bush fire, too small and unchanging. A people fire.

The Porcupines were alarmed, but first thing the next morning, the Moonhawks set out eagerly in that direction. Halfway towards where they had seen the faint light, they met Tun and his party.

This was Tun's story, as Noli heard it over the next few days: he and Var and Yova had worked their way up the canyon, hiding by day and moving at night, while the canyon people were in their caves. When they thought the canyon was as near as it would come to Dry Hills, they had filled their gourds at a pool, climbed out, and crossed the last stretch of desert.

'Four moons back I stood on the mountainside,' said Suth. 'I saw people in the desert. They were three. They woke in the evening. They went towards Dry Hills. I said in my heart, *These are Moonhawk.*'

'Suth, you were right,' said Tun, and went on.

The three had managed to cross Dry Hills and reach the old Good Places. They had found them full of the murdering strangers, but because they knew the land so well, they had been able to hide for a while as they moved around, living like wild beasts. Then they had been discovered and attacked, and had had to flee west into the Demon Places, where there was very little food or water. There they had met a few of the remaining members of the Kins. No one knew what had happened to the others.

They were still in the Demon Places when the volcano had erupted. Everything to the west of it was smothered in ash, but the Demon Places were far enough away to escape the worst. Most of the Kin people decided to go yet further west, but the three Moonhawks had persuaded a few of them to try to make it around the north of the old Good Places and back across Dry Hills and the desert.

They had had a terrible journey, and several of them had died on the way, but these seven had come through, very thin and tired – the three Moonhawks, a man from Snake, another from Fat Pig, and a woman and a girl from Little Bat.

The girl's name was Bodu. She was about the same age as Noli.

They all returned to the place where Noli's group had laired, and rejoined the Porcupines. As they sat around their fire that evening Net said, 'Tun, Bal is dead. Now you are leader.'

Tun sat thinking for a while, then rose. 'Who says Tun is leader?' he asked.

The men stood and touched palms with him. The women, children, and small ones pattered their hands on the rock in front of him, as a sign that they accepted him as leader. He would be a good leader, Noli thought, better than Bal. Bal had been angry and strong. Tun was calm and strong.

Chogi, looking around the circle, said, 'I see Bodu and rejoice. She is Little Bat. Soon she is a woman. Soon Suth is a man. He is Moonhawk. They choose each other for mates.'

Both Suth and Bodu looked startled. This wasn't a thought they were ready for. But this was something the senior women took charge of, and discussed with senior women in other Kins when they met. Little Bat was one of the two Kins from whom the young men of Moonhawk could ask for mates, so in Chogi's eyes the arrangement was acceptable.

Everyone, of course, began teasing Suth and Bodu.

But Chogi stayed serious, and as soon as the laughter lessened, she held up her hand.

'I say more,' she announced. 'Here is Noli. Here is Shuja. Can they find mates? Where are they? They are not here.'

The men shrugged. These were serious questions, but they weren't man stuff. The women discussed them in low voices. Noli didn't listen.

A thought came to her. *When I am a woman, I choose Tor for my mate.*

Everyone was looking at her. She realized she'd spoken the words aloud.

'Who is Tor?' said Tun.

'One of these,' said Net, pointing with his thumb over his shoulder towards the nearest Porcupines.

'This is not good,' snapped Chogi.

Noli barely saw or heard. She was breathing in the familiar dragging lungfuls.

The One came softly, almost hesitantly. She knew at once, this time, that it wasn't Porcupine. It was very young. It spoke through her mouth.

'These are new times,' it said.

As it spoke, she knew it. In her mind she heard the faint rustle of feathers, felt the curved beak nibble gently at her ear, the talons clasp her shoulder.

'Who speaks?' gasped Tun.

'It is Moonhawk,' Noli whispered in her own voice. 'It is not the Moonhawk that comes before. It is new, new. We have new Places to live. We find new ways to live. We are together, a Kin, new in these new Places, these new ways.

'So Moonhawk comes. She is new.'

KO'S STORY

For Sam and Andrew

KO'S STORY

Contents

Chapter One 311
Oldtale: THE DAUGHTERS OF DAT 319
Chapter Two 322
Oldtale: FALU'S PRAYER 334
Chapter Three 337
Oldtale: GOGOLI 346
Chapter Four 349
Oldtale: TWOHEADS 363
Chapter Five 366
Oldtale: BAGWORM 383
Chapter Six 386
Oldtale: STONEJAW 398
Chapter Seven 401
Oldtale: THE FATHER OF SNAKES 416
Chapter Eight 419
Oldtale: TOV AND FALU 430
Chapter Nine 432
Oldtale: TOV'S GIFT 441
Chapter Ten 443
Oldtale: GATA AND NAL 455
Chapter Eleven 458

CHAPTER ONE

No rains came.

For moon after moon after moon the sky stayed the same harsh blue. All day the sun glared down. The nights were very cold, but no dew formed.

The grasses withered, with empty seed heads. The roots that people could eat shrivelled in the ground. If nuts formed they were empty shells.

The river dwindled to a stream, to a trickle, to a few stinking pools. When they were gone, it ran underground, and then the people had to dig down till they reached the water and scoop it out handful by handful.

When they did this, animals smelt the water from far away and came for it, desperate to drink, but weak with hunger and thirst. This made them easy to hunt, but there was not much meat on them.

And people were not the only hunters. There were lions and cheetahs and packs of wild dogs and hyenas. They too smelt the water and came to it, knowing that they would find both drink and food. People might be food, if they didn't set lookouts. Lookout was something a half grown child could do. Even Ko, though he'd had to ask.

Ko had climbed a tree. It was dead, because of the drought, so there were no leaves to screen his view. It was a bit far from the water hole, so he'd really need to shout if danger threatened.

He was pleased with himself. When the men had been arranging their hunt he had nudged Suth and whispered, 'Suth, I do lookout? I, Ko, ask.' Suth had smiled and spoken to Tun, who was leader, and Tun had glanced at Ko and nodded. So Ko was one of the two lookouts. Nar was the other, over on the far side of the dry riverbed. Nar was Ko's private enemy.

'Keep good watch, Ko,' Suth had told him quietly. 'Do not dream.'

But of course Ko dreamed. He was always full of dreams. This time he was the hero of the hunt. Antelope would come to the water and the hunters would spring their ambush, but they'd be unlucky. Someone – Net, probably – would move too soon and the antelope would take fright and race away across the plain. The best of them, a glossy great buck – he must have found good grass somewhere to have all that meat on him – would run close by Ko's tree, and clever Ko had taken a couple of good stones up with him, and now he slung one at the buck, slung it with deadly aim, catching him full force on the side of the head, just in the right spot below the ear, and . . . and . . .

Ko hadn't decided on the end of the dream. Would he kill the buck outright? That seemed a bit much, even for a dream. Perhaps he'd just stun it, so that it lost its bearings and ran back into the arms of the hunters . . .

Anyway, he kept an eye open for good stones as he made his way across to the tree, but there weren't any. How could he change the dream . . . ? Before he'd thought of anything he reached the tree.

It was growing on a sloping slab of bedrock a bit taller than a man at its upper end. The tree-roots ran down the face of the rock into the soil beneath. At the bottom lay a single chunk of rock, almost as large as Ko's head, much too heavy for him to throw. It would have to do. The buck would just have to come nearer, so that he could drop the rock instead of throwing it. Why, he might even kill it, that way . . .

With a lot of effort he heaved the rock up into the tree and managed to wedge it into a fork. Then he found a place where he could perch in the shade of the trunk and start his watch.

Time passed. Ko didn't mind. He had his dream to play with. It was a good dream, wonderful but not impossible, something he, Ko, might really manage to do if he was very lucky . . . There would be a feast that night of course, and praise from the hunters, and he, Ko, would be allowed to make his boast, and no one would laugh at him . . . and Nar would be watching with jealous eyes . . .

Something was happening!

Noises, a shout, men shouting, the shouts of the hunters as they leaped for the kill.

Ko twisted round to where he could look towards

the river, but could see nothing. The shouts were coming from down in the dry riverbed, out of sight. So the prey must have come from Nar's side, and he, Ko, hadn't seen anything, nothing at all . . . Surely his buck would break out now and come racing towards him . . .

No.

He turned back and stared longingly across the plain. Perhaps even now . . .

Far as the horizon nothing stirred on the baked and dreary emptiness, lit clear by the sideways light of the late afternoon sun.

But yes, there!

Much closer than he'd been looking, a movement.

Why hadn't he seen it before?

Because it was almost the same colour as the tawny plain. The lion-coloured plain that hid the lions. But for the movement of their shadows he mightn't have seen them at all as they padded towards the river. Three lionesses and two cubs. Very dangerous.

A lioness with cubs to feed is afraid of nothing.

Ko turned towards the river, cupped his hands round his mouth and yelled the whooping, carrying call that meant *Danger!* Everyone used and understood it, both the Moonhawks and the others from the old Kins, who had words, and the Porcupines who didn't.

Nobody heard. The hunters were making too much noise. A few small deer were scrambling up the far bank and dashing off across the plain.

He called again, even louder. He saw the lions pause in their stride. Their heads turned towards him. His heart thumped. Lions could climb trees. He checked for a branch he could scramble along, too far for a lion to follow him. But the lions padded on towards the river.

Ko waited for a lull in the shouting, and yelled again, *Danger!*

This time somebody heard him. A man appeared from the riverbed. He spotted the lions at once, now nearer to him than Ko's tree. He turned and shouted down to the men in the riverbed. Several men scrambled up the far bank, three of them with the bodies of deer across their shoulders. They ran off, staggering under the weight, while the others followed as guards, looking over their shoulders as they ran.

That couldn't be everyone. No. As the leading two lions disappeared into the riverbed, more men climbed to the top of the further bank. They all had stones cradled on one arm, with the other one free for throwing. They lined up, ready to drive the lions back if they tried to attack.

A moment later two men came in sight to Ko's left, further up the river, and started running towards him. He recognized Suth and Kern, and sighed with relief. They were coming to see that he was safe. Though he might dream of finding his own way back to the lair, alone in the dangerous night, he didn't want to have to do it for real.

But the lioness and her cubs hadn't yet followed the other two down into the riverbed. She too saw the men running towards the tree and at once turned and came after them at a rapid lope. The cubs followed.

Ko yelled and pointed. The men glanced over their shoulders and sprinted for the tree. The lioness quickened her pace, gaining on them all the time.

Ko scrambled round the tree to where he had wedged his rock, heaved it up and rested it at chest level on a sloping branch. Perhaps he could still do something. His heart hammered. This wasn't a dream.

Suth was faster then Kern. He reached the great boulder on which the tree stood and scrambled up it, then turned to help Kern.

Almost at the rock, Kern glanced back. As he did so, his foot caught, he stumbled and fell. He was up in an instant, but the lioness was close behind him. Suth shouted and flung his digging stick. Its sharpened end hit her on the right shoulder, below the neck, a good strong blow that made her flinch and pause a moment. Kern reached the boulder, but hadn't time to climb it. Desperate, he put his back to it and raised his digging stick to strike one last blow.

Hopeless. This was a lioness with cubs to feed.

Ko fought for a kneehold on the sloping branch. Two-handed he heaved the rock above his head. He couldn't possibly throw it far enough. But perhaps, just as the lion sprang . . .

He tensed, scrabbling for a better hold, and slipped.

He grabbed for the branch, and the rock tumbled from his grasp. He watched it fall, straight down, useless.

It just missed Suth, slammed into the very rim of the boulder, and shot forward, catching the lioness full in the face as she sprang. Kern at the same moment flung himself sideways. The lioness buffeted into the boulder and half fell, but staggered up, shaking her head, with blood streaming from her nose and mouth.

Suth yelled and helped Kern up the face of the boulder, and together they scrambled up the tree.

The lioness was still staggering round, trying to shake the blood off her face and out of her eyes, but after a little while she recovered enough to pause and study the three people in the tree. She and her cubs were scrawny with hunger. Every rib showed clear. If she didn't find food soon they would all three die.

Ko, Suth and Kern watched her deciding whether to try to climb up after them. At last she turned and padded draggingly towards the river, followed by her cubs.

They waited until the lions vanished into the riverbed, then climbed down and ran off in the opposite direction before making their way back to the outcrop that was their lair. They took wide circuits round any cover that might hide other lions. By the time the outcrop came in sight their shadows stretched tens and tens of paces in front of them.

'Ko,' said Suth, when they were almost there, 'tonight I tell the Kin your deed. I, Suth, praise.'

'I, Kern, also praise,' said Kern. 'I praise and thank.'

These were words that Ko had longed to hear, ever since he could remember, especially from Suth. So why did they make him feel uncomfortable when they were now at last spoken? He didn't understand.

'The rock was big,' said Kern wonderingly. 'It was high in the tree. How is this?'

Suth looked at Ko.

'I . . . I do not know,' said Ko. 'I found it there.'

He knew that Suth had long ago guessed about his dreams, but Ko wasn't going to say anything about them in front of Kern.

'This was lucky, lucky,' said Kern.

Suth was still looking at Ko.

'Lucky is good, Ko,' he said.

Oldtale

THE DAUGHTERS OF DAT

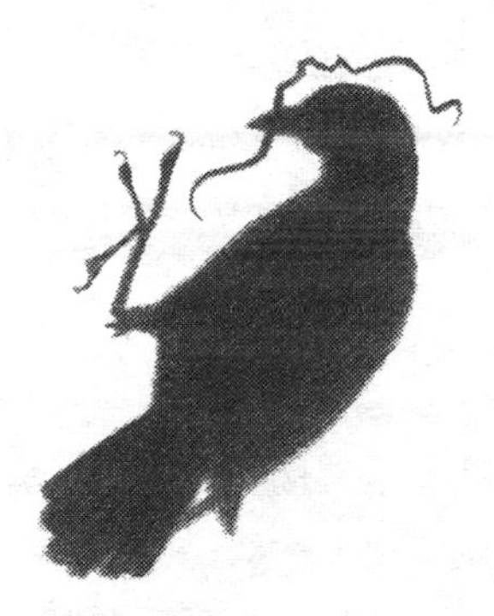

Dat was of the Kin of Parrot. He had two daughters, children only, named Gata and Falu. Their mother, Pahi, was bitten by a red scorpion. At Ragala Flat she was bitten. There she died.

Dat said to his daughters, 'I have no mate. Who now pounds grass seed for me? Who mixes gum-root paste? This is woman stuff.'

Falu said, 'We, your daughters, do these things, my father.'

Gata said nothing.

Dat said, 'One day men come, from Fat Pig and from Weaver. They say to you, 'Gata, Falu, we choose you for our mates. Do you choose us?' What then do you say to them?'

Falu said, 'We say, Go to our father, Dat. Ask him.'

Dat said, 'Is this a promise, my daughters?'

Falu said, 'It is a promise, my father.'

Gata said nothing.

So Gata and Falu did woman stuff for their father,

Dat. They pounded his grass seed and mixed his gum-root paste. He was happy.

Tens of moons passed, and more tens, and Gata was almost a woman. Parrot camped at Stinkwater, and Snake was there also. Gata saw a young man, tall and strong. His name was Nal. She said to Falu, 'Soon I am a woman. I choose Nal for my mate.'

Falu said, 'This is not good. You are Parrot, my sister. Nal is Snake.'

Gata said, 'These are words. I, Gata, choose Nal for my mate. I choose no other man.'

Now Gata was a woman. She was very beautiful. Men came to her, from Fat Pig and from Weaver, and said, 'Gata, we choose you for our mate. Choose one of us. Whom do you choose?'

Gata said, 'My father, Dat, chooses for me. Ask him.'

Gata whispered in her father's ear, 'Choose none of these men, my father. I, Gata, ask.'

Dat said to the men, 'I choose none of you.'

He was happy to do this. He did not wish Gata to leave him.

A new man came from Weaver. His name was Tov. He was small, but clever, and laughter was in his mouth.

Falu saw him. She was a child still, half grown, but her heart sang for him. Tov saw only Gata. He came and came to Dat, saying, 'Give me Gata for my mate.'

Dat said to his daughters, 'This man comes and comes. What do I say to him?'

Gata said, 'Say this to him, my father: First you give me a gift.'

Dat said, 'What gift do I ask?'

Gata said, 'Say this to him, my father: Bring me a tooth of the snake Fododo, the Father of Snakes. Bring me the poison tooth.'

Dat said, 'This is a hard thing I ask. Tov cannot do it.'

Gata said, 'You are right, my father. Tov cannot do it.'

She laughed, and Dat laughed with her.

Tov came yet again to Dat. Falu saw him and followed him. She lay in long grasses and listened to their talk.

Tov said, 'Give me Gata for my mate.'

Dat said, 'First you give me a gift. You give me a tooth of the snake Fododo, the Father of Snakes. You give me the poison tooth.'

Tov laughed. He said, 'You ask a hard thing. Yet for Gata I do it.'

CHAPTER TWO

There was one good thing about the drought – fuel was easy to find. Most of the trees and bushes were dead. Dried by the roasting sun, their branches snapped off easily, and then burst into flame at the first spark.

That night the people sat round the two fires they had built on the top of the outcrop where they were lairing. The moon was full, and the Kin were mostly Moonhawk, so they feasted. Not that it was much of a feast. They had three starved deer, a few small animals they'd hunted or trapped, some lizards and a couple of snakes, some wizened roots, a few handfuls of grubs, and sourgrass, whose leaves were good to chew but choked you if you tried to swallow them. That was all, but they'd eaten scraps of things during the day, and now everybody got three or four mouthfuls, so they finished hungry but not starving.

Kin – Ko and the Moonhawks, and the remnants of the other Kins who had straggled through to the

New Good Places and joined them – sat round one fire, and the Porcupines round the other. This wasn't unfriendliness. They were on good terms, and used to each other. Before the drought they had usually moved about separately, but when they'd met up they'd greeted each other with pleasure. Now, as the last water in the river failed, they were following it down together.

It was the only thing they could do. Already they had come almost as far as any of them had ever been, because to the north lay an enormous marsh, blocking their way. Ko had heard the adults worrying what they'd do when they reached it, but at least there ought to be water there.

The reason why Kin and the Porcupines sat separately in the evenings was very simple. The Porcupines didn't have language. They touched and stroked each other much more than Kin did, and they used a lot of different sounds – warnings and commands and greetings and so on – but they couldn't talk about anything the way Kin did. They couldn't gossip or argue, or praise or boast, or tell and listen to the Oldtales, which was how Kin liked to spend their evenings.

Tor was the only Porcupine who stayed with the Moonhawks, because he was Moonhawk too. When Suth and Noli and Tinu had first rescued him, and Tinu had mended his broken arm, they had given him his name and let him join the Kin, and now he was Noli's mate. Ko didn't remember the rescue. As far as he was concerned Tor had always been there, gentle and kindly, with his strange-shaped arm, because it had mended crooked, though it was perfectly strong.

They finished eating what little there was, but went on passing the meatless bones around to suck and gnaw in turn. While they were doing this the men stood up and made their boasts about what they had done in the hunt.

Suth was the youngest of the men, so he came last. He stood and raised a hand for silence, and looked at Tun, who nodded. Though he was youngest, everyone listened when Suth spoke. They thought well of him. When he was still a boy he had fought and killed a leopard, single-handed. That was a great deed, the deed of a hero. He had the scars of the leopard's claws on his left shoulder, and a small one on his cheek. The other men had man-scars on both cheeks, cut there by the leader of their Kin at the special feast when they had been accepted as men. Suth had only the scar that the leopard had made. It was enough.

'I, Suth, speak praise,' he began. 'I praise the boy Ko. We hunted. Ko kept watch in a tree. Three lions came . . .'

Slowly he told the story – how he and Kern had run from the lioness, and how she had almost caught Kern, but Ko, up in the tree, had thrown a great rock (Suth didn't say 'dropped' – he said 'threw') and had managed to stun the lioness for long enough to let the two men climb the tree and escape.

Suth stopped and sat down. Ko realized that everyone was looking at him, sitting with the women and children on the other side of the fire, opposite the men. Noli, beside him, nudged him gently with her elbow. He stood up and raised his arm and looked at Tun.

Tun nodded gravely. Silence fell. Ko tried to speak,

to make his boast. This was a moment he'd dreamed of again and again, though boys didn't normally get to boast in front of all the adults like this – they boasted among themselves all the time, of course. In Ko's dreams the words came smoothly, proudly. Not now. Whatever Suth said, he knew that he hadn't been the hero of his dreams, clever and brave, saving the day. Yes, he'd maybe saved Kern's life, but it had just been a stupid accident.

He gulped, and managed to speak.

'I, Ko, did this. Yes. I did this. Suth said it. It is true. I . . . I . . . was lucky, lucky.'

He sat down, almost weeping with shame at his stupid boast. Everyone was laughing. He bowed his head in misery. He longed to run away, away, far into the dark night. He felt Noli's arm slide round his shoulders.

'Ko, why do you hide your head?' she whispered. 'You do well, well. Suth praises you.'

'They laugh at me,' he muttered. 'They laugh at my stupid words.'

'No, Ko,' she said. 'Your words are good. They are happy for you. They laugh. Listen. Now they laugh at Kern. It is different.'

It was true. There was a new note in the men's voices as they jeered at Kern for letting the lion almost catch him and needing a boy to save him.

'It is you, Kern, are lucky, lucky,' they said.

'This is true,' said Kern cheerfully.

Ko felt better, but he stayed where he was, leaning against Noli, and she understood what he wanted and kept her arm comfortingly round him. Noli wasn't Ko's mother – she was far too young – it was only eight moons since she and Tor had chosen each other for mates, and now she was fat with her first child inside her. But she had acted as mother to Ko and Mana and her own small brother Tan, since all their real parents had been killed or taken when savage strangers had attacked the Moonhawks and the other Kins and driven them out of their old Good Places.

Ko couldn't remember any of that. He could just remember little bits of the time soon after, when the six of them – Suth, Noli and Tinu, Ko himself and Mana and Tan, who had been called Otan then because he was still a baby – had lived for a while with the lost Monkey Kin in a hidden valley at the top of a mountain. He knew the mountain had exploded. He'd been told about that, but all he could remember was running desperately up a rocky slope in the dark and clutching something he'd been told to keep hold of while rocks rained down all around him and a huge hot orange mass roared and boomed below.

He didn't remember a lot of stuff that had happened after that, like meeting the Porcupines – Suth said that had been in a canyon somewhere – and then coming to the New Good Places and finding Tun and Kern and Chogi and the rest of the Moonhawks.

All Ko's real memories were about living in the New Good Places, along with the people who now sat around the two fires. But he still thought of the six who'd done the things he'd been told about as his own family. Suth was father and Noli was mother, although Suth was mated with Bodu and they had their own baby son, Ogad, and Noli's baby would be born inside a moon.

Tinu was a big sister, or maybe an aunt, though she wasn't a woman yet. And Mana was Ko's younger sister and Tan was his little brother, though really they'd all had different parents. So Ko felt closer to these five than he did to anyone else on the outcrop. Just now he was sitting between Noli and Mana, with Tinu on Noli's other side. Tan was running around between the two fires, playing tag with other small boys, both Kin and Porcupines. You didn't need words to play tag.

While the men were still teasing Kern, Chogi stood up and crossed to the other side of the fire and faced Tun. She bent her knees and dipped her head briefly and made a fluttering movement with her fingers in the air. Chogi was senior woman. Nobody expected her to kneel right down and patter her hands on the ground in front of the leader, as a junior woman would have done.

'Chogi, we listen,' said Tun.

Chogi dipped her head again and moved slowly to the gap between the men's side and the women's, so that everybody could see and hear her. It was obvious that she had something important to say.

She was a short, wrinkle-faced woman. Ko had never seen her laugh. He could remember when she'd been rather fat, but now she was skinny with hunger, like everybody else. Her main business was to see that the Kin kept strictly to their ancient customs, stuff to do with childbirth and choosing mates, and things that were done when babies became small ones, or small ones became children, or children became men and women. Ko thought this sort of thing very dull, so instead of listening to Chogi he started dreaming his boast over, with him, Ko, saying the words he wished he'd said. While he was at it he went back and changed the actual adventure, so that he'd found a couple of good throwing stones on his way to the tree . . .

Something was happening. The men had stopped whispering among themselves, as they usually did when woman-stuff was being discussed. Ko came out of his dream and listened.

' . . . The moon is big,' Chogi was saying. 'We feast. This is good. This is happy time. But now we go to new places, dangerous, dangerous. Do we find food? Do we feast again? When is another happy time? I do not know. So I, Chogi, say this. We do happy time stuff now. We do it here. I see Nar. I see Tinu. Soon Nar is a man. Soon Tinu is a woman. Soon they choose mates. Nar chooses Tinu. There is no other woman. Tinu chooses Nar. There is no other man. They smear salt on their foreheads. This is good. It is happy time stuff. So I, Chogi, say, they do not wait. They do this now. I, Chogi, say this.'

She stopped, but stayed where she was, with the firelight wavering across her old, lined face, and the big moon halfway up the sky behind her. Everyone seemed too surprised to speak. Even Ko understood that what Chogi was suggesting was a break with custom. No one had been surprised when Suth and Bodu had chosen each other. There hadn't been anyone else for them to choose, and besides Bodu was from Little Bat, which was one of the two Kins from which Moonhawk men were allowed to choose.

Even so, they'd waited until they'd both been through the correct customs for becoming man and woman. Then, at a full moon feast, they had stood up from each side of the fire and crossed to the place where Chogi now stood, and touched palms, and said the words of choosing, and smeared salt on their foreheads, just as Nal and Turka had done long, long ago, at the first ever such choosing, by the saltpans beyond Lusan of the Ants – one of the Old Good Places, where none of them would ever go again.

Now chatter broke out as everybody began to talk about Chogi's idea. Even the men were interested. It wasn't just the business of Nar and Tinu choosing each other before they were man and woman. Nar was Monkey. He and his mother Zara had somehow escaped when the mountain where Monkey used to live had exploded. There'd been other people with them, but they'd all died, wandering lost in a desert somewhere. Only Zara had struggled through with her small son, Nar, and come at last to the New Good Places and joined up with the Moonhawks. Now they were the last of the Monkey Kin, and nobody knew who Monkey were allowed to mate with.

The adults thought this sort of thing was very important, though as far as Ko could see it didn't make much sense any more. Who was he supposed to choose when his turn came? The only girls the right age were Mana, who was Moonhawk (Chogi wouldn't like that at all) and Sibi, who was almost a small one still, and besides that she was Parrot, and Moonhawk wasn't allowed to mate with Parrot – and anyway Sibi made it obvious she thought Ko was stupid.

Ko leaned forward and looked to see how Tinu was taking Chogi's suggestion, but she'd shrunk back into Noli's shadow with her hands over her face – her strange, twisted mouth always made her try to hide like that when anyone drew attention to her. Ko hoped she didn't like the idea. He didn't want Nar becoming part of his family, the way Tor and Bodu were now.

Ko didn't really have any good reason for making Nar his enemy. Nar was just another boy, a bit older than Ko himself. Perhaps they should have been friends. There were no other boys anywhere near their age among the Kin. Nar was taller and stronger than Ko, but that was just because he was older – he wasn't a bully or a loudmouth. Other people seemed to like him, but that only made it worse.

The real reason why Ko didn't like Nar was his smile. Nar smiled a lot, almost whenever anybody spoke to him, and when Ko made one of his boasts – claiming he'd done something he hadn't, really, or promising he would when everyone knew he couldn't – Nar would smile that smile and look at him for a moment, a look that said, 'I am almost a man, and you are nothing but a stupid little boy . . .'

Ko stood up, pretending he needed a stretch and a yawn, but really to get a look at Nar and see how he was reacting. He couldn't see him. Where was he? Ah, that must be him, just beyond Zara, but Ko couldn't see his face. Zara was saying something to him. He must have answered, because she shook her head and made a furious gesture with her left hand, as if she were trying to sweep the whole idea away.

Good – Zara didn't want it to happen either. Ko

couldn't imagine Tinu really wanted Nar for her mate. Chogi was just a silly old woman. Why didn't Tun stand up and say so . . . ?

As he settled down again, Ko realized that something was happening to Noli, beside him. She was shuddering, and breathing in slow, deep lungfuls. Now her body went stiff. Her eyes were open, but rolled so far up that he could see only white below the bulging lids. Froth gathered at the corners of her mouth.

Ko wasn't alarmed. He understood what was happening, and was ready when Noli took an even deeper breath and shot suddenly to her feet. She didn't scramble awkwardly up, as she usually did now because the baby inside her unbalanced her. This time it was more as if something had taken hold of her and just jerked her upright.

Everybody stopped talking and looked at her. None of this was strange to them. They waited in silence.

She raised her arms and stood as still as a tree for a while. Then a voice came out of her, not her own voice, not any man's or woman's, but a big, soft voice like an echo from a cave, the voice of Moonhawk, the First One.

'Wait,' said the voice. 'It is not the time.'

As the last whisper of the voice faded into the night, Noli crumpled. This sometimes happened, so Ko was already kneeling, ready to catch her, but she went the other way, into Tinu's arms, and now by the firelight Ko could see Tinu's face. Her twisted mouth was open, with her jaw working sideways and down as if she'd got something stuck there. Her cheeks were streaming with tears.

Mana had seen too. By the time Ko had helped ease Noli down onto the rock, Mana was kneeling on Tinu's other side with both arms round her, hugging her close. Tinu huddled beside Noli's sleeping body, with her head in her hands, sobbing bitterly.

Ko moved round to hug her from the other side.

'Do not weep, Tinu,' he begged her. 'Why do you weep?'

Mana made a face at him to be quiet, but Tinu answered, mumbling through her sobs.

'No man . . . chooses . . . Tinu . . . No man . . . ever.'

Ko, desperate to comfort her, said the first thing that came into his head.

'I find a mate for you, Tinu. I, Ko, do this.'

She took her hands away from her face and looked at him, and he could see that she was trying to smile, but the tears still streamed down. Mana, behind Tinu's shoulder, was frowning at him, shaking her head. He sighed and moved back to the other side of Noli's sleeping body and sat with his chin on his fists, staring at the small, wavering flames as they danced over the heap of glowing embers.

What had he said wrong? What did Tinu mean, saying no one would ever choose her for a mate? There wasn't anything wrong with Tinu, anything that mattered. Her face wasn't like other people's, with its broken, twisted look, and she couldn't talk right. But she did have language – you just had to get used to the mumbling way she spoke. And she was clever, clever with her mind and her hands. She sometimes found good new ways of doing things, which people had never thought of.

Anyway, he told himself, as soon as she was a woman some man was going to choose her for a mate. What man? As Chogi had said, there wasn't anyone except Nar. Forget about Nar. He, Ko, was going to find someone.

Oldtale

FALU'S PRAYER

Falu said to Gata, 'Stay with my father. Pound grass seed. Mix bloodroot paste.'

Gata said, 'My sister, where do you go?'

Falu said, 'I follow Tov. He seeks the tooth of Fododo, Father of Snakes. Tov is clever. Perhaps he gets the tooth. But I set traps in his path. I lead him astray.'

Gata said, 'My sister, this is good.'

Falu went first to Dindijji, the place of dust trees. As she went, she gathered nuts. She dug gumroot from the ground and chewed it, and spat the chewings into her gourd.

She came to Dindijji. She made paste from her chewings and spread it on a rock in the sun. Soon it was very sticky. She smeared it on the branches of the dust trees, and so stuck the nuts to them. Parrots came to eat the nuts, the little grey parrots with the yellow tail feathers.

They stuck to the paste. Falu caught them. From each she took a yellow tail feather.

She gave nuts to them and set them free.

She said, 'Little grey parrots, fly to the First One. Say to him, Falu is our friend. She gives nuts to us.'

She stuck feathers to her buttocks, the yellow tail feathers. She rolled herself beneath the trees, and poured their dust over her head, the grey dust. She said, 'Now I am a parrot, a little grey parrot with yellow tail feathers.'

At nightfall she climbed a tree. To its topmost branches she climbed. The little grey parrots came and roosted around her. They woke at the sunrise and flew hither and thither and sang their song. It was the time of the parrots.

Falu sang also. These words she sang:

Parrot, First One.
I am your nestling.
You brood over me.
You bring me sweet fruits.
Give me Tov for my mate.

Five nights Falu stayed in the tree, neither eating nor drinking. Each morning she sang with the parrots.

On the sixth night she bound herself round with tingin bark and slept. The tingin bark held her safe.

Falu dreamed. Parrot came to her in her dream and said, 'Falu, you are my nestling. I brood over you. I bring you sweet fruits. I give you Tov for your mate. Go where he goes.'

Falu woke in the morning. She looked at her arms,

and they were wings. She looked at her fingers, and they were the grey feathers of the wing tips.

Her chin itched. She scratched it with her foot. She looked at the foot, and it was the foot of a bird.

She opened her mouth and sang. Her voice was the voice of a parrot.

Falu said in her heart, This is good. I go where Tov goes. He does not know me.

CHAPTER THREE

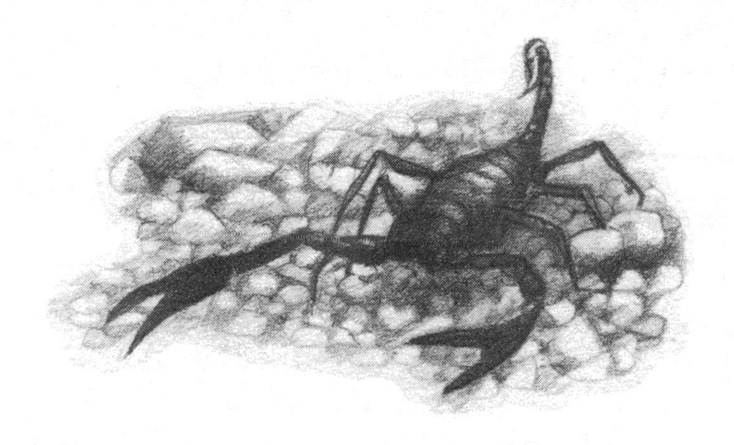

There was no food left where they were, so next day they moved on north. To search a wider area the Porcupines stayed on the east side of the river and the Moonhawks crossed to the west. It was hard going. The land became more and more like true desert. The trees along the river that used to be green all year were mostly leafless and dead. Water was hard to find, even when they dug in the riverbed, and they were lucky if they each got a few mouthfuls of food a day.

For several days they moved on like that. Hunger seemed to follow Ko like his own shadow. He was hungry even in his dreams. Soon he was thirsty too. They could smell the water trickling below the riverbed, but when they dug down they found almost none there. They sucked pebbles and chewed dry sticks to give their mouths something to do.

The women were very anxious about the babies, both Bodu's little Ogad and Noli's unborn child. Was

Bodu getting enough food to make good milk? Was Noli getting enough to make the baby grow inside her? Would she have milk to feed it when it was born? They gave the two mothers everything they could spare, but it wasn't really enough.

The men were worried too. Ko heard some of them talking together one evening after they'd had a stroke of luck and found a patch of good gourds, the sort that would hold water for several moons without going soft, once they'd been well salted and smoked. The men were working at this, while the women prepared the scraps of food that had been found.

'We use all the salt,' said Var. 'It is gone. Now we go far and far. Do we find more salt? Do we find cutter stones? Do we find tingin trees?'

He spoke gloomily. Var was like that, but this time the other men grunted in agreement. These were all things that people used every day. You couldn't make a good digging stick without a cutter, or loops to carry a gourd without tingin bark, and salt was useful for preventing meat from rotting and for making food taste better. But all these things were scarce, too. You could go many days' journey without finding them.

'There is a salt pan out there,' said Net, jumping up and pointing west, as if he was ready to start out that moment. 'Yova found it. It has no name.'

'It is too far,' said Tun. 'There is no food there. No Good Place. Not any more. It is gone.'

Ko knew what they were talking about. He could just remember the times before the rains had begun to fail, when they'd been able to roam over a much wider tract of land, going from one Good Place to another. Now all the Good Places had been swallowed up by the desert.

He stopped listening to the talk and started on a dream in which he, Ko, sneaked off secretly into the dark, travelling by the light of the moon, and after several good adventures reached the salt pan Yova had found and dug out a slab of wonderful white salt, the best sort, so white that it glittered in the moonlight. Then he journeyed home with it and sneaked into the camp while the others still slept, and when they woke in the morning they found it by the embers of the fire and couldn't imagine how it came there. And then he, Ko, told them.

It was a good dream. Ko was still working on it when they all lay down to sleep.

The next few days were worse. The river split up into a maze of smaller rivers, all now dry, separated by islands and mudbanks and immense tangles of dead reed, the kind of dangerous, useless territory that the Kin called demon places. Somewhere over on the far side were the Porcupines – there'd been no sign of them for several days and they were now quite out of reach.

Water was still hard to find. Sometimes they had to wait all morning before they could move on, while a few of the adults fought their way through with the empty gourds and came back with the stinking, muddy liquid.

Several people fell sick. Mana was the worst. She staggered, so that Ko had to put his arm round her and help her along. And she was hot and cold by turns and babbled about things that weren't there.

And then Cal was stung on the foot by a scorpion.

His whole leg swelled up. He was a brave man, but he howled and wept with the pain of it and they thought he was going to die. But by next morning the pain and the swelling were almost gone, and then the leg shrivelled to a stick, so that he walked with a heavy limp.

Ko didn't go to search for water of course. He tried a couple of dreams about doing so, but the demons got into them, and they scared him.

They reached the main marshes very weak and depressed. This was as far as any of them had ever been, even before the rains had failed. They halted at the top of a low rise and looked north.

It was evening, and beyond the first few tens of paces everything was hidden under a strange haze, golden with the light of the setting sun. It didn't seem to be very dense. Ko could see the first few mudbanks and reed patches clearly enough, but then they became vague, blurred shapes, and then vanished completely. There was no sign of a pathway, and it was too late to explore, so they made camp and slept.

When they woke in the morning the haze had cleared, and they could see what they were in for.

The marshes were demon places, too. Ko hadn't known what to expect, so he'd made them up in his mind, mudbanks and tall green reeds with patches of clear water between them. The reeds were there, a vast brown tangle. The mud was there, dried and cracked. There was no water. Insects swarmed out of the reeds and gathered around the newcomers. Ko couldn't see how far the marsh stretched, but beyond it, almost as blue as the glaring blue sky, he could see a wavering line which he knew was distant hills.

Suth pointed.

'We go there,' he said. 'See, it rains. We find Good Places there.'

Ko looked, and yes, in the far distance he could see two separate dark masses of raincloud blurring the horizon.

'Suth, we cannot cross the marsh,' said Bodu.

She spoke dismally. Usually she was cheerful. Ko liked her. She laughed at him sometimes, but she didn't make it sound jeering or scornful – she just liked to laugh. But she was worried about her baby, Ogad, who wasn't yet three moons old. He was very thin and fretful, because she hadn't enough milk to give him. If she didn't find better food soon, Ogad would die.

Ko longed to comfort her. As usual he spoke before he thought.

'I find a way through the marshes,' he said. 'I, Ko, do this.'

Behind him someone laughed and he swung round. It was Nar, not trying to hide his smile. Ko took a pace towards him and stuck his chin out. He felt his scalp stir as it tried to make his hair bush out, though he'd have to be a man before that would happen so that anyone could see.

'I, Ko, speak, Nar,' he snapped. 'I find the way through the marshes. Does Nar say *No* to me?'

Nar wasn't impressed. His smile widened.

'You do this, Ko,' he said. 'Then I give you a gift.'

'What gift, Nar?'

Ko was really angry. He thought he could feel his hair actually moving a little.

'You ask, I give,' said Nar carelessly, making it yet

more obvious he was sure Ko couldn't do what he'd promised. All this was man stuff, the sort of words Var and Kern might have used in an argument. The boys copied the men, of course. For them it was a kind of game. Ko could see that was how Nar was treating it this time.

Ko wasn't. He looked round and saw a boulder jutting up out of the ground a few paces behind Nar.

'Come,' he said, and marched over to it, not looking to see if Nar followed.

He did, and he wasn't smiling now.

Ko laid his right hand on the boulder.

'This is the rock Odutu . . .' he began, but Nar interrupted him.

'Ko, I take back my words,' he said.

'You say I, Ko, find the way through the marshes?'

'No, Ko,' said Nar quietly. 'You do not do this thing. You do not try. It is dangerous, dangerous.'

But Ko was much too angry to listen, either to the words, or the way in which Nar had spoken them. He put his hand back on the rock.

'This is the rock Odutu, Odutu below the Mountain,' he said. 'On Odutu I say this. *I, Ko, find the way through the marshes.*'

He stood back and waited. This was the strongest oath or challenge anyone knew. Odutu was a real place, a huge rock, far in the south of the Old Good Places, standing at the foot of the mountain where the First Ones lived. Ko had been taken there when he was a small one, but he didn't remember. All he knew was an Oldtale, which said that an oath sworn at Odutu was an oath for ever. Since they were all now so far away from the real Odutu, any big rock would do almost as well, provided the right words were used.

Nar hesitated, sighed and shrugged. He put his hand on the boulder and muttered, 'This rock is Odutu, Odutu below the Mountain. On Odutu I say this. *Ko finds the way through the marsh, then I give him a gift. Ko asks. I, Nar, give.*'

He looked at Ko and shook his head disapprovingly, but without saying a word went back and joined the others.

Ko followed. Nobody seemed to have noticed what they were up to. They were just a couple of boys doing boy stuff, and there was something more interesting happening in the other direction.

The solid ground ended in a low bank, and then the marsh began. Everyone was lined up along the bank watching someone – Net, of course; he always rushed into things – picking his way across a patch of dried mud between two tangles of reeds, moving a half pace at a time and testing the surface beneath each foot before he shifted his weight onto it. He was four or five paces from the bank when the surface gave way.

At once he was right in to his waist, but the sticky black mud seemed to be deeper than that, and he went on sinking as he floundered round and tried to wade back.

Soon he was up to his chest, struggling frantically for the bank but not getting any nearer. Everyone was shouting. The other men were down at the edge of the marsh, Tun giving orders.

Suth started to crawl out onto the mud. He was the lightest of the men. Now he lay on his belly and wormed his way forward, spreading his weight across the treacherous mud. Ko watched with his heart in his mouth.

As soon as Suth's feet were clear of the bank, Var knelt and gripped his ankles, and then as Suth moved further out Var too lay down and wormed after him, while Kern and Tor knelt and held Var's ankles. By the time Suth could grasp Net's wrists, Net was up to his neck, Suth and Var were well out on the mud, and Tor and Kern were kneeling and leaning out over it to keep hold of Var.

The angle was awkward. Neither of the two on solid ground could pull with any strength, and the two out on the mud didn't dare risk pulling at all. But now, without waiting for Tun to give the order, the women formed two lines, each woman with her arms round the one in front of her, and the two at the head of the lines gripping Tor and Kern round their waists.

Chogi called, and they heaved, all together. Suth and Var took the strain. Ko could see the muscles of their forearms bulging as they fought to keep their grip. Net stopped sinking. The women heaved rhythmically, Tun calling the time. It wasn't enough. Net remained stuck fast. Ko and Nar and the older children joined the ends of the lines and added their weight. Ko was well up the bank and could still see the men out on the mud.

The surface under Suth gave way but somehow he kept his hold, turning his head sideways to keep his nose and mouth clear while he floated on the filthy ooze.

The changed angle must have helped. Slowly, so

slowly that Ko could hardly see it was happening, Var's feet were coming closer to the bank. The bodies of Tor and Kern were straightening. Net's shoulders were clear of the mud.

And then he came with a rush. The teams on the bank fell over backwards. By the time they were on their feet, Tor and Kern were hauling Var ashore and Suth and Net were slithering back over the surface. And then they were on firm ground, and everyone was crowding round them, shouting with triumph, and jeering at Net for his rashness, while they tried to scrape the stinking mud off their bodies.

But Ko stayed at the top of the bank, staring out over the marsh, with dismay in his heart.

Not that way, he thought. Not even in dreams.

Oldtale

GOGOLI

Tov went to Fon, his father's father. He was very old, and knew many things.

Tov said, 'Father of my father, old Fon, tell me this. Where is the lair of Fododo, Father of Snakes?'

Fon said, 'Tov, son of my son, no man knows this. Only one knows this. He is Gogoli, the Jackal who Knows All Things.'

Tov said, 'Where is Gogoli?'

Fon said, 'He is here, he is there. But at little moon he drinks at the waterhole beyond Ramban. He does not drink, then he dies.'

Tov said, 'I thank Fon, father of my father.'

Fon said, 'Tov, son of my son, be lucky.'

Then Fon died. He was very old.

Tov journeyed to Ramban. There he saw a parrot, a little grey parrot with yellow tail feathers. He said, 'Why is this parrot here? Its place is at Dindijji, the place of dust trees. Surely Gata sends it. Her Kin is Parrot.'

He laughed. The parrot answered, and its voice was laughter.

Tov said, 'Parrot, we are two who laugh. Come with me. You are my guide.'

At that the parrot flew down and sat upon his head.

It was the night of little moon, so Tov journeyed to the waterhole beyond Ramban. He saw a wing nut tree beside the path, and said, 'This is good. I lie in wait behind this tree. Gogoli comes. I leap out. I catch him. Parrot, fly into the tree. Keep watch with me. Make no noise.'

Tov lay by the path and waited. At dusk Gogoli came. Many people hunted Gogoli, to steal his knowledge. So he made a magic as he went, a sleep magic. The hunters slept, and did not catch him.

Now Gogoli made his magic, and Tov slept.

The parrot did not sleep. It was not people. When it saw Gogoli it flew down and cried in Tov's ear. He woke and leaped out.

Gogoli fled, but Tov caught him by the tail. He tied tingin bark to the tail and hauled Gogoli up into the tree.

Gogoli said, 'Man, let me go. This night I drink at the waterhole. I do not drink, then I die.'

Tov said, 'Tell me this first. I seek Fododo, Father of Snakes. Where is his lair?'

Gogoli said, 'It is in the desert, where no man goes. It is west from Tarutu rock, three days. It is north a half day.'

Tov said, 'Where is there water on the way?'

Gogoli said, 'Twoheads has water. It is beneath

him. Bagworm has water. It is there, and not there. Stonejaw has water. It is inside him.'

Tov said, 'Last, tell me this. I seek the tooth of Fododo, the poison tooth. How must I steal it?'

At that Gogoli was very angry. He said, 'How can I know this? No man has done it. It is a thing not known.'

Then Tov untied the tingin bark and Gogoli went to the waterhole and drank. But his sleep magic was still strong, and Tov lay down and slept.

Now it was dark, and the parrot was people again. It was Falu.

Falu said in her heart, Gogoli's magic is strong, strong. Perhaps danger comes. Tov does not wake. Now I, Falu, keep watch.

So Falu watched all night. She did not sleep. In the morning she was a parrot again.

Tov woke. He said, 'Little grey parrot, I dreamed. In my dream I slept. One kept watch. It was a woman. My thought is, It was Gata.'

The parrot answered. Its voice was laughter.

CHAPTER FOUR

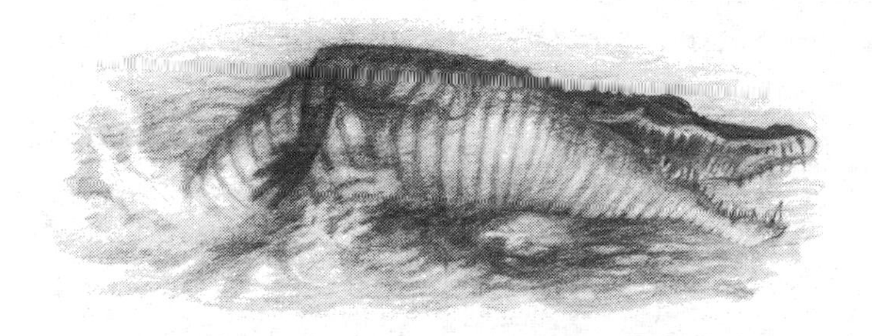

There was nothing to do but turn westward and try to find a way round the marsh. As the sun rose higher the mudbanks began to steam, and soon everything beyond the first few tens of paces was again hidden in haze. Sometimes a pool of water between the mudbanks reached as far as the dry ground, so at least there was enough to drink. But there was no food at all, only the reeds and the mud and the dry, dry land.

So they trudged along all day with despair in everyone's heart. Soon clouds of insects found and followed them, so they moved a little inland to be free of the worst of them. Tun was already looking for a place to camp when Ko noticed Moru heading off by herself to the right. For something to do, he trotted after her.

'Moru, where do you go?' he asked.

'I go see,' she said. 'Perhaps we are lucky.'

She smiled her thin smile. Moru was one of the

stragglers who had come back with Tun when he had gone to see if there was anyone left in the Old Good Places. Her Kin was Little Bat, but her mate was dead, and so was Var's, so they had chosen each other. But Ko felt that she always had a sad look because of everything that had happened to her.

Just before she reached the edge of the marsh she stopped and crouched down. Here the solid ground didn't end in a bank, but in a large, gently sloping patch of soft, sandy earth. With a grunt of satisfaction Moru walked a couple of paces forward, crouched again and gently scooped the earth aside. Ko watched over her shoulder.

She grunted again, scooped even more gently and then carefully lifted something free and showed it to Ko. It was a large egg.

'What bird makes this?' he asked, astonished.

'It is not bird. It is turtle,' said Moru. 'We, Little Bat, had a Good Place. It was at Sometimes River. There were turtle nests. Look, here are many. Call the others.'

Ko ran up the slope, hallooed, and beckoned. Heads turned.

'Come. Moru finds food,' he called, and they all came running. Moru showed them how to look, and in the end they found ten and ten and two more nests, all full of eggs with little baby turtles almost ready to hatch. They carried them well away from the marsh and built a good fire of dead branches and roasted the eggs on the embers. It was the best feast they'd had for several moons.

But the next three days were very bad. They found only two patches of water they could reach, and almost no food at all. On the third day the ground rose, and they walked endlessly along a barren, rocky slope above the marshes. By afternoon even the usually cheerful Kern was looking dismal, and poor Bodu was weeping with anxiety over her baby. Ko was too sick-hearted to dream.

Then, when the sun was low in the west, he felt a faint breeze blowing in his face, with a new smell in it. Water. Not the dead, stinking water of the marsh, but sweet, clean water with green plants growing in and around it.

Everyone smelt it at the same moment. Their weary legs found strength. The loads they were carrying seemed suddenly lighter. Their pace quickened. Some of the men loped ahead. Ko saw them turn and shout and wave, black, spindly shapes against the glare of sunset. Most of the party broke into a run, but Noli was very tired after walking all day with her baby inside her, and by now Suth and Tor were helping her along, so Ko stayed too. They came up with the others last of all, and saw what they had found.

It was a true Good Place, like the ones that Ko could only just remember, before the rains had failed. A narrow strip of the marshes ran south into the desert, but this was a different kind of marshes, with good clear pools and banks of tall green reeds, and leafy bushes growing along the shorelines. Surely there was food there, as well as water.

Hungry and thirsty though they were, they didn't rush down, but stood and looked around for possible dangers. Then Tun pointed to a place where open ground reached down to the water between two patches of bushes. He set lookouts in every direction before he and a few of the adults took the water gourds to refill.

Ko was told to watch back the way they had come, but hardly had he taken up his post when he heard a yell from behind him, one voice, then several, screaming *Danger! Run!* He turned to look. People were racing away from the water. Beyond them something large and dark and glistening was hurtling up the slope. For a moment he couldn't see it properly. A scream rose above the yells. Someone had fallen down.

As the others stopped running and turned back to help, Ko saw the creature clearly.

Crocodiles didn't come that big!

Ko could remember crocodiles basking on the sandbanks of the river when it had still run through the New Good Places, ugly creatures, with thick, scaly hides and long snouts full of jagged teeth. He'd been smaller then, and they'd seemed huge to him, but he knew that they'd really been only two or three paces long, at the most.

This one was more than twice that. It was a monster, a nightmare, a demon from the Oldtales.

He watched it shy away as the people rushed shouting towards it. The men struck at it with their digging sticks as it hummocked itself down to the water. It seemed not to feel their blows. As it slid beneath the surface Ko saw that it had something in its mouth.

Now the people were coming slowly back up from the water. Ko could feel their shock and horror. Four of the men were carrying somebody cradled between them. When they reached the crest where Ko and the others were waiting they laid him on the ground. It was Cal. His left leg, the one that had been stung by the scorpion, was gone, bitten clean off just above the knee. He had fainted. Chogi was trying to staunch the blood flow with her hands, but it pulsed violently out between her fingers.

Ko couldn't bear to watch, so he stared out over the desert. Still nothing moved there, so he turned again and gazed down at the peaceful-seeming stretch of water below, all pink and golden under the sunset. His thirst was suddenly so fierce that he barely noticed when Chogi said, 'Cal is dead. He is gone.'

Everyone groaned, but still Ko could think of nothing but his thirst.

'Tonight we mourn for Cal,' said Tun. 'Now we fill our gourds. This is dangerous, dangerous. First, I do it. Then others, by one and by one.'

Again Ko was set to keep lookout, but kept glancing over his shoulder to see what was happening. One by one the adults dashed down to different places on the bank to fill the gourds, while the others showered rocks and lumps of earth into the water to scare attackers away. Nothing happened, and after a short time they returned to the ridge with brimming gourds.

Everyone had a drink, and then, still keeping careful watch and staying well away from the water's edge, they used the last of daylight to explore for food. To their delight they found several patches of dinka and one of thornfruit. Dinka was a small bush whose young leaves tasted of nothing much but could be swallowed after a lot of chewing. Thornfruit was a sort of cactus with vicious spines. The fruits were tricky to pick, and poisonous raw, but well roasted on embers they became sweet and juicy.

When it was almost dark they carried what they'd found back up the hillside and built their fire and made camp. After they'd eaten Tun stood and raised his hand for silence.

'We mourn for Cal,' he said. 'He is dead.'

The women rose and stood in a line on their side of the fire. The children moved back to give them room. The men, sitting cross-legged opposite them, started to beat out the rhythm with their hands. But before the dance could begin Ko saw Noli stiffen and then walk with slow, jerky steps, as if something were moving her from outside, to the gap between the two groups. The men stopped clapping, and waited. Noli closed her eyes, and when Moonhawk's voice came out of her it spoke so softly that Ko could only just hear the words.

'Fat Pig is dead. He is gone,' said the voice.

It was the saddest sound Ko had ever heard.

Noli bowed her head. For a long while nobody moved or spoke, and then she opened her eyes and moved quietly back to her place in the line.

'Cal was Fat Pig,' said Chogi. 'He was the last. There are no more Fat Pig.'

Even Ko, who didn't often think about such things, felt the solemnity of the moment. The Kins had always been there, ever since the time of the Oldtales. There'd been eight of them (or nine, counting Monkey, but Monkey was different). Now . . . Now, really, there was only one, Ko's own Kin, Moonhawk. Moonhawk and a few scraps. There was nobody from Weaver in the group round the fire, and nobody from Ant Mother. As far as anyone knew, those Kins were dead too, gone. But Cal's death was the first time anyone had actually been there at the moment when a Kin vanished.

Tun gave the signal, the men clapped the rhythm, and the women shrilled the death wail and danced the dance – three stamps of the right foot and three stamps of the left, again and again and again – while the sparks wavered up above the embers of the fire towards the star-filled sky. Mana, sitting beside Ko, took his hand. He looked at her and saw she was weeping, so he put his arm round her and held her close.

Ko didn't feel like weeping but he felt very strange, not like Ko at all, but like somebody much older, much more wise and serious. This person didn't think about Ko stuff. He thought about time, and the people who'd been alive once and weren't any more – all those lives, those ancestors, going back and back and back to the time of the Oldtales, all who had ever been Kin, come down to these few living people left round their fire in the desert.

And they were alive only by the skin of their teeth. If they hadn't found this Good Place, then tomorrow, perhaps, or the day after, Moonhawk would have been gone too, like Weaver, like Ant Mother, like Fat Pig. No Moonhawk, not any more, ever . . .

From where he was sitting, if he looked to his right, Ko could see out over the marshes. The haze that had hidden them all day had gone. What he saw was an immense dark distance, ending in a range of hills outlined against the paler sky. Over there, the rains had not failed, over there were Good Places where

Moonhawk could live and thrive, more lives and yet more lives, going on and on through time . . .

It had to be true.

If only they could get there.

Next morning, they filled their gourds in the same way as they had last evening, some darting in one at a time to different places on the shoreline, while others showered the surface with clods and stones. Ko and the children watched tensely until it was over, but there was no sign of the monster, or of any smaller crocodiles.

Next, according to their custom, they carried Cal's body well away into the desert and mourned again and left it there with his gourd and digging stick and a cutter.

Then they returned to the inlet and explored this new Good Place, foraging as they went. They found plant food, dinka leaves and whitestem and thornfruit, and a bluish root called ran-ran, and various seeds, a far better harvest than they'd gathered anywhere for the last several moons. Even the swarming insects seemed somehow less horrible than in the main marsh. There were plenty of birds deep in the dense thickets, and tracks of small animals beneath them, but no sign of anything larger. Ko heard some of the men talking about this.

'This is strange,' said Kern, who was the best tracker among the men. 'Here is food. Here is water. I see deer tracks. I see pig tracks. They are old, old. None are new.'

'I see no swimming birds,' said Net.

'The crocodile eats them,' said Var gloomily. The other two laughed, because that was the sort of thing Var always said, but a little later, while Ko was hunting for a way into a cactus thicket to reach a juicy-looking thornfruit, he heard a call of 'Tun, come look!'

It was Kern's voice. Ko forgot about the thornfruit and scampered along to see what was up. He found the men looking at one of the patches of open ground that ran right down to the water's edge. Kern was kneeling and pointing at what he'd seen.

'These tracks are old, old,' he was saying. 'Two moons? Three? I do not know. See, five deer come. Two are young. They are slow, careful. And see there, they run, four only. One is young. They run fast, fast. Now see here . . .'

He moved nearer to the water and pointed at an area where the two lines of hoofprints suddenly disappeared, as if a huge fist had been rubbed over the place, wiping them out. Kern pointed at a pattern of dimples amid the mess, and with his forefinger outlined the shape of a large round foot with four spread toes.

'Crocodile,' he said. 'Big, big. Deer go to drink. Crocodile comes from the water. It takes one deer, a young one. See, it drags it . . .'

He pointed to a groove in the earth, running all the way down to the water. Everyone gazed out over the peaceful surface. Ko saw Yova stiffen, then slowly raise her hand and point.

'See, by the reeds,' she said quietly. 'Eight paces from the edge. It watches.'

Ko stared, trying to see what Yova had noticed.

There was a stand of tall green reeds close to the shore. He looked along its edge. How far was eight paces . . . ? Yes! There! Where that reed had twitched with nothing to stir it! Light ripples were spreading away from a small patch of what looked like floating mud and reed leaf that was drifting very gently towards the shore.

In an instant, with a thud of the heart, Ko's way of seeing it changed, so that it wasn't a patch of mud but the very top of a crocodile's head. The slight mound at the near end was the nostrils, and the one at the back was the eye ridge. Ko could see the glisten of a watching eye.

He shuddered and drew back. He wasn't the only one, in fact most were already moving when the crocodile attacked.

It burst out in a sudden violent surge, its tail lashing the water to foam, and rushed towards them. They fled, scattering right and left. Ko risked a glance over his shoulder and saw that the crocodile wasn't pursuing them, but had halted just about where they'd been standing. He stopped and turned, waiting to see what it would do next. He was sure it was the one they'd seen last night – there couldn't be two that huge. The people were scattered up the slope, some still running, others, like Ko, standing to watch, but all tense and ready to run again.

The crocodile rested only a moment or two before starting another charge, hummocking its body up and driving itself forward with its stubby back legs. Again everyone scattered. This time when Ko glanced back the monster was still pursuing, and gaining on him. With horror he realized that it was actually faster than he was. Desperately he raced on and only stopped when he saw Chogi, just ahead of him, look back, and halt and turn.

He turned and stood, with his heart pounding. The crocodile had stopped again, halfway up from the inlet. As he watched it raised its head and gave a deep, thundering roar, unlike any animal Ko had ever heard.

Net answered with a shout, dashed forward and flung his digging stick. It was a well aimed shot, but the stick bounced off the animal's hide like a twig. It swung round and lurched towards Net, forcing him back. Others copied him, still not doing any harm, but after a while the crocodile seemed to realize it wasn't going to catch anyone this time. It turned, dragged itself back into the water, and disappeared. A little later they saw it climb out onto a small island and settle down to bask.

The adults discussed the problem during their midday rest. Normally Ko didn't listen to this kind of talk – it was adult stuff – but the crocodile had really scared him and he wanted to know what they were going to do about it.

'Var is right,' said Kern. 'This crocodile eats all the deer. It eats the swimming birds. They are afraid. They do not come.'

The others grunted agreement and sat in gloomy silence.

'We see only one crocodile,' said Chogi. 'Are there others in this place?'

The men discussed the question among themselves, and agreed that there was probably only this one monster in the inlet. Either it had eaten any smaller ones, or it had driven them away.

'Then I say this,' said Chogi. 'We are weak. We are tired. Bodu must have food. No food, her baby dies. Soon Noli's baby is born – five days, ten, I do not know. Noli must have food. Then she is strong, her baby is strong. Here is food. Here is good water. The crocodile is dangerous, dangerous. But we watch all the time. We see it – it is in one place. We go to another place. It does not catch us. I, Chogi, say this is best.'

'Do the men kill the crocodile?' asked Bodu.

'Bodu, this is difficult,' said Tun. 'The crocodile is strong, strong. It is in the water. We cannot hunt it. Its skin is thick. Our digging sticks do not hurt it.'

'Tun, you are right,' said Chogi. 'You hunt it, then perhaps men die. You are few. This is not good.'

Everyone muttered agreement, and they settled down to discussing the precautions they must take against the crocodile.

Soon after they moved on, they reached the head of the inlet. Surprisingly there was no river feeding it, not even a dry riverbed. The water seemed to well up from below.

On the far side rose a range of low hills, burnt just as dry as everywhere else.

In the afternoon they explored along the further shore of the inlet, keeping well clear of the water. This meant there were promising-looking areas they couldn't safely reach, but they found enough to eat elsewhere.

That evening, to get away from the insects, they moved up into the hills and found a good place for a camp among some large boulders near a grove of dead trees. They could see down to the inlet, but the main marsh was just out of sight behind a low ridge.

When they settled round their fire, Ko didn't sit with Noli and the others. Instead, he found a place where he could hear the men talk, in case they said anything about the crocodile. All day, off and on, he had been thinking about the monster, and remembering the horrible moment when he'd been running away from its charge, and had looked back and seen that it was gaining on him. Perhaps, after all, they'd think of a way of killing it. They were strong and brave, especially Suth. Ko was sure they could do it, somehow.

But to his disappointment they spent the evening discussing what they'd do with their time until Noli's baby was born. There wasn't anything to hunt here, and the women and children could forage for everyone. So the men decided that in a day or two some of them would explore further westward along the marsh, while others would head inland to the salt pan Yova had found – less than a day's journey from here, they thought – and bring back fresh supplies of salt.

At least that let Ko lie down to sleep that night, happy with the dream he'd had before, about how he would go off alone to the salt pan and bring back the wonderful white salt.

His waking dream turned into his sleeping dream, and that turned into a nightmare, a bad one. He was walking proudly along in the moonlight with a lump of glittering salt, as heavy as he could carry, but then it started to get smaller and dirtier, and the moon set, and there was nothing in his hands, but it was too dark to see where he'd dropped the salt – or put it down, he couldn't remember – but there was something near by in the dark – he could hear its snorting breath . . .

He started to run, but his feet were heavy as rocks and now he could hear and feel the deep thump of that hummocking charge . . .

He woke with his yell stuck in his throat. The thump was the slamming of his own heart. Every muscle was locked stiff. His arms and legs were like digging sticks. He couldn't move a finger . . .

Slowly the terror faded. His hands loosened, and then his limbs. Shuddering, he pushed himself up and looked around. There was a half moon high in the west, shining on the dark bodies sleeping quietly among the boulders. Stupid Ko. It hadn't been real, just a bad dream. It was all right.

As he was lying down again to try to get back to sleep, somebody stirred. Noli, only a couple of paces away. It was a sudden movement, as if she'd already been lying awake and had heard somebody whisper her name.

She sat straight up and seemed to stare directly at Ko. The moon shone full in her face. Her eyes were wide open, but they looked stony and dead in the moonlight.

Slowly she raised an arm, stretched out a finger and pointed at Ko. She spoke, not in her own voice, but in a soft, deep whisper, the voice of Moonhawk.

'Kill the crocodile.'

Oldtale

TWOHEADS

Tov journeyed to Tarutu Rock. There he drank at the dewtrap and filled his gourd. Then he went west into the desert, into the Demon Places.

The parrot went with him, perching on his head. All day it slept.

Tov found no water. The sun was behind him, and over him, and shone in his eyes, and his gourd was empty. He came to Twoheads.

Twoheads grew from the desert, as a tree grows, with roots that go deep, deep. He had arms but no legs. The parrot woke and saw him. It left Tov and flew to a rock.

Tov said, 'Do you have food? Do you have water? I see none.'

Twoheads answered, both mouths speaking together. 'We have food. We have water.'

Tov said, 'I am hungry. I am thirsty. My gourd is empty. Give me food and water.'

Twoheads said, 'This is our place. We know no

other. Our food and our water are beneath us, deep, deep. We do not give. We are Twoheads.'

Tov laughed.

Twoheads said, 'What is this noise?'

Tov said, 'It is laughter. I laugh at your folly. I say in my heart, See this Twoheads. He has this one place. He knows no other. A stranger comes. He knows many places. He has many tales. Twoheads gives food and water. The stranger tells tales. He speaks of many places. They are happy together, Twoheads and the stranger. They laugh.'

Twoheads said, 'We do not give. We do not laugh. We are Twoheads.'

Tov said, 'Twoheads, hear me. I make you laugh. Then you give me food and water. I do not make you laugh, I go away. Is this good?'

Twoheads said, 'This is good. We do not laugh.'

Tov said, 'I tell you a tale of folly. There is a man. His name is Tov. He sees a woman. Her name is Gata. She is beautiful, beautiful. He goes to her father. He says, Give me Gata for my mate.'

Now the parrot flew softly from its rock and perched between the heads of Twoheads. Twoheads did not feel it. Tov continued the tale.

'Gata's father says, First you bring me a gift. Bring me the tooth of Fododo, the Father of Snakes. Bring me the poison tooth. Tov answers, For Gata I do this thing . . . Was not this Tov a great fool?'

Now the parrot cried between the heads of Twoheads. Its cry was laughter. It flew away.

The left head turned to the right head. It said, 'You laughed.'

The right head answered, 'It was you.'

They were angry. They fought. They bit and struck blows. The left hand struck the right head and the right hand struck the left head.

Their blood flowed. It fell to the ground. Tov ran with his gourd and caught it as it fell. It was yellow, like honey, and sweet. It was food, it was water, as is the juice of stoneweed.

Tov filled his gourd and went on his way. The parrot went with him.

When it grew dark Tov said, 'Parrot, this is a place of demons. One must watch all night. All day you slept on my head. Now I sleep and you watch.'

He lay down and slept. In the dark the parrot was Falu. All night she watched.

Tov woke in the dark. By starlight he saw the shape of one who watched. He said in his heart, This is Gata. He called her name.

Falu answered, 'Tov, you dream. Gata is far and far. Sleep.'

Tov slept. In the morning he woke. Falu was a parrot again.

CHAPTER FIVE

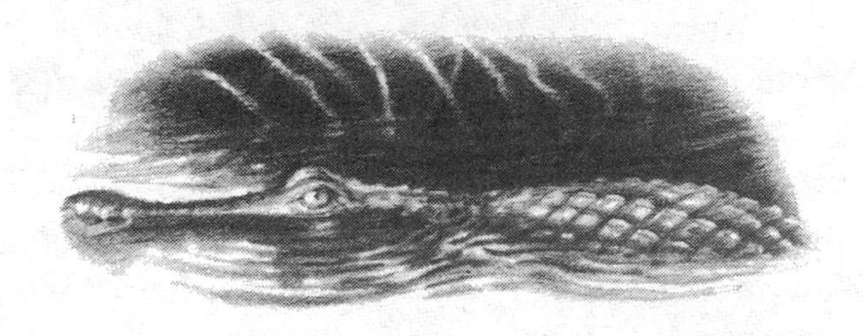

Ko lay awake till dawn, miserable with fear. He was more afraid of the crocodile than he'd ever been of anything in his life. Everyone else was afraid of it too, even Tun and Suth, but to them it was just a big, dangerous animal. To Ko it was something else. He'd recognized it the moment he'd seen it. The crocodile was a demon. It was the thing in his nightmare, alive and real in the daytime world.

Who could he talk to about it? Who would understand, and not just try to comfort him by saying, 'Don't be afraid, it isn't a real demon. It's only a nightmare'? Not even Suth, he felt. Noli, perhaps, and he could ask her too what she'd meant when she'd pointed at him like that. Or what Moonhawk had meant. If Noli remembered – she didn't always. Anyway, he'd ask her. At least she wouldn't laugh at him.

But when the others woke and started to get ready for the day, Noli was busy with Tor. Tor was worried about the Porcupines, whom they'd last seen when they'd separated onto opposite sides of the river. How were they doing? Had they also found food and water? If they hadn't, they'd all be dead by now. Because Tor and Noli couldn't talk to each other, they made up for it by spending much more time together than most pairs of mates did, sitting close and hugging and stroking each other. Noli seemed to understand what Tor was thinking, without any words, and she said he understood her the same way. Only it was all far slower than words, and much more to do with feelings and things like that.

Now she was trying to comfort him, and tell him she was sure his friends were all right, so Ko settled down a little way off and waited for them to finish. After a while Mana came and sat beside him and offered him a bit of roast blueroot left over from last night. He shook his head.

'Ko, you do not cat,' she said. 'Why is this?'

'I am not hungry,' he muttered.

'Ko, you are sad,' she said. 'What is your sadness? Tell.'

He sighed, and in a low voice, not looking at her, told her about his dream, and waking. She didn't answer at once, but took his hand in hers and sat thinking. Then, without letting go, she rose to her feet.

'Come,' she said. 'Now you tell Tinu.'

'No,' he said, without moving. 'I do not want this.'

'Come,' she repeated firmly. 'This is good for Tinu.'

She pulled him up. Both reluctant and relieved he followed her to where Tinu was grinding grass seed by spreading it out on a flat boulder and rocking a rounded stone back and forth across it. Since the feast when Chogi had suggested that she and Nar should choose each other for mates, Tinu had been even quieter and more withdrawn than usual. Now she hardly seemed to notice as Ko muttered his story again, and when he'd finished she continued rocking the stone back and forth, and sweeping the seeds back together as they spread out, without saying anything.

'Tinu,' said Mana. 'How do we kill this crocodile?'

Tinu stopped her work and looked directly at Ko. For the first time in days he saw her smile her twisted smile.

'Ko . . . This is . . . difficult,' she mumbled. 'I think.'

Ko thanked her, and left her to her seed grinding.

Tinu did think, too. Ko could tell, because several times while they were foraging down at the inlet he saw her standing by herself, quite still, heedless of the cloud of insects swarming round her and crawling over her body. Then her hands would start to weave invisible shapes in front of her, and she'd frown at them and shake her head and irritably brush the insects away and go back to foraging.

This made Ko feel that he didn't need to worry about the problem for himself, so he went off into a good dream in which he, Ko, found a secret way across the marsh and led everybody over to the wonderful Good Places on the further side. Before long he was far away, enjoying the imaginary feast when they'd caught their first deer, and of all the boasts and praises round the fire none was better than Ko's, who had found the way across the marsh.

Without warning the ground gave way under his feet. He landed with a bump and shouted aloud with the shock of it. Suth, just ahead of him, turned and laughed.

'Ko,' he said. 'The hunter watches where he puts his foot.'

Several other foragers had seen what happened and were laughing too. Nar was one of them. Ko scrambled out of the pit he'd dropped into – it was only waist deep – and kicked angrily at the mat of fallen grass stems that had hidden it.

'I watch,' he snarled. 'See, this grass hides the hole.'

Suth laughed again and turned away. Ko was still uselessly trying to think of something else to say when Tinu came and knelt beside the hole.

Carefully she rearranged the grass stems to cover it and then scattered some handfuls of loose earth over them.

'Tinu, what do you do?' asked Ko.

'Ko . . . We kill . . . crocodile . . .' she answered. 'You show . . . how.'

During the midday rest Ko watched her chip out a little circular pit in the ground, and then fiddle with twigs and stems to cover it, and finally hide it under a layer of fine earth. When she was ready, Ko fetched Suth and Tinu showed him how the crocodile could be lured onto the trap and made to fall through into the pit. She used a stubby twig for the monster and a smaller one for the person who would be the living bait to tempt it out of the water.

'Like we kill the demon lion?' said Suth. And then, smiling, 'Ko, you are bait again?'

Ko scowled. This was a tease he didn't enjoy,

because it was about one of his stupid-Ko times, so long ago that he didn't remember. But he kept getting told how he'd gone running off into a dangerous place, and Noli had come after him. Then this demon lion had almost caught them, but Noli had run with Ko to the trap that the men had built, which meant that someone up above could drop a rock on the lion and kill it.

When Tinu had rebuilt the model Suth fetched the rest of the men and showed them her idea. They discussed it round the fire that evening, but they weren't very interested.

'This is much, much work,' said Kern.

The others laughed, because Kern always avoided serious hard work if he could, but then Var said, 'Kern speaks truth. There is food here for five days, six days, I do not know. There is no meat. Soon we must go. Do we make ourselves weak, digging this hole? I say no.'

Net said, 'I say we fetch salt. Some fetch salt. Some journey west. They look for a new Good Place.'

They discussed it to and fro, but decided in the end to spend next day gathering extra food for the two expeditions to take with them, and then to set out on the day after that. If the group exploring the edge of the marsh came back without finding a fresh source of food, then they would think about trying to kill the crocodile.

That night Ko had his nightmare again, just as bad as before, only this time he was by the inlet and the crocodile was coming and cleverly he was running towards the trap the men had dug . . . but they hadn't, they'd gone to fetch salt instead, and Ko was alone,

alone in the dark desert, lost, and his legs wouldn't run, and the horrible thud was coming nearer and nearer . . .

This time when he woke Noli didn't stir. It was the same again next night. He was too terrified to get back to sleep, so he crept out of the camp in the dark and made his way up to the ridge, and settled down there to stare out over the marshes.

During the night the heat haze cleared away, and bands of pale mist formed, very beautiful under the setting moon. Then, just as the sun rose, these too cleared, and for a little while he could see the whole marsh, reed beds and mudbanks and water, with fair-sized islands here and there, some of them with real trees on them. Ko would have liked to stay on and search for signs of a path, but by now the camp was stirring, and he didn't want to answer questions about where he'd been, so he slipped back and join the others.

He was afraid of the crocodile during the day too, but it was a different kind of fear, the same as everyone else's. They all stayed well clear of the water whenever they couldn't see the monster basking on one of its islands, but most of the time it was no worse than a serious nuisance. Only when the call went up from one of the lookouts to warn everyone that the crocodile had left its island, did Ko feel a shadow of his night-time fear. Then he would gaze out across the peaceful surface of the inlet, and know that the monster was hidden somewhere underneath, almost certainly coming nearer and nearer, trying once more to catch somebody being careless . . .

*

As soon as the men had set out on their expeditions Chogi called the women together.

'Hear me,' she said, in her solemn, anxious manner. 'I, Chogi, say this. The men are gone. Now we women dig the pit. The men come back. It is done. The men kill the crocodile. We have meat. We reach more plant food. We stay here ten days, and ten more. Noli's baby is born. It is strong. We are strong. We gather food. We store it. Then we journey on, far and far. Is this good?'

They all agreed, and started as soon as they had found enough food for the day. They chose a spot about twenty paces up one of the patches of open ground that sloped down to the water, cut themselves digging sticks like the men's, and started to dig.

Meanwhile the older children, Ko, Mana and Nar, broke branches off bushes and built a low barrier between the shoreline and the pit, so that they could keep watch without the crocodile being able to see them so dangerously close to the water. When the barrier was ready, the three of them spread out along it, crouched down and stared across the still waters of the inlet. Each of them had a pile of stones beside them, ready to throw.

It wasn't long before Mana called softly and pointed. Ko stared. Yes! There! A dark shape like a piece of waterlogged wood just breaking the surface, but moving very gently, closer and closer . . .

Nar was at that end of the barrier. Mana and Ko ran to join him. As soon as the crocodile was in range they stood up and flung their stones. They'd all been throwing stones at targets almost since they were babies, because that was one of their vital skills. A good hunter would expect to knock a bird out of a tree at least one time in three if he got a clear shot at it. Now a shower of rocks rained suddenly down around the monster's snout. At least one scored a direct hit. There was a violent swirl in the water beyond, and when the surface settled the crocodile was gone.

Ko went back to his place and crouched there with his heart pounding. Time passed, and then he and Mana both saw the same dark patch some way out, again coming slowly shoreward. This time it vanished below the surface before it came in range, but the inlet was so still that Ko could see the faint ripple made by something large, moving just below the surface, aiming for his end of the barrier. He called, and the others ran to help. When the ripple was near enough they showered the place with rocks, and again there was that sudden heavy swirl in the water as the crocodile turned and fled.

It tried once more that morning before it gave up and returned to its island. It stayed there, basking, through the hottest part of the afternoon, so Ko and Nar went to help carry soil away from the pit, while Mana kept watch alone.

It was heavy work. Tinu had woven mats from reeds. Two of the women loosened the earth with digging sticks. Four others scooped it out onto mats with their hands, and the rest dragged it clear on the mats. After a while these fell apart, but there were plenty of reeds, so Tinu was kept busy weaving fresh mats. Any stones they dug out they put aside, the smaller ones for throwing at the crocodile, and the big ones for the men to use later, when they'd caught it.

After a while Mana called to say that the crocodile had left its island, so Ko and Nar ran to help drive it away. Four times more that afternoon the enemy came nosing in, each time seeming bolder, getting nearer, and staying longer. The last time, instead of heading back out of range, it turned along the shoreline, as if it were searching for a way past them, while they followed it, yelling and flinging their stones, until it disappeared beyond the thicket that lay along the water's edge.

By now it was getting dark, and they could no longer keep watch in safety. The diggers were exhausted too, so they gave up and trooped back to their camp. On his way, Ko jumped into the pit and found it was already waist deep.

He lay down that night feeling pleased and cheerful. With a little help from Mana and Nar, he, Ko, had kept the demon crocodile at bay all day. He'd beaten it. If he could do that once, he could do it again. He could do it in his dreams.

But no. The daytime triumph made no difference to the night horror. He was crouched behind the barrier, watching with the others, but then he was alone, and it was dark, and he was staring out over the moonlit inlet, waiting for the attack, and the rocks that he'd piled ready were somehow gone, and the monster was already ashore, behind him in the dark . . . and now the thud of that terrifying charge began . . .

He woke then as usual, and crept out of the camp and up to his watch point, where he sat staring over the dark marshes, waiting for sunrise.

The next two days were much the same. At some

point the children must have scored some good hits on the crocodile, which had hurt it even through its armoured hide. At least it seemed warier for a while, turning away as soon as the first rocks splashed down. But it didn't give up.

Meanwhile the women kept digging. The work became harder as the pit got deeper, and by the time the men returned with the salt on the second afternoon, the sides had to be shored up with branches to stop them falling in. Half teasingly, the men praised the women, but they didn't stay to help. Their excuse was that on their way back, already laden with salt, they had found a place where there were good cutter stones, so next morning they set out to collect them, leaving the women to work on alone.

On the fourth day there was a change. The crocodile wasn't on its island, and when they reached the inlet they found to their alarm that it had been ashore in the night. The barrier had been pushed aside in two places, and they could see the creature's huge footprints and the dragging groove of its tail all over the area around the pit. They rebuilt the barrier and Ko and Nar crouched tensely down to watch while Mana went to collect more rocks.

Almost at once the crocodile attacked. It came in a single rush, without warning, straight out of the water, lashing the surface to foam and beginning that awful pouncing leap as it burst through the middle of the barrier with the water still streaming from its dark scaly flanks. If Mana had been at her place it would surely have got her.

Ko had a stone ready in his hand. He yelled and flung it, and raced up the slope. The women were helping each other scramble from the pit, and then they were all fleeing from the attack. At the top of the slope they turned and watched the monster snuffling frustratedly around the pit, smelling the traces of the good fresh meat it hungered for.

Ko studied it, shuddering. Sometimes, when he was only thinking about it, he wondered if he wasn't making it even bigger in his imaginings than it really was. But he'd been right. It was massive and horrible. He wondered if the pit was going to be big enough to hold it, supposing the men could lure it into falling in. At last it gave up and dragged itself back to the water and disappeared. When they saw it climb out onto the nearest island they went back to work, with one of the children to keep an eye on it.

Twice more that morning it attacked, but it didn't seem to realize that the watcher could see when it left the island, so everyone was safely out of reach by the time it came ashore. The interruptions were maddening, because the women were determined to finish before the men came home that evening. So they worked on through the dense, steamy heat of midday, with the sweat streaming from them and a cloud of insects as thick as the marsh haze swarming around them.

By early afternoon the pit was deep enough and they started to roof it in with reeds, propping them up at the centre on twiggy branches. That took a long while. When the sun was more than halfway down the sky, and Ko was dragging an armful of cut reeds up the slope, he heard Nar call from the barrier. The crocodile had once again left its island. He dropped the reeds and was moving to safety when Chogi called to him from the pit.

'Ko, bring the reeds. Go to watch. Mana go too. Stay far from the water. Almost we finish. You see the crocodile. You shout. You run. We run. Say this to Nar.'

So the three watchers took up their posts well above the barrier, to give themselves enough of a start if the crocodile attacked again. Ko waited, tense as ever. By now he could judge almost exactly how long it would take the crocodile to cross from the island . . . Just a little longer . . .

'He is there,' called Mana, and pointed.

Ko saw it at almost the same moment, the slight churning of the still surface, ten and ten paces out, coming faster now . . .

'*Danger!*'

All three watchers shouted together. Ko was already running. Thc women were scrambling out of the pit, just ahead of him. He looked to the right. Mana was racing up the slope . . .

Where was Nar?

He glanced back. Nar was there, running too. But there was something wrong with his leg. The crocodile was already hurtling out of the water, leaping at the barrier, bursting through . . . It saw Nar limping ahead and turned towards him. Nar was too slow . . .

Suddenly his leg got better and he started to run, not up the slope but slantwise across it, straight into the crocodile's path. The crocodile was almost on him. It hummocked itself up into a final spring.

Nar flung himself violently to his left, almost at the edge of the pit. At once he was up and running on.

Behind him there was a tearing crash as the crocodile landed on the half-finished roof of the pit and tumbled through.

The women yelled and rushed down the slope. As they reached the pit the crocodile reared up out of it, scrabbling with its forelegs for a grip on the rim. Zara struck full force at its head with her digging stick. Yova picked up one of the big stones they'd laid ready, raised it two-handed over her head and flung it. The stone thudded into the monster's neck. It bellowed and fell back.

But it was huge. As Ko had thought, the pit wasn't really big enough to hold it. Left to itself it could have scrambled out without difficulty, but each time it tried the women drove it back. Ko darted in when he got the chance and flung anything he could find. Then the rim gave way on one side, right under Tinu's feet, but Yova caught her by the arm and hauled her to safety. The monster started to crawl up the slope, but Moru darted forward and struck at it from the side, right in the eye.

It bellowed with pain and rolled away, slithering back into the pit with its great tail lashing uselessly around, finishing half on its side amid the mess of reeds and branches in the bottom. Chogi and Yova were already heaving up a boulder so large that the two of them could barely lift it. Judging their moment they swung it out over the edge and let it fall. It struck the crocodile on the foreleg below the shoulder. There was another bellow of pain. The crocodile thrashed violently and managed to right itself, but the leg was now clearly broken, and when it tried to clamber up the slope it couldn't get a hold and fell back while more stones rained down on it, until there were none left to throw.

Women and children stood around the pit, panting, and waited for the monster to die. It made a few more feeble efforts to climb out, but at last simply lay and twitched, and then was still.

'We kill the crocodile,' said Chogi solemnly. 'We women do this.'

The men came back in the sunset, both parties together. Ko had gone up to the camp to wait for them, and from his watch place he saw them trudging wearily along the rough slope that led down to the marsh. From the way they walked he could tell that they had found no fresh Good Places.

Happily he ran to meet them and took Suth's hand.

'Do not go to the camp,' he said. 'Come to the inlet. There is a thing to see.'

'What thing, Ko?' said Suth, with a tired smile.

'The women finish the pit,' guessed Var, who was one of the ones who had seen it half dug.

'No,' said Ko. 'It is more, more. Come.'

Suth came, and the others followed. Ko raced ahead and shouted from the top of the slope, 'The men come! The men come! I do not tell them, *The crocodile is dead!*'

The women had been sitting at the top of the clearing, waving leafy twigs to keep the insects from settling. Now they rose and waited to greet the men, then led them to the pit.

The men gazed down, astounded.

'Chogi, this is good, good,' said Tun at last. 'Tonight we feast.'

By now it was getting dark, but Tun sent Nar to fetch hot embers down from the camp, and they built a small fire and lit twists of dry reed, one after another, to give them enough light to see what they were doing. With a huge effort they dragged the body out of the pit and paced out its length. From snout to tail-tip it was seven good paces.

Next they butchered off a section of the crocodile's tail, which they carried up to the camp and set to roast, while others piled rocks over the rest of the body to keep it safe.

Then they feasted. For the first time for several moons there was meat enough for everyone, and it was wonderful after days of plant stuff.

When they had eaten Tun rose and held up his hand for silence.

'Hear me,' he said. 'I, Tun, speak. We men went to the sunset. We went far and far. We found bad places, Demon Places, no food, foul water, marsh water. We come back. We are hungry, we are sad. Fear is in our stomachs.

'We find the women. They say happy words to us. They kill the crocodile. To you, men, I say, *This is a deed of heroes*. Let Chogi speak. Let her make her boast.'

Everyone shouted. Chogi rose and held up her hand and waited. She didn't look any different from usual, Ko thought, though he'd never heard of a leader inviting one of the women to boast like this.

'Hear me,' she said when everyone was silent. 'I, Chogi, speak. I speak for the women. I praise all the women. First I praise Tinu. She saw Ko fall into a pit. She said in her heart, *This way we kill the crocodile*. It is Tinu's thought. She is clever. Next I praise the women. I praise Yova, Zara, Dipu, Galo, Bodu, Runa, Moru, Noli, Shuja. We dug the pit. The work was hard, hard. I praise Tinu again. She made clever mats. They carried earth, much and much. I praise the children who watched for the crocodile. They watched well. They threw stones. They drove it away. I praise the boy Nar. Nar was clever. He was brave. The crocodile came from the water. We ran. We ran fast. Nar ran. He ran slow. He ran like a boy with a hurt leg. The crocodile sees him. It says in its heart, *This boy's leg is hurt. I catch him*. Nar runs to the pit. The crocodile is close, close. Nar jumps to the side. The crocodile does not see the pit. It falls in the pit.

'We women come. We fight the crocodile. We strike it with digging sticks. We hurl great rocks . . .'

Ko had stopped listening. He felt his heart would burst with shame and anger. He could have borne it, perhaps, if Chogi had just named and praised Nar, but why did she have to name Ko too, not for anything clever or brave he'd done, but only reminding everyone about that stupid business of falling into that hole? And she hadn't even bothered to name him for the scrap of praise she'd given him. He was just one of the children who'd kept lookout and driven the crocodile off with rocks. Ko was certain some of his rocks hadn't only scored hits – they'd actually hurt the monster, and scared it from attacking more in those first three days. *And* he'd helped in the fight round the pit . . . But all anyone was going to remember about his part in the adventure would be that he'd fallen into a stupid hole! And Tinu wouldn't even have been thinking about killing the crocodile if Ko hadn't asked her to . . .

And then, worse still, they let Nar stand up and make a separate boast of his own, and he did it well, not tongue-tied or stammering, as Ko had been when he'd accidentally driven off the lioness and saved Kern's life, but choosing good words and saying them easily.

Ko lay down to sleep still hurt, still furious. Strangely, his nightmare didn't return, but he woke in the early dawn with two fixed thoughts in his mind. Somehow he, Ko, was going to find a way across the marshes. And when he'd done that he was going to find a mate for Tinu. To prove to himself that he really meant it, when no one was looking he stole a small lump of the new salt and put it in his gourd, so that he would have it handy to give to Tinu and the man, whoever he was, when they chose each other.

Oldtale

BAGWORM

Tov journeyed west. The parrot went with him, the little grey parrot with the yellow tail feathers. All day it perched on his head and slept. The sun was behind him, and over him, and shone in his eyes, and his gourd was empty. He came to the place of Bagworm.

Bagworm lay in the desert. He was a great worm, and his belly was a bag. It was full of water. He put his ear to the ground, and heard footsteps. He said in his heart, One comes. He finds no water. He dies. I eat him.

He spewed his water onto the ground and crept away. Tov saw the water and ran towards it. Bagworm sucked with his mouth, and the water returned to his belly and was gone.

Again Tov saw water, and ran, and the water was not there. He said in his heart, This is magic stuff. But I am Tov.

A third time he saw water, but he did not run. He

said, 'Wake, little parrot. Fly high. See the water. Soon it goes. Follow it.'

The parrot flew high. Then Tov ran. Bagworm heard him and sucked with his mouth and drew the water to him. The parrot followed.

Now Tov went softly, following the parrot, until he came to the place where Bagworm lay. Tov came on him from behind, and leaped into the air, and landed on the great fatness of his belly, so that the water all spewed out.

Then Tov caught Bagworm by the throat and crammed his mouth with earth. With the butt of his digging stick he rammed it firm. Now Bagworm could not suck the water into himself.

Tov drank, and filled his gourd. He saw creatures in the water, whose name is fish. They are people food. He took them, and journeyed west.

At nightfall he camped, and ate fish until his belly was full. The parrot did not eat. Fish are not parrot food.

Tov said, 'Little parrot, I am weary. All day you slept on my head. Now keep watch while I sleep.'

Tov slept. The parrot perched on a rock at his feet. In the dark she became Falu. She was hungry, and ate the fish, spitting out the bones. Then she kept watch.

Tov woke. By the light of the stars he saw Falu, where she sat on the rock at his feet. He called, 'Gata?'

Falu answered, 'It is not Gata. She is far and far. Tov, you dream. Now sleep.'

Tov slept. When it was day, he woke and saw the

parrot, where it perched on the rock at his feet. Beside the rock he saw the bones of fish.

He said in his heart, I do not dream these bones. This parrot is clever, clever. But I am Tov.

CHAPTER SIX

The next morning, with great difficulty, the men cut the head off the crocodile, and set it on a pole beside the camp, to show what the women had done. Now that the monster was dead, they could safely harvest far more of the inlet, wading into the water if they needed to reach parts of the dense thickets that grew along the shoreline. And there was enough crocodile meat for several days, though it started to go bad almost at once in the steamy heat. But their stomachs were strong, and even when it truly stank they ate it without falling ill.

The extra food meant that they could now stay until Noli's baby was born, so they decided to wait.

Soon Ko was very restless. If he got the chance, he would sneak off down to the shoreline, looking for places where the mud seemed drier and firmer than elsewhere. Once he ventured out a few paces onto a dried mudbank, but then it got softer, and he remembered how suddenly Net had fallen through and just barely been dragged out, so, shuddering with fear, he edged his way back to safety.

But he found other patches where flattened tangles of reeds had fallen across the mud, and here the stems seemed to spread his weight so that he could walk with confidence. These patches didn't lead anywhere, of course, but suppose he cut a whole lot of reeds and laid them down as he went . . .

He was thinking about that one evening when he remembered the mats that Tinu had woven to carry the earth away when the women were digging the crocodile trap. The next day he went and found several of them still by the pit, not too battered. At his next chance he took them along to the main marsh and tried them out. They didn't feel safe only one layer thick, so he laid them down double, making a good, firm path three mats long, and carefully crawled onto it.

When he reached the end he realized that he could now drag the first pair of mats round and lay them down in front of him, and so move one mat farther. And again. And again.

He was ten and more paces out onto the mud before he lost his his nerve, and turned round and worked his way back until he could stand, quivering with relief, on solid ground and wipe the worst of the mud off his arms and legs.

I walk in the marsh, he thought as he sneaked back to join the others. *I, Ko, find the way. But it is slow, slow.*

Suth noticed his return.

'Ko, where do you go?' he asked.

'Suth, it is secret,' Ko answered.

Suth smiled. Ko guessed what he was thinking – *Boy stuff. Boys are full of their small secrets.* But this wasn't a small secret. It was big, big. Ko decided he wasn't going to tell anyone about it until he had actually reached the first island, a little west of the inlet.

For that he needed more mats. It was far too slow, crawling along with only three pairs of mats. If he had five pairs he could lay down a longer path and move three pairs at a time. That would be much faster.

When the men weren't foraging, they were making fresh cutters with the stones they'd brought back. Kern was teaching Nar how to do it, but Ko's hands weren't strong enough yet, so he'd asked Suth to make him a small cutter of his own. It was a good one, with an edge both sharp and strong, which would last some while before it blunted. No one thought there was anything unusual about Ko wanting to try it out – all boys were like that with cutters – and the obvious thing was for him to go off on his own and cut a few reeds, so it was easy for him to get away and carry on with his plan.

But making mats was much trickier than he'd thought. Ko copied Tinu's as carefully as he could, but his weren't nearly as good. It took him all his spare time in two days to make another pair, and he then decided that would have to be enough. On the third day he collected the eight mats and started off on his adventure. He was scared now, both of the danger and of what Suth would say about it, but he wasn't going to give up.

He had studied the island he was aiming for from

his lookout above the camp, just after sunrise when the mists had cleared, and before the haze hid the marshes again. It wasn't all that far from the shore across a level stretch of mud. And it had real trees on it.

So he didn't follow the shoreline, but went some distance up along the slope, because from there he could see the tree tops poking above the haze. As he came opposite them and was about to start down to the marsh, a little swirling dust storm came scurrying out of the hills, straight towards him. Just in time he flung his mats on the ground and knelt on them so that they shouldn't be carried away, and then crouched with his hands over his face while a hail of grit and twigs, caught up by the flurry, slashed against his skin.

In a few moments it was gone, and he rose and watched it whirl crazily down the slope and out into the marsh, tearing the haze apart and leaving a clear patch which moved across the mudbank, dying as it went. It vanished just as it reached the island, so Ko caught only a glimpse of its eastern tip. But in that glimpse he saw a man.

The man was standing on one leg, at the edge of the water, still as a heron. His other leg was bent, with the sole of that foot resting against the straight knee. His right arm was raised to his shoulder, holding a long, slim stick. His head was bent, peering at the water. Ko understood at once that he was doing what herons do. He was fishing.

Then the haze closed up and hid him.

Of course Ko knew what he ought to do. He should run at once and tell Suth and Tun what he had seen.

But he wasn't going to. He told himself the man was there now. By the time he'd reached the others and brought them back, the man might be gone. And there were only eight mats. They wouldn't be strong enough to carry the weight of a grown man. But if Ko could reach the island and watch this stranger, without himself being seen, and perhaps follow him when he left . . .

Why?

Because the man must have got to the island somehow. That meant he knew a way across the marshes!

Before he could change his mind Ko ran down to the shore, chose a place and laid the first pair of mats on the mud. He crawled onto them, reached back for the next pair, and then the next, and the next. Only when he'd crawled back to fetch the first two pairs, and so cut himself off from firm ground, did he hesitate, biting his lip. It still wasn't too late to go and fetch Suth.

No. He, Ko, was going to do this thing.

So he set off, working as he had the day before, moving his little path steadily out across the mud. Soon he was in a rhythm. The surface was caked hard, and he could barely feel it move when he crawled forward onto the next pair of mats. Now he could see the island, a vague brownish mass in the dense haze. And looking back he could no longer see the shore. He must be halfway there, at least

Then the surface changed, becoming softer and stickier. His mats became clogged with mud, and when he dragged them forward they started to fall apart with their own weight. He did his best to be careful, but each time he moved one it became looser, and pieces fell away. The two he had made himself were useless almost at once . . .

He looked back, and saw nothing but mud and the sticky ooze he had crossed. He looked ahead and the reedbed that lined the island seemed very near. He could see the individual stems. He would have to get there. His mats wouldn't last long enough to get him back to the shore. Perhaps he could make himself fresh ones on the island.

For the last few paces he abandoned the ruined mats and lay on his belly and squirmed his way forward over the stinking, clinging ooze, until he could haul himself out onto a layer of fallen reed stems.

With intense relief he stood and walked carefully along beside the dense tangle of growing reeds, looking for an opening. But after a little while the mudbank ended at a patch of open water, so he was forced to turn back. He chose a place where the tangle didn't look quite as hopeless as elsewhere and started to wrestle his way through the reedbed.

It was horrible. Soon he could scarcely move. With a great effort he would force his way through a gap, find himself trapped, struggle on a little further, and be trapped again. The sweat streamed down. Swarms of insects, disturbed by his efforts, gathered eagerly round him. He could no longer tell which way he was heading. He felt helpless, desperate, terrified, utterly alone. Even if he got free of the reeds, he'd never get back across the mud. The others would never find where he was. He was going to die, caught in this horrible place, this Demon Place – stupid, stupid Ko.

To his shame he started to sob. His breath as he dragged it in moaned in his throat. His tears blinded him. He groped forward.

And something caught him by the wrist.

He yelped with the shock of it, and in the next instant realized that the thing was a hand. It dragged him forward and flung him down on a patch of clear ground. He heard a hiss like the hiss of an angry snake and looked up, raising his arm against the expected blow.

Through the blur of his tears he saw a face. It was the face of a demon.

His mouth wrenched itself open, but the scream jammed in his throat. The face was the shape of a man's face, but striped bright yellow, like the tail of a parrot, and with purple blotches round the eyes.

The demon snorted. Ko cringed, and then some corner of his mind that hadn't frozen with terror recognized the sound. It was almost the same snort that Tor used when he was surprised or puzzled by something new to him. Tor didn't have words. He couldn't say, 'What is this?' Instead, he snorted.

Ko's voice came back to him.

'I . . . I . . . I . . . Ko . . .'

All he could think of was to offer the demon a gift. He knew that in the old days, when a Kin came to a Good Place that belonged to some other Kin, this was what they used to do. He scrabbled in his gourd and found a hard lump. Yes, the bit of salt he'd stolen. Salt was a real gift. He cupped it in his hands and offered it to the demon.

The demon snorted again with surprise and took it. The hand didn't have great, hooked talons, like a demon's in the Oldtales, but ordinary fingers, people fingers. There was a yellow circle on the back of it, but seeing it up close Ko realized that wasn't the colour of the skin. It was some sort of yellow stuff that had been smeared on. The skin itself was brown, not as dark as Ko's, but like Tor's skin.

The demon was a man. He had coloured stuff smeared onto him to make him look like a demon.

With a gasp of relief Ko watched the man raise the salt to his mouth and lick it, and then grunt. Again Ko recognized the sound. It wasn't the same, but it was something like the grunt Tor used to mean he was pleased.

Feeling much better, Ko rose to his feet and stood while he and the man looked at each other. Now that he wasn't stupid with terror Ko saw that the man could easily have been one of Tor's people, the Porcupines. He was taller and skinnier than Tor himself, but he had the same thin face and sharp, hooked nose and protruding teeth. After a while he looked at the lump of salt in his palm and offered it back to Ko with a questioning grunt, as if he wasn't sure Ko meant him to keep it.

Feeling steadily more confident, Ko raised both hands, palms forward, fingers spread, and moved them towards the man. At the same time he made a brief double hum in his throat, the second part lower than the first. This was more Porcupine stuff. The Porcupines were always giving each other small gifts. It was one of the things they did instead of talking. Ko had once seen three of them passing the same coloured pebble to and fro all through a rest time, and then when they'd moved on they'd left it behind. It had been the giving that had mattered, not the gift.

The man made his pleased sound again, even louder. He was wearing what looked like a strip of reed leaf round his waist. From it dangled several short wooden tubes, not any kind of wood Ko knew, but more like very thick reed stems. Some of them were stoppered with a wad of leaf. The man opened one, dropped the salt into it, and stoppered it up. He picked up his long stick and turned, gesturing to Ko to follow him, then led the way along the narrow path on which they'd been standing.

It came out on the open space at the tip of the island, where Ko had first glimpsed the man. Here he kneeled and moved some fallen reeds aside, revealing three fish. He chose one, bit a chunk from its back, took the morsel out of his mouth and offered it to Ko.

Ko knew about fish. There'd been some in the river that ran through the New Good Places. The Porcupines had sometimes managed to catch one in their bare hands, but the Kin hadn't bothered until the river started to dry up and they found them stranded in pools. Ko made the *I thank* noise and chewed the mouthful up. It was very good.

The man went back to what he'd been doing before, standing one-legged, motionless, right at the tip of the island, staring at the water.

Ko waited. An insect settled on his neck and bit. He slapped it, and instantly the man turned his head and hissed for silence, then returned to his fishing. Ko moved back along the path as far as he could without losing sight of him, picked up a broken piece of reed to use as a swat, and waited again.

Time passed. The man seemed not to move a muscle, not even to breathe. This is good hunting, thought Ko. There was a saying among the Kin, *The hunter is strong – good. The hunter is swift – better. The hunter is still – best.* People were always telling Ko that, because he wasn't very good at stillness.

But now he did his very best to be almost as still as the man. It wasn't just that he didn't want to be left alone on this horrible island, with no way back to the Kin. But also, having got this far, having started to make friends, Ko wasn't going to give up easily. The man had to know the way across the marshes. There would never be a better chance of finding it.

The stillness ended in a movement as sudden and sharp as the strike of a snake. The left arm shot out. The bent leg straightened into a huge stride. The body flung forward, with the right arm hurling the long stick ahead of it, out and down, in a thrust that lanced it cleanly into the water. An instant later the man splashed in behind it and disappeared under the foam.

When he came up he was grasping a fish in both hands. Ko had never seen one as large. It was as long as his arm, with a gaping jaw and thin, curving teeth. The man's stick was still in it, piercing it through, but it was alive and thrashing around in the water while the man fought to hold it. Somehow he shifted his grip and got both hands on his stick, one on each side of side of the fish's body, and then dragged it to the bank and heaved it ashore. Ko ran and caught it by the tail and hauled it well clear of the water while the man climbed out. Laughing with triumph the man put his foot close behind the head, pulled the stick out and stabbed down, piercing the fish through again but this time pinning it to the ground. It lay there, flopping and gasping, and at last was still.

While they waited for it to die Ko looked at the stick. It was taller than the man, about as thick as Ko's thumb and very straight but with knobby rings at intervals along it. He thought it must be another kind of reed. What impressed him was how sharp it must be, to pierce clean through a big fish like that, and how good for throwing. It was lucky the man hadn't thought Ko was some kind of animal while he was struggling among the reeds, making all that noise. He could easily have thrown his stick at the sound. Or perhaps Ko had been lucky to be weeping aloud, making the sort of noise that only people make.

It looked as if the man thought he'd now done enough hunting for the day. As soon as the fish was dead, he picked it up with his stick still through it, then threaded the three smaller fish onto the point. He lifted the stick and its load onto his shoulder, nodded to Ko and made a double grunt. Again it was a bit different from the Porcupines', but close enough for Ko to realize it meant both *I go* and *Goodbye*.

'I come too,' said Ko firmly. He had no intention of being left behind.

The man looked puzzled, but Ko didn't waste time trying to explain what he meant with signs. Knowing Tor and the Porcupines so well, he realized that this wasn't the sort of thing he could quickly get across to this man.

'Tor is not like Tinu,' Noli had once explained. 'Tinu's mouth is hurt. It cannot make good words. But Tinu has words in her head. Tor does not have words in his head. There is no place for them. I make signs with my hands. These signs are hand words. You understand my signs. For you it is easy. For Tor it is hard, hard.'

So now Ko guessed it would be no use tapping his own chest and then pointing across the marshes to say *I want you to take me over there*. Instead he simply grasped the man's free hand and started off along the path. The man still looked puzzled, but he came. The path wasn't wide enough for two, so Ko let go of the man's hand, waited for him to pass, and then followed him. The man looked round, shrugged, and walked on.

Oldtale

STONEJAW

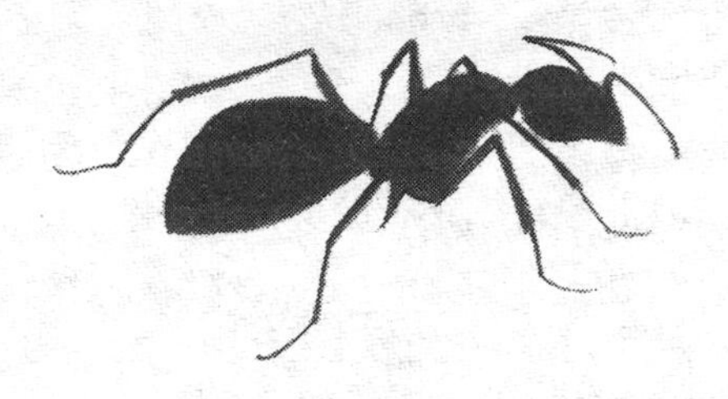

Tov journeyed west. The parrot sat on his head, and slept. The sun was behind him, and over him, and shone in his face, and his gourd was empty. He came to the place of Stonejaw.

There he saw a great rock. That was the head of Stonejaw. There was no body, no arms, no legs, only the head. In the rock was a cave. That was the mouth of Stonejaw. Out of it came his song.

Come into my cave.
In it is water.
Hear the sweet water.
It is cool, cool.

The song was magic. When Tov heard it he forgot the skills of the hunter. He ran to the cave, not looking, not seeing.

The parrot woke and screeched in Tov's ear, so that he could not hear Stonejaw's song. Now he looked and saw. He said in his heart, This is Stonejaw. The cave is his mouth.

Beside the cave Tov saw a great rock. He rolled it into the mouth of the cave, between the jaws of Stonejaw. Then he walked through.

The jaws closed on the rock, but could not close further. Tov went to the water and drank, and filled his gourd. Beside the water he saw a dead gazelle, a gazelle of the desert. Stonejaw had caught it. Tov took it and carried it out of the cave.

He said, 'Come, little parrot. We have food, we have water. Stonejaw, farewell.'

Tov camped, and ate of the gazelle. The parrot did not eat. Gazelle are not parrot food.

Tov said, 'Little parrot, all day you slept on my head. Now I sleep. You watch.'

When he lay down he put a sharp thorn beneath his ribs. He did not sleep.

In the dark the parrot became Falu. She was hungry, and ate of the gazelle, sucking the marrow from the bones. The noise was loud. Tov heard it, and opened his eyes, and saw her where she sat sucking the marrow bone. He crept softly towards her and caught her by the wrist.

Falu cried aloud. She said, 'Tov, let me go.'

Tov said, 'I do not let you go. Soon it is morning. I see who you are.'

Falu wept. She said, 'Tov, do not do this. You hold me, you see me. Then your parrot dies, the little grey parrot with the yellow tail feathers.'

Tov said in his heart, I cannot do this. I need my little parrot. She is clever, clever.

He let go of Falu's wrist, and lay down and slept. In the morning Falu was a parrot again.

CHAPTER SEVEN

The path came out on the far side of the island. Looking past the man, Ko could see a stretch of mud, and beyond it another island. The man stepped confidently onto the mud, and at once started to sink. The mud closed over his foot, but then he stopped sinking and took another pace, and another, checking his foothold each time before he moved on.

Ko followed him, stepping exactly in his footprints, and found that there was something solid just below the surface. Curious, he stopped after a while, balanced on one leg and carefully felt down with his other foot beside the line of footprints. There was nothing there, and nothing on the other side, only this single narrow path.

He bent and probed through the mud with his fingers and felt around. The solid stuff seemed to be a thick layer of reeds, laid all in the same direction. That couldn't have happened by accident. He realized that they must have been put here.

He hurried after the man, before the mud could close over the footprints. Looking back he saw that it had already done so where they'd started from the first island. So if you didn't know exactly where the path was, you couldn't use it.

On the far side of the next island there was a more open shoreline. Some way along it two women were fishing, using sticks like the man's. The man called to them. They turned, stared for a moment, and came running.

The man showed them the fish he'd caught and they clapped their hands and made the chortling *wo-wo-wo-wo* that Tor used when he wanted to praise someone. They hugged him, and fawned on him and stroked him, while he laughed with triumph. Their faces weren't coloured like the man's, but they wore the same sort of belt that he did, with the wooden tubes on it. One of them had a baby inside her. Ko guessed she must be the man's mate, but he was puzzled by the other one, because she was behaving in exactly the same way. She looked a bit younger than Noli, but he didn't think the man was old enough to be her father.

When they'd finished letting the man know how wonderful he was they turned and stared at Ko, making sounds of astonishment. They bent and sniffed him and poked him, and the younger one licked his skin, and then rubbed hard at the place with her fingers, while he tried to squirm free. The other two watched, laughing, until she realized that Ko's skin colour wouldn't come off, and gave up.

They set off together in single file, winding from island to island, mostly using the hidden paths across the mudbanks, but sometimes wading through water up to their waists. After a while they came to another of these open channels and Ko saw a group of people standing on the shore of the next island. The three Ko was with stopped and squatted to watch, making quiet mutters of excitement, though as far as he could see the other group weren't doing anything special. Then he noticed that one of the men was crouched down, holding one end of a fishing stick with its other end beneath the water, and jiggling it gently to and fro.

Nothing happened for a while. The usual horrible insects gathered and settled and stung. Ko switched at them with a piece of reed. The marsh people didn't seem bothered by them. The air was dense and hot and steamy. He couldn't see the sun, but it must be high overhead. The Kin would be having their midday rest. No, they'd have noticed by now that Ko was missing. They'd be angry and worried and unhappy, and they'd be looking for him despite the heat. They'd find the trail he'd left with his mats on the dried mud near the shore. Perhaps they'd see the bits of broken mat far out across the marsh. They'd think he'd sunk in the mud out there, and drowned. *Stupid, stupid Ko*, they'd say. He said it now to himself. *Stupid, stupid Ko*. Why hadn't he run and told Suth about seeing the man on the island? He felt very miserable and alone and far away from his friends.

Now the man he was with picked up the big fish and began to chew at its back. He had trouble getting started, because he couldn't get his mouth round it, so Ko felt in his gourd and offered him his cutter. It was already a bit blunt, after cutting all those reeds for the mats, but there were still some sharp places on its edge. The man frowned at it, puzzled, until Ko knelt by the fish and sliced a chunk out and gave it to him, then did the same for each of the women. Though he didn't feel hungry he cut a small piece for himself. The man took the cutter and felt its edge with his thumb, grunted approvingly and handed it back.

Then he opened one of his belt tubes, took out the lump of salt Ko had given him, and crumbled a few crystals onto his piece of fish. Immediately the women started wheedling for some for themselves, and very grudgingly he broke them off a few grains each, but when they begged for more he snorted crossly and shook his head.

Ko groped again in the bottom of his gourd and found several crystals that had fallen off the main chunk, so he scraped them out and gave them to the women, who crowed with delight over them.

Suddenly there was a shout from the other bank. Ko's three guides were on their feet, jumping with excitement. He ran to look. The man with the stick was standing up now, straining back to stop himself from being pulled into the water. A couple of others were helping. Several more had jumped in. There was a flurry of splashing, and glistening arms and bodies heaving about as they struggled with something below the surface. The stick came loose, and the three holding it tumbled on their backs. The ones in the water were lifting a large creature out, working all together as it thrashed around, and now Ko could see that it was a crocodile, a small one, not much longer than his own body. Despite that, it took six people to hold it, one to each leg, one to the tail, and one to grip the jaw and hold it shut.

They hauled it onto the bank and pinned it down while one of the men stabbed it again and again through the eye sockets until it was dead.

Now Ko's party picked up their fish and waded in and crossed, splashing the water around and shrieking and yodelling as they went. Ko was pretty scared. He guessed this must be a bad crocodile area. None of the Kin would have dreamed of wading into water like this. But he wasn't going to be left behind, so he followed, keeping as close as he could and shrieking and splashing like the others, and climbed out onto the far bank with a sigh of relief.

Everyone gathered round the dead crocodile. They were mostly men, all with differently coloured faces, and a few women who were hugging and stroking some of the men, and making *Praise* noises to them. The man who seemed to be the chief hunter was standing proudly with his foot on the crocodile, and he had three women to himself, while others had none.

Ko stared at the scene, bewildered. And then an extraordinary thought came to him. Perhaps these men had more than one mate each. His friend had two, and this chief hunter had three. Which must mean that some of the other men had none at all! Ko couldn't imagine how anyone could live like that. It was too weird.

At first the new people were too excited by their catch to notice him, but when they did they weren't friendly. They made their sounds of surprise, and some of them prodded and rubbed his skin, but they snatched at him when they wanted to look at him and shoved him roughly away when they'd done.

Then one man tried to grab Ko before another had finished with him and neither of them would let go. He yelled as he was pulled to and fro, until the man he'd first met joined in and there was the sort of snarling match he'd often seen among the Porcupines, because they didn't have words to argue with. In the middle of it one of the men gave a sudden jerk and got Ko to himself, but then just slung him aside while he went on with the snarling match.

Ko crashed into someone's legs and fell, half stunned. As he struggled up, determined not to let anyone see the tears that were starting to come, a hand took his arm and pulled him, much more gently, away from the men. It was the younger of the two women he'd come with. She patted him comfortingly and pushed him behind her until the spat was over.

When the man joined them, she and the other woman stroked him and cooed at him for a bit, as if he'd done something almost as wonderful as catching the big fish, and then they left the hunting party to their celebrations and moved on.

Soon the journey became easier. The hidden paths across the mudbanks were firmer, and nearer the surface, and the trails through the reedbeds and islands were wider. From time to time Ko saw people fishing from different islands, both men and women, standing in that one-legged heron pose, waiting in total stillness. Though he could see that what they were doing was a kind of hunting, it seemed very different from the sort of hunting he was used to. His sense of loneliness deepened. He didn't understand these marsh people at all. He felt as helpless as a baby in their world.

And he was completely lost, more lost than he'd ever been in his life, among the shapeless tangle of reedbeds and islands, and with no way of knowing where the sun was, above the dense haze. At last they came to somewhere different, a much larger patch of open water with a cluster of small islands in the middle of it, just mounds rising above the water, almost bare of reeds or trees, with people moving about on them.

Ko couldn't see any way across to the islands, but the man led them on round the edge of the water until they came to what looked like a long, narrow mudbank running out from the reedbeds to the nearest island, with a reed path laid along the top. As they approached the place Ko's guides each scooped up a handful of mud, and then as they crossed to the island they chose a spot and put the mud down and carefully stamped it in to strengthen the path.

These people were clever, Ko thought. They didn't have words, or know about cutters, but they knew a lot of things that the Kin didn't know. They must have built the hidden paths through the marshes and chosen these islands for their lair, and made them safe for themselves.

Where the path reached the first island there was a strange, low wall, with a gap in the middle, and a row of poles behind it with objects on top of them. As he came nearer, Ko saw that these were crocodile heads – and then, with a thud of the heart, that the whole wall was also made of crocodile heads. Some of them were so old that the flesh and hide had fallen away, leaving only the grinning white skulls. None of them was half as big as the monster that the Kin had killed, but there were tens and tens and tens of them.

Ko found them really scary. They gave the entrance the look of a demon place. But the man simply halted at the gap, touched the snout of the largest skull with his hand and led the way on. The women followed without any fuss, so Ko did the same.

There were several women and a lot of children on the island, who cried out the moment they saw Ko and came crowding round, sniffing and touching him and muttering with surprise. Then a man came striding through, pushing them roughly aside. His face, too, was coloured like a demon's. He stared at Ko, snorted with anger, grabbed him by the shoulder and flung him back towards the entrance.

Immediately a ferocious snarling match began between the two men, but as Ko picked himself up he could at once see who was going to win it. This new man was older and more important than Ko's guide, who was already backing away from him when the two women took Ko by the arms and hustled him down to the water and along the edge of the island to another path. This led to a smaller island which they crossed, again going round by the edge, and so on, past two more islands, till they reached one right at the outside of the group, where they let go of him and put their burdens down. Ko guessed that this must be their home. A few moments later the man arrived, looking both anxious and angry.

The three marsh people did their usual petting and stroking as they settled down, and then the man laid his fish on the ground and pointed at Ko's gourd and made a *Give* sound. Guessing what he meant, Ko took out his cutter and handed it across. Awkwardly, because he wasn't used to the tool, the man hacked off pieces of fish for everyone. Scraping in the bottom of his gourd, Ko found enough crumbs of salt for himself and the two women.

The whole surface of the island was littered with scraps and splinters of reed, and when they'd had enough to eat the women scooped a hollow in this, laid what was left of the fish in it and covered it over. The man settled down to sharpening his fishing stick by rubbing it with a short piece of pole dipped in gritty mud. The women made storage tubes from pieces of reed, using their teeth to nibble the splintered ends clean. All three seemed jumpy and kept glancing anxiously towards the large island by the entrance path.

After a while Ko heard rhythmic shouts floating across the water, mixed in with a strange rattling noise a bit like a lot of woodpeckers tapping on a hollow tree. The three marsh people jumped up and stared. Ko followed their gaze and saw a procession winding its way through the reed beds on the far side. The man took Ko by the shoulders and gave him a firm push to tell him to stay where he was, and then he and the two women hurried off towards the entrance.

Ko waited and watched. The procession was mostly hidden by reeds until it reached the path across the water. Then he saw that the men at the front were marching close together in single file with something held at arm's length above their heads. It was the body of the crocodile they had caught. People were running out onto the path to meet it, and then dancing back in front of it. The rattling sound increased, but Ko still couldn't see how it was made. Killing a crocodile must be a big thing among these people, he realized. He wished he could have shown them the monster that the Kin had killed.

He waited for a long time, until the grey haze started to turn to gold, and he realized that soon it would be sunset. The colour was deeper on the side away from the entrance, so he reckoned that had to be west. He settled down with his chin on his knees and watched the slow change. It filled him with sadness. Though he seemed for the moment to be in a place of safety, he felt very, very lonely. This was the time of day when the weary foragers and hunters would be coming home to their lair, and roasting the meat they had caught, and pounding roots and seeds. Then they would eat, with the firelight flickering on the dark faces, and the eyes glinting with reflected sparks, and talk and tease and boast – Ko's people in Ko's world, a world he understood, his home. Not this dense, steaming marsh, these strangers, with their uncomfortable customs . . .

New shouts, different, angry.

Coming nearer.

He rose and turned, and saw the two women running across the nearest island, followed by their man. Close behind them came several more men, yelling furiously. The women dashed across the connecting path, but the man stopped when he was halfway over, and turned and faced the attackers. He had no weapons, but he stood in a fighting pose with his hair bushed right out and bellowed at them.

Ko watched, terrified. This had to be something to do with him. Now that the men were back from the crocodile hunt their leader had brought them to get Ko. They didn't want this strange child in their place. They were going to kill him, or else throw him off their islands, out into the dreadful marshes, alone in the night. That would be almost as bad.

They halted, yelling, on the shore. Their leader pushed through onto the path and confronted Ko's host. Ko expected him to back down, as he'd done when the same thing had happened on the main island, but he stood his ground, snarling. *This is my island*, he seemed to be saying. *On it I am leader, not you*. The women watched, murmuring anxiously. The older one grabbed Ko's arm and pulled him behind her, where he couldn't be seen.

After a little while the other man snorted and turned away, and the attackers moved off, growling. Ko's host strutted back onto the island and the women petted and praised him, but he stood frowning at Ko, until Ko knelt in front of him and rapped his knuckles together, three times, as he'd have done if he'd been asking a favour of his own leader, Tun.

'I, Ko, thank,' he said. 'Also I, Ko, ask. Tomorrow I go. You show me the way.'

He twisted and pointed south, to show what he meant. The man grunted uncertainly, but rumpled Ko's hair for a moment, and Ko felt he was trying to tell him he would look after him if he could.

By now it was almost dark. The women scooped a

large hollow in the reed-litter and the three marsh people settled into it, lying close together with the man in the middle. Ko made himself a hollow of his own and lay down in that strange and frightening place, longing with everything that was in him to be away from there, lying among his own people, close to the good red embers of their fire. He wept quietly in the dark, and fell asleep still weeping.

He was shaken awake, and had no idea where he was. His left side was covered with insect bites. A woman's voice grunted softly and he remembered. He sat up and looked around.

It was dark still. The heat haze was gone, and the familiar stars overhead shone almost clear. To the east the sky was faintly grey. Now the woman, softly again, made her *Come* sound. Ko rose, groped for his gourd and slung it over his shoulder. He followed the other three down to the path and across to the first island. They worked their way round it, paddling at the very edge of the water, and so on to the main entrance, never setting foot on anyone else's island. By the time they reached the reed beds it was almost light. Ko saw that the younger woman was carrying the half-eaten fish.

The man led the way in silence, not stopping till they had crossed several more islands. Then they paused only long enough to hack off four portions of fish, and moved on, chewing as they went. As the sun rose the heat haze formed, and soon Ko lost all sense of direction once more. All this time the man had barely looked at him, and Ko began to have a sick feeling that he was just being taken away into the marshes, to be got rid of, and then he'd be left to find his own way home. But the women stayed friendly, especially the younger one, and after a while he recognized the place where the crocodile had been killed, so he started to feel much better. He was going home.

More mud flats, islands, reedbeds, water crossings. And then, on yet another path across yet another island, the man stopped. All three of Ko's guides turned and looked at him. The man grunted, *All right?* Ko frowned and looked around, and saw that this was the place where the man had first met him, fighting his way through the reeds.

But how was he going to get off the island, across that last dreadful stretch of mud? Perhaps the man knew a way.

Come, he grunted, doing his best to imitate the way the marsh people made the sound. He led them along the path to the tip of the island where the man had been fishing. The haze wasn't yet quite thick enough to hide the solid land where he'd set out. Ko pointed at it and made the light, anxious sounding moan that meant *I beg*.

The man frowned, snorted uncertainly and turned back along the path. Halfway down it he stopped and studied the reeds on his left, shook his head, moved on a little further, grunted and pushed his way in. As he followed the others Ko realized that they must be using an old path, now partly overgrown, but still nothing like the impossible tangle of reeds to either side.

They came out directly opposite the land, with only

a few tens of paces of mud still to cross. The man prodded around with the butt of his fishing stick, nodded, and stepped out onto the mud. He sank deeper in than usual, halfway up his shin, but then found solid footing. He took a couple of paces more, but this time the women didn't follow him, and he turned and came back. Once more all three of them looked at Ko. This was an old hidden path across the mud, they seemed to be telling him. If he was careful he should be able to use it on his own. The man took his shoulder and gave him a push towards it.

Ko grunted, *I thank*, and felt in his gourd for a gift. He had nothing left except his cutter, so a bit reluctantly he offered it to the man, who took it without hesitation, obviously pleased. The women were watching, waiting. They didn't seem to expect anything, but Ko felt strongly that he ought to give them something too. They'd stood by him just as much as the man had, and been friendly too.

At least he could show them he didn't have anything else to give, so he tipped his gourd out over his cupped palm. Several grains of salt glittered amid the other crumbs. Not nearly enough for a gift, but the women pressed eagerly forward and picked them out and put them on their tongues with little gasps of pleasure.

Ko had a sudden thought. There was plenty of salt at the camp, if he could persuade them to come there. And then perhaps Ko could fetch Tun and Suth and the others to meet him. And then, wonderfully, he might show them the way through the marshes.

And it would be all Ko's doing.

Before the women could grab the last couple of

grains he closed his fingers over them and held them tight. With his other hand he tapped the knuckles, and then pointed out across the mud.

The women were trying to pry his fingers open, laughing at their game. He snatched his fist out of reach and pointed again and made the encouraging *food* noises that Porcupine parents used to call their children to come and eat.

They stopped laughing and stared at him, and at his cupped hand when he opened it and showed them the salt and pointed again. They stared out at the dimly seen slope of hill beyond the mudbank, and he realized they'd understood.

So had the man, and he obviously didn't like the idea. The women took his hands and wheedled, but he pulled them away, grunting angrily. They fell on their knees and stroked him and fawned on him, until he gave a heavy, exasperated sigh and led the way onto the last hidden path.

Oldtale

THE FATHER OF SNAKES

Tov journeyed north. The parrot sat on his head. It slept. The sun shone on their right, and was over them, and they came to a great hole. Beside it was a tree, a tree of the desert, that does not die. This was the place of Fododo, the Father of Snakes.

Tov said, 'Hide, little parrot. Birds are snake food.'

The parrot flew into the tree and hid.

Tov put his hands to his mouth and called, loud, loud, 'Fododo, come out of your hole.'

Fododo heard, and came. His body was ten and ten paces long, and ten and ten and ten more. His width was the width of a man's body, and his colour was white, like bone, an old bone in the desert.

He looked at Tov, and the look was magic. Tov could not move.

Fododo said, 'Tov, you are a great fool.'

Tov said, 'You know my name. How is this?'

Fododo said, 'I know all, all.'

Tov said, 'I, Tov, know a thing. You, Fododo, do not know it. It is this. There is one. Day comes. This one has laughter and no words. She has wings and no arms. Night comes. This one has words, she has laughter. She has arms and no wings. Fododo, Father of Snakes, who is this one? You do not know.'

It was true, and thus Fododo lost his magic. Above his head the parrot cried. Its cry was laughter. Fododo looked up, and Tov could move. He ran behind the tree, quick, quick.

The parrot flew down in front of the head of Fododo. He struck at her, but she flew behind him. He followed her with his head, close, close, but she flew under and over and round, and again, and yet again. All the time Fododo followed her with his head.

Then she flew up into the tree, and he reached to catch her. But his body was now a great knot. Reaching, he pulled it tight, so that he could not move.

Tov came out from behind the tree, and went behind Fododo and took him by the neck. Fododo opened his mouth to bite him, but Tov was ready. He thrust his digging stick between the jaws of Fododo, from the side, so that the poison fangs were in front of the stick.

Tov took hold of the left fang and pulled hard, hard. The fang came out, and Tov held it and rejoiced. He took his stick from the jaws of Fododo. Still Fododo could not move.

Tov said, 'Come, little parrot, we have finished.' He left.

Fododo called after him, 'Tov, be careful, careful. My fang is full of death.'

Tov answered, 'Fododo, you are right. But it it is not the death of Tov, nor of his parrot.'

CHAPTER EIGHT

By now it was mid-morning. Ko guessed that everyone would be foraging down at the inlet, but as he led the way up the slope he heard a shout to his left and saw Mana running towards him. He made *Wait* signs to the marsh people and raced to meet her. They flung their arms round each other and hugged close. Ko was so happy to see her that it took him a while to realize she was sobbing.

He held her by the shoulders and looked at her.

'You cry, Mana,' he said. 'Why is this? I come back. I am happy, happy.'

'Oh, Ko,' she sobbed. 'I look for you long, long. I say in my heart *Ko is dead*. I am sad, sad.'

She took his hand.

'Come,' she said. 'See Suth, see Noli, see Tinu. Oh, Ko, we are sad!'

'No,' he said. 'First you greet these people. They bring me back. Mana, they are like Tor. They do not have words. Then I take them to our lair. I give them salt. It is my thank gift. You go to Suth. You tell him *Ko is back.*'

He took her to meet the marsh people and she knelt and pattered her hands on the ground in front of the man, as she would have on greeting an important man from the Kin. He looked puzzled, but more confident. There was no way he could be afraid of Mana.

She rose and put her arms round Ko and made *Thank you* sounds to the women, and then ran off, while Ko led the way on. The moment they reached the ridge and could see the camp below them, the man halted and gave a sharp bark. All three stared wide eyed down the slope. Ko followed their gaze, bewildered. There was nobody down at the camp, nothing but the embers of the fire, and the crocodile head on its pole . . .

Of course, the crocodile head! Ko remembered what a celebration there'd been when the marsh people had brought home the little crocodile they'd caught – and the crocodile heads on the poles around the entrance to their lair, none of them anything like the size of this monster.

The man turned and stared at Ko. Ko smiled confidently.

'We kill the crocodile,' he said. 'Our women do it. I, Ko, help.'

He tapped himself on the chest. It was good to be able to boast a bit in front of this man, after all that grovelling and pleading in the marshes. He made the *Come* sound and started down the slope. The marsh people followed, murmuring doubtfully, and then hanging back, and finally stopping completely.

Ko waited. He wasn't impatient. He needed them still to be here when Suth came, because that would put off the time when Ko had to face him alone. And surely, however bad he'd been, Suth would see that some good had come of it, and be easier on him because, after all, he had found the marsh people. Didn't that count for something?

So he watched the man gesture to the women to stay where they were, and then walk with slow, stiff strides towards the crocodile head. A few paces from it he stopped and barked, three times, with long pauses between each bark. Then he knelt and crawled to the pole and knocked his forehead on the ground at its foot, and finally rose and stood directly in front of the monster. He raised his right arm in a kind of salute and stood in silence for a while.

Very slowly, like a man going through some kind of big test in front of his whole Kin, he moved his hand forwards and rested the fingers against the monster's snout, waited a little and withdrew it. Still saluting he took several slow paces backward, knelt, knocked his forehead on the ground again, and then rose and came back to the women.

They fawned on him as usual, but this time with gentle, wondering movements, as if he were part of something magical. Each of them took a hand, and together they led him to join Ko, and then on into the camp, where they carefully sat him down as if he couldn't do even that for himself.

Ko didn't interrupt. He had some idea what was happening. Noli often needed help like that after Moonhawk had come to her. The man had been doing First One stuff. So Ko quietly went and fetched three small blocks of salt from under the rock where it was stored, and then waited until the man gave a violent shudder, and sneezed, and shook his head and stared around as if he had no idea where he was, until his eye fell on the crocodile and he remembered.

He grunted and looked questioningly at Ko. Ko went over and formally presented him with the largest chunk of salt. The man took it and thanked him and then just as formally gave Ko back his own cutter, and Ko thanked him as if he'd never seen it before. Quickly he gave the two women their salt. They crowed with delight, but instead of thanking him they fawned on him, the same way they did on the man, while the man looked on benignly.

They hadn't finished when Ko saw Suth loping up from the inlet. He signed to the man to stay where he was and ran to meet him. Suth stopped and waited, making Ko come to him. Ko had seen him looking angry before, but never so stern.

'Oh, Suth,' he gasped. 'I am bad, bad. I, Ko, know this. But hear me. I went to the marsh. I found people. Suth, they live in the marsh. They know all its paths. Three brought me back, one man, two women. Suth, they are here. Come greet them. Perhaps they show us the way through the marsh.'

Ko's voice trailed away. Suth didn't answer. Beyond him Ko could see Noli, Tor, Bodu and her baby, Tinu, Mana and Tan coming up the hill. Tor was carrying Tan on his shoulders.

'Ko, you are bad, bad,' said Suth. 'I tell you later. Come.'

On the way back to the camp Ko explained as much about the marsh people as there was time for

– how they didn't have words, but used sounds and gestures like Tor and the Porcupines, and the men coloured their faces like demons, and they mostly ate raw fish because they didn't have fire, and the crocodile was some kind of First One, and so on. Suth said nothing.

They found the three marsh people standing close together with the man in front. He looked very tense, and was holding his fishing stick point down but ready to raise and strike. Moving calmly and confidently Suth laid his digging stick on the ground and walked forward with his right hand raised, palm forward, fingers spread. As he reached the man he made a low humming noise in his throat. This was how the Porcupines greeted each other when two men met.

Instead of the hum, the man gave a soft bark, but his gesture was the same as Suth's, and the two men touched palms. Ko sighed with relief. So far, so good.

Next Suth put his arm round Ko's shoulders and drew him against his side and made *Thank you* noises, and then presented the man with his cutter. The man gave him in exchange two of the wooden tubes from his belt. Suth looked at them, puzzled, and the man took them back and struck them against each other, showing that they made a sweet, ringing noise. Smiling, he beat out a pattern of sound with them, *tic-atic-tack*, *tic-atic-tack*, and Ko recognized the strange woodpecker sound that had reached him across the water when the hunters were carrying the crocodile home. Suth smiled and took the tubes and tried for himself, while the man made encouraging murmurs.

By now Noli and the others had arrived. While Tor greeted the man, the rest of them hugged Ko, laughing and crying, and then bowed and fluttered their fingers to the man and went to greet the women. In no time Noli and the older woman were stroking each other's rounded bellies with admiring coos and a lot of laughter from the other three.

Then they all sat down, and Mana took round a small gourd of seed paste, and showed the marsh people how to dip a finger into it and lick the paste off. But before long the marshman started to become restless, and as soon as Suth stood up he jumped up too and called to his women to come.

Before he left the camp he knelt in front of the crocodile head again, and rose and touched his fingertips to the crocodile's snout, and to his own forehead, and then backed away.

Suth and Ko walked down to the marsh with the visitors, and on the way Suth tried to get the man to understand hat he needed someone to act as a guide across to the far side, but the man didn't understand, so they made *Goodbye* noises on the bank, and watched the marsh people pick their way along the hidden path until they disappeared into the haze.

'Now, Ko, I speak to you,' said Suth, and told him in a quiet, even voice, without anger or contempt, how bad he had been. It was very bad indeed. Ko wept.

They walked up the slope in silence, but before they reached the camp Suth said, 'Hear me, Ko. Soon people come to rest. Tun calls you. He says, *Ko, tell what you have done. Tell what you have seen.* You tell all. Think now of your words. But hear me, Ko. You were lucky, lucky. Lucky does not boast.'

'Suth, I hear,' said Ko. It struck him that Suth could have waited until everyone was there, and then told Ko in front of them all how bad he'd been. He was very grateful that he hadn't, but that didn't make it any easier when Ko had to stand in front of Tun and the others and tell his story. Even Kern looked horrified as Ko explained how he'd glimpsed the marshman and crawled out across the dangerous mud and tried to reach him, without telling anybody.

But as soon as he got to the meeting, their faces changed, and they started to ask questions. And when he told how the women had tried to lick and rub the darkness off his skin somebody laughed, and he started to feel better.

There were a lot more questions. The rest time lasted halfway through the afternoon, and then Ko took everyone down to the marsh and showed them the hidden pathway. It was easy to find now, because the dried mud near the shore was still trampled where Ko and the marsh people had crossed it, but further out the wet mud had closed over their footprints, and there was no trace at all.

They foraged until dark. Ko felt wonderfully happy to be back where he belonged, among friends. To his surprise Nar came to talk to him, and asked several questions, and then laughed and said, 'Ko, I think you find the way through the marsh. Soon I give you my gift.'

'Tomorrow is tomorrow,' said Ko, loftily, and Nar laughed again.

*

Nothing much happened for the next two days. By now they'd almost stripped the inlet of food, and would have liked to move on, but there was nowhere to go. Var and Net explored the way into the marsh, taking salt in case they met any of the marsh people, but they got only as far as the first island, and Ko's friends hadn't been there. They couldn't find the path to the next island.

On the third morning Ko and Mana were deep in a thicket, excitedly digging out a burrow Mana had found. They were almost at the nest, and could hear the frenzied squeaking of the little creatures trapped below, when Suth called. Disappointed, Ko wormed his way out and found Suth, with Tan standing puzzled beside him.

'Noli's baby begins,' explained Suth. 'Men and boys go.'

Ko understood at once. The same thing had happened when Ogad had been born, a few moons back. It had been night time, and they'd been asleep, but Suth and Ko and Tan and all the other males old enough to walk had left the lair and gone away into the dark and waited until they heard the birth song rising from around the fire. Then they'd gone back, and Suth had seen his baby son for the first time.

Childbirth, more than anything else, was woman stuff. Men and boys weren't allowed near it. Only small babies like Ogad could stay, because they were still feeding from the breast, and needed their mothers. So now all the males trooped back up to the camp to wait in the mottled shade beneath the leafless trees. The men settled down to playing their usual game, tossing pebbles into a circle drawn in the earth and trying to knock someone else's pebble out of the circle.

Ko was very restless. After his adventure in the marsh he'd promised he wouldn't go out of Suth's sight without permission. There was nothing he wanted to do under the trees. He was too young to join in the game. He had no one to play with, only Nar. He had begun to feel differently about Nar since their strange little conversation a few days back, but he didn't know how to start making friends after working so hard at being enemies for so long.

Ko went and watched the game until Suth had finished his turn, and then knelt beside him and whispered, 'Suth, I go up the hill. I look at the marsh. I stay there. I do not go down to the marsh. I, Ko, ask.'

Suth glanced at him. Ko could see he was trying not to smile. 'Go, Ko,' he said, and turned back to the game.

So Ko climbed to his watch place and sat with his back to a boulder, staring longingly out over the marshes. He could just see the tops of the trees on the island where he'd met the marshman. So close . . . Perhaps the man was there again, at this very moment . . . Suppose Ko borrowed the soundsticks he'd given to Suth, and went down to the shore and banged them together . . .

He'd hardly got into the dream when Nar came and squatted beside him.

'What do you do, Ko?' he asked.

'I wait,' said Ko. 'Perhaps I see something. Perhaps I hear something.'

'I wait with you?' asked Nar.

'Good,' said Ko, and made room for him to put his back against the boulder. Below them the marshes steamed in silence.

After a while Nar said, 'My mother Zara is sad, sad. All of our Kin are gone. Dead. Lost. We lived on the mountain. We were happy. The mountain burnt. It threw up great rocks. One hit my father, Beg. He died. We fled. We came to a desert, no food, no water. Many died there. My sister Illa died. Others were lost. Now my mother says to me, *We two are all our Kin. Here is little food. Soon it is gone. Then we die. You die, my son, Nar. Then our Kin is dead.* Ko, my mother is sad, sad.'

Ko murmured sympathetically. He remembered the strange feeling he'd had when Cal had been killed by the crocodile. His whole Kin, Fat Pig, had died with him. Until that moment there'd always been a Fat Pig Kin, ever since the First Ones had raised the children of An and Ammu in the First Good Place. Ko could imagine how he would feel if he knew that he was the last of Moonhawk, and there would be no more after him. It would be worse than his own death.

No wonder Nar was so interested in finding a way through the marshes.

Ko couldn't think of anything to say, so they sat in silence. Though there was no wind, the haze over the marshes seemed to move around all the time, with thicker and thinner patches coming and going. At times Ko could see the dim outlines of several islands, but a few moments later they would all have vanished.

He was getting restless again when Nar straightened, peered and pointed.

'A thing comes,' he whispered. 'People? Animals?'

Ko stared, and he too saw the vague, dark shape coming slowly through the haze towards the land. It was roughly where the hidden path was. It was too big to be an animal. It could only be several people, moving close together.

Both boys rose. Ko took a couple of paces down the hill. In the nick of time he remembered his promise to Suth. He turned, and together they raced back to the men, and knelt and rapped their knuckles together. The men looked up, frowning at the interruption.

'Tun, I, Nar, speak,' said Nar, and at once went on without waiting for permission. 'People come from the marsh. Ko sees this also.'

The men snorted with surprise, broke off their game and ran up to the ridge. By the time they got there the vague shape that Nar and Ko had seen had reached the shore and was clearly visible. It was indeed people. Seven or eight marshmen. They formed themselves into a line and marched up the hill with their fishing sticks gripped menacingly above their shoulders.

Oldtale

TOV AND FALU

Tov came to Stonejaw. The parrot was with him. The rock still held the mouth of Stonejaw, so that it could not close. Tov went into the mouth and found water. He drank and filled his gourd, and left the cave. Beside Stonejaw he camped and ate meat from the gazelle. Night came.

Tov said, 'Now I sleep, little parrot. Keep watch.'

He lay down and slept.

It was dark, and the parrot was Falu again. Now she sang with her own voice. These were the words of her song:

Parrot, First One,
I am your nestling.
You brood over me,
You bring me sweet fruits.
It is day, I am a parrot.
It is night, I am a child.

Let me be these no more.
Make me a woman.

Then Falu went into the cave, into the mouth of Stonejaw. She washed the yellow feathers from her buttocks, and the grey dust from her body, and made herself clean. When she left the cave she was a woman.

Tov slept. All night Falu watched over him.

In the morning Tov woke and saw Falu. He did not know her.

He said, 'Now, woman, I see you. Tell me your name.'

She said, 'I am Falu, daughter of Dat. I was a child. She is gone. I was a parrot, a little grey parrot with yellow tail feathers. It is gone. I am here. Tov, I choose you for my mate. Do you choose me?'

Tov said in his heart, Gata is more beautiful, but Falu is clever, clever. She is brave. She helps me. He said, 'Falu, I choose you for my mate. Now we smear salt on our brows.'

Falu said, 'No, Tov, we wait. My father Dat has my promise. He chooses for me. Now we go to him. You give him your gift, the tooth of Fododo, Father of snakes, the poison tooth. You say to him, Give me Falu for my mate.'

Tov said, 'I do this. It is good.'

Tov and Falu journeyed together. The sun was in their faces. They were happy, happy.

CHAPTER NINE

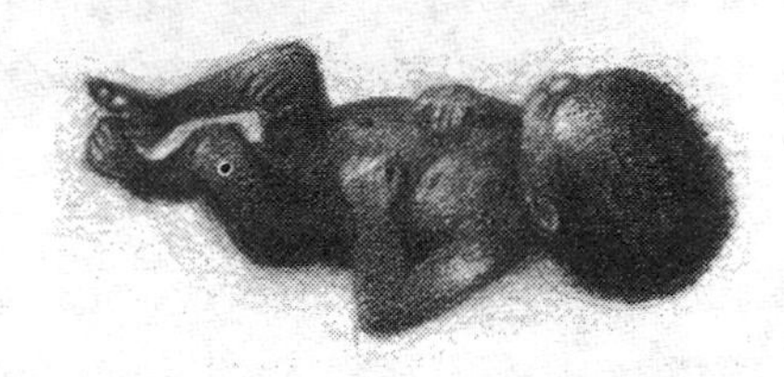

The marshmen came steadily up the hill. Their whole bodies, not just their faces and hands, were blobbed and streaked with demon colours.

The Kin men massed to face them. A low growl rose from their throats, and their hair began to bush out.

The marshmen's hair bushed in answer. They didn't growl, but made a weird, high yapping sound that was just as frightening.

Halfway between the two parties Ko watched, appalled. The marshmen were going to pass only a few paces from him, but they weren't looking at him. He mightn't have been there at all.

Without warning Net yelled and charged down the hill. Tun shouted at him to stop, but Net charged on. The marshmen halted. Their throwing arms went back.

Ko had seen what those fishing sticks could do, how sharp they were, how far the marshmen could throw them. Without thought he dashed forward, shouting a warning.

'Danger! Sticks are sharp, Net, sharp!'

He stood in Net's path, shouting and waving his arms. Crazy. How could a child stop a grown man in a fighting rage, the rage of a hero? Net charged straight through him.

Ko was slammed aside and flung sprawling down the slope. The breath whooshed out of him. He lay stunned, bruised, croaking for air. His head seemed full of a strange whooping sound.

As he struggled to his feet he realized that the sound was coming from outside him. Dazedly he looked around. Net was lying face down on the slope just below him. Dead? No. He was trying to get up, but croaking and gasping, even worse winded than Ko had been. Just beyond him stood the marshmen. They had lowered their sticks, and their hair was no longer bushed. With their free hands they were pointing at Net and whooping with laughter. Tears streamed down their bright-coloured faces. Some were stamping their feet, and others were almost doubled up. They were helpless. If the Kin men had attacked now they couldn't have fought back.

Bewildered, Ko turned. The Kin men had lowered their digging sticks and their hair too was starting to lie down. Kern was smiling and shaking his head. Ko saw Tun speak to Var and beckon to Tor, and then walk calmly down the slope with Tor beside him. Bruised and scraped and still totally bewildered, Ko helped Net to his feet and fetched his digging stick for him. Net didn't seem to want to fight anyone now. They waited to see what Tun would do.

A few paces from the marshmen he halted and signed to Tor to do the same. They laid their digging sticks on the ground and walked on, with their right hands raised, palms forward, the sign of peace. They halted again and waited for the laughter to end. Ko thought Tor looked anxious, but Tun seemed quite confident. As soon as he could make himself heard without shouting he turned and spoke to Net.

'Go back, Net. Take Ko. I, Tun, speak.'

Obediently Net limped up the hill, not looking at Ko. Ko could feel his shame, that he had let himself be so jeered at by these strangers. He couldn't imagine anything more awful. He was afraid Net was now very angry with him, because Ko had got in the way of his hero charge down the hill. What was Ko, a stupid little boy, doing meddling with man stuff?

Kern came to meet them and put his arm round Net and consoled him as he limped back to his friends. Trailing anxiously behind, Ko saw Suth beckon. By the time he reached him Suth was busy watching Tun and Tor dealing with the marshmen.

'Suth, what happens?' he whispered. 'Do we fight the marshmen?'

'No. You, Ko, stopped the fighting.'

'I think Net is angry with me for this. Am I bad, Suth?'

Suth snorted, amused.

'No, Ko. This time you are not bad.'

Ko was relieved, but still baffled. Only a few minutes ago everything had seemed so terrifying and hopeless, but now . . .

'Why do the marshmen laugh, Suth?' he asked. 'Why do you smile?'

'Ko, I cannot say. This was laughter stuff, that is all. Net charges. It is a hero charge. Who can stop him? A boy stands in his path. The boy waves his arms, he shouts. The hero does not see the boy. He hits him, he falls, he cannot breathe. The hero is gone . . . I see it, I laugh. It is laughter stuff . . . Ah, see, we do not fight. They come. Now Tun gives them salt.'

Ko looked and saw Tun leading the way up the hill, waving to the marshmen to follow. They did so, keeping close together, silent and purposeful, and not seeming at all friendly, but not in the fighting postures with which they had first arrived. Now Ko recognized their leader as his friend from the marshes, but the man didn't seem to notice him.

As they crossed the ridge their leader gave a loud bark, and stopped dead. The others lined up on either side of him. Tun turned and waited. The marshmen paid no attention to him. A low, astonished moan came from their lips. Ko realized what was happening. They had seen the great crocodile head for the first time.

'Suth,' he whispered. 'They do not come for salt. They come for our crocodile.'

'Ko, you are right,' muttered Suth. 'I tell Tun.'

He caught Tun's eye, and the two men moved aside and talked quietly together. Tun nodded and went on down towards the camp.

With slow, stiff steps the marshmen approached the great head, and halted a few paces in front of it. One by one they knelt, crawled forward, knocked their foreheads on the ground at the foot of the pole, then rose and touched their fingertips to the vicious snout and their own foreheads. They stood for a while, breathing deeply, and walked backwards to their places in the line. Just as Ko had done, the Kin men recognized all this as First One stuff, and watched in silence.

The leader came last. He also took a few paces backward, but instead of returning to the line he halted and came forward again, with his hands raised in front of him, obviously now intending to lift the head from the pole. Ko heard murmurs of anger from the Kin men. This wasn't right. It wasn't the marshmen who'd killed the crocodile, it was Chogi and the women. The head belonged to the Kins. Ko started to feel anxious again. Was there going to be fighting after all?

But Tun had other ideas. As the marshman had been moving back he had come and waited beside the pole. Now, before the marshman reached it, he lifted the head free and carried it forward to meet him. Startled, the marshman halted.

Tun held out the head and made the double hum in his throat that meant *I give*. The man stared, even more astonished, and then reverently took the head and made his *I am pleased* sound, loudly, three times.

The whole line of marshmen made noises of wonder and delight as the leader carried the head back to them. He laid it carefully on the ground, hesitated, picked up his fishing stick and looked at Tun. Suddenly he seemed unsure of himself. Ko could see just what he was thinking. He didn't have a gift nearly magnificent enough to offer in exchange for the crocodile head. Would Tun accept the fishing stick, or would he be offended?

But Tun was ready for this. He made a *Come* noise, beckoned to Tor and led the way back up to the ridge.

'Nar, Ko,' said Suth. 'Go. Find the women. Say to Chogi, *Wait for Noli's baby. Then come quick, quick. Bring food.*'

'What happens?' asked Ko as he and Nar loped down towards the inlet.

'Tun spoke with Suth,' said Nar. 'I hear their words. Tun gives the head of the crocodile. This is his gift. The marshman gives the path through the marshes. This is his gift. Now Tor says this to him.'

Ko understood at once. Though he and all the other Kin knew the Porcupines well and were expert at using their sounds, it was still often impossible to get them to understand something that Kin could explain to each other in a few words. But the Porcupines had ways of doing it among themselves, with a lot of touching and grunting and gestures, until they agreed on whatever it was. Ko's friend must have done something like this to persuade the other marshmen to join him on his expedition to fetch the crocodile head. And Tor would have the best chance, now, of explaining to him what Tun wanted.

As they neared the inlet Ko heard the sound of women's voices, singing high and happy, rising and falling in waves, three or four voices together, others lacing in and taking over, then a single voice, the chief woman's, Chogi's, ringing with joy, and the first voices answering again, and yet again – the Newborn Girl Song that the daughters of An and Ammu in the Oldtales had invented to sing together when Turka's first child was born.

They halted and waited. It was too soon for men or boys to be let anywhere near the birthplace, however urgent the message. As the last notes died Mana came running towards them.

'Noli's baby is born!' she cried. 'It is a girl. She is beautiful, beautiful. Nar, Ko, why are you here? What happens?'

'A big thing happens, Mana,' said Nar. 'Go. Find Chogi. Tell her *Come quick*.'

Mana hesitated a moment, but she could see this wasn't just boy stuff. Nar was serious. She scampered back down among the thickets. A little later Chogi appeared, frowning even more deeply than usual, obviously displeased by the interruption of important woman stuff. Impatiently at first she listened to Nar's explanations, but then nodded and said, 'This is good. The birth is easy. Noli is strong. We come soon. Tell this to Tun. Now, go.'

When the boys got back to the camp they found that Tun and Tor had somehow persuaded the marshmen to guide them into the marsh. Now, while they waited for the women, the men were sitting in the shade of the trees, with the crocodile head perched on a nearby boulder, and the marshmen were learning how to play the pebble game.

Before long the women arrived. Noli, tired but laughing with happiness, showed Tor his daughter. Tor hugged and stroked her, and then carried the baby round to show to the men, coming to Ko last of all. As far as Ko was concerned the baby was just a baby, wrinkled and floppy the way newborn babies always were. Her skin was paler than Noli's dark brown, much nearer the tan colour of Tor and the

Porcupines. Ko made the correct *Praise* sounds while Tor beamed with pride and delight.

Meanwhile the Kins shared food with their visitors. Nobody got more than a mouthful or two, as the store was almost empty, and they hadn't foraged long that morning before Noli's baby had started to come. But it was important to do everything they could to signal to the marshmen that they wanted them to be friends and allies. To make up for the scanty meal, Tun gave each of the visitors a palmful of salt, and they were delighted.

Now it was time to go. While the Kins packed their gourds with anything they had to carry, and Ko helped Tinu fill and seal the fire log, the visitors laid two of their fishing sticks side by side on the ground, settled the crocodile head between them and lashed it firm with reed leaves. When they were ready their leader arranged them in single file, pushing them around till he had them where he wanted.

Ko watched, fascinated. Only five days ago this man had let himself be driven back to his island by the other marshmen, but now he was completely in command, and nobody questioned him. It was because of the crocodile head, Ko guessed. He had discovered it, and now Tun had given it to him. That made him a big man, important.

When he was satisfied the leader barked, once. The two men at the head of the line bent and picked up the fishing sticks and lifted them onto their shoulders, one at each end, with the crocodile head sagging between them. The leader took two of the wooden tubes from his belt, and the four men at the back did the same. He placed himself at the head of the procession and marched off, rattling his tubes together as he went. The four at the back joined in and the whole line followed him up to the ridge, with the Kins, men, women and children, trailing behind.

As the haze-hidden marsh came in sight the leader gave a shout of triumph, and the other six answered with cries of praise. A few paces farther they repeated it, and again and again as they marched down the slope.

Ko found the noises strangely exciting, The woodpecker sound of the tubes had a kind of pattern in it, and the cries were part of the pattern. There was a meaning there too, almost as clear as he had learnt to hear in the grunts and barks of the Porcupines. The meaning was happiness. It was glory.

Oldtale

TOV'S GIFT

Tov and Falu journeyed all day, and came to Bagworm. His water lay beside him. His mouth was full of earth, and he could not suck it away. There were fish in the water. Tov and Falu took them and ate and drank and filled their gourd. Bagworm saw this. He was very angry.

Night came. Tov and Falu kept watch in turn, each while the other slept. They woke, they journeyed, they came to Twoheads. His heads fought still, and the yellow blood dripped from them. Tov and Falu drank it and filled their gourd. Night came, and they slept and kept watch as before.

They woke, they journeyed, they came to Tarutu Rock. Weaver camped there, Tov's own Kin. Tov said, 'Tell me, my kinspeople, where is Dat?'

They answered, 'Parrot camps at Dead Trees Valley. He is there.'

Tov and Falu journeyed to Dead Trees Valley.

When Gata saw them coming she hid, close, in long grasses.

Tov stood before Dat and said, 'Dat, I bring you the gift you ask. I bring you the tooth of Fododo, Father of Snakes. I bring you the poison tooth. Here is Falu, your daughter. She is a woman. I choose her for my mate. She chooses me. Dat, do you say Yes to this?'

Dat said, 'Give me the tooth of Fododo, Father of Snakes. Give me the poison tooth.'

Tov gave him the tooth. Dat held it in his hand. He said, 'My promise was not for Falu. It was for Gata. I say No to your choosing.'

Tov was very angry. He said, 'Give me back my gift.'

Dat said, 'The gift is given. It is mine.'

He closed his hand on the tooth, tight, tight, so that it bit into his palm and the poison went into his blood. He died.

Then Tov and Falu smeared salt on their brows, and were chosen.

All this Gata saw and heard, hiding in the long grasses.

CHAPTER TEN

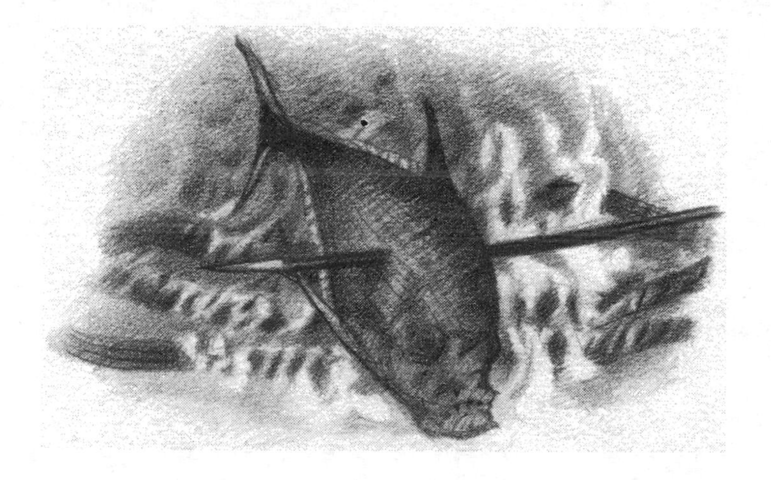

Slowly the procession picked its way along the hidden pathway. By the time everyone was ashore on the first island the buried reeds were beginning to give way, with so many people crossing all together. The crossing to the second island was worse. They had to hold hands and form a human chain to pull the last of them safely through.

The marshmen paid no attention, but strutted on ahead. They were well out of sight by now, though their wild music still floated eerily across the marsh. The Kins hurried after the sound and saw them disappearing across a mudbank into the haze ahead. But the marshman's two mates were there, waiting to help. They were obviously amazed to see so many people winding out from the trees, but the younger of them recognized Ko and ran to greet him, marsh fashion, with hugging and stroking.

She crowed with delight over Noli's baby and called to the other woman to come and admire her, and then they set about organizing the next crossing. They made the Kins go over a few at a time, with each party carrying a bundle of reeds to tread in anywhere the path felt weak. With plenty of workers, and cutters to gather the reeds, this didn't take long, but even so the sound of the marshmen's procession grew steadily fainter as they drew ahead.

Then it started to get louder again, and the Kins actually caught up on the far side of the fifth island, where several people had been fishing along a channel of open water, and the marshmen had stopped so that the men there could do First One stuff with the crocodile head. They were just finishing when the Kins came up with them.

The women ran to look at the strangers, and clucked and cooed over the baby, though some of them made sorrowful sounds and looked Noli in the eyes and sighed sympathetically.

'Why are they sad, Ko?' asked Mana.

'Mana, I do not know,' he answered. 'I think they say, *It is only a girl. A boy is better.* For them, men are big, big. Women are small. See, these new ones. Three men. Five, six women. I told you this. The women are the men's mates. A man has two mates, or three. It is strange, strange.'

Mana was staring at him, wide eyed. Perhaps she hadn't taken it in, hadn't really believed it, when he'd explained about it earlier.

'Ko, this is not good,' she whispered.

He heard mutters of agreement from around and realized that several of the others had been listening, Yova and Var as well as his own family. Suth nodded encouragingly to him. It was a curious feeling for Ko, being listened to as if what he had to say was something his hearers wanted to know about. He was pleased, but at the same time uncomfortable. It was as if he had been somehow changed by his adventure, but wasn't quite ready for the change.

All afternoon the procession threaded its way across the marsh, going more and more slowly as it picked up fresh followers. The men joined on at the front and added to the patterned din, while the women and children thronged laughing behind. By the time they reached the central camp the line was snaking almost across two islands and the channel between them.

Already the sun was a fuzzy blob low down on their left, all the shrouding haze glowed gold, and the lake surrounding the island shimmered with the coloured light. Across its shining surface Ko watched the men at the head of the procession move onto the raised path to the islands. Their reflections moved with them, scarcely rippling on the silky water. The echoes of their music floated away over the distant reedbeds. Five of them now were carrying the crocodile head at arms' length above their heads. Even seen at that distance through the marsh haze it looked a fierce and dreadful thing. Ko shuddered, remembering his nightmares. He well understood why this was First One stuff for the marshmen.

A small procession came out to meet the main one and did their greeting in the middle of the pathway, then turned and led the trophy home, with the whole long line of people shuffling behind. The music, tens and tens and tens of marshmen rattling their soundsticks and shouting their cries, didn't stop for an instant. By the time the Kins reached the pathway it was dusk.

They found the area round the entrance to the main island already crowded with excited people, so they pushed their way through to the further side and settled down where they could hear themselves talk.

'We were eight Kins at Odutu,' Ko heard Chogi say. 'All of the Kins, men and women and children. Yet these marshpeople are more.'

'Chogi, you are right,' said Kern. 'But what do we eat? We have little food here.'

'We eat fish,' said Suth. 'Come, Kern. Come, Zara. Come, Mana and Ko. Bring salt. Ko, you know these people. You say to the women, *You give me fish. I give you salt.*'

It was still just light enough to see. The women were sitting in groups, with the fish they'd caught piled between them. Suth chose a group that seemed to have plenty, handed Ko a chunk of salt and gave him an encouraging pat on the shoulder.

Hesitantly Ko went over. The women were already watching him, nudging each other and making their chuckling noise of interest and amusement. He crumbled some grains of salt into his palm and offered them round. The women took them and put them to their tongues and begged for more. Ko picked up a fish and made the *I ask* grunt. All the women grabbed for fish and thrust them at him, with eager I *give* noises. One by one he took them and passed them back to Suth and handed over another morsel of salt.

The job wasn't made any easier by the women who'd already had their share pinching and rubbing at his skin, or scratching it with a fingernail, to see if the colour was real. He could hear Suth and the others laughing behind him as he tried to slap the hands away, not let go of the precious salt, and pass the slippery fish back to them.

They worked on from group to group. Sometimes one of the marshmen would come strutting up and bark at the women, who would give him a fish and fawn on him while he munched it. He paid no attention to Ko and the others, and as soon as he'd eaten he'd strut away to rejoin the noise makers.

By now it was fully dark, but when Ko and his party got back to the others they found a fire going, with everyone scavenging along the shoreline for broken and discarded reed, which burnt brightly, but without much heat. Luckily there was masses of it, and after a while they were able to bury fish among the ashes and wait till they were cooked and rake them out with sticks to cool. They were delicious, as good as the crocodile tail had been that first night.

The marsh people didn't seem to have fire, but they must have known about it, because soon they were coming with dry reeds and thrusting them into the blaze and then they ran with them to piles they'd already built and got their own fires going. By the time the Kins had finished eating, the island was dotted with patches of light, with dark figures moving to and fro between them. The brightest blaze of all was over by the entrance, where the main crowd was, and where most of the noise came from.

Ko was intrigued.

'Suth, we go see?' he begged.

Suth rose, saying, 'Come, Tinu. Come, Mana and

Tan. This is a thing to see. We do not see it again. Noli, do you come?'

In the end everyone came and joined the crowd at the entrance. None of the marsh people paid any attention to them. Ko couldn't see over all those bodies, but he managed to squirm his way through to the front. There he found an open space around the wall of crocodile skulls and the line of larger skulls on poles. The head of the monster crocodile was now on the central pole. In front of it a fierce fire blazed, with the firelight glinting off the ragged fangs and throwing flickering shadows across the scaly hide. The mass of marshmen stood in front of the wall, slamming their soundsticks together and yelling their cries. The women and children formed a circle round the scene. Inside this circle one man strutted to and fro, leading the shouting and brandishing his fishing stick above his head every time he yelled.

Ko didn't recognize him until a pregnant woman came up from the pathway and flung fresh reeds onto the fire and then fawned on him briefly. She was the elder of the two women he'd met when he'd first found his way into the marsh. But then, a little later, a strange young woman appeared with more reeds and did the same. Before she'd finished, the younger of those first two women came with more reeds, and then joined her. She didn't seem to mind about the other young woman being there already.

Ko was watching this, open mouthed, when the one he knew spotted him and dashed across and dragged him, laughing, in front of the man. Now Ko could see by the firelight that it was indeed his friend, the man he'd met five days ago. He'd thought it must be, but he wouldn't have known him, with the mad, proud look on his face. His eyes were so wide open that the whites showed all the way round the irises, and the glisten of the flames added to the wildness.

Since noon the man had been leading the procession and then strutting in front of the crocodile head, and all the time yelling his triumph cry. His voice was hoarse, his coloured body shone with sweat and shuddered with effort, but he was still full of hero strength. He barely paused in his strut when he saw Ko, but laughed and snatched him effortlessly into the air and sat him on his shoulder while he paraded round the ring.

Now Ko found himself sucked into the frenzy, as he swayed above the heads of the crowd and looked out from the firelit island across the misty waters to the shadowy dark distances of the marsh. He clutched the man's hair with his left hand and raised his right fist above his head and shook it to the beat of the soundsticks, and when the man yelled his cry he joined in at the top of his voice.

It was thrilling, a wonderful, wordless boast, a boast like no other boast that ever had been or ever would be, a boast to remember all his days, and there was no shame in it at all.

His throat was sore by the time the man at last put him down, and the crowd let him through and patted his back as he ran laughing to join his friends. They too were laughing, with him, not at him. They watched a little longer and then went back to their fire.

As they were lying down to sleep Ko heard Var

say, 'This man makes a promise. He leads us through the marsh. Does he remember his promise tomorrow?'

'Var, I do not know,' said Tun. 'He is like a drinker of much stoneweed. Perhaps he remembers nothing'

They are wrong, Ko thought. In the middle of his triumph the man recognized me. He knew what he owed to me, even if I didn't do anything of it on purpose. He'll remember his promise.

Ko was right. The man did remember. He came next morning with his three mates and two other men and three more women – the two men's mates, Ko guessed, though he didn't yet have a chance to work out who was whose. All of them carried fishing sticks, and the women had several fish strung on each of theirs.

Ko's friend looked utterly exhausted, and when he tried to grunt or bark he made faint croaking sounds, but he still seemed completely sure of himself and greeted Tun as leader to leader. He let his senior mate make the *Come* sound, but he led the way off the island.

By now most of last night's crowd were gone, but the great crocodile head still stared grimly to the north, with the lesser heads on either side. The marshmen touched its snout reverently as they left. Ko looked at it for the last time. It was just a crocodile head. Dead. It didn't scare him any more.

They had crossed only a few more islands when Ko's friend halted and started to croak *Goodbye* sounds. After a moment's puzzlement Ko realized from the way they were all behaving that his friends were now going to turn back, while the other five led the way on. The man presented Tun with the fishing stick one of his mates was carrying, with several fish on it, and Tun gave him a gourd and salt in exchange, with more salt for the women, and then with a great chorus of different sorts of *Goodbyes* they parted.

Now the going was different, no longer islands and reedbeds with hidden pathways between them, but one endless vast reedbed where they trod not on squelching earth but on a solid network of reed roots just below the water. A maze of paths ran through it. Sometimes one of their guides would turn off down one of these, and a little later come hurrying up from behind with another fish to add to the collection.

Ko was curious. He found the ways of the marsh people weird but fascinating. So next time one of the women turned off he followed her. She heard him and looked back, but smiled and led the way on. Soon the side path ended. The woman put a finger to her lips, moved stealthily on and knelt beside a hole among the reed roots. From one of her belt tubes she sprinkled a few crumbs of something into the water, and then waited, motionless, with her fishing stick raised. Ko saw her tense. She struck, and with an expert movement of her wrist twisted the spear so that the fish didn't flap itself off as she was pulling it out.

Ko clapped his hands. She laughed, and gave him the fish to carry as they ran to catch up with the others.

They took no midday rest, but splashed steadily on, passing fish down the line to eat. Ko had never known this kind of moist heat. The haze was so dense that it was hard to breathe. Insects swarmed. Sweat streamed down. There was a kind of buzzing tingle in the air. It felt as if the haze was somehow being stretched, tauter and tauter, and at any moment it was going to rip apart from horizon to horizon and let the clear sky through.

Noli's baby was whimpering and wouldn't be comforted.

'Her head hurts,' said Noli. 'Rain comes.'

'Noli, you are right,' said Suth.

And then, in what seemed like the middle of nowhere, the procession halted. Ko was near the tail of it and couldn't see what was happening, but after some while Tun and Chogi came back down the line with their guides. Ko watched, puzzled, while they made *Goodbye* noises and exchanged yet more gifts. The marshpeople were obviously very anxious, and kept adding *Danger* sounds onto their farewells, but in the end they turned and went back the way they had come.

'They go no further,' Tun explained. 'They are afraid. There is a path. It is not good. It is old.'

'Tun, what is this danger?' Bodu asked.

'Bodu, I do not know,' he answered. 'We go on. We see. We are careful.'

After that they struggled slowly on for a while along what had once been a good path but was now almost blocked with new reeds. And then Ko came round a bend and saw that ahead of him the line of people seemed to be rising into the air, and a moment later he realized that they were climbing a solid slope. The haze thinned. Now Ko too was out of the reeds and climbing. Ahead of him he could see a whole hillside, strewn with rocks and boulders. This was the northern edge of the marshes. They had come through.

The Kins stood and looked around. The sun was already low. They were standing on what seemed to be a spur of hill jutting out into the marsh, so that both east and west they looked out over the same haze-hidden reeds. Though the hillside itself seemed barren, the shore was lined with thickets, but before he would let them forage Tun sent scouts up the hill and along the edges of the marsh. They returned saying that the promontory seemed to stretch a long way north but they had seen no sign of danger.

'The marshpeople were afraid,' said Chogi. 'Why is this?'

'They know this place,' said Var in his gloomiest tones. 'It is dangerous. We do not see this danger. It is here.'

'Var speaks,' said Kern, and they all laughed as usual, but nervously. The very stillness and emptiness of the hillside seemed a little menacing.

'I say this,' Kern went on. 'They are marshpeople. They do not like hard ground. It is not their Place.'

There were murmurs of agreement, but all the same Tun sent Shuja and Nar to keep lookout while most of the others foraged along the shoreline for what they could find until it was almost dark.

But Suth and his family gathered fuel and climbed the hill and chose a site for their camp, in a hollow between two ridges, so that no stranger could see their fire from a distance. Now Tinu anxiously opened the fire log. The reeds they had burnt last night had turned to ash, not embers, but she had saved the few bits of wood they had found to the last, for this purpose. When she tipped the fire log out and blew on the blackened pile a few sparks glowed, and she was able to nurse a flame from them.

So they all gathered round in the near dark, and sang the song that the Kins had always sung, whenever they moved to a fresh camp and relit their fire. Then they cooked their food and shared it round. When they had eaten, Tun rose and held up a hand for silence.

'Hear me, Tun,' he said. 'I praise the boy Ko. Often Ko is foolish. Often he is bad. So it is with boys. But we cross the marshes. Ko found the way. This was his deed. Now let Ko speak. Let him boast.'

Ko hesitated, astonished, then rose. This time he didn't feel nervous or tongue-tied. He had had his great boast last night, sitting on the marshman's shoulder, and that was enough. He remembered something that Suth had said to him not long ago.

'I, Ko, speak,' he said. 'Hear me. Tun is right. I was foolish. I was bad. But I was lucky, lucky. Lucky does not boast.'

He sat down, feeling that this time he'd got it right. The others seemed to think so too, and cheered quietly and laughed without any jeering. He even saw Chogi smile at him and nod. He felt very good.

Nar came and squatted beside him and said, 'Ko, you keep your promise. You find the way through the marsh. Now you tell me my gift to you.'

Ko smiled teasingly at him.

'I tell you tomorrow,' he said.

Oldtale

GATA AND NAL

Gata said in her heart, My father, Dat, is dead. My sister, Falu, is a woman. She chooses a mate. Now I, Gata, have no one.

Men came to Gata, from Little Bat and from Ant Mother. They said, 'Gata, you are beautiful, beautiful. I choose you for my mate. Do you choose me?'

To each of them Gata answered, 'I do not choose you.'

In her heart she said, I choose only Nal.

Gata left her Kin and journeyed alone to Ragala Flat. Snake camped there. She waited and watched until Nal hunted alone. Then she stood before him and said, 'Nal, I choose you for my mate. Do you choose me?'

Nal answered, 'Gata, you are Parrot. I am Snake. This is not good. It is bad, bad.'

Gata said, 'Good is a word. Bad is a word. I do not know them. I know only this. I choose you, Nal, for my mate. I choose no other man, ever.'

Nal looked at her. She was beautiful, beautiful.

He said, 'Gata, how do we live? Who is our Kin? Nobody. Where are our Good Places? We have none. Where do we hunt? Where do we forage?'

She said, 'We go far and far. Perhaps we find Good Places. Perhaps we die. I choose you, Nal. I choose also this.'

Nal said, 'Let it be so. I choose you, Gata, for my mate.'

Then they smeared salt on their brows, and were chosen. Their Kins said to them, 'This is bad, bad. Go far and far.'

Gata and Nal went to the Dry Places, the Demon Places. They found no food and no water. They lay down together and said, 'Tomorrow we die.'

They slept, and Gata dreamed.

Parrot came to Gata in her dream, and sang. This was his song:

Gata, my daughter, my nestling,
I do not brood over you.
I bring you no sweet fruits.
Tomorrow you die.
But I say this to you, this:
There are Kins, men and women,
They have children, they grow old, they die.
And their children, and their children's children.
They sit round fires, they tell Tales.
They speak your name, Gata.
They say, Beautiful, like Gata.
They are sad, sad.

The First Ones too were sad for Gata and Nal. They changed them.

Two rocks stand in the Dry Places, a day's journey and another day's beyond Ragala Flat. No other rock there is like them.

One rock is smooth and black. When the sun shines, see, it is full of bright stars. It is beautiful. It is Gata.

The other is tall and strong. It is Nal.

CHAPTER ELEVEN

Everyone was exhausted with the long day of toiling through the marsh, and there seemed to be no immediate threat of danger, so Tun didn't set sentries, and they lay down thankfully to sleep by their fire.

In the middle of the night,with a colossal crash of thunder, the rain came. The sleepers leaped awake and stood and raised their arms to the sky and let the warm, dense downpour sluice over their bodies. Hastily Tinu packed the fire log before the precious embers could be dowsed. Then they trooped up out of the hollow and watched the jigging legs of lightning prance to and fro over the marshes while the thunder bellowed on and on.

The storm ended as suddenly as it had begun, and the dark hillside tinkled with streaming water, and the smell of rain on dry earth filled the night with sweetness, and Ko lay down to sleep again on the soaked ground and thought *Ah, this is good, good.*

He managed to wake himself early next morning, in the first grey light. He knew exactly what he was going to do. He crept across to where Tinu lay and touched her gently on her shoulder.

She woke instantly, and he put a finger to his lips for silence and beckoned to her and stole away up the short slope and over the brow, out of sight of the others. While he waited for her to join him he studied the hillside for any sign of danger, but it seemed as empty as ever. Then he looked around for somewhere a little hidden and private, so that there wouldn't be any interruptions. The rain had washed the air so clear that he could see all the way across the marshes, and across the New Good Places, to a faint blue line that he knew must be Dry Hills, the range of mountains on the further side of the southern desert, many long days' journey away.

There were some promising-looking places among the bushes beside the marsh to his left, so when Tinu joined her he took her by the wrist and said firmly, 'Come.' She stared at him, but he tugged at her arm and she went obediently down the hill with him.

He found a little open space between some bushes and the marsh, well screened from up the slope. He studied the ground for paw prints, and sniffed the air, which carried scents richly after the rain. There was nothing to suggest any dangerous beast might be lurking close by.

'Wait here, Tinu,' he said. 'I bring you a thing.'

Before she could object he scurried back up the hill. By now the camp was stirring. He caught Nar's eye and waved to him to join him. At once Zara called to ask Nar where he was going.

'I go with Ko,' Nar answered cheerfully, making it sound like boy stuff. 'We have a thing to do.'

Ko led him a couple of paces down the slope. He put his hand in his gourd and drew it out with the fingers closed to hide what he was holding.

'Now I tell you the gift you give me,' he said.

With his free hand he pointed towards the marsh.

'Tinu waits there,' he said. 'Go to her. Take this.'

He opened his hand and showed Nar the palmful of salt he had prepared, the whitest he could find, crumbled fine and mixed with a little spit and seed-paste so that it would stick.

'This, Nar, is the gift you give me,' he said. 'You choose Tinu for your mate.'

Nar stared at the salt.

'Ko, I cannot do this,' he said.

'You made your promise,' said Ko firmly. 'On Odutu you made it, Odutu below the Mountain.'

Nar started to smile, as if this were boy stuff he was now too old for. Ko kept his face serious. What he was asking was perfectly fair. A gift didn't need to be a thing. It could also be a deed, a favour. Nar's smile faded. He knew that he had promised on Odutu below the Mountain, and that was something he couldn't go back on.

He turned his head for a moment and looked back towards the camp. From where they were standing they could just see the heads of the people moving around in the hollow, and Ko guessed Nar was looking to see if his mother was watching. He remembered how furious Zara had seemed when Chogi had first suggested that Nar and Tinu should choose each other. What, her lovely son, the last of his Kin, mate with this girl whose face was all twisted and wrong, and who couldn't even talk right! No! He could wait till Mana was old enough, or Sibi.

Nar had always been a very good son, and done whatever his mother wanted. Zara wasn't going to like this at all.

He looked at Ko and nodded.

'I do it,' he said slowly. 'Give me the salt. Come.'

They walked together down the slope, but Ko stopped before they reached the bushes.

'I stay,' he whispered. 'You go alone.'

Nar seemed to be deep in thought, barely noticing where he put his feet on the rough hillside, but he nodded. Obviously it would be better for Tinu to think he was asking her of his own accord. Ko waited till he was out of sight, then crept down until he could see Nar and Tinu through a screen of branches. He was just in time to watch Nar hold out his hand and offer Tinu the salt.

She stared at it. Her jaw moved to and fro, the way it did when she was too excited, or too upset, to force her mouth to make words. She took half a pace back. Now a branch hid her face from Ko. As he moved to where he could see her again a twig cracked beneath his foot.

At once Tinu's head turned. Ko froze, cursing himself. Stupid, stupid Ko, always getting it wrong just when it mattered. Oh, why hadn't he looked, like a hunter, to see where he was putting his foot?

Tinu was staring directly at him, though he was sure she couldn't see him behind the bushes. Her face went stiff. She turned back to Nar and mouthed a question – *Who is there?* Ko guessed. Nar answered.

Now a longer question. Oh, let him lie, let him lie! Let him tell Tinu that he, Nar, had asked Ko to take Tinu there to wait for him so that he could offer her the salt without everyone watching. But of course he wouldn't. This was a way out for him, a way he could give his gift to Ko and still not make his mother furious. Stupid, stupid Ko, when he'd got everything else so right, and then at the last minute spoilt it all.

Nar was speaking. Tinu listened. Once or twice Ko had seen people's faces after they'd died. Tinu's was like that. When Nar finished she bowed her head and at the same time pushed away the hand that was holding the salt.

Nar stared at it, then turned and walked back the way he had come. Tinu looked up to watch him go. Her face was so twisted that it didn't seem like a human face at all. Tears streamed down it. Ko couldn't bear to watch, but at the same time couldn't look away.

A few paces from Ko, but still on the far side of the bushes, Nar stopped. The hand with the salt moved gently up and down, as if he were judging its weight so that he could throw it as fiercely as possible into Ko's face. He had the look of a grown man, the same look that Suth had had when he'd told Ko how bad he'd been, going out into the marshes alone.

'Hear me, Ko,' he said, just loudly enough for Ko to catch the words. 'I, Nar, speak. My gift to you is given. I promised upon Odutu, Odutu below the Mountain. It is done. Now go. Go back to the others.'

'I go,' whispered Ko miserably, and trudged back up the hill.

He couldn't bear to face anyone, so he climbed

across the slope and round to the far side of the spur. He sat down well below the ridge, put his chin on his fists and stared glumly west.

It was a wonderful day. He couldn't remember a day like this, so clear, so fresh. The marsh stretched limitlessly away, first the immense reedbed, and then the maze of islands and mudbanks and channels. Birds rose in flocks, circled, settled. The air was full of their calls. Another rainstorm was massing in the distance, a black bank of cloud trundling slowly towards him with its veil of rain beneath it. To left and right of it rose the outer ends of a rainbow, and between them flashed the sudden spikes of lightning. Already he could hear the unsteady burr of thunder.

Wonderful, but Ko barely saw it. All he could think of was that he had ruined his chances, and – far, far worse – ruined Tinu's chance of happiness. Everything was pointless, stupid, and it was all Ko's fault.

Vaguely he noticed the voices of people, chattering excitedly. Something must be happening in the camp, but he wasn't interested. It didn't matter. Nothing mattered. If they'd never got across the marshes, if they'd all died in the desert, it wouldn't have been any worse.

A hand touched his shoulder. He looked round, ready to snap. It was Mana, with a broad smile on her face. Even Mana was laughing at him for being so stupid.

'Go!' he snarled.

She shook her head, still smiling.

'Come, Ko,' she said. 'Suth says this. Come now.'

She took his wrist, dragged him to his feet and started to pull him up the slope. He came, grudging every step. From the ridge they looked down into the hollow.

Ko couldn't make out what was happening. Everyone was massed in an excited group on the other side of the fire. He could see Tun and Chogi and Suth near the centre, talking to a woman who had her back to him. Chogi was speaking earnestly to her.

The woman shook her head angrily. From the way she did it Ko recognized her as Zara. Chogi went on speaking till Tun held up his hand and spoke briefly to Zara.

He moved aside to make space for someone standing behind him. Nar.

Nar and Tinu, standing close together, with their fingers laced into each other's, Tinu, of course, had her head bowed to one side with shyness, but Nar faced his mother directly. He began to speak to her, firmly. His forehead was smeared with white stuff. So was Tinu's.

Ko stared, bewildered.

'What happens? What happens?' he muttered.

Mana laughed.

'Nar tells us,' she said. 'He goes to Tinu. He chooses her for his mate. It is his gift to you, Ko. A twig breaks. Tinu hears. She is clever, Ko. She asks, *Is that Ko? Why does he watch?* Nar tells her. She says, *Tinu is not Ko's gift. Nar, I do not choose you. Go*. Nar goes. He sends you away. He comes back. He says, *My gift to Ko is given. Now, Tinu, I choose you for my mate. It is my choosing. Do you choose me?* Then Tinu says, *Nar, I choose you.*

'Oh, Ko, Tinu is happy, happy!'

MANA'S STORY

For Rosemary and George

MANA'S STORY

Contents

Chapter One 469
Oldtale: THE DILLI HUNT 480
Chapter Two 484
Oldtale: THE RAGE OF ROH 494
Chapter Three 496
Oldtale: THE WAR OATH 507
Chapter Four 511
Oldtale: BLACK ANTELOPE'S WAKING 524
Chapter Five 527
Oldtale: SIKU 535
Chapter Six 538
Oldtale: FARJ 546
Chapter Seven 549
Oldtale: THE PIG HUNT 567
Chapter Eight 570
Oldtale: THE MAMBAGA CROSSING 580
Chapter Nine 583
Oldtale: THE GAME OF PEBBLES 596
Chapter Ten 601
Oldtale: THE UNSWEARING 613
Chapter Eleven 616

CHAPTER ONE

Mana was fishing, alone, among the reeds.

She had her own fishing hole. Suth and Tor had helped her to make a path into the reedbed, laying the cut reeds flat on the net of roots, for her to walk on. Ten and ten paces in they had made a small clearing, and in the middle of this they had cut a circular hole down through the roots, leaving a little pool of clear water, less than a pace across.

They'd known what to do because Ko had seen one of the marshwomen fishing like this. But after that they'd had to find stuff out for themselves – what sort of bait was best; how a target in the water was never where the eye saw it, but above; and, most important of all, how to wait and wait in utter stillness, and then fling the power of every muscle in arm and shoulder and side into a strike as quick and sudden as the strike of a snake. Any twitch, any hesitation before that moment, and the fish would startle, and flick away. Mana was good at waiting.

Tinu had first found the trick of it, and shown the others. Then Suth had made the children practise and practise. He'd put a leaf on the end of a thin reed and moved it around under the water, as a fish might move, and they'd used that for a target. When Mana's fishing stick pierced the leaf three times out of four, through several trials, Suth and Tor made the path for her.

So now for the first time she crouched by her own fishing hole, with her stick – a strong reedstem, sharpened to a point – resting on her shoulder, ready for the strike. This part of the reedbeds was full of fish. It was strange that none of the marshpeople came here to hunt them, but they seemed wary of coming so close to the shore, as if there was something here that scared them badly.

She could see three little fish, silver with a green stripe along the side, the size of her middle finger. That was good. They were much too small to spear, but their movements would tell larger fish that there was food here. Gently she edged her left hand forward and dribbled another few dragonfly eggs onto the surface. As the white specks wavered down through the water the little fish darted at them and sucked them in. Two more appeared from the darkness beneath the reeds, one the same sort, and the other slightly larger, dark brown and blunt nosed.

Was that a movement, a shadowy something stirring at the edge of the darkness?

Mana's heart started to pump. More slowly than ever she drifted her left hand forward and dropped a few more of the precious eggs. The shadow came nosing out to take them, a fish as long as a man's foot, deep-bellied, blue-black with a red spot behind the eye. It was too late. The little fish had got there first.

Mana released another dribble of eggs. All six fish rose for them, competing, and began to follow them down.

Now!

As the dark back turned away, Mana struck. The point jarred for an instant against a toughness, but she drove it on. At once the spear came alive in her grip, snatching itself to and fro as the fish fought to wrench itself free. Hands and arms remembered their endless lessons, so she didn't make the instinctive move, pulling the stick back along the line on which she'd thrust it in – that would risk pulling it out of the fish – but grabbed it with her left hand as far forward as she could reach, and then pulled up and sideways, leaning her body back to heave the stick out with its point just clearing the far edge of the hole. A hand's breadth down it, pierced clean through, the fish flailed in the air.

With a sigh of happiness Mana rose and stood, absent-mindedly brushing the insects from her body. They'd swarmed around and on her all the time she was fishing, but she'd scarcely noticed them. Several had bitten her. She guessed how she'd be itching by nightfall, but she didn't mind. It was all so worth it. At her first try, at her own new fishing hole, she'd caught this beautiful fish.

She forced the stick further through it so that it couldn't wriggle itself free, then laid it on the path. When the water was still she took a different sort of bait from her gourd – not the dragonfly eggs, which were hard to find, but crumbs of the stuff left over after pounding blueroot paste – and sprinkled them onto the hole. They floated on the surface, so that the fish that had been frightened away would find them when they came back, and think this was a good place to look for food again. The one fish she'd caught was enough for Mana, enough happiness, enough food for herself and someone else. She put her stick over her shoulder with the fish hanging behind her, and left.

Now, climbing the hill, she realized how glad she was to escape from the marsh insects. This happened every time anyone went into the marsh. Clouds of the horrible creatures gathered around them in the steamy heat, mostly just to settle and tickle as they drank their sweat, but some to bite in and suck their blood. They had all learned to put up with it, to forget about it as they did what they were there for. But as soon as they could they climbed back up the hill, into the fresher, drier heat, where the insects mostly didn't come.

When she was high enough she sat down to wait. Now, of course, more than anything, she wanted to show someone her lovely fish, but they were all busy fishing at various fish-holes in the huge reedbed that reached along the shoreline below her. She'd chosen a place where she could see anyone who came out, so that she could run at once and show them. But she wasn't impatient for them to do so. She was happy to wait, happy in her own happiness, not needing anyone to share it.

The hill on which she was sitting was like the tail of some vast crocodile, a craggy, steep-sided promontory rising to a central ridge, where the crocodile's spine would have been. From north to south it was a whole difficult day's journey in length.

Mana was sitting on its eastern flank, with the morning sun shining in her face. In front of her and to her right the mist-veiled marshes stretched away. Somewhere out there Var and Net and Yova and Kern should now be making their way back from the far side, using the paths that the marshmen had shown them.

They had gone to fetch fresh supplies of salt. They'd used up almost all of what they'd brought with them, as gifts for the marshmen, and Tun had decided they might need more, to help make friends with any new people they met when they journeyed north to look for new places where they could live. It was something to do while they waited for everyone to get well from the marsh sickness.

Two of them had died, Runa, and Moru's little daughter Taja. Most of the others had been very sick. Mana had been the first, before they'd even started to cross. Chogi said that it was from sleeping in the marshes, or too near them. But now everybody was well again, though some were still a bit weak, and as soon as the salt party returned they would be ready to travel north.

Mana felt anxious about the move. She knew they couldn't stay here for ever. Plant food was already getting scarce along the shorelines, and they couldn't live on nothing but fish. Besides, this wasn't the sort of life they were used to. But Mana didn't really like change. She preferred things she knew and understood. That was one of the reasons she'd been so pleased about catching her fish – it meant that there was something useful she could do. Fishing gave her a place among the Kin, a purpose. It helped her to know what she was there for. And now that she thought about it she felt suddenly sad that soon she would be leaving her fishing hole. She would be going to places where, perhaps, she would never have the chance to fish again.

She rose and looked north, along the way they were going to travel. Tun had sent scouts up there to explore. They'd come back and reported that after half a day's journey they'd not reached the end of the promontory, but it had become steadily steeper until its flank was almost a cliff, with neither room nor soil for anything much to grow between the plunging rockface and the marsh.

So now Mana gazed along the hillside, trying to imagine the difficult journey, and wondering what might lie at the end of it. Would it be a great wide open landscape, perhaps with a river running through it, and clumps of shade trees and patches of bushes, like the Good Places she could just remember, before the rains had failed?

The imaginary landscape filled her mind, so she wasn't really studying the actual one that lay in front of her. Even so, a quick movement caught her eye. She stiffened, and stared.

Yes, there. Brief, furtive, a brown flicker between two boulders. Gone.

A fox or jackal? Too big. Not a deer's motion. Anyway, they'd seen no creatures that size in this place. The promontory was too barren for grazing animals, and there wasn't enough prey for the meat eaters.

There again! Though Mana saw it clearly this time she still couldn't tell what it was. A round, black head, a brown back behind it, the movements rapid but awkward

Only when it had vanished did she realize what she'd seen. The creature slinking up the hillside was human – a woman, Mana thought – one of the marsh people, judging by the colour of her skin. She was moving in that strange way because she was crouching low and at the same time clutching something in both her hands, held close to her chest . . .

There she was again. But the hands weren't clutching anything. They were holding it cupped between the palms. The woman paused, peering round a boulder, not towards Mana but away from her, north, as though she was hiding from a danger that might be coming from that direction. She scuttled on, still with the same awkward gait as she tried not to spill whatever she was carrying.

It could only be water, Mana decided. Why was a marshwoman carrying water up over the barren rocks? The marshpeople never came out onto the promontory. There was something out here they were desperately afraid of – and certainly the way the woman was behaving showed that she shared that fear. And why was she carrying water in her hands, instead of one of the reed tubes that the marsh people used for that sort of thing?

Curious, Mana picked up her fishing stick, with the fish still impaled on it, and set off across the hillside. She wasn't afraid. The marshwomen were pleasant and easy to deal with, and the men weren't dangerous, for all their proud ways. But since the woman had been moving so warily Mana slipped behind a boulder the moment she reappeared, and waited until she was well down the hillside before moving on.

When she was near the place from which the woman had come she laid her stick down and crawled silently on until she could peep round a rock to see what lay beyond.

She looked down into a small, steep-sided hollow. At the bottom lay a man. His eyes were shut. His face was pulled into tight lines of pain. Blood oozed from a ghastly wound below his left shoulder. His right arm was flung out across the stony ground. A small boy, almost a baby, sat clutching his fingers and staring around with a look of terror, misery and bewilderment.

The man's face wasn't painted with bright colours, as the marshmen's always were. Nor did he wear their kind of braided reed-leaf belt, with wooden tubes dangling from it. These weren't marshpeople after all.

It didn't cross Mana's mind that these people were nothing to do with her, and she needn't try to help them. The look on both their faces told her she must. She glanced down the hill and saw the woman already starting to climb back up with a few more precious mouthfuls of water for the wounded man. Better wait for her.

Mana crept a little way back and hid, but as soon as the woman had vanished into the hollow she eased the fish off her stick and crawled with it to where she could again look down.

The woman was crouched over the man, dribbling water onto his mouth. Half of it splashed aside, but his tongue came out and lapped the rest in. When it was almost gone she held the last palmful in front of the boy and pushed his face down into it so that he could suck it up. Mana waited till she'd finished, then hissed softly.

Instantly the woman spun round, snatching up stones with both hands, and crouched snarling in front of the man.

Mana knelt up with her hand held palm forward in the sign of peace and greeting. The woman stayed where she was, with her teeth bared, snarling like a cornered jackal. Mana held out the fish and made the double hum which people who hadn't got words used to mean *I give*.

The woman frowned, uncertain, and stopped snarling, but stayed in her fighting crouch with her eyes flickering from side to side. Mana smiled, shrugged, and flipped the fish down into the hollow. It landed at the woman's feet.

The woman hesitated, staring to and fro between Mana and the fish. At length she made up her mind, dropped the stone from her left hand and, without taking her eyes off Mana, groped for the fish. Still in her fighting pose, with the stone in her right hand ready to strike or fling, she bit a mouthful out of the back, chewed it, spat the chewings into her hand and forced them between the man's lips. He munched feebly while she chewed some for the child.

Still with her eyes on Mana she took a mouthful for herself and while she chewed it backed up the further side of the hollow until she could see out over the rim. Here at last she turned and scanned the hillside to the north, but kept glancing back at Mana to make sure she hadn't moved. Then she came back and carried on feeding the three of them.

This would obviously take some time, so Mana emptied the contents of her gourd onto a flat rock and hurried down the hillside, keeping under cover just as she'd seen the woman doing. Judging by the man's wound, they had every reason to be afraid. She filled the gourd at a marsh pool and carried it back up.

This time she picked her way down into the hollow. The woman snarled and made ready to strike, but Mana smiled at her and showed her the gourd, brimming with water. The woman hesitated, so she put the gourd down and climbed back out of the hollow. The woman relaxed a little, picked up the gourd and started to help the man drink from it.

Mana turned and looked south along the shore. Two people had now come out of the reedbed. Even at that distance she recognized the smaller one as Ko. No one else had that special sort of look-at-me way of standing, eager and uncertain at the same time. The other one looked like Moru. Ko was showing her something. He looked proud and happy about it. He must have had luck with his fishing too.

With a pang Mana realized that now she would never show anybody her beautiful first fish. By the time these strangers had finished with it there would be nothing left but the bones. But she'd had to give it to them. There'd been nothing else she could have done. And now she had to go and fetch help for them. That was obvious too.

She called softly down to the woman, pointed, smiled and made the *I go* sound. The woman didn't react. Mana wondered whether she used the same noises as the other wordless people she knew. She had made no sounds at all so far, apart from snarls.

In fact, Mana realized as she hurried across the slope, she didn't know anything about these people at all. If they hadn't been in such desperate trouble when she'd found them, would they have been friends or enemies? She couldn't tell.

All she had known was they were in trouble, and in danger. She could even guess, from the man's wound, what sort of danger that might be. It wasn't the bite or the claw-mark of some big fierce animal. Something hard and sharp had struck the man a savage blow, and driven deep into him. It might have been the horn of an animal, but it looked too wide for any antelope Mana had ever seen. And if it had been something like that, why should the woman be so deadly afraid, so instantly ready to fight? Antelope didn't chase down the hunter they'd wounded.

No, Mana thought. People made that wound. She had never seen a wound from the thrust of a digging stick, but that was what it would have been like.

This was bad, she thought, bad. Now perhaps she and all her friends were in the same danger as the three she had left in the hollow. But she still felt she couldn't have done anything else.

Oldtale

THE DILLI HUNT

Black Antelope slept. His sleep was long, long.

Fat Pig and Snake drank stoneweed. They were happy.

Snake boasted. He said, 'See my man, Gul. No hunter is swifter. No hunter has keener eyes. He throws a stone. No hunter has truer aim.'

Fat Pig said, 'Snake, you lie. My man Dop is better. He strikes a rock with his digging stick. It shatters apart. He follows the track of the dilli buck. He does not lose it. In the dark night he smells it.'

Snake said, 'Fat Pig, you lie. Gul is better.'

They quarrelled. Their voices were loud.

Weaver said, 'You two, stop your shouting. My wives cannot hear my orders.'

Fat Pig and Snake said, 'Judge between us, Weaver. See our men, Gul and Dop. Which is the better hunter?'

Weaver looked from the top of the Mountain, the Mountain above Odutu.

He said, 'See that fine dilli buck. He has a black patch on his rump. Go now. Make him two. Now you have two dilli bucks. Set one before Dop. Set one before Gul. Make each dilli buck run to Yellowspring. One man comes there first. He kills his buck. That man is the better hunter.'

Fat Pig and Snake said, 'Weaver, this is good. We do it.'

But Weaver said in his heart, This is nothing to me, which hunter is better. Yellowspring is far and far. Now we have quiet here.

Gul hunted. Dop hunted. Each saw a fine dilli buck. It had a black patch on its rump. It ran before them. It was clever. It turned aside, it ran on rock, it hid in thick bushes. The hunters did not lose the tracks. The bucks came near Yellowspring. Both came there together, but Dop followed closer.

Snake saw this. He was not happy. He said in his heart, My man loses the contest. We made two bucks from one. Now I make one from two.

He put a stoneweed in Fat Pig's path. Fat Pig found it. He drank. He did not watch the hunt. Snake caused Dop's buck to run behind a thicket. Then he made two bucks into one. Dop's buck was gone.

Dop came behind the thicket. His buck was not there. Its tracks ended. He hunted this way and that. He could not find it.

Gul followed his buck to Yellowspring. There he killed it. He was happy.

Dop was thirsty. He went to Yellowspring. He saw

Gul. He saw the dead buck. It had a black patch on its rump.

Dop said, 'Gul, you killed my buck. All day I hunted it.'

Gul said, 'Dop, you lie. The buck is mine. All day I hunted it.'

Dop took the buck by the hind legs. Gul took the buck by the forelegs. Both pulled. Neither was stronger.

Gul loosed one hand from the buck. He picked up a stone. He flung it. His aim was good. The stone struck Dop on the side of his jaw. He loosed his hold from the buck.

It was sudden. Gul was not ready. He went backwards. His foot caught on a grass clump. He fell.

Dop leapt at Gul. He struck at him with his digging stick, a fierce blow. Gul twisted aside. Dop's digging stick drove into the ground.

Gul laughed. He said, 'Dop, an anteater is swifter, a blind anteater.'

He struck at Dop, a fierce blow. Dop turned it aside. He laughed. He said, 'Gul, a nestling is stronger, a featherless nestling.'

Each mocked the other. They were filled with rage, the rage of heroes. They fought.

Snake and Fat Pig saw this. They said, 'This is good. Now we see which is better.'

All day Dop and Gul fought. They gave fierce blows. They threw stones. They struck with their fists. They bit with their mouths. Blood flowed.

The sun sank low. Gul saw this. He turned away. He ran towards the sun. Dop followed.

Now Gul turned again. He faced Dop. He struck

him a great blow, the blow of a hero. It was of this sort:

See this tree, this father of trees. No tree is taller, none stronger. Now is the time of rains. See this cloud. It is black, it is slow, it is filled with thunder. It stands over the father of trees. It bursts. Out of it falls the lightning. The sun is not brighter. The lion's roar is not louder. The father of trees is stricken, he falls, he lies on the ground.

Such was Gul's blow at Dop.

The sun was in Dop's eyes. He did not see Gul's blow. It struck him on the head, the side of the head, behind the eye. His sight was darkened. His knees were weak. He fell to the ground. He did not move.

Gul picked up the dilli buck. He carried it away. He was happy.

CHAPTER TWO

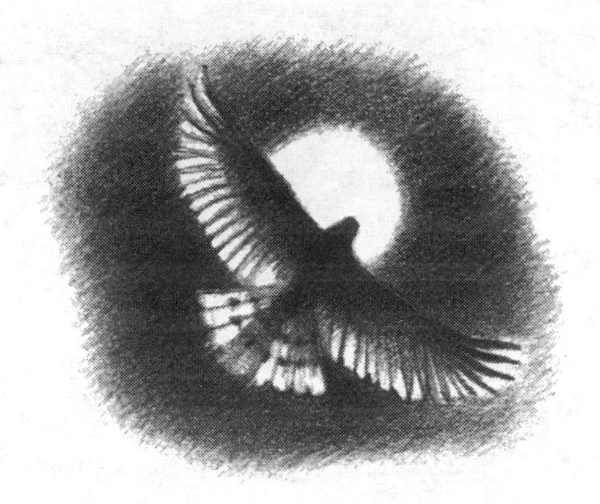

The man couldn't stand, let alone walk, so Suth and Net linked hands to make a seat between them, and with his arms round their shoulders carried him moaning back to the camp. His wound reopened and bled the whole way. The woman seemed to have decided that these strangers were friendly. She walked anxiously beside the man, carrying the child and glancing back over her shoulder every few paces.

They made the man as comfortable as they could on a bed of reedstems, and Mana fetched water for the woman to wash his wound, and then put what was left of her fish on the ashes of the fire to roast for them.

By now it was time for the midday rest, but first Tun sent Ko and Nar to keep a watch to the north, one on either flank of the hill. The rest of them sat in the shade, eating what they had caught or found, and talking in low voices about the strangers. Mana couldn't hear what the men were saying on the far side of the fire, but the women round her all agreed that the man's wound had been made by something like a digging stick, and that the woman was very scared. They guessed it was because she thought that whoever had caused the wound might still be following them.

Nobody said a word of blame to Mana for what she had done. Like her, they all seemed to feel that she'd had no choice.

Before the rest ended Mana went up the hill with Shuja to take over as lookouts. They stayed there most of the afternoon, until Zara came up with Dipu to relieve them. As they were making their way back down the hill Shuja stopped and pointed ahead, towards the tip of the promontory.

'See,' she said. 'Var comes. And Net and Yova and Kern. They have salt. This is good.'

Mana looked. The haze that covered the reedbeds all day was starting to turn golden as the sun moved towards its setting. Four weary people, each with two heavy gourds slung from their shoulders, had just emerged from it and were starting to climb towards the camp. Others had seen them too. She heard shouts from down the hill to her left, and everyone came running up from the fishing holes to greet the expedition.

By now they'd caught and found plenty of food to go round, and down in the marsh the insects were always worst in the evening, so they built up the fire and prepared their meal while they caught up with each other's news. Ko had caught three fish, which he shared with Mana. They were all smaller than the one she'd given away, but she didn't tell him.

At sunset, while they were still eating, the stranger woman gave a loud, wailing cry, and began to tear with her nails at her face and chest, till the blood came. Mana didn't need to look to know that the man was dead.

At first the woman wouldn't let anyone touch him, but after a while they insisted. They were certainly not going to sleep with a dead man near them. A body might attract demons, come to eat the spirit that was still tied to it. Some of them held the woman while the others carried the corpse well up the hillside and piled stones around and over it, and then in the last light the women did the death dance for the stranger, to set his spirit free, while his woman knelt wailing at the foot of the cairn.

Mana was too young to join in the dance. The stranger had let her take charge of her baby while she mourned for her man, and now Mana was sitting behind the line of women, with the little boy asleep in her arms, when she saw Noli break from the stamping rhythm, stiffen and sway. Bodu, beside her, caught and held her. Tinu took little Amola from her. The rest of the women stilled. The men, on the far side of the cairn, stopped their slow handclap and their groaning chant. Last of all the stranger woman looked up and fell silent, staring bewildered as the voice of Moonhawk came slowly between Noli's lips, deep and soft, but filling the long hillside with its sound.

'Blood falls,' said the voice. 'Men follow.'

Noli's head dropped and her knees buckled, but Bodu and Tinu held her steady until she shook herself and snorted and looked around her. She murmured to Tinu and took the baby back. They all stared questioningly at each other. For a while no one said anything.

Mana could feel their fear and uncertainty. She knew they were all thinking the same thing. Moonhawk's brief message was frighteningly clear. *Blood falls.* The stranger man's wound had been oozing when Mana had first seen him. It must have dripped all the way as he had fled from his enemies, and had broken out afresh and left a still clearer trail as he'd been carried to camp. *Men follow.* Not just a single enemy, then. At least two, perhaps several.

'Do they follow this trail in the dark?' said Var. 'Do they smell it?'

'I say they do not,' said Kern, who was the best tracker among them. 'I say they wait. Tomorrow it is light. Then they come.'

'How many men,' asked Chogi. 'Can Noli tell?'

'I do not see them,' muttered Noli. 'They are hunters, fierce, fierce.'

Murmurs broke out. Mana saw Noli hold up her hand, but she seemed to be too dazed still from Moonhawk's visitation to assert herself. Bodu had seen the movement, though, and called out, 'Wait. Noli tells more.'

Everyone fell silent again, straining to hear. This time Noli's voice was dreamy, and very quiet, but her own.

'I was a child,' she said. 'We laired at Dead Trees Valley. I dreamed. Men came, fierce, fierce. They killed our men. They took our women. This was my dream. Moonhawk sent it. It was a true dream. These men came.'

Everyone knew what she was talking about, though Mana herself had been only a small one when it had happened, and couldn't remember it, except sometimes at the shadowy edges of a nightmare. The eight Kins had been living peaceably in the Old Good Places, as they'd done ever since the time of the Oldtales, when a horde of murdering strangers had burst upon them, killing all the males they could catch and taking the women for themselves.

Only the Moonhawk Kin had had any warning, because of Noli's dream, but they hadn't believed her.

Now they did. There was a horrified silence before Chogi asked the question in everyone's mind.

'These are those men?'

Noli hesitated.

'I do not know,' she muttered. 'I think . . . I think they are others.'

Tun took charge.

'Hear me,' he said. 'We keep watch tonight, by three and by three. We hide the fire. Tomorrow we wake in the dark. We are ready. We set lookouts. They see who comes, how many. Few men, we meet them. They see we are more. They go away. Many men, we go into the marsh. We know the paths. They do not. Is this good?'

There were mutters of agreement, and they went back down to the camp, deciding as they went who should do what, and how they should confront the strangers if it came to that.

Only the dead man's woman stayed mourning by the cairn. In the middle of the night she crept into the camp. By then her baby was restless and whimpering, but she took him and suckled him for a while, and then lay down at Mana's side and slept.

Huddled in her lookout, almost at the ridge that ran along the top of the promontory, Mana waited for Ko's signal. He was further along the hillside, at a point from which he could see a long way north. The hunters were sure to be following the blood trail. Very early that morning Kern had tracked it as far as the point at which Ko would first see them appear, so he knew exactly where to look. Mana couldn't yet see him, as he was below the skyline on the far side of a low spur.

Slowly the shadows of the rocks shifted as time dragged past. Around mid morning Mana saw Ko appear, crawling beween two boulders. As soon as he was again below the skyline he stood and raised both arms. Mana did the same, to show she had seen the signal. Now Ko lowered his right arm and raised it again, once, twice, three times, four . . .

Four hunters only. She sighed with relief as she answered the signal, then moved to where she could pass the news on down to the camp. Suth waved back, turned and spoke to the people at the camp, waited for an answer and turned back to her. He raised both hands and pushed them towards her.

Stay there.

There were few enough hunters for the adults of the Kin to wait at the camp and face them. Mana waved and passed the order back to Ko, who answered and crawled out of sight. Then she waited, dry mouthed, heart hammering, her eyes on the point where the blood trail crossed Po's spur, a long way down from his lookout.

Below her the hillside seemed empty. Suth had vanished. The marsh was hidden under its usual haze. Somewhere out there, a safe distance along the winding paths, the mothers were waiting with the babies and small ones. Everyone else was concealed among the boulders round the camp.

The hunters came much sooner than she'd guessed, slinking across the skyline. One, two, three, four, swift and stealthy, pausing, peering ahead and then darting on to the next piece of cover. They weren't hiding for fear of meeting some enemy, only because they didn't want to alarm their prey. Every now and then their leader would crouch, point and peer for a moment at something on the ground. Mana knew what he'd found – another speck of the blood trail. It didn't take them long to reach the hollow where Mana had first discovered the strangers.

They crouched at its edge for a moment, and slipped down out of sight. Mana ducked behind a boulder and signalled to the camp. Suth didn't risk an answer, but she was confident he'd seen her. She returned to her watch.

The hunters were out of sight for a while. They would be reading the signs that Kern had found – the man had lain here and bled, the woman had knelt here, the child had pissed here, chewed fishbones had been spat out here. Then others had come. The man had been helped, lifted. His wound had broken out afresh . . .

Now she saw them again, but this time it was only a single head peering over the rim of the hollow, studying the hillside ahead. Yes, they had read the signs well. Now they knew they had more than one woman and a wounded man to deal with.

All four came out of the hollow and moved on, crouching and darting, taking more trouble to hide, but moving just as confidently as before. As they passed below her Mana got her first clear view of them. They were different from any people she knew, with long, thin arms and legs, and skins as dark as her own, but not her deep clear brown. Theirs was greyer, with a faint purple tinge beneath the surface. They wore belts with one or two strange pale gourds slung from them, and carried pointed sticks, longer than ordinary digging sticks, but shorter and stouter than the fishing stick Mana had been using yesterday.

Every now and then one of them would freeze and stare around, and Mana would freeze with him and hold her breath, sure that this time as the fierce gaze swept across the slope he would notice the glisten of an eye behind the crack between two boulders. It was hard not to sigh with relief as the gaze moved past her and on.

Despite these pauses they covered the ground quickly. Soon they had almost reached the camp. When they were still about ten and ten paces away from it, Tun, Suth, Var and Kern, with their digging sticks in their hands, rose from behind rocks. Tun took a pace forward with his left hand raised in greeting and his hair peaceably still.

The strangers scarcely hesitated. Instantly their hair bushed out. They gave a sharp, barking shout and charged. The four Kin shouted in answer and raised their digging sticks. Mana saw Kern, nearest her, parry a thrust, but then the rest of the Kin rose from their hiding places and rushed to join the scuffle. Their cries echoed along the hillside, savage and furious. One of the strangers broke from the throng and raced away. Nobody but Mana saw him go. She stood up, pointed and yelled, but her voice was lost in the uproar. By the time the fighting stopped he was well along the slope.

She yelled again. Heads turned. She pointed. Net and Tor raced off after the man, but he had too great a start and they soon gave up. Mana turned back to the others. She could see one body – no, two – lying on the ground, part hidden by people's legs. Somebody was sitting on a rock, nursing a wounded arm. Chogi was looking at somebody's hurt head. Suth waved, and pointed towards Ko's lookout, out of sight from the camp, then waved again, beckoning. Mana passed the message on and ran down the hill.

It was Tun whose arm was wounded, a deep gash from a thrust in that first attack. Yova's eye was swollen shut. She'd been hit by the butt of somebody's digging stick as he'd drawn it back to strike. Shuddering, Mana looked at the bodies, three of them, the third one down in the hollow by the fire. They were all those of the strangers. The two she'd first seen lay face down, but the third, bloody and battered, stared blindly at the sky. At his side lay the thing that had hung from his belt. It wasn't any kind of gourd. It was a human skull.

Appalled, terrified, Mana turned away. Suth was at her side, staring down at the dead man and the dreadful thing beside him. She clung to him and buried her face in his side, while he put his arm round her and held her.

'This is demon stuff,' he muttered.

Oldtale

THE RAGE OF ROH

Dop fought with Gul. Gul won. Fat Pig and Snake saw this.

Snake said, 'See. My man Gul is better.'

Fat Pig said, 'The sun shone in Dop's eyes.'

Snake said, 'Gul made it so. He was clever.'

He laughed. He went back to the Mountain, the Mountain above Odutu.

Fat Pig was angry. He went to Dop. He breathed on him. He healed his wounds. He filled him with strength.

Still Dop slept. Fat Pig sent him a dream. In the dream he spoke to him. He said, 'Dop, my piglet, you are dishonoured by Gul. He took your dilli buck. Now he boasts to his Kin. He says, 'I fought with Dop. I beat him. He was grass before my blows.' Dop, what do you say to my Kin? What boast do you make?'

Dop woke. He remembered the fight with Gul. He

looked, and saw the dilli buck was gone. He was filled with fresh rage.

He journeyed to Sam-Sam, to the cliff of caves. Fat Pig camped there. Their leader was Roh. He was Dop's father. He was old.

Dop stood before him. He said, 'Roh, my father, I am dishonoured.'

Roh said, 'Dop, my son, who dishonours you?'

Dop said, 'Gul dishonours me, of the Kin of Snake. It happened thus and thus.' And he told of the fight.

Roh was foolish. He did not say in his heart, 'My son fought all day with Dop. I see his wounds. They are healed. This is First One stuff.' He did not think. He was filled with rage. It was of this sort:

See Sometimes River. The bed is empty. It is dry stones. Deer drink at the pools. Now the flood comes. It is a hill of water. It rushes through the bed of the river. The deer flee. They are swift, but the water is swifter. It sweeps them away. They are gone. The river is filled with water. It roars.

Such was the rage of Roh.

He called the men of Fat Pig about him. He spoke fierce words. He filled them with rage. He said, 'Where do Snake camp?'

They answered, 'Roh, Snake camp at Egg Hills. It is their Place. It is not ours. We do not go there.'

Roh said, 'Now you go to Egg Hills. You lie in wait for a man of Snake. You take vengeance on him for the dishonour of Dop.'

The men of Fat Pig put food in their gourds. They sharpened their digging sticks. They set out to Egg Hills.

CHAPTER THREE

Nobody was willing to stay near the dead men, let alone touch them. Without any more talk they moved well away from the camp, while Nar went up the hill to keep lookout and Ko ran down to the marsh to fetch the mothers and children.

Still holding close to Suth, Mana listened to the talk. Every so often another fit of shuddering welled up inside her from the memory of what she'd seen.

'Are these men?' said Kern. 'Are they people? Are they demons?'

'I say they are people,' said Var. 'Their First One is a demon.'

'Mana found a man,' said Tun. 'Four hunted him. We kill three. One runs. Now, does he bring others?'

'I say this,' said Chogi. 'Noli is right. Moonhawk showed her. We were in the Old Good Places. Strangers came. They gave no warning. They killed men. They took women. These are like those.'

Mana heard mutters of anger at the memory. It

was no wonder that the normally peaceful Kin had fought so fiercely.

'Those others had words,' said Kern. 'Do these? This man – he runs. He finds others – other demon men. He says to them *This happened*. How does he say this?'

'Kern, I do not know,' said Chogi. 'I say they come.'

'Those other strangers were many, too many,' said Var. 'We could not fight them. These four carried sharp sticks. They were not digging sticks. They were not fishing sticks. I say they were fighting sticks. These are fighters, they are people-killers. Soon many come. We cannot fight them.'

For once nobody laughed at Var for his gloomy forebodings. What he said was only too likely to be true. The four strangers hadn't been hunting the wounded man for vengeance, or for any reason that the Kin could understand. They had hunted him because they were killers. The skulls at their belts said that.

'Hear me,' said Tun decisively. 'I say this. We do not stay here. This is a demon place.'

Nobody argued. With those dead men in and around the camp, how could it be anything else?

'We do not sleep in the marsh,' Tun went on. 'There is sickness. We do not go north. These men come from there. It is dangerous, dangerous. We go to the other side of this hill, far and far. We walk on hard rock. Our feet are careful. We leave no trail.'

'Tun,' said Kern. 'On that side the reeds are dry. They are dead. They have no fish.'

'Kern, you are right,' said Tun. 'We make paths in those reeds. We hide our paths. Out beyond is water.

We fish there. All the time we keep watch on the hill. These demon men come. Our watchers see them. We hide in the reeds. Perhaps they find our paths. We make the paths narrow. These men come by one and by one. We fight them by one and by one. We lie in wait. For them it is dangerous, dangerous. Perhaps they do not come in the reeds. They are afraid.

'Hear me again. This is difficult. It is dangerous. It is not good. But what other thing do we do? Other things are worse.'

They discussed the plan for a while. Nobody liked it, but as Tun had said, what else was there to do?

'I have a bad thought,' said Var. Again, nobody laughed at him. 'The rains go. Soon is west wind time. These men stand on the hill. Does the wind blow away the haze? Do the men see our paths?'

'Suth, what is this?' whispered Mana, puzzled and anxious. She didn't clearly remember a time when the rainy season had been a regular thing. Rapidly Suth explained that after the rains had been over, a steady wind used to blow from the west. Var was suggesting that if that happened here, the demon men might be able to see far out across the marshes and work out where the Kin were hiding.

By the time she listened again, Kern – always much more cheerful than Var – was reminding them that soon after they'd arrived on the promontory he had explored far up its western side, and found very little by way of food.

'This man runs away,' he said. 'He finds others. How long is this? One day, two? I do not know. He says, *Men and women are in that place. Come. We hunt them*. This is another day. They bring food.

They come. They do not find us. They eat their food. They have none. They find no food here. Do they know fishing? I say they do not. They go away. We come out of the marshes. We fish. We keep watch. We do not hide all the time. This is better.'

The rest of them talked it over, sounding slightly more cheerful. Mana felt Suth pat her comfortingly on the shoulder.

'Mana, you fish at your fishing hole,' he said. 'Is this good?'

She took his hand and squeezed it, but still she found herself imagining what it would be like to crouch at her fishing hole, still and tense, waiting for a fish to come sidling into the open, but all the time wondering if one of the demon men mightn't have slipped unnoticed past the lookouts and be creeping along the path behind her. Another fit of shuddering shook her.

Suth knelt and took her by the shoulders and looked her in the eyes.

'You are afraid?' he asked gently.

'They are demons,' she muttered.

'Mana, you are Moonhawk,' he said. 'We are brave. We are clever. We are strong. Moonhawk helps us. These men are not demons. They are people. They say in their hearts, *All are afraid of us. All run before us*. But Moonhawk are not afraid. We do not run. First we hide. We make plans. We wait. We choose good times. We beat these men, these people-killers. We, Moonhawk, do this. You do it, Mana. You help.'

She nodded and pulled herself together, squaring her shoulders and standing erect. Tun was right. It was going to be difficult and dangerous, but there was nothing else to do. And Suth was right too – Moonhawk could do it. But not if they let themselves be scared stupid.

Now the mothers came sombrely up from the marsh with their small ones. Ko had told them the news. As they climbed the hill they must have been having much the same discussions as Mana had just heard. They stood and listened in silence while Tun explained his plan. His words meant nothing to the stranger woman, of course. She looked around, spotted Mana, and came and made questioning noises to her.

To save trying to explain with grunts and signs Mana led her up the hill and across to a point from which they could look down onto the camp. The woman stared, gave a gasp of astonishment, thrust her child into Mana's arms and dashed off, not slackening her pace until she reached the spot. As soon as she'd regained her breath she knelt by the two bodies that were lying face down and heaved them over onto their backs. Then she rose and stretched both arms to the sky and gave a great shout, like the scream of a furious beast.

She bent again and dragged the body by the fire up to the other two and laid it beside them, then started to dance around them, alone on the rocky hillside, clapping her hands and singing at the top of her voice.

The others heard the glad and savage chant and came to see what it could mean. They watched the dance in silence for a while.

'This is good,' said Tun. 'The demons do not come near her. They are afraid. Now Tinu fills the fire log.'

Tinu scampered down the hill and did as he suggested. Mana wondered if perhaps she wasn't in any case as scared of demons as the rest of them. When she returned the stranger woman came with her, no longer the cowering, desperate creature she had been till now, but walking erect and smiling.

They climbed to the ridge, on a slant that took them further to the north. Even the smallest children were careful to step where they would leave no footprints. Yova and Moru worked their way along the top to keep lookout, while the others slanted on down the other side of the promontory towards the western shore.

Below them lay another arm of the great reedbed they had come to know so well, but here the reeds grew not in good water, but out of an immense mudbank. That had dried out, and as a result large patches had died completely, leaving a confusion of dead stems. Though the rains had come and gone, even where the reeds still lived the first green shoots were only just beginning to spear up through the brown, dry tangle.

It was midday by the time they reached the shoreline. Normally they would have rested through the heat, but most of the adults started at once on the slow and difficult task of cutting a hidden path into the reeds. Suth, though, said, 'Come, Ko. Come, Mana. We find lookout places,' and led them up the hill.

Mana might not have spotted the feather if she hadn't been watching where she put her feet. She bent and eased it out from a cranny between two rocks – a single plume, of a dull, bluish dark grey. When she twisted it at an angle to the sunlight the blueness seemed to rise to the surface and shimmer to and fro over the sombre undercolour. She knew only one bird that had feathers like that.

'Suth, see what I find!' she said, and showed it to him.

He stopped and took it from her, making it do its trick with the sunlight.

'Moonhawk,' he said. 'Mana, you find a good sign.'

Smiling, he handed it back and they climbed on.

From the top of the ridge Mana gazed back. Yes, she thought, Var had been right. The marsh haze was their friend. If an enemy stood where she was standing, he would see the reedbed clearly for the first few tens of paces, and the people who were working there now, but beyond that everything would be vague brown distances. Not even a broad trail would show up. But if the west wind came and brought clear air, then it would be far harder for the Kin to hide themselves.

They found Yova and Moru tucked down among the boulders on either side of the ridge, each with a clear view north along her flank of the promontory.

'This is good,' said Suth. 'Now Mana and Ko keep lookout. Yova and Moru go down. They cut reeds. I look for a thing.'

So Ko took over from Moru on the eastern side of the ridge while Mana stayed on the western side. She settled and began to study the landscape to the north. The slope wasn't regular, but full of dips and rises. She looked for places where any attackers would need to cross some kind of ridge or spur, and she would have her best chances of spotting them. Below her Suth moved to and fro, searching the hillside. Mana had no idea what he wanted until he heaved up a flat slab of rock and staggered with it up the hill. He was gasping with the effort by the time he reached her.

He knelt and propped the slab upright, just above the lookout. Now Mana saw that all its surface was covered with glittery little specks, which made it much paler than any of the other rocks around.

When he'd recovered his breath he said, 'One watches by the path into the reeds. He sees this rock. He says in his heart, *No enemy comes*.'

He laid the rock flat.

'The watcher does not see this rock,' he said. 'He says in his heart, *It is gone. An enemy comes*. He tells others. They hide. Is this good?'

Mana remembered how fast the demon men had covered the ground in their first attack. There wouldn't be time for the watchers to run down to the shore and warn the others. Even to shout, or to stand and wave, might be dangerous. But . . . Her heart tightened with renewed dread.

'But the watchers, Suth?' she whispered. 'Where do they go?'

He nodded confidently.

'I find a place,' he said.

Again he searched the slope, pausing often to gaze north and crouching low whenever he crossed open ground. Mana returned to her watch, but as she scanned the hillside her mind kept telling her, *This is danger. All the time it is danger. All the time we move like Suth. We watch. We run. We hide. We are afraid.*

Suth didn't find what he wanted in front of her or below her, so he moved out of sight behind her, and after a short while called softly to her to come. She did so, moving as he had moved, and found him squatting beside a large slab a little way down the hill, doing something with a few smaller rocks at its lower end. As she knelt beside him he lifted one of them away and showed her a narrow opening beneath the slab.

'I am too big,' he said. 'Can you go under this rock? Take my digging stick. Look for scorpions.'

Cautiously Mana wormed her head and shoulders into the slot and prodded around with the digging stick. When her eyes were used to the dimness, she made out that further in the space widened enough for her to wriggle through and squirm round until she could see out into daylight.

'This is good,' said Suth. 'See. Take this.'

He passed one rock in to Mana and placed the rest across the opening, leaving a narrow gap, then removed them and made her practise reaching out and dragging them into position, before fitting the one he'd given her into the final gap. Then he fetched Ko and tested whether there was room for him to fit in beside Mana. There was, just, but he had to work his way in feet first and then almost wrench his chest through the slot. When Suth was satisfied he let them come out.

'Suth,' said Ko. 'This place is small. Does Yova go in there? Does Moru?'

'Ko, they do not,' Suth answered. 'Few can keep lookout. Tinu and Shuja – they are small. You, Ko, and Mana. That is all. Now, Ko, you go back to your place. I bring Tinu and Shuja. I show them. Mana, wait.'

So she crouched beside him on the roasting hillside until Ko was out of sight. Then he looked her in the eyes and said, 'Mana, you do this? You are not afraid?'

She swallowed. The slot beneath the rock looked like the mouth of a burrow. Mana had many times dug small animals out of their burrows, listening eagerly to their terrifed squeakings as she came nearer to the nest. Now it would be her and Ko in the burrow. She knew that Suth must have guessed what she was thinking, or he wouldn't have asked. She looked down at her hand and realized that she was still grasping the moonhawk feather.

'Yes, Suth, I do this,' she answered.

She watched him stand and use the sole of his foot to blur away any betraying scrape marks that the rocks might have left as they were dragged to and fro. Then she crept back to her lookout while he made his way down to the marsh.

For the first time ever that Mana could remember they made no camp that night. There was no cheerful fire. The workers had cut an open circle at the far end of the path they had made, and floored it with mud and built their fire out there, banking it around with more mud and leaving two small openings above and below, so that there would still be embers hot enough in the morning to start a fresh fire. Like that it was invisible from the shore, and there was no danger of any spark setting light to the great reedbed on which their safety depended.

The reedbed was now their home. The hillside was only a place where they could sleep, away from the night-time sickness of the marsh. Every evening from now on they would choose a different place on the hillside, and try to leave no trace that they had been there. Anyone old enough to control themselves must make dung and pass water out among the reeds, and the mothers must clean up as best they could after their babies.

They were settling down among the unfamilar rocks when Mana heard someone say, 'Be quiet. Listen.'

Her heart stood still. Had the speaker heard a footfall, or the click of a pebble dislodged as unseen figures crept towards them?

No. From north along the promontory came a high, harsh shriek, thrice repeated, *yeek-yeek-yeek*, then a pause and the call again, and yet again, the cry of a moonhawk leaving its nest at nightfall to hunt among the rocks for its prey, the shy little scurriers that came out of their burrows only in the dark.

'She is here,' someone whispered. 'She is with us. This is a Moonhawk place.'

Mana knew she was not the only one to feel comforted.

Oldtale

THE WAR OATH

The men of Snake said, 'Today we hunt.'

Jad was among them. His mate was Meena, from Little Bat. They were new mated. They were happy, happy. All saw their love. It was of this sort:

See this man. He says in his heart, Now I make a cutter. He chooses a good stone. He strikes it thus, and thus. His aim is true. The chips fly from the stone. The edge is sharp, strong, a clean curve. He holds the cutter in his palm. His fingers close round it. Cutter and hand, they are one thing. He is glad, glad.

Such was the love of Jad for Meena, and of Meena for Jad.

Meena said, 'Jad, I come with you? I see you hunt?'

Jad asked the men. They laughed. They said, 'Let her come.'

They came to the deer pastures. They spread apart. Jad said to Meena, 'Come behind me, ten paces. Do not be seen.'

The men of Fat Pig lay in wait. Mott was among them. Rage was in his heart. Jad came close. Mott gave no warning. He sprang out upon Jad. He struck him with his digging stick, on the side of the neck. Jad fell. Blood flowed. Mott raised his digging stick for another blow.

Meena saw this. She ran between the men. Mott did not see, he did not think, his rage filled him. He struck again. His digging stick was sharp, it was heavy. It hit Meena between the breasts. It broke through her ribs. It entered her heart. She fell on Jad's body. They were dead.

Now the rage left Mott. He saw Jad's body, and Meena's. He did not rejoice. He said in his heart, I have done this thing. It is bad, bad. He dragged the bodies under bushes. He ran from that place.

The men of Fat Pig saw him. They said, 'Mott runs. We run also.'

So they fled.

The men of Snake rejoiced. They said, 'Fat Pig are weak, they are cowards. We are brave and strong. But where is Jad? Where is Meena?'

They searched. They found the bodies of Jad and of Meena. They were filled with rage.

Ziul was Jad's brother. He said, 'Fat Pig did this thing. Now we, Snake, take vengeance. Come.'

They pursued the men of Fat Pig. They came to Sam-Sam, to the cliff of caves. The men of Fat Pig met them. Again they fought. The men of Snake fought better. They struck fierce blows. They killed two. The men of Fat Pig fled.

The men of Snake rejoiced. They said, 'We have vengeance for Jad.'

But Ziul said, 'It is not enough. We do not have vengeance for Meena.'

He entered the caves. He found Dilu, Tong's mate. She hid there. She was from Ant Mother. Ziul struck her. She died.

He returned to the men of Snake. He said, 'Rejoice. I have vengeance for Meena.'

The men of Snake did not answer. Shame was in their hearts. They went home.

The men of Fat Pig said, 'We take vengeance for Dilu. But the men of Snake are too strong. We need friends.'

They sent to Ant Mother and to Weaver and to Parrot.

To Ant Mother they said, 'Take vengeance on Snake for Dilu, who was your daughter.'

To Weaver they said, 'Sam-Sam is your Place. There Fat Pig killed Dilu, a woman. You are dishonoured.'

To Parrot they said, 'You fought Moonhawk in our father's time. We helped you. Now help us.'

The men of Snake said, 'Fat Pig send to their friends. They take vengeance on us for Dilu. Let us send also, to Little Bat, and to Crocodile and to Moonhawk.'

To Little Bat they said, 'Fat Pig killed Meena, who was your daughter. Take vengeance upon them.'

To Crocodile they said, 'Ant Mother fights against us. Yellowspring is their Place. You want it. Now help us. We beat them. You take Yellowspring. It is yours.'

To Moonhawk they said, 'Parrot fights against us.

You have blood debts to settle. Help us. We help you.'

The Kins spoke among themselves. Some men did not want this. They said, 'Mott did this, and Ziul. Let Mott be given to Snake. Let them kill him. Let Ziul be given to Fat Pig. Let them kill him. It is finished.'

These men were few.

Other men said, 'Let us fight. Let us go to Odutu. Let us swear the War Oath.'

These men were many.

So all gathered to Odutu. First came Snake and Fat Pig. They laid their hands upon the rock. They swore the war oath. The others watched. They said, 'Tomorrow we too swear. It is war.'

CHAPTER FOUR

For ten and two more long days they saw no sign of the murderous strangers. There were two lookouts, one on either side of the ridge, each with its own signal stone. Morning after morning Mana crouched at one of them, scanning the now familiar hillside for the faintest flicker of movement. Her tension never lessened. She knew in her heart the enemy would be back in the end, and if they weren't spotted far off there would be no time for everyone to hide, and then there would be fighting and slaughter. However bravely the Kin fought, if the attackers came in too great numbers, then Moonhawk and all the other Kins would be gone for ever. The demon men would kill all the males – Tun, Suth, Tor, Ko, and the others, even little Ogad – while the women and girls – Yova and Noli, Bodu, Tinu, Mana herself, all of them – would be taken away to become the mates of these demon men, and bear their demon children.

Perhaps Moonhawk would send a warning, as

she'd done before. Perhaps not. You could never tell with First Ones.

So Mana watched unwavering, with Ko on the other side of the ridge, doing the same. They took turn and turn about, so that they didn't become stale with watching the same hillside all the time. They were alone.

If Mana was on the western flank and looked down to the marsh, she could see nothing of her friends. But she knew they were there, cutting the main path further and further across the mudbank, or side paths and blind alleys to confuse anyone who didn't know the way. Out there, somewhere, the precious fire was burning, but she could see no sign of it through the haze, and smelt no whiff of smoke.

If she was on the other flank and looked down she would see a few people foraging along the shoreline, or perhaps coming or going along one of the paths that led to a fishing hole. If an attack came while they were there, there would be no time for them to climb and cross the ridge and reach the safety of their main hideout. So they had cut another path here, also hidden at the entrance, and with its own maze of traps and side turnings. If danger threatened they could hide there. At least two of the men were always there to defend the path if they had to.

Like everything else, this was dangerous, but they were forced to take the risk because there was so little food of any kind on the western shore, and their main path had not yet reached the far side of the great mudbank to an area of water where they could fish.

At midday Tinu and Shuja came stealthily up from

the western marsh to take over lookout, and Mana and Ko, watching every step they took, crept back down the hill. By then Mana's head would throb and her eyes would be sore with endlessly gazing at the rock-strewn slope, lit by the glaring sun.

Somebody was down at the shore, waiting for the moment that the pale rock by the lookout vanished, signalling that the enemy had been seen. Ko and Mana greeted the watcher and then, at a particular point in the great tangle of reeds along the shoreline, lifted a broken mass of stems and crawled into the gap beneath them, and on for several more paces along a twisting tunnel, until they reached the path. There were three such entrances, so that everyone out in the open could get quickly into cover.

The path itself twisted to and fro to make it harder to see from the hillside. Twice in that first stretch they stopped and, instead of going straight on – those were blind alleys – sidled between reedstems to where the real path continued beyond.

On the third day, just beyond the second of these places, they found Net and Var toiling away, with sweat streaming from their bodies in the steamy heat. They had cleared the cut reeds from the floor of the path and were using their digging sticks to loosen the mud beneath.

'Var, what do you do?' asked Ko.

'We make a trap,' said Var. 'It is Tinu's thought. See, we make the mud soft . . .'

He stepped onto the patch he had been working on. Immediately his leg started to sink.

'We finish,' he went on. 'We put the reeds back. We walk on them. This is safe. But demon men come.

They find our path. We run. We cross here. We take reeds away. We wait this side. Demon men come. They walk on the mud. They sink. We fight them with digging sticks. They are in the mud. This is good for us.'

The men went back to their work, and Ko and Mana made their way on.

By now the path had reached what had once been an island, with trees and bushes growing on it. Most of these had died in the drought, so there was good fuel for the fire, as well as a safer place for it to burn without setting fire to the whole vast reedbed.

This was now their daytime lair. By the time the children reached it most of the others would have gathered there for their midday rest and meal, but as soon as they'd finished eating they all went back to work. Mana helped with whatever needed doing – collecting fuel, preparing food, laying and firming reeds in the pathways or searching for birds' nests, and for insect bait for fishing. As the sun dipped towards the horizon everyone except the lookouts gathered again on the island for their evening meal.

This was scanty for the first few days, with most of them either on watch or working desperately to make their hideout secure, and to drive the path to the far side of the mudbank, where they could fish in safety. This left only a few of them to fish among the eastern reeds and forage along that shore. But they ate what they had and were glad of it.

Then, as dusk fell, moving as carefully as ever, they came ashore and climbed to wherever Tun had chosen for them to lair. Mana at first dreaded these times, and knew that she was not the only one to do so.

The moon was small, and the nights were very dark. The dark belonged to the demons. Everyone knew that. That was why, however hot the season, and whether or not there was food to cook, when the Kin made a fresh camp the first thing they always did was to light a fire, so that they could sleep in its friendly glow and know that the demons would be afraid to come too near.

But they could have no fire now, with its flame far-seen in the night and its betraying ash left on this hillside in the morning. They were forced to sleep in the dark, and from time to time Mana would wake, tense with terror, and hear a small one whimper or an adult sigh, and know that someone else was awake too, and as afraid as she was.

But then, from north along the promontory, she would hear one of the moonhawks call. These were just a pair of ordinary moonhawks, each hunting in turn, while the other one fed the chicks with what it had just caught, but hearing that cry Mana would sense that Moonhawk herself was hovering near her in the dark, ready to warn, ready to guard the last of her Kin. Then she would master her fear and sleep again.

The maze of paths and traps was almost finished. The moon grew half large, and still there was no sign of the demon men. Mana heard the adults discussing whether they were going to come back at all. Var, of course, was sure that they would, and Kern just as sure they wouldn't. The others' opinions were in between.

'Hear me,' said Tun at last. 'They come, they do not come, who knows? But we say in our hearts *They come*. This is best. Every day we are careful, careful. The moon grows big. It grows small again. Then we decide. I, Tun, say this.'

So they didn't relax their watch, but went about their business as if an attack might come that very day. Though they had reached the further side of the mudbank, the fishing there turned out to be disappointing, so several of them still returned to their old fish holes on the eastern side. When there was nothing more for her to do around the island lair Mana asked Suth if she could go and join them after she'd finished her stint on lookout.

She caught nothing on her first afternoon, but two nice little fish on the second. On the third afternoon the tiddlers had found the bait and started to feed, and she was waiting eagerly for something larger to nose into view, when she heard from the shoreline the whistling call of a small brown bird.

Mana laid her fishing stick down and waited, holding her breath. The bird had been common in the New Good Places on the southern side of the marsh, but nobody had seen it here. That was why they had chosen its call.

Again the bird called, but this time, listening for it, she could tell that it wasn't a real bird. Kern, on guard at the entrance to the hidden path, had seen the signal stone disappear above the eastern lookout, and had given the danger signal. The watcher there had seen someone or something approaching from the north.

Mana let out her breath and rose with her heart

pounding. She couldn't stay here. The entrance was obvious from the shore. She picked up her gourd and fishing stick, checked quickly around that there was no other trace of her presence, and ran back down the short path. Crouching low, she scuttled along the shore to where Kern was waiting.

'Good,' he said. 'Soon Moru comes. Then all are in.'

He lifted a stack of reedstems and she crawled through. Just as on the other side there was a tunnel before the path began, and a little way beyond it a trap like the one she'd seen Var and Net making. Tun was there, and the stranger woman with her child on her hip. (Noli had given them names, Ridi and Ovoth. As soon as Ridi had worked out that Tun was leader she had simply attached herself to him, and went everywhere he went.)

Mana had crossed the trap and was about to run on when Tun said, 'Wait. My arm is not good. Take reeds from the trap. Not all. Some. Moru comes soon, and Kern. Then take all, quick, quick. Show Ridi. Why does Moru not come?'

Mana had never heard him sound so anxious. She laid her gourd and stick on the path and signed to Ridi to put Ovoth down. While Tun stood guard on the far side of the trap she gathered up an armful of loose reeds, passed them to Ridi and gestured to her to carry them back along the path.

The reeds were laid crisscross in several layers. Beneath them was clear water. She stripped two layers away and tested the ones she'd left by walking on them. She could feel them quake beneath her.

'Tun, do I take enough?' she asked.

He looked over his shoulder.

'Take from that side,' he said. 'Leave those.'

She did as he'd said, and was about to ask him again when she heard shouts from the entrance to the path – men yelling in anger – and a moment later Moru came racing along the path towards them.

Tun stood aside to let her pass. Mana shouted to her to keep to her right as she crossed the trap but she didn't hear and trod on the weak part. Her foot went through and she started to fall, but Mana grabbed her outstretched arm and dragged her over.

Before Mana could follow a demon man appeared at the bend of the path, with another behind him. The leading one saw Tun, raised his fighting stick, and rushed at him with a yell.

'Back!' shouted Tun.

Mana turned to run. Ridi, bending to pick up Ovoth, blocked her way. She looked back and saw that Tun had retreated to the near side of the trap and standing with his hair bushed full out and his digging stick raised to strike.

The man rushed at him and launched himself into his thrust. His front foot landed, hard, on the trap and sank straight through. He stumbled and started to fall. His momentum carried the thrust past Tun's thigh, and just missed Mana behind him. Ridi bent, grabbed the end of the fighting stick with her free hand and wrenched, just as Tun's blow slammed down into the man's back.

He screamed and collapsed, but as he fell his free hand reached out and grasped Tun's ankle. Tun was already moving back for another blow. Suddenly unbalanced, he fell on top of Mana. She was beginning to struggle up as the second man rushed towards them.

Ridi was the only one still standing. The first man had let go of his stick as he fell, but she'd kept hold of it. The second man paused for an instant, judging his leap across the trap. In that instant Ridi managed to reverse the spear, and as he sprang she screamed and darted to meet him, jabbing forward two-handed with all her strength. He didn't seem to see her. All his attention was on Tun. In the middle of his leap he drove himself onto the sharpened point of the stick. It sank into his stomach, just below the rib cage.

Ridi was knocked over backwards by the force of their meeting, but by now Mana was on her feet. Tun was still on the ground, trying to kick the first man's grip from his ankle. He had let go of his digging stick. His left arm, wounded in the earlier fight, was still almost useless to him. Mana saw the stick lying at her feet, snatched it up, took a pace forward and hammered down on the first man's head. He gave a deep grunt and let go of Tun's ankle. While Tun was getting to his feet she hammered twice more, to make sure. The last blow felt different. Something gave way beneath it. The man lay face down in the water and didn't move.

The second man was kneeling up on the edge of the trap where Mana had left the extra layers of reeds. The stick point was still in his stomach, and he was grinning taut lipped, with all his teeth showing. He dragged the stick free and started to try to rise, with the blood streaming down his belly. Tun took the digging stick from Mana, aimed, and struck him savagely on the side of the neck, above the collar bone. Still grinning, he toppled sideways on top of the other man.

They stood side by side, panting, with the dead men at their feet.

'Mana, I thank. Ridi, I thank,' said Tun. 'I fear for Kern. Where is he?'

While Tun guarded the path Mana and Ridi rearranged the reeds over the trap so that they hid the water below but wouldn't take any weight. Then they waited a long while, but no one else, friend or foe, appeared along the path.

'Go, Mana,' said Tun. 'Find others. Tell them our doing. Say *Come. Make this trap strong.* I look for Kern.'

Mana hurried away. She found Yova, Moru, Rana and Galo waiting anxiously just beyond the first place where a false trail led onwards and the real path was hidden behind a screen of reeds. Moru was obviously very distressed, and the others had been trying to comfort her.

'Kern does not come?' she asked desperately.

Mana shook her head.

'It is my doing,' Moru said, croaking with grief. 'I did not hear the whistle bird call. Kern came. He found me. We ran. The demon men saw us. They were five. They found the path. Kern said, *Run, Moru. I fight them.* I ran. Oh, Yova, Kern is dead.'

It was true. When they returned to the trap they found Tun there, looking very grim. He had gone to the end of the path and seen blood on the trampled reeds at the entrance. The signal stone was not in its place by the lookout, so he'd known there must still be demon men about. There was nothing to do but leave the trap as it was and wait.

Towards evening the signal rock appeared, and at last they came out. They found Kern's body some way up the hill. They knew it had to be his from the colour of the skin. Otherwise they wouldn't have known. The head was missing.

Tun stared sombrely down at the body, saying nothing. The others waited. Mana started to sob and couldn't stop. Rana knelt and held her. Dimly she was aware of Moru's voice, also racked with sobs, blaming herself over and over, and the other women trying to comfort her, though they were weeping too.

At last Tun said, 'We do not leave him here.' So they lifted the battered body, two at the shoulders, two at the thighs, and Mana carrying the trailing feet, and with Tun leading carried it up to the cairn they had piled over the stranger man. They laid it down beside the cairn and heaped more rocks over it.

It was exhausting labour, but it felt to Mana that at least she was doing all she could for Kern, and this seemed to ease her grief. Before they had finished some of the others came up from the western marsh. They had seen the signal stone on their side reappear, so they knew the danger was over and had come to see what had happened.

In the late dusk they crossed the ridge and found the rest of the Kin already assembling on the hillside. They had brought food with them, but Mana was unable to eat. Someone had already run down down to the marsh with the news, so instead of settling down to sleep they sat and talked it over.

The half moon was rising, but not yet above the

ridge, so this slope was still in deep darkness. Only now, sitting there, unable to see the faces but listening to the well-known, troubled voices, did Mana begin to feel something deep inside her that she hadn't until now realized was there.

In the terror of the sudden attack, that had been all she had felt – terror, almost drowning her wits, spurring her to run, and then to fight. After that the immense relief of victory, and then the long anxiety of wondering what had happened to Kern, and the horror and grief of the answer.

But now, as she sat and gazed unseeing over the vague distances of the moonlit marsh, a different thought came to her.

I have killed people.

Yes. The attackers had been demon people, but that didn't make them any less people. Mana wasn't sorry for what she had done. If she hadn't done it, perhaps Tun would now be dead, and little Ovoth too, and she and Ridi and Yova and the other women who had been there would be being herded away to the north by their savage captors. She had had to kill the man. She was sure of that.

But despite that, everything had changed, and Mana herself would never be the same again.

She had killed people.

At last the moon crossed the ridge, and suddenly the whole slope was bathed in pale light, mottled by the dense black shadows thrown by the rocks. Tun rose.

'Hear me,' he said. 'We do no death dance for Kern. The demon men take his head. They take his spirit. He is not here. I say again we do no death dance for Kern. We do this. Come.'

He led the way to a large boulder. He waited for the rest of them to gather round, and then reached up and laid his dark hand against the paler stone.

'This rock is Odutu,' he said in a low clear voice. 'Odutu below the Mountain. On Odutu I say this. *These men kill Kern. He is Moonhawk. They take his head. For this I kill them, all, all. Not one lives. I, Tun, do this.* On Odutu I say these words.'

One after another all the adults, women as well as men, came to the boulder and laid their hand against it and swore the same oath. Moru could scarcely get the words out, and she was not the only one.

As she finished the triple call of a hunting moonhawk rang through the night stillness.

Oldtale

BLACK ANTELOPE'S WAKING

Black Antelope slept. He dreamed good dreams. Then a thing woke him. His waking was of this sort:

See this man. He sleeps by the fire. A log falls. Sparks jump out. One lands on the arm of the man. The pain is sharp, sharp. He wakes. He cries, 'Oh!'

Such was Black Antelope's waking.

He said in his heart, Men came to Odutu, Odutu below the Mountain. They laid their hands upon the Rock. They swore the War Oath.

He looked down the Mountain. He saw the rock Odutu. He saw the Kins gathered about it. He breathed through his nostrils. His breath was thick mist.

The men slept. They woke. They were in thick mist. They could not see. They searched for the rock, Odutu. They could not find it.

Black Antelope called the First Ones about him.

He said, 'The Kins swear the War Oath. Why is this? Let Moonhawk speak.'

Moonhawk said, 'Parrot fights against Snake. My Kin has blood debts to settle with Parrot.'

Black Antelope said, 'Parrot, why does your Kin fight against Snake?'

Parrot said, 'My Kin owes Fat Pig a debt. When they fought against Parrot, Fat Pig helped them.'

Then Crocodile told the reason, and Parrot and Ant Mother and Little Bat.

Black Antelope looked at Snake. He said, 'Your man Ziul killed a woman. Why is this?'

Snake said, 'He sought vengeance for the death of Meena. Fat Pig's man Mott killed her.'

Fat Pig said, 'Mott was in rage, the rage of a hero. He did not see it was a woman.'

Black Antelope said, 'What made this rage?'

Fat Pig said, 'My man Dop hunted. Snake's man Gul hunted. There was one dilli buck. Each man said it was his. They fought. Gul won by a trick. My man Dop was dishonoured. My Kin was dishonoured.'

Weaver said, 'Now I remember. Snake and Fat Pig drank stoneweed. There was much shouting. Each said his man was better. The men were Dop and Gul.'

Black Antelope said, 'Is this the seed of it?'

Fat Pig and Snake were filled with shame. They hid their heads.

Black Antelope spoke to the First Ones. He said, 'You six, go now to your Kins. They did not swear the War Oath. Speak in their hearts. Say to them, This is folly. Send them back to their own Places.'

They went down the Mountain, those six. They spoke in the hearts of their Kins. It was done.

Black Antelope spoke to Snake and to Fat Pig. He said, 'This folly is your folly. You must undo it.'

They said, 'We go now to our Kins. We say to them, Unswear your War Oath.'

He said, 'This is not enough. On Odutu they swore, Odutu below the Mountain. How must they unswear? In their own hearts they must do it, not from your telling. I know you two. You say in your hearts, 'I cheat Black Antelope. My Kin is mine. I wish a thing, they do it.' So now I do this to you.'

He put his nose against theirs. He breathed in. He drew their powers out of them. Fat Pig was Fat Pig no more. He was a pig of the reedbeds. He was fat.

Snake was Snake no more. He was a tree serpent, green and black. He was long.

They said, 'Our powers are gone. Our Kins do not hear our words. We cannot speak to them.'

Black Antelope said, 'I give you this. Go to your Kins. One sees you first. That one hears your words, that one only. Now, go.'

CHAPTER FIVE

They woke with the first light. As they searched the hillside for any traces of their stay, Mana could hear a different note in their voices. Anger, as well as fear. She felt the difference in herself. The fear itself was different too, like a different taste in the mouth, not thin and acid as before, but rounder and stronger. The taste of something she could feed on, use.

She thought about it later that morning, crouching in her lookout, and decided that if it had been possible she would sooner have had the old fear back. Of course, if she needed to, she would again fight as fiercely as any of the adults who had sworn the oath. If the chance came to kill another of the demon men she would seize it. Horrible, but she'd had no choice. Why should she alone be spared the horror?

But there had been a different Mana yesterday, one who had never killed people. That Mana had been happier, despite her fear.

She and Ko watched all morning, but saw no sign of danger. There was no question now of fishing in the eastern marsh, with the path no longer hidden and the spirits of the dead men bringing demons to lurk among the reeds. So they went down the other side and out to the island and ate scraps for their midday meal. But Suth came in with the cheering news that the path had now reached a new area of water where the fishing was better, and several fish holes had already been cut. When they had eaten they went out to see, and were allowed to fish for a while at one of these. They took turns. Mana caught nothing, but Ko speared a good fish, short but deep bodied, and carried it back to the island in triumph.

Not far into the night, as she slept on the hillside, Mana was woken by the moon rising above the ridge. It was now more than half full, its light even brighter and the shadows it cast even blacker than they had seemed the night before. The moonhawks were again busy, coming and going in quick succession as the stronger light made it easier for them to find their prey.

Someone close by was moaning in her sleep. The sound stopped, and Mana saw a dark figure – Noli – push herself up and stand with arms wide spread, facing the moon. The bottom half of her body was in shadow, but the top half was clear in the sharp, pale light. The voice of Moonhawk breathed in slow syllables into the silence.

'Big moon . . . Men . . . bring Kern . . .'

Mana rose and crept to Noli's side, ready to ease her fall.

'Big moon . . .' sighed the voice again.

Noli shuddered. Mana put her arms round her. Her body went as rigid as a log, and then, just as quickly, slack. Mana was almost knocked over by the sudden weight, but she managed to lower her to the ground, still asleep but again moaning softly, while everyone else, wide awake now, sat up and wondered in whispers what the message could mean. It was a long time before any of them slept again.

Next morning went much the same as the day before. Mana and Ko kept lookout and saw nothing. But as they went down the hill at noon they felt a change. There was a wind blowing in their faces. The adults were already talking about it as they reached the island.

'I say this,' said Var. 'These men find no food here. They go back to their place, they get food, they bring it. This is two days. It is three. I do not know. Now west wind comes. They stand on the hill. They look far. They see the marsh. Do they see our path? Our island? I say they do.'

'Moonhawk says big moon,' said Net. 'Three days is not big moon.'

'Hear me,' said Suth. 'I say this. Var is right. Net is right. Say in your hearts, *I am a demon man*. Now say, *Men, women are in this place. We are many. We hunt them. Where are they?* What do you do? I say first you come, few, few. You hide. You are not seen. You look this way, that way. You see the marsh. The mist is gone. You say, *They are there*. You search the rocks. You smell baby dung. You find people hair. You say, *They sleep here*. You say, *At night we come, at big moon. Moon is strong. We find these men, these women. They are asleep*. I think you do all this.'

'Suth, you are right,' said Chogi.

'This wind is bad, bad,' said Var.

A slight movement caught Mana's eye. Tinu, sitting a few places to her left. She had reached across Bodu to touch Noli's wrist. Bodu shifted out of the way, and while the others continued to talk Tinu squatted beside Noli and mumbled into her ear. Mana couldn't hear what she was saying, but she could see how eagerly she struggled to get the words out through her twisted mouth.

After a while Noli signalled to Suth, who rose from among the men on the far side of the fire and came round. Tinu shuffled herself back and she and Suth crouched together, he listening and sometimes asking a question, Tinu mumbling excitedly away, scratching on the ground with a stick, rubbing the marks out, and drawing again.

Mana saw Nar watching them anxiously. Since he and Tinu had chosen each other, though they were not yet mates, he had been very protective of her. And Tinu had grown more confident, but still she would never have dreamed of standing up in front of everyone and telling them some idea she had had, though they would all have been ready to listen.

Now the rest of them continued to argue about when and how the next attack would come, but somehow aimlessly, as they waited to hear what Tinu was telling Suth.

At last he moved back to his place among the men, but didn't sit down. He looked at Tun.

'Speak, Suth,' said Tun. 'We hear.'

'Hear me,' said Suth. 'This is not my thought. It is

Tinu's. I say it for her. Var is wrong. This wind is not bad. It is good.'

Stage by stage he told them Tinu's terrifying plan.

They argued about it for a long while, some of them adding ideas and details, others making objections. Var kept saying how dangerous it was, and how many things could go wrong. What if the wind died? What if the demon men realized it was a trap? What if only a few of them came after all? What if . . . ?

Every time he raised one of these doubts Mana heard mutters of agreement.

'Hear me,' said Chogi suddenly. 'I remember this. There was a demon lion. The men made a trap. Noli was bait, and Ko. We killed the demon lion. It was Tinu's thought. There was a demon crocodile. The women dug a trap. Nar was bait. We killed the demon crocodile. This also was Tinu's thought. Demon men came to the reedbed. Tun fought them, and Ridi and Mana. They killed them. At a trap they did this. It was Tinu's thought. Now I say this. We make a new trap. We are bait, we women, our men, our children. I say in my heart, *This is dangerous, dangerous. But it is Tinu's thought. It is good.*'

'Hear me,' said Tun. 'I say this. Var speaks well. Chogi speaks well. Who is right? I do not know. But I have another thought. It is this. I swore an oath. On Odutu I swore it, Odutu below the Mountain. In my oath I said, *I kill these demon men*. How do I do this? It is difficult, difficult. Tinu shows me the way. It is enough.'

That settled it. Even Var stopped arguing. He too had sworn the oath upon Odutu below the Mountain and, however dangerous the undertaking, that oath was binding. The risk had to be taken.

They started at once on the task, Tun allocating the different jobs that had to be done, mostly cutting a huge new curving path through the dried-out reedbed between the island and that shore, but also hollowing out crude fire logs from whatever they could find, and cutting extra traps along the main entrance path.

But of course they still needed to eat, so Mana was sent off to fish at one of the new holes. As she settled down beside the little patch of water she felt that she would never catch anything. All of her, body and spirit, seemed to be vibrating, silently buzzing, with a new mixture of excitement and hope and fear. The long, poised stillness needed for fishing seemed quite impossible, but she found that her feelings seemed to weave themselves together, telling her that what she was doing, as well as what she was going to do, was all part of the plan. They were things within her power, not beyond her. If she did them right, the Kin would survive. If not, then not.

So focused, she fished eagerly, passionately, all afternoon, and it seemed to her that her waiting was stiller than usual, her aim surer, her strike swifter. She made five strikes in all, and as the sun went down towards the west and the strange clean air glowed with gold light, she came back to the island with five good fish threaded on her stick.

For the next three days Mana saw very little of the work that everyone else was busy on. In the mornings she kept lookout on the ridge, at midday she went back to the island and gobbled whatever had been left over for her, and then went straight out to one of the fishing holes for the rest of the afternoon.

On the second day came a stroke of luck. Net, Yova, Nar and Tinu, cutting the northern arm of the new path, reached the nesting area of a colony of marsh herons. Nar ran to fetch help, and while the adult birds circled, squawking furiously, the people robbed the nests of tens and tens of half-grown fledgelings. There was a feast that evening on the island, and a change from the endless diet of fish. They left the marsh as darkness fell and climbed the hill with a strange, unreasonable feeling that all might yet be well.

That night, for the first time, they laired in the same place as the night before, a little way down the hill from the hiding place that Suth had found for the lookouts. When they left next morning they made no attempt to conceal the fact that they'd been there – indeed they deliberately left a few traces, a handprint in a soft patch, the spine of a small fish, a few strands of human hair.

Tinu's plan had several versions, depending on when and how the enemy chose to attack, and whether scouts would come first to spy out their ways. That would be best, for then the scouts would find a place where people had laired in the night, and the demon men would come and try to catch their prey sleeping unawares one night when the moon was big.

Noli was no help with any of this guesswork. Though Mana and many of the others had heard Moonhawk's message, Noli herself had no memory of it at all, only the shadowy knowledge that she had dreamed, and Moonhawk had been there in her dream.

So each morning as Mana climbed the hill in the brief half-light she told herself that today would be the day. She settled into her place as the sun rose and concentrated everything that was in her into a steadfast search of the hillside, working her way over it rock by rock by rock, making sure that she missed nothing at all, not the slightest movement or change.

Each day the wind blew ever more steadily, rattling the dead reedstems together and scouring the haze away, just as Var had said it would. By the second day Mana, slinking down the hill with Ko after their stint on watch, could see the bright glimmer of water far out across the marsh, and beyond that other reed-beds and islands, stretching all the way to the western hills.

But to her relief, though she knew where the path was, she couldn't actually see it winding its way through the tangled reeds. The nearest island must be the one where they laired, but there was no sign of the fire, or of people living there.

Oldtale

SIKU

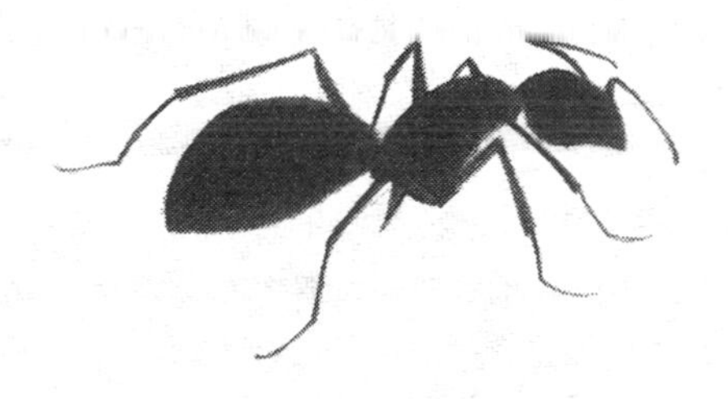

Fat Pig and Snake went down the Mountain. Black Antelope made himself invisible. He went with them. They did not see him.

They were afraid. They said in their hearts, We have no powers. Men hunt us. They kill us. They roast our flesh on embers. They eat it. We are gone. This is bad, bad.

Fat Pig said, 'My Kin lair at Windy Cliff. They do not eat Pig. I go there. I hide in long grasses. I wait. I see Roh, their leader. I show myself to him. He sees me first. He hears my words. This is good.'

Fat Pig journeyed to Windy Cliff. Black Antelope went with him. Fat Pig did not see him.

Now Kin fought with Kin, Snake against Fat Pig. They raided, they lay in wait, they set traps. They struck fierce blows, they threw stones, they bit with their teeth, blood flowed, men died. Those times were bad.

The men of Fat Pig said, 'The rains are gone. Soon all the Kins go to Mambaga. The white-tail buck cross the river. The Kins hunt them. We do not fight at Mambaga. It is a Thing Not Done. But see, now Snake lair at Old Woman Creek. They go to Mambaga by way of Beehive Waterhole. We go now. We lie in wait for them there.'

They sharpened their digging sticks. They set out. The women stayed. They were sad.

Siku was a child. She had no father, no mother. She foraged with the women. No one watched her.

She came to the cliff. A bloodberry vine grew there. It was of this sort:

See, Gata the Beautiful. Her hair was long, long. It shone. It flowed down over her shoulders. Her skin was hidden. So the bloodberry vine flowed down the cliff.

Siku saw good bloodberries. She said in her heart, They are too high. The vine is weak. The women are heavy. They do not climb to them. But I am a child, light. I climb.

She took hold of the vine. She climbed. The vine broke. She fell. She fell upon a soft thing. It was Fat Pig. He hid behind the vine.

Siku spoke as a child speaks, thus: 'Pig, why do you hide? My Kin is Fat Pig. We do not eat pig.'

Fat Pig did not answer. He said in his heart, Must I speak to a child? Must she carry my words to my Kin? Who hears me?

Siku said, 'Oh, pig, I am sad, sad. Men lay in wait. They killed my father. I have no father. My mother grieved. She did not eat. A sickness took her. I have no mother.'

Fat Pig said in his heart, This is my doing. He spoke. He said, 'Siku, I hear you.'

Siku said, 'Oh, pig, you have words! How is this? Is it demon stuff?'

Fat Pig said, 'Siku, it is not demon stuff. I am Fat Pig.'

Siku knelt down. She laid her forehead on the ground. She fluttered her fingers. She said, 'Oh, Fat Pig, I am your piglet. The men go to Beehive Waterhole. They lie in wait for Snake. Say to them, Do not do this.'

Fat Pig said, 'Siku, they do not hear me. Only you hear me.'

Siku said, 'Fat Pig, how is this?'

Fat Pig said, 'Black Antelope made it so. I do not tell you more. It is my shame.'

Siku said, 'Fat Pig, this is not good. Our women said to the men, Do not go. The men said, There is rage in our hearts – we go. How do the men hear me, Siku? I am a child, a girl child.'

Fat Pig thought. He said, 'We find Snake. He is at Old Woman Creek.'

Siku said, 'That is far, too far.'

Fat Pig said, 'Climb on my back. I go quick.'

Siku climbed on his back. All day he ran, and all night. Black Antelope went with them. They did not see him. They came to Old Woman Creek.

CHAPTER SIX

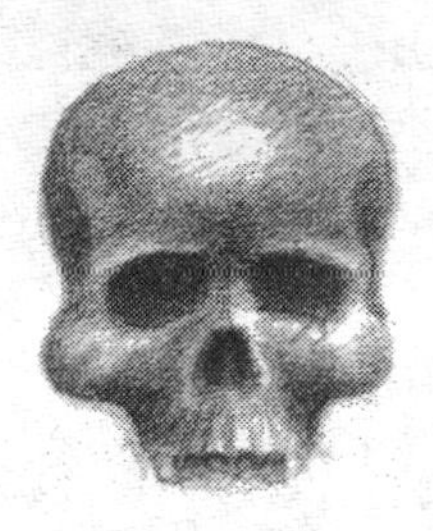

On the fourth morning demon men appeared again, soon after Mana had started her watch at the top of the western slope above the dried-out reedbed. So single-mindedly was she concentrating on searching the hillside before her that she almost missed Ko's signal from the eastern side of the ridge.

Had she really heard it? The call of the whistle-bird, suddenly cut short? Or had she imagined it so strongly that the sound seemed to have crept into her memory without having come there through her hearing? Better make sure.

She gazed once more at the hillside but could see nothing new, so she left her post and crawled up towards the ridge. If Ko was still in his lookout she'd know it was a false alarm.

She was almost at the top when she heard the light click of a dislodged pebble. She froze. A moment later Ko came crawling into view.

'Mana, do you not hear me call?' he whispered. 'Why do you come? Why do you not hide?'

'Ko, I think I hear,' she told him. 'I do not know. You saw a thing?'

'Men come,' he said. 'Three? Four? I do not know. They are careful. They move slow. They hide. Come. See.'

He turned and crawled back to the ridge. More anxiously than ever Mana checked her own side of the promontory and then followed him. He was lying behind a boulder, peering down the further side. She wormed in beside him and very slowly raised her head to see past his. The long hillside seemed as empty as ever.

'See the big rock,' he whispered. 'It touches the reeds. See further, and up, a small cliff . . .'

Before he had finished a brief flicker of movement caught her eye, well to her left, near the bottom of the slope.

And again.

This time, ready for it, she saw it more clearly, a dark someone or something darting between two boulders. Now the hillside was empty again. But again that quick, darting movement, across the same gap – another man, the second, and a third, and a fourth, each with his fighting stick held low, at least one with a skull at his waist.

There was something puzzling about their movements. Though they were obviously taking a lot of trouble to keep under cover, they weren't being clever about it. There, now, that one crouching behind that boulder. His head and right shoulder and arm were still in clear view.

'Ko, they hide badly,' she whispered.

'They came before,' he suggested. 'People were in those reeds. They found them. Now they say in their hearts, *People are there*. They hide from these people. They do not hide from us.'

Yes, that must be it. And now the four demon men were creeping down to the entrance to the path into the reedbeds. Just above it they stopped and searched the ground, once or twice pointing to some sign or mark one of them had spotted.

'What do they see?' said Ko.

'I do not know . . .' Mana began, but then the answer struck her. 'Ah – Kern's body was there. We lifted it. We carried it away. They see this.'

More cautiously than ever the four men moved to the entrance of the path and followed each other in.

'They do not find us in the reeds,' said Ko. 'Do they find their dead men? Mana, what do they do then?'

'I do not know,' she said. 'I think they look more. They come up the hill. They see the other side. Ko, now I move the white stone. I say to the others, *Demon men are here*. Is this good?'

'Mana, it is good,' he said. 'I stay here. I watch.'

So Mana turned back, but before she started down the western flank she checked it carefully once again. Perhaps the demon men had sent a second party of scouts, and they were already there below her. But still nothing moved, so she crawled down to the lookout and laid the signal stone flat. Bodu, with Ogad on her hip, appeared briefly at the edge of the dead reeds, waved, and slipped out of sight again.

Satisfied, Mana returned to the ridge and lay down beside Ko.

Time passed. Every now and then Mana crawled back to check the western flank, saw nothing, and returned to Ko. At long last the demon men emerged and stared around. What had they found? Mana wondered. Were the bodies of the two that she and Tun and Ridi had killed still floating in the water of the trap, or had they sunk out of sight? What did these men feel if they'd found them? Were they angry, as the Kin had been about Kern, full of feelings of revenge, more savage than ever? Or was it like when a jackal was killed, and the others of the pack just sniffed for a moment at the body and moved on? Both thoughts were dreadful, but the second one was worse.

The demon men weren't making any attempt to hide now. It didn't seem to occur to them that anyone might be watching from above. They hesitated a while, touching each other from time to time. The one with the skull at his waist began to point in various directions. Then they split up, one heading on along the shoreline towards the tip of the promontory, two working across it at different angles and the fourth climbing up towards the two watchers. All four zigzagged to and fro as they went, keeping low but not taking any special trouble to hide, and covering as much ground as they could.

Mana and Ko knew at once what they were doing. This was how a hunter moved when he'd lost the trail, and was searching for some sign of his prey, a hoofprint, a stone disturbed from its bed, fur caught on a thorn, droppings.

'Soon he comes close,' Ko whispered. 'Now we hide.'

They left the ridge and crawled rapidly back down to the boulder with the slot beneath it. Mana was smaller than Ko, so he wriggled in first and she then passed him the rock they would use to fill the final gap, checked that the others were in easy reach, and worked her way in beside him. As soon as she was settled they fitted the screening rocks into place, leaving themselves with three narrow cracks of light. By twisting her neck until her cheekbone was hard against the rock beneath, Mana could get her eye to the right-hand crack and see a narrow stretch of the hillside, and the reedbed beyond. Ko was better off. He could reach both of the others, and see a different bit of the slope through one, and through the other a long way out over the marsh, including the island where the Kin laired and had their fire.

So they lay in the dark and waited. While they had been watching unseen, up on the ridge, Mana had barely been afraid. Her heart had thundered at first, but more with excitement than terror. Then, as time had passed, this had quietened to the sort of steady, intent awareness that she felt while fishing.

Now, though, the heavy pulse began again, and would not calm. Time passed, slowly, slowly, with nothing to measure it. It was not yet midday, so the sun was behind her, and every shadow on the patch of hillside that she could see was hidden by the rock that cast it, and she was unable to watch it shrink.

At last she felt Ko reach for her hand and squeeze it. She moved to let him put his mouth close against her ear.

'One is below,' he breathed. 'He waits. He looks here. He raises his hand. I think another is near us . . . He moves . . . I do not see him.'

Mana eased her head back to her spyhole. The wind was blowing steadily up the slope and whistling into the crack, so that if she tried to watch for any length of time her eye started to weep in the draft. She could see nothing new, but heard a soft call from somewhere down below. It was answered from very near by. A moment later Mana's narrow line of sight was briefly blocked by a dark something moving across it, and on.

'One is here,' she whispered. 'He goes your way.'

'I see him,' Ko breathed. 'He goes down the hill, fast, fast. Now another comes . . . I think they find our sleep place.'

Under the almost voiceless whisper she could hear his excitement, and shared it, despite her fear.

For some while they saw nothing more. It was very frustrating. A little below their hiding place, but out of sight for both of them, was the area where the Kin had spent the last three nights, and deliberately left the signs of their having done so. They could only guess whether the demon men had found them. But Bodu would still be watching from the reeds. She would have seen. Nar would now be racing along the path to bring the news to the island that the lair had been found . . .

Ah! There was a demon man!

Bent low, searching the ground, he crossed Mana's sight line and vanished.

'Smoke rises,' whispered Ko.

The man came back in the other direction, nearer.

Before he moved out of sight Mana heard the same furtive call. The man looked up, turned, and stared out across the marsh, shading his eyes. Mana held her breath. This was a crucial moment. Would they work it all out? Would they understand the signs, and realize that their prey stayed far out in the marsh by day but slept the night here on the hillside? And then would they make up their minds that if they wanted to catch the Kin without having to fight their way along the maze of paths in the reedbed, full of traps and ambushes, they must come by night?

That was what the Kin were hoping for. Though Tinu's plan might work in other ways, a night attack would be far the best. Even then, the thought of all that could go wrong filled Mana with dread.

Now her man moved out of sight. Her eye was so sore from peering into the draught that she could scarcely see. She withdrew and rested it, blinking away the tears. She could hear nothing but the hiss of the wind and far birdcalls from the marsh.

She wondered what the demon men would be doing. From the way they had behaved when they had come out of the path in the eastern reedbed, it didn't look as if they had words. That was how the wordless people Mana knew, the Porcupines and the marshpeople, worked out what they were going to do. They touched each other and grunted and gestured until they had all agreed. Tor was Porcupine, and Noli was Tor's mate, but she still didn't know how they did it.

'This one sees that one's mind, I think,' she'd told Mana. 'With Tor I do this little, little. For me it is hard. My mind is full of words.'

It was strange to think of the savage killers on the hillside being in any way like the kindly, gentle Tor. But there was no escape from it. They were people too. People, like Mana herself, and Ko and Suth and Noli. And she, Mana, had killed one of them. Now she was helping to try to kill many more.

The horror of the thought shuddered through her. Ko felt it, but didn't understand.

'Do not be afraid, Mana,' he whispered. 'This is good. Our trap works.'

She sighed, knowing that it was no use explaining. If she'd tried, he still wouldn't have understood.

They lay in their hiding place until long past noon. Shadows appeared on the uphill side of the rocks and started to creep towards them. From time to time Noli peered through her crack, but saw no more of the demon men. Ko could reach his cracks with either eye, and give the other one a rest. He saw them several more times, lurking along the edge of the marsh. The entrance to the path was out of view, so he didn't know if they'd found it.

At last, halfway through the afternoon, Mana saw them again, climbing purposefully northward across the slope.

'I think they go,' she whispered.

They waited some while more before pushing their screening rocks aside and crawling out, aching and stiff with long stillness. They climbed to the ridge and studied the further flank, but they could see no sign of the demon men, so they lifted the signal stone into place and crept down to the marsh.

Oldtale

FARJ

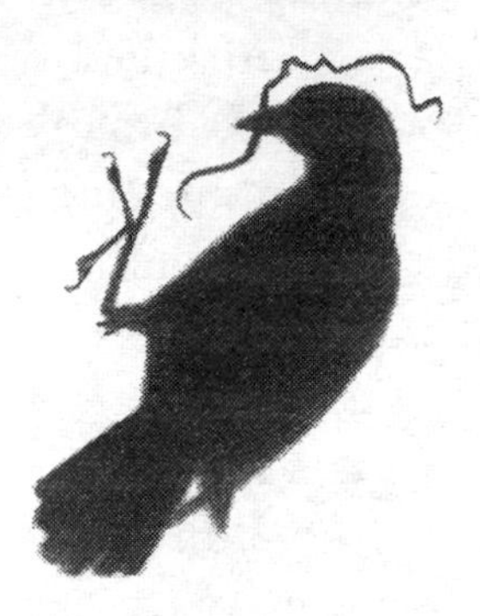

Snake said in his heart, Fat Pig's plan is good. I do it too. I go to my Kin. They are at Old Woman Creek. They do not eat snake. I hide in long grasses. I wait. I see Puy, their leader. I show myself to him. He sees me first. He hears my words.

He went to Old Woman Creek. The men hunted zebra. The women foraged. Farj tended the fire. He was old. His limbs shook. He did not see far.

Snake said in his heart, I do not speak with old Farj. He was a strong man. He was leader. That is gone. Now he is old, he shakes, he mutters, he sees few things. No, I wait for Puy.

Farj prayed. This was his prayer:

> *Snake, you are strong, you are wise.*
> *You guard your snakelings.*
> *Hear me, Farj. I am old. Soon I die.*
> *These are bad times, bad.*
> *Rage is in the men's hearts.*

My first son is dead, he is killed.
My second son seeks vengeance.
Soon he is killed also.
Let me die before this.
I, Farj, ask.

Snake heard him. He said in his heart, This is my doing. He spoke. He said, 'Farj, my snakeling, I am sad for you, sad.'

Farj did not see him well. He said, 'Who speaks?'

Snake said, 'I, Snake, speak. I am your First One.'

Farj knelt. He knocked his head on the ground. He clapped his hands together. He said, 'Snake, First One, stop this fighting. Today the men hunt zebra. They dry meat, they put stores in their gourds. Tomorrow they seek out the men of Fat Pig. They fight yet again. Speak to them, First One. Take the rage from their hearts.'

Snake said, 'Farj, I cannot do this. The men have sworn the War Oath. They must unswear it. From their hearts they must do it, not from my telling. My powers are gone. Black Antelope took them. Only one of my Kin hears my words. It is you.'

Farj said, 'First One, this is hard. Rage stops the men's ears. I speak, they do not hear. What do we do?'

Snake said, 'Farj, I do not know.'

He laid his ear to the ground. He heard a noise. It was of this sort:

See the mountain. Fire is inside it. Now it bursts out. Rocks fly through the air, they are red, they are hot. The mountain shakes, it roars. Far off men hear it. They listen. They say in their hearts, This is not thunder – it is more. Such was the noise Snake heard.

He said, 'We wait. One comes. He runs fast. He is heavy. It is Fat Pig.'

Fat Pig came. Siku was on his back. They were tired. Black Antelope came with them. They did not see him.

Fat Pig spoke to Siku. Farj could not hear him. Siku said, 'I am Siku. This is my First One. His powers are gone. Only I hear his words. We bring news. Soon the Kins go to Mambaga. They hunt the white-tail buck. You go by Beehive Waterhole. The men of my Kin sharpened their digging sticks. They set out. Now they lie in wait at the waterhole. Say to your Kin, Do not go there.'

Farj said, 'This is not good. The men have rage in their hearts. They say, Ah, ah! Men of Fat Pig lie in wait for us. We go. We creep up on them from behind, softly, softly. We kill many.'

Siku said, 'Do you tell the women?'

Farj said, 'Some are foolish. They speak to their men. Now, wait. I think.'

He thought. He said, 'We do thus and thus.'

Black Antelope heard the words of Farj. He said in his heart, This is good. Now I speak to the zebra. The men do not catch any.

CHAPTER SEVEN

Three nights till big moon.

The attack could come on any of them, or on several more nights after. Any of those would be light enough.

What if there were demon men, already spying on the Kin's doings from further along the ridge? This is what they would have seen. All day, the bare hillside, and the occasional puff of smoke from the island, streaming away in the wind. Then, as the sun went down, two or three people coming cautiously out of the reedbed and anxiously scanning the hill for signs of danger. Apparently satisfied, they would turn and gesture, and other people – ten and ten and several more of them – would come out of the reeds, climb confidently up the hill and settle down for the night with a couple of sentries on watch.

Soon the moon would be up and the short dusk over. Now the whole western flank would be in deep shadow. So the watchers wouldn't see most of those people rise from their places and move down the hill and sideways to a different place – a place screened from the north by a fold in the ground – and settle down again there.

But two people didn't go with them. One stayed at the old sleeping place, while the second – smaller than most of the others – climbed to the ridge and vanished.

This last person could only be Ko or Shuja or Mana. Everyone else but Tinu was too large to hide under the boulder. Tinu couldn't do it because she was unable to call the signal. The three chose pebbles from Suth's closed fist to decide their order. Shuja watched the first night and saw nothing. Ko watched the second, and it was the same. So Mana watched on the night of big moon.

She came out of the reeds with the others, climbed the hill, and pretended to settle down. When Tun whispered the word, all but two moved off to their real sleeping place. Yova stayed where she was – at midnight Zara would climb the hill and take over, so that Yova could get some sleep. But Mana had to stay awake all night.

Bent low, she climbed the hill and into the moonlight. By now she knew the best route, crawling over the ridge itself along a shallow dip, down a gully beyond, and then left up the low spur that had the lookout at its top. By the time she was there the moonhawks were busy, calling from their nest site, north along the other flank, skimming over the ridge, and hovering above the moonlit slope as they searched for prey.

Moonlight is deceptive. It seems almost as bright

as day, but even the heaviest, darkest day is much brighter. Under the full moon Mana could see far into the distance along the rugged flank of the promontory, dark in the silvery light. She would have expected to be able to spot the demon men, several tens of them, from a long way off as they came, however carefully they hid as they crept towards her.

But as soon as the details of the plan had been worked out, even before the four demon men had come as scouts, Suth and Var had taken Mana, Ko and Shuja up to the ridge in the moonlight and told them to watch while the two men walked away from them, making no effort to hide. In a terrifyingly short time they seemed to vanish. Only their moving shadows betrayed them, flickering over the grey rocks.

'They come this way,' Var had said, pointing north along the shoreline. 'They know it.'

'Var, you are right,' Suth had said. 'Few lead. They show the way. Many follow. They come by the shore. Then they climb the hill. They come here. It is above our lair. It is close. They wait. The moon goes up the sky. First it is this side. The other side is dark. Then the moon is high. It shines on the other side. Then they attack.'

Mana could only hope they were right, but it seemed the obvious plan for the demon men, approaching by the route they knew, with a few scouts in advance, massing at the top of the ridge and waiting for the moment when the moon rose just far enough to light the western slope, so that they could see their prey as they fell on them.

That was why Mana couldn't simply wait in the

hiding place and give the warning from there. She wouldn't see them in time for the Kin to reach the safety of the reeds. The attack would already have begun.

So now she crouched, as she had done so often by daylight, and watched the colour of the hillside change slowly as the heavy shadows shrank towards the rocks that cast them. Above her the wind hissed and whistled between the boulders of the ridge, but down here she was in stillness. She didn't feel sleepy. She had spent the afternoon dozing on the island, and now in the certainty of danger, terror and excitement mingled into her bloodstream, pulsed through her at each beat of her heart, and kept her intensely awake and aware. Through the thick skin of her soles she could feel the grainy surface of rock, not just as surface but as individual grains that she could have counted if she chose. And she wasn't merely seeing the moonlit hillside. Her eyes seemed to feed on it, to suck it into her, until every mottling of the long slope seemed to be part of her, a tingle at a nerve end.

A flicker of movement. She tensed. Where? Ah, not among the rocks but above them. A star had vanished for an instant as something had passed it, a moon-hawk swooping across the ridge to hunt in the brightness. She watched it briefly at its work, a shadow against the lit sky, speeding out along the wind, then swinging wide, slowing, hovering with fluttering wingtips while it peered with night-seeing eyes for anything that moved below it. She saw it plummet. Above the wind's hiss she heard the light thump of the strike, and shrill squeal of the prey.

For an instant, hearing that squeal, Mana herself was the victim, cowering among these rocks, with the demon men poised to strike. Then she thought, No, they were different. The moonhawk did the thing it was made for, or it wouldn't be a moonhawk. But the demon men were people, just as she and the Kin were people. Each did the things they chose. The demon men chose to be demon men. But she, Mana, and the Kin chose to say, *No, we are not your victims.* Watching here on the hill was part of that choice.

She returned to her task, barely noticing the moonhawks any longer as they came and went. The night wore on. The moon climbed. Soon it would be high enough for its light to cross the ridge and reach the western flank. Soon, soon, surely, the attack must come, if it was coming tonight at all. Or had the demon men decided on a dawn raid? Or . . .

What was that? Down to her right?

No, it had been only the sudden plunge of a moonhawk, followed by . . .

Not a squeal, not the thump of the strike, but a light squawk, and . . .

Why had it caught her attention? Why that strike, when she'd long stopped paying any attention to them?

She watched the bird circle up, but this time, instead of heading for the nest site with its prey, or hovering again as it did when it missed a strike, it circled on, higher still, until she saw its spread wings actually cross the bright disk of the moon. No prey dangled from beak or talons.

Yes. That was it. She'd noticed the strike because something had been wrong with it. The hawk hadn't struck home. Even when it missed there was always the light thump of its impact with the ground. But not this time. And the squawk. Not from the victim, but from the hawk itself. A squawk of surprise. Of alarm.

What had it struck at? What quick, furtive movement? What shadow twitch, tricking it into danger? Surely it wouldn't strike at anything as big as a man. But a man crawling through a patch of shadow but allowing something, the tip of a fighting stick, a heel, a hand, to reach for a moment into moonlight?

Perhaps.

With her heart now slamming with panic, Mana stared. Where had the hawk dived? There.

So near?

She stared, but her night vision was dim for a while from looking directly at the moon. Slowly it cleared, focused on a single patch of the hillside . . . one low boulder . . .

Yes!

Barely even a glimpse, but something had moved, the tip of a larger something, a second man, perhaps, crawling behind the first. There was no time to wait for a third and make sure. They were so much nearer than she'd guessed.

Willing herself to move slowly she withdrew her head until she was completely under cover and sped back the way she had come, until she reached the top of the western slope. It was still all in deep shadow, but the line where the moonlight met the darkness lay sharp along the dead reedbed, only a few tens of paces from the shore. The steady wind hissed over her.

While she waited to bring her heaving lungs under control she listened for the next call of the moonhawk. It didn't come. Of course – the bird had been alarmed. It was shifting its hunting ground. It wouldn't call again for a while.

'Wait,' Suth had said. 'Let the bird call. Call after. Then you do not call together. We know it is the signal.'

But she couldn't wait.

She cupped her hands, moistened her lips, drew a deep breath and called, as loud as she could, because she was calling directly into the wind.

Yeek-yeek-yeek-yeek.

The call of the hunting moonhawk, made not three times but four. She and Ko and Shuja had practised it again and again down in the marshes, until even Var was satisfied that they had it true.

At once she took another breath and repeated the cry.

That was the signal, two calls, each of four shrieks. The closer the calls to each other, the closer the enemy.

They are here! They are close, close!

As the final shriek left her lips she rose and hurried to the hiding place. The demon men were already terrifyingly near, but she didn't dare run. She had to feel for each footstep in the almost pitch dark. Any noise she made would carry to them on the wind.

At last, with her heart now thundering with the tension of stealth, she crouched down by the boulder and checked by feel that everything was where she needed it. But she didn't at once slide in under the rock. She could see too little from there. Instead she laid her body down along its lower side, with her head projecting far enough beyond it to let her watch the jagged line of the ridge against the sky, paler and almost starless now as the rising moon drew nearer.

From below her she could hear nothing but the movement of the wind, though by now the sentries would have woken the sleepers on the hillside and they would all be moving stealthily through the darkness. A few of them would be climbing up to join Yova at the old lair – when the alarm came, the attackers must think that they had all been sleeping there all night, unsuspecting. The others would be creeping down to the reedbed. Most of these would immediately hurry along the hidden path to the island, but several of the men, with Tinu, would hide close by among the reeds. And Yova would be fully alert and tense, staring like Mana for the first glimpse of a movement on the skyline.

Again time passed, slow as the rising moon. Mana thought it would never reach the ridge, though the sky there now seemed almost as pale as dawn. Had she made a mistake and given a false alarm? Had the moonhawk's behaviour tricked her into seeing a movement that wasn't there?

What was that?

Not a movement, but a sound, a brief, faint scrape, barely reaching her through the wind. Wood on stone, perhaps? The trailing end of a fighting stick touching for an instant against a rock?

And now she saw a movement, a slow change on the jagged black skyline, as a head was stealthily raised to peer down the slope.

The man seemed to stay there for ever, watching what lay below him, though it was all still deep in shadow. Had he night vision, like a moonhawk? Would he see Mana herself, despite the darkness? He was so close above her.

She remembered something she had heard Suth say to Ko when he was telling him how the hunter must think while he lay in wait for his prey. *I hide among grasses. I am grass. The buck does not see me.*

I am rock, she thought. I lie long on this hill. I am still, still.

At last the head withdrew, but Mana stayed where she was. It was too soon to give the next signal. For that she must wait until the enemy began to move down the hill, and from the hiding place she wouldn't be able to watch that happen. Would they attack immediately from the ridge as the moon rose, or would they, more likely, try to use the darkness to creep nearer to their prey?

Ah, now they came. Mana saw several of them at once, slinking over the skyline and starting down the hill. Their fighting sticks were held low at their sides. All but one, and this man moved more awkwardly. Mana could see why. He was having to hold his fighting stick two-handed because its point was weighted down by a round mass.

With a wrench in her stomach she guessed what it was. A human head. And she guessed whose.

She swallowed twice, mastering the shock of horror, and silently squirmed herself back and then sideways, feet first, into the slot beneath the boulder. She didn't drag the smaller rocks into place, because the sound was certain to betray her, and she still needed to see out. So now she lay with only the top of her head protruding from the slot. With her right hand she reached out and felt for the base of the long reed that lay there, ready for the instant. At its other end was a small cairn of rocks, carefully balanced by Tinu at the top of a sloping slab.

She waited, scarcely breathing. She could no longer see the ridge, but instead she had a clear view down to the marsh and along the flank of the promontory to her right. Below her the line of shadow had almost reached the shore. The slope was still in darkness, but the sky above was brilliant with stars and bright with the nearing moon. Before long, against that brightness, Mana saw the line of demon men creep past, spread out along the hill. The nearest one was not ten paces from her.

Just after he'd gone by she gave the reed a tug. The cairn unbalanced and rattled noisily down the slab.

The demon man halted, turned, stared. Mana held her breath. Would he guess what had happened? Or would he think that he had somehow dislodged the cairn as he passed it? Yova's yell of *Danger!* gave him no time to make up his mind.

Shrieks and screams rose from the lair, the handful of people there shouting at the top of their voices, sounding like three times their number, and continuing to make the hillside echo with their panic as they raced down the hill.

The line of demon men charged after them, their war cries doubling the din.

Mana raised her head to watch. The moonlight had reached the edge of the reeds. She could see the heads of people milling around by the path entrance, their bodies still in darkness – not many, but making it seem as if others had already passed through, and these were the last few struggling to get in, screaming with panic as they waited for their turn. The final one vanished into the reeds while the attackers were still charging down the hill.

This was the next critical moment. The leading demon men didn't hesitate but plunged in through the now obvious entrance. Would they all follow? Would anyone stay on guard? No. They all gathered at the place and crowded through.

Now Mana crawled from the slot and, crouching in the shadow of the boulder, looked left and right along the hillside. No demon men watched there, either. Cautiously she raised her head into the moonlight and checked the ridge. That too was empty. She turned, cupped her hands round her mouth and screamed the moonhawk call at the top of her voice, twice and twice, *yeek-yeek . . . yeek-yeek*.

She waited and repeated the signal.

They are all gone in. None keeps watch.

Unsure if her voice would carry that far against the wind she climbed onto the boulder, raised her arms over her head and waved them up and down, until she at last saw people slipping out from the reeds to the left and right of the entrance.

They waved to her to show that they had seen her, and all but one disappeared along the path where the demon men had gone to start dragging the reedstems off the series of fresh traps that had been prepared for this moment. The last one, Tinu, came racing up the hill with a bundle over her shoulder. Mana ran to meet her, took the bundle – dry reeds – and arranged them into a loose pile on a jutting rock.

Tinu opened the fire log she was carrying and tipped the contents onto it.

There was no need for her to blow on the embers. The wind did that, setting them glowing at once. Mana fed them with loose wisps of leaves, which curled, crackled and burst into flame. Within instants the whole pile was ablaze.

Out on the island, and along the curving path to left and right, watchers were waiting for the signal. They too had dry reeds piled and fire logs ready. Now it was Mana and Tinu's turn to stand with pounding hearts and stare and wait . . .

There! An orange spark!

And there! And there! Soon the reedbeds were alight at each place, and the sparks became brightnesses as the flames roared up, and fresh sparks shone and grew between them as the people out there raced along the path with twists of flaming reeds in their hands to start fresh fires, working all the time from the outer ends towards the safety of the island, in case an eddy of wind should cause the flames to swirl backwards and set light to the reeds behind them.

But the wind held steady and drove the flames before it, spreading them to left and right, joining the separate blazes together, so that soon the two watchers on the hillside saw two curving lines of flame stretching towards each other while the smoke, bright silver in the moonlight, streamed in front of them as they roared towards the shore, building a wall of flame to trap the demon men inside it and drive them back the way they had come.

By the time the two lines joined into one they were moving as fast as a man could run, certainly faster than a group of men who had been following what had seemed one simple path and then suddenly found themselves lost in a tangle of paths that led only into blind alleys in the middle of the reedbed – and then, when they realized their danger and turned to race back to the safety of the shore, found that path blocked by places where the footing suddenly gave way beneath them, leaving them floundering in thick engulfing mud, which they must either struggle through or fight their way round through the mass of reeds.

And all the time the smoke was streaming over them, and nearer and nearer they could hear the growl and crackle of the flames . . .

Tinu was jumping up and down in her excitement, clapping her hands, exulting not just in watching the destruction of these terrible enemies, but (perhaps even more) at the glory of seeing her huge trap working, just as she'd planned it. But Mana felt no such thrill. Mainly she felt a huge relief that things had gone so well, so luckily, and that the hideous danger they been living under would soon be over.

But at the same time, with another part of her, she felt the horror of how it had needed to be done. That men, people, should die like this. Even at this distance, she could now hear the bellow of the flames, and mixed into them, faintly (or was that only her imagination?) screams. There'd been no help for it. It had had to be done. But it was wrong, wrong.

She could no longer bear to watch or listen. She put her hands over her ears, turned away and faced up the slope. By now the moon was clear of the ridge, no longer silver, but browny orange behind the veil of smoke. Into the round of its disk flew a bird.

One of the moonhawks again, of course. But this time it didn't fly on. Full in the face of the moon it poised, hovering with wings spread wide. It seemed to be watching the scene below, just as Mana and Tinu had been doing. Perhaps it wasn't one of the nesting pair after all. Perhaps it was Moonhawk herself, come to see that all went well for her Kin.

A prayer formed itself in Mana's mind. Silently she breathed it between her lips.

Moonhawk, I praise.
Moonhawk, I thank.
Let it be finished, Moonhawk.
Soon, soon.

With a tilt of its wings the bird swung away and was gone. Comforted, Mana turned back to the marsh.

The smoke was denser around them now as the flames marched closer. It streamed up the hill, hiding the shoreline. Shouts came suddenly from it, the voices of men in rage – the five of the Kin who had gone along the path to open the traps and had then returned to wait in ambush by the entrance, ready to strike down any survivors as they struggled through into the open. The path was only wide enough for one of the demon men at a time, as they were forced out by the closing flames, groping, blinded with smoke.

Tinu gave a cry, pointed, snatched up a stone and raced to her right. Someone was running up the slope.

Two others were chasing him, with digging sticks held ready to strike. Without thinking, Mana seized a stone and ran to cut the first man off, to delay him for just an instant.

All four shapes – Tinu, the two men of the Kin, and their quarry – disappeared in a swirl of smoke. It cleared, and she saw Tinu's throwing arm lash forward as the man rushed past her. He staggered, missed his footing, half fell. Before he could recover his pursuers were on him, beating him down with savage strokes.

Mana dropped her stone and turned away. Only later did she think how strange it was. Suppose she had been the first to see the man escaping, she would have done exactly as Tinu had done, and rushed to try and delay him so that the men could catch and kill him. But seeing it happen, as she had, it filled her with horror.

That was the last of the demon men to try to escape from the reeds.

When the tips of the curving line of flame met the shore they died away, and the curve itself closed inward until the two ends met, and the fire died. Now there was nothing left for it to burn, but ribbons of smoke continued to stream for a while out of the charred mess beyond. Then they too dwindled and died and the night grew clear.

The group on shore, Mana, Tinu and the five men, climbed halfway up the hill and waited, though they didn't expect the others to try to find their way out of the marsh until it was daylight, and the embers of the great fire were cool enough to walk on, and they could see their way for sure.

Some kept watch, but Mana herself lay down and dropped into a wonderful, deep and dreamless sleep, and didn't wake until it was broad day. The others were already coming and going from the island or searching along the shore and around where the paths had been.

She could see the bodies of demon men lying by the entrance. Beyond them stretched a great black space, from which the wind picked up sudden flurries of ash flakes and floated them up the hillside.

Mana didn't go down to join her friends but waited until she saw the whole party gather together and come trooping purposefully up the hill. Tun led the way. In his hands he cradled a dark round thing. Kern's head. Mana guessed that the first thing they had done, as soon as it was light, was search for the leader's body, and found the head lying beside it.

Net had a wound in his side, where a blind thrust from one of the demon men had caught him as they fought at the entrance. Moru had painful burns from a freak explosion of flame, backward into the wind. Several of the others had lesser burns, and many had eyes still weeping from the smoke.

Chogi had already done what she could for these hurts. Now, before they fed or rested, Tun led them along the hill and up the headland to the cairn. They unpiled the rocks from Kern's body. Tun settled his head into place. They rebuilt the cairn.

The women lined up to the east of it, with the rising sun behind them. The men sat facing them, and beat out the rhythm with their hands, groaning in slow deep notes through closed lips. The women stamped to the time of the beat and set up the shrill interlacing wail that would loose Kern's spirit from the place where he had died and send it on its way to the Good Place on the Mountain, the Mountain above Odutu, where the First Ones lived.

Mana watched and listened, feeling all round her the others' feeling of rightness, of release at a dreadful act being at last undone and made well. She shared the feeling. She was glad for Kern, glad for herself and the Kin. But there were other spirits still bound to this hillside and the marsh below it. She could sense their presence also, the spirits of all the demon men who had been killed that night, and earlier. She could almost feel them around her, almost hear them wailing faintly in the sweet morning air.

When the dance was over they went quietly back along the hillside, but as they crossed the spur that brought them in sight of the eastern marsh, the leaders halted. The rest climbed up to see why they had stopped. Down on the shoreline a single figure was dancing wildly to and fro. Ridi. Her wild chant of triumph reached them on the wind, as she exulted in the vengeance that had fallen on her enemies.

Mana watched for a little while, thinking, *No, I am not like that*. She realized that Noli was standing beside her.

'Noli,' she whispered. 'Help me. I have a trouble in my heart.'

Noli seemed to be in some kind of dream. The death dance was First One stuff. Maybe she had been some of the way with Kern on his journey. Now Mana saw the ordinary brightness come back into her eyes.

'Mana,' she murmured. 'What is this trouble?'

'Noli . . . it is these others . . .' said Mana. 'They are demon men . . . They are dead . . . spirits . . . Where do they . . . How . . . ?'

Noli understood the stammered question. She shook her head, smiling.

'Mana, I do not know,' she said. 'It is not our stuff. Soon we leave this place.'

'Noli, it is my stuff,' Mana insisted. 'It is a trouble in my heart. What do I do?'

'Mana, I . . .' Noli began, shaking her head again.

She stopped, shuddered and clutched Mana by the shoulder. A dribble of froth appeared at the corner of her mouth. Mana put an arm round her, ready to stop her from falling, but it wasn't needed. The whisper of Moonhawk's voice was so soft that only Mana could hear it.

'Wait.'

Noli sighed, shook herself and looked around. She frowned at Mana, puzzled. 'Moonhawk was here?' she asked. 'She spoke?'

'Yes,' said Mana. 'It was for me.'

The others were starting to move on. Noli nodded, shook herself again, and followed them. She didn't remember what had just happened, Mana realized, perhaps not even Mana asking her question.

That didn't matter. Mana knew what to do now. Wait.

Oldtale

THE PIG HUNT

The men of Snake came back from their hunting. They were tired. They were hungry They brought no meat.

They said, 'Yesterday we saw many zebra. Today they are gone. We saw their tracks. All went together. We followed them far and far. We did not find them.'

The women mocked the men. They said, 'You are foolish hunters. The zebra are more clever. Tonight you eat plant stuff only. Your strength is gone.'

The women laughed at the men. Their laughter was of this sort:

See, it is dusk. The starlings gather to their roost, the blue starlings. The sky is dark with their wings. They clamour with shrill voices. A lion roars. He is not heard. So loud are the voices of the starlings.

Such was the laughter of the women at the men of Snake. The men were ashamed.

*

It was dusk. Fat Pig went to the reedbeds of Old Woman Creek. He spoke to the pigs in their wallows.

He said, 'The water goes. Soon these wallows are dry. Beehive Waterhole has good mud. Come now. It is night. The sun does not burn us. The moon is big. We see the way.'

The pig rose from their wallows. They went with Fat Pig.

Now a great snake lay in their way. By the moonlight they saw him. He reared himself up. He hissed. Fat Pig said, 'Run! Run! It is a demon snake! It eats us all!'

Pig are not wise. One does a thing, they all do it.

Fat Pig ran east, toward Yellowspring. The others followed. They came to Long Rock Ridge. Fat Pig stopped. They all stopped.

They said, 'The snake is gone. Now we go to Beehive Waterhole.'

They went. They walked on Long Rock Ridge. They made no tracks.

Fat Pig did not go with them. He went to Old Woman Creek. There he found Siku. She hid in long grasses. He said, 'Climb on my back. I take you to Windy Cliff, to your own Kin.'

It was morning. The Kin of Snake woke. They filled their gourds. They set out for Beehive Waterhole. Men led the way.

Soon they cried, 'Ho! What is this? Here are tracks of pig, many, many. See, they go this way, toward Beehive Waterhole. Pig are not zebra. They do not run far and far. Now we hunt these pig. We kill them, we eat them. Fat Pig are our enemies. We take their strength from them. Women, follow these tracks. We go fast.'

Now they cried, 'Ho! What is this. The pig turn aside. Something makes them afraid. See, they run fast. Soon they are tired. We catch them.'

They followed the tracks. They came to Long Rock Ridge. The tracks were gone.

The men said, 'Now they turn aside. Which way do they go? Beehive Waterhole is this way. Yellowspring is that way. It is nearer.'

They went towards Yellowspring. The rock ended. They saw no tracks. They came back. The women were there.

The men said, 'Now we go to Beehive Waterhole.'

Farj said, 'Yellowspring is nearer.'

The women said, 'Farj is right. Our small ones are tired. Our water gourds are empty. We go to Yellowspring. Men, do you come with us? We have plant food.'

The men said in their hearts, Plant food is better than no food. They went to Yellowspring.

The men of Fat Pig lay in wait at Beehive Waterhole. No people came. Many pig came. The men did not hunt them. Fat Pig do not eat pig.

CHAPTER EIGHT

Days of peace followed the battle. Tun set lookouts still from dawn to dusk, and from dusk to the next dawn, but all the Kin knew in their hearts that they had dealt with the menace from the north. No great raid of demon men, people hunters, would come again. Nor were they likely to attack by twos and threes. If any were left where these had come from, surely they were now afraid. And more than all that, Moonhawk was strong in this place. She would warn and protect her Kin.

Before anything else they took the bodies of the five demon men they had killed in the earlier skirmishes and carried them round into the burned area on the west. This cleared the eastern side of the promontory of anything that might attract demons, so that the Kin could settle back there to lair and fish and forage, and allow Tun's wound and Net's to finish healing and Moru to recover from her burns.

All the time she wasn't on lookout Mana spent at

her fishing hole. She usually caught something, and one wonderful afternoon came back to the lair with four fish, all handsome and fat. But she was perfectly content to wait poised beside the hole, and watch the minnows come and go, and catch nothing.

Fishing was good for her. She felt that she too had a wound to heal, a wound inside her, in her spirit. It had come to her with a blow from a digging stick. She had struck that blow with her own hand and arm as she had stood by the trap in the path through the reeds, with Tun sprawled beside her struggling to kick himself free from the demon man's grasp. She had hammered down on the demon man's head with Tun's digging stick, and at that third blow had felt the demon man's skull shatter. That was the moment she'd killed him. That was the wound in her spirit.

She had burns, too, not as deep as the wound, but sore. She would wake in the middle of the night and everything would be still, apart from the faint hiss of the wind crossing the ridge above her. But Mana would be sure that just before she'd woken she'd heard noises borne by that wind, the screaming of men trapped in the western reedbed, as the wall of flame swept over them.

It was something like what had happened to Moru. While Mana had been standing with Tinu on the hillside watching the smoke stream off the reedbed as the burning arc closed and closed, an eddy of wind had swirled over her, filled with the dark flame of the men's dying, and scorched her spirit as it passed.

She didn't talk to anyone about this. As far as she could tell, the others, even Noli, felt nothing but triumph and relief for what they had done. Mana felt those too. She was happy that all of them except poor Kern were still alive, happy that the days were quiet and they could lair in safety round their fire on the hillside, happy in the beauty of the world, now that the wind had come to blow the haze off the marsh and let her see far into the sparkling distances. Happy to fish.

On the second day after the battle two of the marshmen appeared from the reeds and climbed cautiously up to the camp. Shuja was on lookout, but didn't at once spot them as she was mainly watching for danger from the north. Then she turned and saw them, but recognized them as friendly, so stood and hallooed down to the others, who were all foraging along the shore, or fishing, or searching the reeds for insect bait.

Mana came out from her hole and saw Tun and Var climbing the hill to greet the visitors. This wasn't child stuff, so she returned to her fishing. She heard what had happened when they were all sitting round the fire that evening.

'One man is our guide,' said Var. 'He brought us to this place. Then his two women were with him. They did not leave the reeds. Not the man, not the women. They were afraid.'

'I saw this,' said Net. 'They were afraid.'

There were murmurs of agreement. They could all remember.

'Again we saw this man,' Var continued. 'We fetched salt – I, Var, and Net and Kern and Yova. We met him in the reeds, on a path. He sees us. He is afraid. He turns away. I call, *We meet well.* He runs. I call again. He stops. He comes back, slow, slow. He touches me. He smiles. He is happy. Now he is not afraid. He calls to his women. They come, afraid, afraid. They touch me. They are happy. I say in my heart, *These people think Var is dead. He is a spirit.* They touch. I am warm. I am not dead. They are happy.'

'Var, you are right,' said Yova. 'I saw this.'

'I say this,' said Tun. 'The marshpeople fear the demon men. They say in their hearts, *These strangers are fools. They go to the places of the demon men. The demon men kill them.* They hear fighting in the night They see great burning. Then they see our fire on the hill. It is still there. They ask, *Do the strangers live?* They come. We take them to the dry reeds. We show them the bodies of demon men. They are happy. They are like Ridi. They give great praise. Soon others come. They see too.'

They talked it over for a while, and agreed that Tun was probably right, but they weren't ready for the way it happened. This time Mana was on lookout. She heard a strange noise rising from the marsh behind her, and coming nearer and nearer. After a little while she realized that she'd heard it before, when the procession of marshmen had carried back to their central island the head of the monster crocodile that the Kin had trapped and killed.

It was the sound the marshpeople made by banging together two of the reed tubes they carried at their belts. But this time it was different. When Mana had heard it before it had been a wild, dancing rhythm, mixed with shouts of triumph. Now it was slow and solemn and monotonous, with no intermingling of human voices. Mana recognized at once that it must be a death sound.

All the Kin seemed to have heard the sound too, and gathered from whatever they'd been doing to watch the procession. Tens and tens and tens of marshpeople, men, women and children, came out of the reeds and climbed the hill towards the camp. Then there was the usual exchange of gifts. Even from the lookout point well up the hill Mana could see that the marshpeople had brought far more than the Kin could possibly give them in exchange.

After that they moved out of her sight, round to the western side of the promontory, but their sad music was carried to her on the wind all morning. As soon as Nar came up to take over as lookout she climbed to the ridge and looked down.

Far below her on the scorched mudbank women and children were moving to and fro, searching the ground, while the men stayed at the shoreline, steadily banging their tubes together. Every now and then one of the searchers would stoop, pick something up, and carry it to the shore to add to a pile that was already there. Though she couldn't see them for sure at that distance, Mana realized at once that they were collecting the skulls that the demon men had carried at their belts.

And she knew too – the noise from the sound sticks told her – that what they were doing wasn't demon stuff. It was the opposite. They were taking the skulls not as trophies of their own, like the great crocodile head, but so that they could do something good with them. Some of these skulls must have been the heads of marshpeople, but they didn't know which, so they were taking them all. They would feel about them much as the Kin had felt about Kern's head, so they'd want to do something like the Kin had done, when they had returned that to Kern's body, where it belonged, and only then done the death dance for him.

When they had finished they said their farewells and filed off into the reeds, with the sad music of the soundsticks growing fainter and fainter as they moved away.

They had left a great pile of gifts, mostly fish, but also fishing sticks and crocodile teeth and braided belts and belt tubes. Some of the tubes had coloured paste in them, used by the marshmen to paint their faces, so the children had a great time covering each other with red and yellow and purple blotches and streaks. That night they feasted until everybody's stomach was crammed.

Next day Var and Suth set out on a scouting expedition to the north. Three anxious days later they returned, tired but well, to say that they had gone all the way up the promontory along the same, endless barren slope, and then climbed a range of hills that were almost mountains, almost barren too, with no sign of Good Places for the Kin to live in. They'd nearly run out of food and were getting desperate by the time they reached the top, but had gone on a little further and looked down into a huge valley, full of promise, just the sort of area they'd been looking for. They'd explored a little, and seen few signs of people, but they'd found plenty to eat.

When they had finished their report Tun praised

them with strong words. Then he said, 'This is good. Tomorrow we go. Be ready.'

Next morning, as soon as it was light, Mana went for the last time to her fishing hole and dribbled scraps of bait into it, then watched the little fishes come to gobble them up. To her delight a beautiful large fish appeared, silver, with a yellow stripe along its flanks. It was one of the best sort, with pinkish flesh, juicy and firm, but she didn't try to catch it. Instead she gave it extra bait, and blessed it, and the little ones, and the water they swam in, and left feeling both sad and happy.

They travelled steadily up the promontory all morning, picking their way along the awkward slope with two men scouting ahead for danger. While they were resting Mana noticed Suth stop what he was saying to the other men and point out across the marsh. She looked, and at once saw what he'd seen. A long way out a line of tiny figures was wading thigh deep across a patch of open water.

'Ho! The marshpeople come too!' said Zara. 'Now they are not afraid.'

Net jumped to his feet, cupped his hands to his mouth and hallooed and waved. After a pause Mana saw the marshpeople stop and turn. Everyone stood up and waved. The marshpeople waved back and moved on, while the Kin sat down, feeling cheered that they were not alone in their adventure.

'They use an old path,' said Var. 'They know it.'

'Var, you are right,' said Chogi. 'I say this. All the marsh was their place. They fished here. They came to the dry land. They were not afraid. Then demon men came. They killed men, they took women. The marshpeople were afraid. They went away. Now we kill the demon men. They are not afraid. They come back.'

'Chogi, you are right,' said Net, and they all agreed it looked like that.

That evening they camped early, a little up from the base of the promontory, where the shoreline swept away eastward at the foot of a great range of hills. As Var and Suth had warned them, these gave no promise of food, so they needed time to fish, and forage among the shore plants.

As usual when they camped anywhere new they made their fire in a hollow, so that it couldn't be seen from any distance. Tun set lookouts, and they scattered to their various tasks. There were rich pickings. No one seemed to have foraged here for many moons. Mana found a fong beetle's burrow with the guardian beetle lurking inside the entrance. It had a viciously poisonous bite, but she lured it into the open by tickling it with a grass stem, and then squashed it with the stone she had ready in her other hand. Now it was safe to dig into the burrow and scoop the juicy brown bugs into her gourd.

Just as she finished she heard a brief whistling hiss from the reeds beside her. She looked and saw a bright-painted face peering at her between the reed-stems. She held up her hand and called a soft greeting, and the marshman came cautiously out. She didn't recognize the pattern on his face, but he seemed to know who she was. He returned her greeting, but looked past her, studying the hillside, and made a questioning sound, like a light bark, but with his lips closed. Though it wasn't the grunt the Porcupines would have used, it was obvious what he was asking her.

Is it safe? Have you seen any demon men?

Mana smiled and grunted reassuringly and said, 'Come, I take you to Tun.' But when she started to lead the way he barked at her to wait and called to somebody among the reeds. Several more marsh-people came creeping out, men and women, all obviously very scared and anxious. One of the women offered Mana a couple of fishes as a gift, but wrinkled her nose in disgust when Mana tried to give her a few fong grubs in exchange.

Tun arrived, and led them up to the camp. More marshpeople appeared, and by dusk ten and five more of them were sitting round the fire with the Kin, and toasting their fish on its embers.

They went back down the hill to sleep among the reeds – they didn't seem to mind about the sickness – but next morning Mana was hardly awake when she heard a soft call from one of the lookouts. Five marshmen were climbing the hill. There were no women with them, but this time their whole bodies, not just their faces, were painted in brilliant colours.

'They come to fight,' said Suth. 'I remember this. They came to take the crocodile head. It was ours. They said in their hearts, *These people do not give us the head. We must fight them.* But Tun gave it to them. We did not fight. Then they were painted like this.'

'Suth, do they fight us?' said Ko.

'No. This is my thought. They fight the demon men.'

The marshmen had brought no gifts this time. They

exchanged greetings, and then just stood around, obviously waiting for the Kin to move on. As soon as Tun gave the signal three of them ran on ahead as scouts, while the other two fell in beside Tun. They clearly knew where they were going, so he let them lead the party at a slant across the hill until they reached a spur, which they then followed towards the summit.

It was a long and tiring climb. At last Mana saw that the scouts were beginning to move more cautiously, and when they finally disappeared over the skyline the two men walking with Tun made everyone else stop and wait until the scouts returned and signalled that it was safe to come on.

They climbed to a pass, with hills rising on either side, and wound for a while along it, until the ground began to drop away at their feet and they could look north.

Mana heard a sigh from many mouths, and then a whisper from her left. She didn't know who'd spoken, but it was her own thought. It was everyone's thought.

'These are Good Places. Good. Good.'

Oldtale

THE MAMBAGA CROSSING

Black Antelope went to the white-tail buck, the Mambaga buck. He said to them, 'The rains are gone. These pastures are dry. Now you go south to new pastures, to Ragala Flat. Do you cross the river at Mambaga? Men wait for you there. They hunt you. They kill many.'

The white-tail buck said, 'Black Antelope, we know the Mambaga crossing. We do not know another.'

He said, 'Now I show you another way. Come.'

He led them east, and then south, to Smoke Gorge. In those days the river was full of water. At Smoke Gorge it fell over a cliff.

The white-tail buck said, 'Black Antelope, we cannot cross here. The gorge is too wide. It is too deep. The water smokes. It roars. We are afraid.'

Black Antelope struck the northern cliff with his hoof. It fell into the gorge. He leapt the gorge. He struck the southern cliff with his hoof. That too fell.

The rocks lay across the gorge. The water was stopped.

Still the white-tail buck were afraid. Black Antelope leapt the gorge again. He said, 'Come quick. The water rises. Soon the rocks are pushed away.'

He led the white-tail buck across the rockfall. Their crossing was of this sort:

See, it is dawn. The ants leave their nest. All day they come, they go. They forage here, there. Now it is dusk. They gather to their nest. Who can count them? The ground is black with them. Through a narrow place they go into the nest. They are all gone.

Such was the crossing of the white-tail buck. The water rose beside them. The last buck crossed. The water burst through. It pushed the rockfall away.

The white-tail buck went south to Ragala Flat. There the grass was fresh, it was green. They were happy.

All the Kins gathered to Mambaga. They waited for the white-tail buck. None came to the crossing.

The men spoke to each other. They said, 'Why do the buck not come? This is strange.'

Farj had a daughter, Rimi. Her mate was Nos. He was Crocodile. Farj went to him. He said, 'Nos, mate of my daughter, hear me, Farj. I am old. I have seen many things. This I have not seen. Always the white-tail buck come to Mambaga. At this season they come. Now they do not come. Why is this? I, Farj, say this. I am Snake. Our men swore the War Oath. Anger is in their hearts. The men of Fat Pig swore the War Oath. Anger is in their hearts also. The white-tail buck smell this anger. They are afraid. They do not come.'

Nos said, 'Farj, you are right. I speak to the other Kins. I tell them your words.'

All the men listened. They said, 'Nos is right. Farj is right.'

They went to the men of Snake and of Fat Pig. They said, 'Stop this war, this foolishness.'

The men of Snake and of Fat Pig answered, 'We cannot stop it. We have sworn the War Oath.'

The men of the Kins said, 'Our young men do not come to you. They do not say, We choose your daughters for mates. Your young men come to us. We say to them, Our daughters do not choose you for mates. First you end this war.'

The men of Snake answered, 'Let Fat Pig end the war first. Let them unswear the War Oath. Let them give us Mott. We kill him. Then we unswear the War Oath. We give them Ziul.'

The men of Fat Pig answered in the same way. Both said, 'We do not do it first. We do not lose face.'

The women said, 'You are fools.' They did not laugh.

Farj and Siku listened to this talk. They told it to Snake and to Fat Pig.

Fat Pig and Snake said, 'The men are ripe berries. They are ready. Farj, you are old, you are wise. What do we do now?'

Farj thought. He said, 'Now we do thus and thus.'

CHAPTER NINE

It was as if they had come into a different world. Behind them lay the long dry hillside and the pass – rocks, gravel, clumps of harsh grass, thorny, stunted bushes scattered here and there, all brown and burnt and weary, even after the rains. A world that was almost dead.

But here, so short a distance to the north, was a world of life, green slopes where deer could browse, wide-branched trees with cool shade beneath them, birds answering and calling, vines, bushes, smells of sap and pollen, the hum of honey bees, movement of creatures in the mottled shadows – good earth, good air, good foraging, good hunting – one immense Good Place spread out below them.

A thought came to Mana. She couldn't quite put it into words. Suth was standing beside her.

'Suth,' she whispered. 'The demon men . . . They had this . . . all this . . . Why?'

Why had they left this wonderful valley to hunt

and kill, not animals for food, but men, to cut their heads off and carry them away as . . . ? As what? What did they want them for? Could their First One be really a demon? Did it tell them this was what they must do to please it? That was too ghastly to imagine.

Suth seemed to understand her stammerings. He frowned, shaking his head.

'Mana, I do not know,' he said. 'It is strange, strange.'

Tun, of course, set lookouts, and the rest of the Kin started to forage. This wasn't what the marshmen wanted. They waited for a while, and then tried to persuade Tun to move on. When they realized he wasn't going to, they were unhappy, but hung around a little longer, grunting and gesturing and touching each other, and then went off down the hill, moving warily and holding their fishing sticks ready for fighting.

The Kin worked cheerfully, finding all they wanted, nuts and fruit and roots, grubs and birds' eggs. It had been well after midday when they'd started, and they hadn't had their usual rest, but the air was cooler at this height, and the excitement and pleasure of exploring this new home buoyed them up. Late in the afternoon Mana heard the shouts of hunters, and a little later Net and Nar appeared, triumphantly carrying the body of a large anteater they had surprised and killed.

By then they'd harvested more than enough, so Tun led them back up to the pass and found a good hollow for their lair. The night would be cold up here, but it was safer to sleep in the open, with lookouts on watch, than it would have been lower down, with so much cover for any enemy or wild beast to use to creep up on them.

In the dusk the five marshmen returned. With them came a woman, who looked just like one of the marshwomen. She had a girl baby.

The marshmen were in high spirits. They'd arrived making gestures of triumph, punching the air with their fists. Two of them carried skulls, which they laid carefully down a little way from the fire. Then they proudly showed their fishing sticks to Tun and the other men.

'What is this?' whispered Moru, watching from the women's side of the fire.

'I smell blood,' said Noli. 'I think they kill people.'

Mana too had smelt the unmistakable odour, but hadn't guessed what creature it might belong to.

'Who is this woman?' said Shuja. 'Do the marshmen kill her mate? Do they take her? She is not sad.'

The woman had come to sit with them opposite the men, and as Shuja had said looked dazed, but not unhappy. She ate without seeming to notice what she was doing, and kept her eyes fixed on one of the marshmen the other side of the fire.

'I say this,' said Chogi decisively. 'These were not always marshmen. The marshmen were their friends. But these lived here. These Places were theirs. Then demon men came. They killed men, they took women. These men fled into the marsh. The marshmen said, *Be with us. Learn our ways*. They did this. Now we kill many demon men. These men say in their hearts, *We go back to our own Places. We find our women. We see a demon man. We kill him.*'

'Chogi, you are right,' said Yova.

'Why do they bring skulls?' asked Bodu.

'A demon man kills their friends,' suggested Moru. 'He takes their heads. Now these men kill him. They take the heads back. This is good.'

They discussed the idea to and fro for a while, but Mana was still thinking about the demon men. She could understand what the marshmen seemed to have done. That was revenge. It was dreadful too, but it was people stuff. What the demon men did was different.

Did that mean they weren't people, after all? No, she knew in her heart they were. It was being people that was the worst thing about them. If they'd been just people-shaped animals, they'd still have been terrifying, but it would have been a different sort of terror. The demon men were men, like good, strong Tun and Suth, like excitable Net, like gentle Tor – that was what made the difference. And that was why Mana carried a wound in her spirit, because she had killed one of them.

One day, perhaps, she would understand. Moonhawk had told her to wait. So Moonhawk had known that Mana's wound was a real wound. She'd known that the demon men were people, or she wouldn't have said that.

The Kin slept by the fire, huddled in piles for warmth. The marshmen and the woman they'd found, and her baby, made another pile of their own. In the morning they exchanged goodbyes and the marshmen headed off back to the marsh, while the Kin went down into the valley to explore further.

This time they moved faster, with scouts in advance, only stopping to forage if they came to a specially rich area. They found a small stream, splashing from boulder to boulder, and drank its clean, fresh water, but didn't trouble to fill their gourds.

They were following the stream, spread out in a loose line either side of it, when Mana saw Tor, scouting in front of her, crouch and peer ahead, at the same time making a quick downward gesture with his left hand. Instantly she ducked into the cover of the nearest bush. When she looked to left and right the rest of the Kin seemed to have vanished, apart from Tinu, crouching on the other side of the same bush.

They waited while Tor and Net crept out of sight.

Before long Tor returned and beckoned them on, but then made the same downward gesture as before – *Come. Keep low.* Everyone rose from their hiding places and stole forward.

They reached the rim of a dip, halted and looked down. The bank was short but steep. Below her Mana saw what she instantly recognized as someone's regular lair. There was a dead fire with a large mound of ashes heaped up from steady burning over many days, a stack of branches for fuel, a trampled patch of earth, a flat boulder with drifts of seedhusks round it, and so on. The only unfamiliar thing was a pair of posts driven into the ground on either side of the trail that led on down the hill.

A body lay face down beside the fire. Its skin was very dark grey, faintly tinged with purple, and streaked with blood from several small, deep wounds.

Mana heard a mutter beside her. Bodu.

'The marshmen killed him. They used fishing sticks.'

Yes, a speared fish had a hole like that in its side.

Chogi had been right in her guess last night. The body wasn't that of a demon man, though. It was too small. He'd been a boy – about Mana's own age, she guessed. A demon boy.

With a heavy sigh she bowed her head and turned away. Why? And why in this beautiful place, this lair by the tumbling stream . . . ?

She couldn't bear to stay there, but crept off, with the tears beginning to stream down her face for the dead boy. She wept for him as she had wept for Kern. For the moment it was the same death.

She stole quietly on through the haze of tears, letting her feet choose the path. She knew that this was wrong of her, bad, allowing herself to lose sight of the others in this unfamiliar place with its unknown dangers. But she needed to be alone, to endure her grief without anybody speaking to her, trying to comfort her. She wasn't ready for that.

She stopped because she could go no further, and wiped her tears away with the back of her hand and looked around. She had reached a small clearing beside a fallen tree. She could still hear the whisper of the stream behind her. She wasn't yet ready to turn back. She felt unravelled, as if the sudden upwelling of pure grief had loosened the strands of her inward self – much as the braids of grass stems that she used to carry her gourd sometimes came untwisted – and she needed a little time to weave them firm again.

She was standing there, sighing and shaking her head, when someone shouted behind her. She jumped with alarm, then realized it had been only Suth calling for her. As she was turning to answer something hissed low down beside her. Again she jumped, then backed away, staring. A thin, dark arm slid out from under the fallen tree and beckoned to her. She knelt and peered into the dark space beneath the trunk. Two wide eyes glistened. She could barely make out the shape of the face around them. A girl? A woman?

Suth called again, nearer. The arm beckoned impatiently. Mana held up her hand, palm forward – *Peace* – and answered over her shoulder, 'Suth, I am here.'

She rose and went to meet him.

'Wait, Suth,' she said softly. 'One hides. She is afraid. She says in her heart, *These men kill me*.'

'I fetch Noli,' he said, and ran off. Mana returned to squat by the fallen tree where the woman could see her, and smiled and made calming noises in her throat, until Noli arrived with Amola. She crouched and looked in under the tree trunk and made the usual hum of greeting. When the girl – or woman – didn't move, Noli settled down cross legged and put Amola to her breast, where she immediately began to suck happily.

Mana saw the round eyes widen. Slowly and cautiously their owner crawled into the open. She was a strange little woman, obviously an adult but not as tall as Mana when she stood up. Her skin was darker than Mana's, almost black. She had large, protruding buttocks, and her face was wrinkled, like a new-born baby's, but otherwise she didn't look very old. Her eyes kept darting from side to side. She was as shy as a startled deer.

Noli rose, smiling, and took her hand.

'Come,' she said, and led the way back towards the lair. The moment the woman saw Suth she gave a gasp of alarm, snatched her hand from Noli's and backed away. Suth gave the *Peace* gesture and hummed a greeting. Hesitantly the little woman edged back to Noli and let her lead her on.

Before they reached the lair Suth called out to the others, 'Hear me. We bring a stranger woman. She is afraid, afraid.'

A few of the Kin climbed up the bank to meet her, and once again she stopped and backed away. Then, suddenly, she seemed to make up her mind that these newcomers meant her no harm, but she ignored their greetings and hurried on past them and out of Mana's sight down to the lair. Mana couldn't bear to look at the dead boy again, so when they moved on she asked Shuja what had happened.

'She turned the boy over,' said Shuja. 'She looked at him. My thought was *He is her son*. But she did not grieve. She went to the fire. She took ash. She put it on his face. She stood a little. She turned away. It was finished.'

'This is strange,' said Bodu. 'Is she a demon woman? I say No.'

They talked about it as they moved on, working generally eastward along the slope and not going further down into the valley, so that they wouldn't have far to climb to the open ground when they wanted to lair that night.

'I say this,' said Chogi at last. 'Her skin is black The skin of the demon men is dark, like ours. The boy's skin is darker. A demon man took this woman. He was the father. The boy is her son. She does not want him. But he is her son.'

'This is sad, sad,' said Bodu.

The little woman didn't seem to think so. She had tagged along with them, seeming much more confident now, behaving as if she had always been one of their party, and foraging unconcernedly with them whenever they paused to do that. She seemed to have forgotten all about the dead boy.

But around midday, when they were starting to look for somewhere pleasant to rest and eat, she made one of her strange sounds and smiled and raised her hand in what was obviously a goodbye gesture, and then ran off down the hill. A little later they heard her call. Two more distant calls answered, one after the other.

'She finds friends,' said Bodu. 'Do we go see?'

Before anyone could answer Mana saw Ridi fall on her knees in front of Tun, making the moaning whine that meant she was begging a favour. She pointed the way the little woman had gone.

'These are women's voices,' said Tun. 'We find them. We give gifts. They are friends. Is this good?'

They set off, with Ridi hurrying ahead, and every now and then turning to wave to them to follow faster. After a bit she stopped and halloed. An answering cry came from below. Ridi broke into a run and disappeared.

They followed and met her further down the hill, leading another woman back towards them. This one had a child on her hip, a girl a little younger than Tan. The mother looked very like Ridi, or one of the marshwomen, but the child's skin was darker, with a greyish tinge. The mother and Ridi were obviously old friends, laughing and crying with the happiness of their meeting.

They greeted Tun, and then led the way to another lair, like the first but larger, and with its fire still burning. There were two more women here, the one Mana had found that morning, and another who might have been her sister, with the same wrinkled face, black skin and enormous buttocks. She had a small baby, also very black. There was an older girl, black too, and a little boy with a much paler skin. Ridi's friend seemed to be his mother.

The other difference about this lair was that there were four posts at its entrance. At the top of each of them was a human skull.

This was a sight they were going to see several times over the next few days, a long-used lair, with a fire burning at its centre, women and children preparing food or foraging somewhere near by, and two or more poles, topped by their ghastly trophies.

The women were mostly like the marshpeople, slight and pale skinned; some were like the strange little woman Mana had found by the lair with the dead boy; but a few were tall and thin with the same purple tinge to their dark grey skin as the demon men. The children were mixtures of these shapes and colours, but again a few of them had the true demon people look.

When the Kin chanced on one of these lairs, the little women at once scuttled off and hid, and the pale-skinned ones started to do the same until Ridi called to them, when they came hesitantly back. But if there was a demon woman she would rise and face them proudly, with her demon child at her side. Neither of them looked as if they knew what it was like to be afraid.

The first time this happened Mana just stared at the two of them, but when the Kin moved on she found herself wishing she'd done more – greeted them, smiled, spoken – anything to show them, and show herself, that she and they were the same – they were people. So next time, a couple of days later, she walked up to the demon woman and greeted her with the raised hand and the hum that the marshpeople used for that.

The demon woman glanced at her, and away. The boy – a small one, just old enough to run without falling down all the time – stared back at Mana with dark, unfriendly eyes. She smiled and reached out a hand to touch him.

Instantly the mother hissed like a snake and snatched her son out of reach. Mana backed off, still trying to smile, but the mother stared fixedly away. When Mana turned she saw several of the Kin watching her. Chogi shook her head, frowning. Mana felt very depressed when they moved on. She didn't try to make friends with a demon woman again.

All this was bad enough, but then there came a yet more dreadful change. By now the Kin had ventured further down into the valley and were working their way back west, exploring as they went. Now when they chanced on one of these camps it was like the first one they'd found. The skulls had been taken from the poles. The fire was dead, or dying, and sometimes there would be a body, or bodies, lying beside the cold embers, demon women and dark-skinned children. Any other women and children were gone. Though Ridi called and called, no one answered.

The Kin stared at these scenes with a horror like Mana's. For a man to kill a woman or a child was a shame beyond shame. His own Kin were outcast until they had hunted him down. His own brother, if he had one, would strike the blow. There would be no death dance. Instead his body would be carried to one of the demon places and left there for the demons to eat his spirit. His name would be deliberately forgotten. In the long history of the Kins only three such names were remembered, as a kind of warning. Da. Mott. Ziul.

The Kin saw no demon men at all, dead or alive, and to Mana's relief they met none of the marshmen who had done these killings. They had always seemed to be friends to the Kin, despite their strange ways, but now she didn't know how she could have faced them.

'We do not stay here,' said Tun. 'This place is full of spirits. They are demon spirits. No one does the death dance for them.'

So he led them rapidly on westward and then north until they reached a much less fertile area where there seemed to be no old lairs at all. This was like the country they had been used to, more open, with its Good Places scattered far apart and almost barren stretches between them, rock, sand, gravel, coarse sunbaked grass, and harsh, thorny bushes.

Here they all found that they were more comfortable in their own spirits. It was as if life on those north-facing slopes had been too easy, too rich, too generous. They were talking about this by the fire one evening when a strange idea came to Mana. She thought about it a little and then touched Noli's arm.

Noli looked at her and raised her eyebrows enquiringly.

'I have a thought, Noli,' Mana whispered. 'The demon men. They trouble me. Why do they do these things? I say this. Those other Places – they are too good. The women do everything. They forage, they set traps. They find food, plenty, plenty. What do the men do? They hunt, they catch deer, two, three – there are many deer, many. They cannot eat all these deer. They say in their hearts, *I have nothing to do – I hunt people*. Is this man stuff, Noli? Does Tun do this? Does Suth?'

Noli took the question seriously, and thought about it, frowning.

'Mana, I do not know,' she said. 'I know Tun does not do it. I know Suth does not do it. But men must do something. A man says in his heart, *Let people see me. Let them say, "This is a man"*.'

Yes, Mana thought, that was it. Men needed to stand by the fire and boast about what they'd done. In the Kin they usually boasted about hunting, because hunting was difficult, and a successful hunt was something to boast about. But suppose hunting had been easy, what else was there? There was fighting, man against man. If a man killed another man, he was the better man. And to back up his boast, he might take the dead man's head to prove it.

She fell asleep that night feeling very depressed and still thinking about it.

Was it so? Did it have to be so?

Oldtale

THE GAME OF PEBBLES

The Kins left Mambaga. They said, 'Let there be no fighting. Let Fat Pig go west, by Beehive Waterhole. Let Snake go east, by Yellowspring.'

The Kin of Fat Pig journeyed a morning. A pig stood in their way. The pig was fat.

They said, 'This is strange. This pig does not run from people. Why is this?'

Siku said, 'I, Siku, show you.'

She went forward. She was small. The pig lay down. Siku climbed on its back. The pig stood up. Siku said, 'Come.'

The pig went towards Yellowspring.

They said, 'Do we follow? The Kins said, 'Go by Beehive Waterhole.' We go to Yellowspring, they are angry. But see, this pig does not run from us. A child, a girl child, climbs on its back. She speaks thus to the elders. She is not afraid. Is this First One stuff? We follow this pig. We see.'

They went towards Yellowspring. By the west trail they went.

The Kin of Snake journeyed to Yellowspring by the north trail. They came near the place. A snake lay in their path, a great tree serpent, green and black.

They said, 'This is strange. Here are no trees. Here is this tree serpent. It does not hide from people. What is this?'

Farj said, 'I, Farj, show you.'

He went forward. The tree serpent raised itself. It coiled around him. Its head lay on his shoulder. It did not squeeze him.

He said, 'Wait.'

His Kin looked at him. They said, 'This is old Farj. He shakes. He mutters. But see, the snake coils round him. It does not squeeze him. Is this First One stuff? We wait.'

It was evening. The sun was low. The Kin of Fat Pig came near to Yellowspring. The pig stopped. Siku climbed from its back. The pig ran. It was gone. The people were thirsty. Their gourds were empty. They went to the spring. They came to it by the west trail.

So with the Kin of Snake. The tree serpent uncoiled itself from old Farj. It was gone. The people were thirsty, their gourds were empty. They went to the spring. They came to it by the north trail.

At Yellowspring the two Kins met. The men saw their enemies. They said, 'Now we fight. Here this war began. Here we end it.'

The women seized their arms. They said, 'This end is foolish, foolish. Do not fight.'

The men said, 'People were killed, blood fell from wounds, fierce blows were struck. All this must be paid for. A death for a death, a wound for a wound, a blow for a blow.'

Farj stood before his Kin. Black Antelope went behind him. No one saw him. He breathed upon Farj.

Farj cried in a strong voice, the voice of a leader, 'This is good. I, Farj, make the count for you. I count our deaths, our wounds, our blows. We are Snake. A snake coiled itself about me. It laid its head on my shoulder. This was a sign to you. I am chosen.'

The men said in their hearts, Fat Pig killed his son. He does not forget this. He seeks vengeance.

The women said in their hearts, One son lives still. He does not want his death. He seeks peace.

Both said, 'We saw this sign. Let Farj make the count for us.'

Siku stood before her Kin. Black Antelope went behind her. No one saw him. He breathed upon Siku.

Siku cried in a clear voice, the voice of a senior woman, 'This is good. I, Siku, make the count for you. I count our deaths, our wounds, our blows. We are Fat Pig. A pig stood in our way. It lay down. I climbed on its back. It led you to Yellowspring. This was a sign to you. I am chosen.'

The men said in their hearts, She is a child. She makes the count. We do not like her counting. We say, 'A child did it. It is nothing. Let us count again. Let a man count.'

The women said in their hearts, Her father is killed. Her mother died. She knows war, what it does.

Both said, 'We saw this sign. Let Siku make the count for us.'

Farj said, 'This is good. Now we make the count. We play the game of pebbles.'

Farj and Siku went to the spring. He was tall, he was proud, he was a leader. She was small, she was a child, a girl child. They put their hands in the water. They took out pebbles, black and yellow and grey. They emptied their gourds. They went to their Kins. They counted deaths, wounds and blows. For each death they put a black pebble into their gourd. For each wound a yellow pebble. For each blow a grey pebble.

They went to the spring. They knelt down. The Kins stood around them. No one moved. No one breathed. They watched Farj and Siku.

Farj said, 'I play black. I play five deaths.'

He put his hand in his gourd. He took out five black pebbles. He laid them down in a line.

Siku put her hand in her gourd. She took out black pebbles. She laid them down beside Farj's line. They were five.

Siku said, 'I play yellow. I play ten and three more wounds.'

She put her hand in her gourd. She took out ten and three more yellow pebbles. She laid them down in a line.

Farj put his hand in his gourd. He took out yellow pebbles. He laid them down beside Siku's line. They were ten and three more.

Farj said, 'We play grey. We play blows. We play by one and by one.'

Each put their hand in their gourd. By one and by one they laid down grey pebbles. Ten and ten and two more each laid down.

Farj said, 'My gourd is empty.'

Siku put her hand in her gourd. She took out a grey pebble. She laid it down.

She said, 'My gourd is empty.'

They rose. They faced each other. Farj was tall, he was proud, he was leader. Siku was small, a child, a girl child.

Farj said, 'Siku, strike me a blow.'

Siku struck Farj a blow. With a child's strength she struck him. He fell down. He howled. He said, 'Oh, oh! I am struck with a strong fist! Oh, oh!'

All saw. All heard. None spoke. They said in their hearts, What is this? What does it mean?

Farj lay on the ground, a big man, a leader. He howled.

Siku stood over him, a girl, a child. She shook her fist in the air, she triumphed.

A boy laughed. All heard him. They said in their hearts, This is laughter stuff. They all laughed. Their laughter was of this sort:

See, it is the time of rains. The air is thick, it is heavy. Men snarl, they pick fights. Women shrill, they say fierce words to their mates. Children whine, they are bad. Now, see, the rain comes, it goes. The air is light, the earth makes sweet smells. All are happy. All are kind.

Of such sort was the laughter of the two Kins.

Farj rose. He went to the spring. He took out a grey pebble. He laid it down. The lines were equal.

He said, 'All is paid. Now we go to Odutu, Odutu below the Mountain. We unswear the War Oath.'

CHAPTER TEN

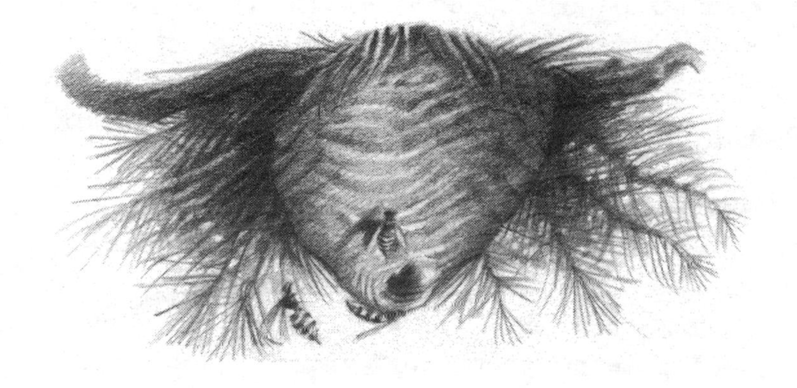

Mana was foraging. Not far off, Bodu and Nar were standing under a stinkfruit tree, waiting for Tinu to crawl far enough along a branch to knock the fruit down with her fishing stick. Ripe stinkfruit were very soft. If you tried to knock them down by throwing stones at them they would either burst when you hit them, or when they fell and hit the ground. So the trick was for somebody to climb the tree and knock them down one at a time, while someone else waited below to catch them.

The trick was trickier still this time, because there was a hornets' nest dangling among the ripest fruit, with the hornets coming and going. That was why Tinu was using her fishing stick, so that she didn't get too near. Several of them had kept their fishing sticks because they were useful for a lot of other things besides fishing.

Mana wasn't helping because she didn't much like stinkfruit. Some people thought they were delicious, though even they needed to hold their noses to eat them. She didn't much like hornets either, so she'd gone off to look for something else. The four of them had already been at the end of the line of foragers when Bodu had spotted the tree a little distance away, so Mana was now even further from the rest of the Kin.

Out on her own like this she went warily, with all her senses keyed, and paused to peer and sniff and listen each time she moved on. She heard the coming sounds when they were still far off – someone running, running desperately, with rasping gasps for air and unsteady tread. In a moment she knew the runner would pass close by.

Stranger comes. Hide. See him. Then choose. Does he see you?

That was a rule Mana had been taught from the moment she'd first known words. She ducked down and waited. The runner came into sight.

It was a demon woman.

Mana glimpsed only her head and shoulders over some bushes before she disappeared behind a larger clump. Beyond these was open ground. Mana waited for her to reappear. She could still hear the heavy, exhausted breathing, but the woman seemed to have stopped.

Now she moved on, and burst into sight, a tall, slim, dark woman whose unbalanced, floundering pace showed how near she was to the end of her strength. She crossed the open ground and disappeared.

Mana stayed where she was. She already knew what would happen next. How could she help? Run to the other foragers, beg them to come? There wasn't time – from the way the woman was running her pursuers must be close on her heels. Besides, most of the men were away, hunting. And anyway they wouldn't come – she'd heard the adults deciding some time ago that what happened between the marshmen and the demon people was no concern of the Kin.

All Mana could do was creep in under the bush and lie there with grief in her hear, and wait.

Wait.

The voice of Moonhawk seemed to whisper in her mind.

Almost at once she heard the cries of hunters hot on the trail, spread a little apart so as not to miss the signs if their prey turned aside, calling to tell each other as they ran that they had seen some fresh trace. And then their easy breathing, and the pad of their footsteps.

Now she saw them, four marshmen, the nearest going past in full view not ten paces from her, the others beyond, moving with the swift lope of huntsmen, smooth and confident, sure that their chase would soon be over. The second man from Mana was the one actually following the trail. Like the woman, he too appeared for a moment over the lower bushes and vanished behind the larger ones, but he came out far sooner into the open ground beyond. All four ran out of sight.

What had the woman done there? Why had she stopped, with the trackers so close? Rested? No. When a runner rests, gasping for air, the breathing slows, deepens. But hers had quickened, if anything.

She had been doing something, doing it in a desperate hurry . . .

Looking for a hiding place, then? Perhaps, but . . .

Anyway, Mana must get back to the others, so that they would know where she was. She crawled out, and with sickness in her mouth and in her spirit started off for the stinkfruit tree. Nar and Bidu were there, no longer looking up at Tinu but watching the chase. A man's voice shouted in the distance, behind her and to her left. Others joined in, savage and triumphant. The hunt was over. The woman would not have screamed or pleaded for life – she was a demon woman . . . strange that she had run at all . . . They'd found her hiding somewhere . . . A demon woman, lurking and hiding . . . ?

Mana remembered the demon women in the lairs, facing the Kin when they had come, expecting to be killed, but too proud to flinch or show fear.

But the whisper in her mind just now hadn't been memory. *Wait*, Moonhawk had said, telling her something as she lay there.

Mana turned and hurried back to where she'd lain, and then carefully on, picking the hardest ground, to the further side of the bushes. Here the soil was sandy, and she could see two sets of tracks, the woman's and the hunter's close beside them. Mana looked to her right. Both sets of tracks vanished at a patch of gravel and resumed. On the sand, neither set faltered. The woman must have stopped actually on the gravel.

Quickly Mana scanned the area for a way of reaching the place without leaving tracks of her own, but couldn't see one. The hunters would be coming back along the trail soon, looking for what they'd missed, so she ran to the gravel, bent, and lifted aside a low, sweeping branch of the largest bush.

The demon baby was lying there, awake, but not making a sound. He was a boy, about one moon old. He stared at Mana with large, vague eyes as she lifted him out and carried him back the way she'd come.

Nar and Bidu were watching her now from under the stinkfruit tree, but she didn't head for them at once. To confuse the marshmen, if she could, she set off toward another patch of bushes, deliberately leaving a few footprints, just as the woman had done. Once there she planned to try to make it look as if she was hiding among the bushes, and then go back to the foragers, leaving no trail. As she was nearing the bushes she heard Nar's warning shout.

'Mana! Marshmen come!'

She turned and ran for the tree. To her left she could see two of the marshmen loping back along the trail. They'd already reached the open area just before the gravel patch. They must have seen her, but the baby was hidden behind her body. In a moment they'd find her footprints and realize. Clutching the baby against her she raced on.

She was already gasping with the effort when she heard the marshmen's shout. Nar and Bodu were on the far side of the tree now, yelling to the foragers to come and help. She took a quick glance to her left, and saw the marshmen racing to cut her off. She was nearer than they were, but they were faster, and closing all the time.

She reached the tree only a few paces ahead of them. She'd run there without thought, because that was where her friends were, but it was only Nar and

Bodu, and Tinu up in the tree, against the angry marshmen. Nar was hurrying back to help. Bodu was waving frantically to the foragers. For a moment Mana thought of trying to throw the baby up to Tinu, but it was useless. She knew she hadn't the strength.

She turned and faced the marshmen. It was the only thing to do.

There were two of them. The other two were out of sight. They raised their fishing sticks. Mana could see and smell the fresh blood smearing the vicious points. 'No!' she shouted. 'You do not kill him! This is bad, bad!'

They glanced at each other and half lowered their fishing sticks, but Mana could see they were still furiously angry. She didn't recognize them, but she was sure they knew she was Kin, and they wouldn't want to hurt her if they could help it, because the Kin were allies and friends, and if it hadn't been for the Kin the marshpeople would still be hiding in the marshes and living in dread of the demon men.

One of them made the *Give* sound – ordering, not asking – and took a pace towards her, reaching out for the baby as he came. She was backing away when something fell from the tree, right at the man's feet, and burst.

He stopped in his tracks, startled. There was an instant's pause, and a cloud of furious hornets rose roaring round him.

Mana turned and ran. The sudden terror of the hornets gave her a burst of strength. Bodu and Nar were already racing ahead. Someone was running beside her. Tinu. She must have dropped from the tree the moment she'd dislodged the hornets' nest.

But Mana was gasping again. Her knees were starting to buckle. She couldn't see – there was blackness in her head. Her foot caught on something. She stumbled, started to fall, still clutching the baby, trying to twist herself so that she didn't fall on top of him . . .

A hard arm caught her and held her up. A man's voice grunted. Tor. Then he grunted again on a different note, startled. He'd seen the demon baby.

'What happens?' said several voices together. Mana was unable to speak. Her lungs were dragging the air raspingly in through her throat, her heart was slamming against her ribcage, her head was full of the red darkness. She heard Nar starting to explain what he'd seen – not everything, but enough . . .

By the time she had recovered enough to look around more than half the foragers had joined the group and the rest were still gathering. Each newcomer needed to be told the story afresh. Mana stood in the middle of them with her head bowed over the baby, not daring to look at their faces. She could tell from the voices that no one was glad of what she'd done. What she heard was doubt, disapproval, anxiety, bewilderment.

There were throbbing patches of pain in her left shoulder and thigh. Hornet stings. She hadn't felt them at the time.

Now she sensed a movement around her, looked, and saw that the four marshmen were approaching and the Kin were grouping to face them. She went and stood behind Bodu, looking over her shoulder but keeping the baby out of sight. All four marshmen were there now. The two in front walked normally, but the third was helping the fourth to hobble along. He was obviously in great pain.

The wound in Tun's arm had gone bad for a while, and was still not well, so he'd decided to rest it and not go hunting. Now he gestured to Tor and walked forward with him to greet the marshmen. It looked for a moment as if they were going to shove him aside, but he stood his ground with his usual confidence and their leader brusquely returned the greeting.

Immediately he began to grunt and gesture. His hair bushed out. He shook his stick with a stabbing motion, beckoned with his head to the other three and once more started to stride past Tun.

Tun moved to bar his way. His hair also bushed, but only partly, showing he meant business but didn't want a fight. The marshman put up a hand to thrust him aside but Tun caught him by the wrist with his good arm and drew him close, staring down into his eyes, unblinking.

The second marshman hesitated, and raised his stick. The Kin gave a shout and surged forward. Though they were almost all women, these weren't the fawning, servile women the marshmen were used to. They backed off and lowered their sticks. Tun let go of the leader's wrist, and he too took a pace back. His hair settled, and Tun's did the same.

'This is good,' he said calmly. 'We make fire. We eat. We talk. Nar, go find the hunters. They went that way. Say to them, *Come*.'

He made the *Come* sound to the marshmen and

without looking to see if they were following led the way towards a group of shade trees.

While most of the women made fire and prepared a meal, Chogi and Bodu pounded garri leaves and mixed them with a little water to make a paste, which they daubed onto the hornet stings. Though Mana and Tinu had both been stung they dealt with the marshman first, because he was much the worst hurt. The garri paste didn't cure the pain, but numbed it enough to make it bearable.

By the time Chogi reached Mana the demon baby was at last beginning to whimper a little, and make sucking movements with his lips.

'He is hungry,' said Chogi crossly. 'Mana, this is stupid. You cannot feed him. You have no milk. He dies.'

'Chogi is right,' said Zara. 'He is a demon baby. One day he is a man. Then he is a demon man. He is not Kin. Let him die now. Give him to the marshmen. This is best.'

'The marshmen are friends,' said Yova. 'Do we make them enemies? This is not good. Give them the baby.'

'I say no,' said Bodu. 'The baby dies – he dies. This is one thing. We give him to the marshmen – we say, *Take him. Kill him*. This is another thing. I cannot do this.'

'Bodu, this is stupid,' said Zara. 'This *one thing, other thing*. They are the same. The baby is dead. Do you say to him, *Live*, Bodu? You have milk. Do you give it to the demon baby?'

By now Mana was weeping. She looked at Bodu through her tears. The round, cheerful face was frowning. Bodu had been eating well for more than a moon now, and she probably had milk to spare, but nothing like enough for two babies. And the second one a demon baby?

Mana could see her struggling with Zara's question, and that she couldn't quite bring herself to say yes. It was too much to ask.

There seemed to be only one thing for Mana to do, though it was worse than anything she could have imagined. She stood up.

'I take this from you,' she croaked. 'It is my stuff. I go away. I go far and far. The baby dies. This is my stuff also.'

A voice shouted from behind the women. Ko. Mana hadn't realized he'd been listening.

'Mana, I come with you. Your stuff is my stuff. I, Ko, say this.'

Through a fresh upwelling of tears she heard Tinu's quiet mumble.

'Tinu comes, I come,' said Nar. Mana could hear that he had willed himself to say it.

'Suth is hunting,' said Bodu slowly. 'I know in my heart he says, *We go with Mana*.'

'This is stupid, stupid!' cried Zara. 'Nar, my son, you do not go! This is not your stuff!'

'Wait,' said a voice.

Silence fell. Everyone rose from whatever they'd been doing and turned and stared at Noli. She had been sitting against a tree trunk, feeding Amola, but the baby had let go of the nipple and was waiting like the rest of them, as if she too had recognized the voice of Moonhawk.

After a long pause the voice came again, no more

than a whisper but seeming to fill the shadowed space beneath the trees and breathe far out across the sunlit plain beyond.

'His name is Okern.'

There was an astonished gasp from every mouth, and then another silence. There was always one person in each Kin to whom their First One came, and that person chose names for newborn babies. So Noli had named Ogad, as well as her own Amola, and long ago she'd also named Tor, after the Moonhawks had rescued him and accepted him into the Kin. She had done this in her own voice, not Moonhawk's.

But it wasn't only that this time she had spoken with Moonhawk's voice. It was the name she'd chosen. The names of babies started either with an O sound, if it was a boy, or an A sound, if it was a girl. Then, when they stopped being babies and became small ones, these sounds were dropped. Mana herself had once been Amana, and Tan had been Otan. When the time came Ogad would become Gad, and Amola would become Mola. And Okern would become Kern.

Names were repeated. They had to be. There weren't that many possible names to go round. There must have been many Manas before Mana. Some she knew about and some she didn't. But usually there was a gap of several generations. Mana had never heard of a name being repeated like this, almost at once, when they could all remember a Kern they had known and loved – a Kern who had then been horribly killed, and one of whose killers might have been the father of the baby who now bore his name.

At last Tun rose from where he had been squatting beside the marshmen, treating them as honoured guests.

'Moonhawk spoke,' he said solemnly. 'The boy is Okern. He is Moonhawk. His blood is our blood. This is good. Now I tell the marshmen this. We leave these places. We take the boy. We go far and far. They do not see us again.'

He turned back to the marshmen. Mana stood where she was, too bewildered to think, too blinded with tears to see. The baby was struggling now, and on the verge of crying. Somebody touched Mana's arm.

'Mana, give him to me,' whispered Bodu. 'I have milk. He lives.'

Oldtale

THE UNSWEARING

The First Ones spoke to their Kins. They said, 'Go now to Odutu, Odutu below the Mountain. Snake and Fat Pig go there. They unswear the War Oath. See this. Let it be done before you all. Then feast.'

The Kins hunted. They foraged. The First Ones drove game to the men. They caused trees to bear nuts out of season. They ripened the berries on the bushes and the seed in the grasses. They swelled the rich roots.

The Kins journeyed to Odutu. Their gourds were heavy.

The men of Snake stood before them, and the men of Fat Pig. By two and by two they went to the rock, one from each Kin. They laid their hands upon the rock. They unswore the War Oath.

The Kins rejoiced. They gathered fuel. They built great fires. They roasted flesh, they baked seed paste, they popped nuts. They said, 'Come, now we feast. The war is ended.'

But the men of Fat Pig said, 'It is not enough. Shame is still on us. We have killed a woman. We killed first.'

They put Mott in front of them. They took his digging stick from him. They said to the men of Snake, 'Kill him.'

But the men of Snake said, 'Not so. Our shame is greater. Rage was in Mott's heart. He did not see, he did not think, he struck. Ziul chose. He saw Dipu. He said in his heart, I kill a woman. It is vengeance for Meena.'

They put Ziul in front of them. They took his digging stick from him. They said to the men of Fat Pig, 'Kill him.'

Fat Pig and Snake hid in long grasses. They saw this. They went to Black Antelope. They said, 'Let there be no more deaths.'

Black Antelope put his nostrils to theirs. He breathed out. He gave back their powers.

Fat Pig and Snake made themselves invisible. They went to their Kins. No one saw them. Fat Pig hid Mott. Snake hid Ziul. Their hiding was of this sort:

See, this mountain. A cloud lies upon it. A man climbs. He is in the cloud. It swirls all about him, it is cold, water covers his skin. He cannot see the trail. He is lost.

Such was the hiding of Mott and Ziul. Then Fat Pig and Snake carried them far and far. They were not seen again.

Now the Kins feasted. They were happy.

The First Ones went back to the Mountain, the

Mountain above Odutu. They too feasted and were happy.

But Black Antelope said to Snake and Fat Pig, 'Let no stoneweed grow in the Places of your two Kins.'

They made it so. It is so to this day.

CHAPTER ELEVEN

Several moons later Mana was watching Okern trying to catch Amola. This was difficult for him, as he could only roll, while Amola could already crawl. She was busy with Amola stuff – mostly spotting something that interested her, crawling to get it, and then testing whether it tasted good – so she had no idea what Okern was up to. But he knew.

Now he tried again. He'd almost got her last time, before she'd crawled away to check out a dead leaf. He'd been rolling when she'd moved off, and hadn't seen her go, but she wasn't there when he next looked. Mana saw him frown and gaze around, turning his neat, dark head in little jerks, like the movements of an insect.

Ah, there she was. Patiently he lined himself up for another roll. He hadn't found how to roll in straight lines, so he approached his target in a series of curves, often going in quite the wrong direction before he stopped to check, and then having to line himself up again. He was an extremely determined baby.

This is man stuff, thought Mana, smiling. He has this idea in his head. He does not let it go. This is how men are.

Then a chill thought struck her. It was a new version of an old thought, one that had lived in the back of her mind ever since the Kin had accepted Okern as one of themselves. Sometimes, as now, it came creeping out to trouble her.

Or is it demon man stuff? Does Okern hunt Amola? One day he would be a man. What kind of a man would he be? A savage killer, like his father? Or strong and gentle like Kern, whose name he bore?

He was a very good baby. Even Chogi said so – at least she said, 'For a boy, good. A girl is better.' He hardly ever cried, and then quietly, though often he had to wait for food while Bodu and Noli made sure their own babies had enough. Mana had to make up by chewing food for him and spitting it into his mouth. At first he used to spit it straight back, but he got used to it, and she found things he seemed to enjoy, and that didn't make his bowels run. She liked to feed him herself, because it was a way of telling him he was hers. From early on he seemed to have decided that she was his, and came gladly to her as soon as one of the other mothers had finished giving him milk.

A prayer formed in her mind. She whispered it under her breath.

Moonhawk, I praise.
Moonhawk, I thank.

See Okern, Moonhawk.
You gave this name to him.
Let him be Moonhawk, like Kern.
Let him not be demon.
I, Mana, ask.

She sighed and looked around. This was a new camp, right at the furthest end of the northern slope of the immense valley. From where she sat Mana could see, rimming the horizon many days' journey to the south, the range of hills they had crossed when they had left the marshes. But they had come here by a far less direct route, for Okern's sake keeping well clear of the southern slope, which the returned marshmen were now reclaiming as their own.

Once or twice, as they had slowly explored this new territory, they had glimpsed one of the frightened little black women, but no men. Apart from that, nobody seemed to live here at all.

It was strange. Though nothing like as rich as the southern slope, these were still good places. This camp, for instance. It was a fine camp, with two caves and a stream nearby. Why was there no sign of anyone using it?

'The small people had these Places,' Chogi had suggested. 'They were theirs. The demon men came. They killed the men. They took the women. They are all gone.'

It was as good an explanation as anyone could think of.

The camp was as far as they had yet explored, and it looked as if they wouldn't be able to go much further. Ahead lay a chain of real mountains, capped with snow. As always, when they first settled at a new camp, Tun had sent scouting parties out to look for possible dangers and good food areas. The mothers, including Mana, had stayed with their babies to forage nearby, gather fuel and prepare for the evening meal.

The sun was going down, all the other scouts were back and the meal was ready before Suth and Tor returned. Though they both seemed well, Suth wouldn't talk about where they'd been. He was strangely grave and silent, and Tor kept shaking his head in a troubled way.

When they had finished eating, the leaders of each scouting party stood up and told everyone where they'd been and what they'd found. Suth was the youngest, so he came last.

'I, Suth, speak,' he said. 'I went with Tor. We went this way . . .' He pointed directly towards the mountains and went on, describing everything of interest to the Kin, areas of food plants, a place with the right sort of ants' nests, deer tracks, another stream, and so on.

'Now we found a path,' he said. 'It was a people path. We followed it. We were careful, careful. No one came, no one went. We came to mountains. The path went up. We climbed far. There were many trees. They stopped. We came to a valley. It was in the mountains. There we found a thing. I do not tell you now – I do not have words. Tomorrow you see it. Noli comes. It is First One stuff.'

That was all he would say, but instead of returning to his place among the men he beckoned to Noli and took her aside to the edge of the firelight. They settled down and sat talking in low voices for a long while. When Noli came back to the fire she looked puzzled and anxious.

They left as soon as they were ready next morning and travelled east along the route that Suth had described. They weren't exploring, as he and Tor had been, so they made good time and reached the path he'd told them about well before midday.

It was a well-worn path, broad enough for two people walking side by side, though there were signs that it hadn't been recently used. If they'd turned right they would have been heading for the southern side of the valley, but they went the other way, directly towards the mountains.

Over the past few moons Mana had often seen those white peaks, unreachably far away. Now she was looking at a single one, so close that it seemed to tower above her.

The path began to climb, twisting to and fro. Still climbing, it entered an area of woodland – not the dense, tangled, steaming forest that grew along the river in the New Good Places, but cool and sweet smelling, with open glades among the trees.

Net and Tor were scouting ahead, with Tun and Suth leading the main party. Mana, Noli and the rest of Suth's 'family' were close behind, with the rest of the Kin spreading down the path. Sometimes after they'd rounded a bend Mana could look down and see between the tree trunks the tail-enders still toiling up the previous stretch.

All at once Noli halted, and froze. The others

jostled to a halt behind her. Suth and Tun heard the slight commotion and turned to see what was happening.

'Goma is here,' said Noli quietly.

They stared at her, then looked at each other, bewildered. Goma was one of the Porcupines, with whom the Kin used to share the New Good Places. She'd been a special friend of Noli's, because she was the one to whom their own First One, Porcupine, came. But apart from Noli's mate, Tor, who was Porcupine, the Kin had seen nothing of them since they'd split up to travel either side of the river as they'd all journeyed north to escape the drought that was killing the New Good Places. How could Goma be here, after all this time?

'Ko,' said Noli in the same quiet voice. 'Run. Find Tor. Bring him.'

Ko raced off. Noli waited, gazing up the slope above the path.

'She comes,' she said. 'Others are with her.'

She called the Porcupines' *I come* sound and started to scramble up. Before she'd gone far, someone stole out of the trees higher up, peered for a moment, gave a cry of joy and came slithering and bounding down. She flung her arms round Noli and they hugged each other, laughing and crying. Only when they stood apart and gazed at each other could Mana see that this really was Goma.

By then three other women had appeared. Mana recognized two of them as Porcupines. They looked far more scared and uncertain than Goma, until they recognized that the people on the path were their old friends, the Kin, and came down and greeted them.

Then Net, Tor and Ko came hurrying down the path, and there were yet more greetings and cries of gladness, but Mana didn't take much part in them because she was still watching Noli and Goma. She saw Goma admire Amola, and realized at the same moment that Goma's little son wasn't with her. She heard Noli's questioning grunt. Goma's face turned sorrowful and Noli started to weep. He was dead, Mana realized, and wept too.

After that the two women stood for a little while, touching and stroking each other and making murmuring sounds, before they came down and joined the others on the path.

'What happens to Goma?' Noli said as they climbed on. 'I do not know. I feel bad times. I feel sadness. I feel fear, blood, another sadness. My thought is this. The Porcupines come round the marsh. They find little food. Some die. Men come. They fight the Porcupine men. They kill them. They take women, Goma too. They bring her to this place. She is afraid, afraid. It is not the men she fears. They go. They do not come back. These women are with her. They run away. We find them. Still she is afraid. I feel her fear. I feel the thing she fears. It is demon stuff, bad, bad. Suth says this also.'

They climbed on, cautiously now, though they had still seen no sign of anyone using the path for a long while. Then the slope eased and they came out into a long, narrow clearing. It was the bottom of a valley between two steep spurs of the mountain. Trees clung to the slopes on either side, with dark cliffs above them. A thin stream rippled along the floor of the valley. Some way on, on the left side, the cliff ran sheer down to the clearing. Against it lay a low, treeless mound.

They stopped at the edge of the wood and stood staring. Mana could see no sign of danger, but she could sense something. It was as if the air was full of whispering voices that she couldn't quite hear, while invisible hands were fingering her skin, too softly for her to feel. She shuddered and looked at Okern, but he was fast aleep in the sling Tinu had made for him. His small face was untroubled.

Noli turned to Yova. She was breathing deeply, as she sometimes did just before Moonhawk came to her, but there was no froth on her lips, and she seemed in full control of her own body.

'Yova, take Amola,' she said. 'This is my stuff. It is Goma's stuff. We go first.'

Goma was already beside her, looking anxious and frightened, but she took Noli's hand and together they led the way on. The Kin followed, keeping close together, but the three women who had been with Goma in the wood refused to come any further.

The path ran straight towards the mound, which lay on the far side of a low rise, so that they saw only the upper half of it until they reached the top of the rise. By then they were only a few tens of paces from it, so that its meaning burst suddenly upon them.

Just in front of them two large boulders stood either side of the path, forming an entrance. On top of each of them was a human skull. Rings of skulls circled their bases. Beyond the boulders two lines of posts, topped with skulls, led down to the mound. More posts and skulls ringed the mound. Where the path reached the mound there was a low slab of rock. Behind it, in the mound itself, was a dark opening.

Noli paused, but not from uncertainty. She seemed to be waiting for something. She looked at Goma, who was holding herself more confidently now. They nodded, as if one of them had spoken.

'Moonhawk is here,' said Noli, still quietly. 'Porcupine also. He slept. Now he wakes.'

The two women, still holding hands, walked on towards the mound. The Kin followed, spreading out into a line on either side of the path, but Suth and Tun stayed on it, and Mana followed them down.

When Noli and Goma were about ten and ten paces from the slab a man came out of the opening behind it. He was old. His hair was white, his eyes bloodshot and gummy, and he used a staff to walk with, though he held himself as straight as a young man. Mana didn't need the colour of his skin, or the skulls that dangled from his belt, to tell her that this was a demon man. She would have known by the way he moved, by the look on his face, by the feel of his presence. Though he was old and feeble, he seemed far more terrible than any of the savage young hunters they had fought in the marshes.

The red-rimmed eyes stared at the newcomers. The man raised his staff and gave a harsh, croaking cry, which echoed from the cliff above him.

He waited for the echo to die, and cried again, and then again. Each time the cliff repeated the sound. Mana's stomach felt cold inside her. The echoes sounded to her like more than echoes. They sounded like the demon speaking from the rock.

The Kin murmured uneasily. She guessed they were

having the same thought, the same dread. Then Okern stirred against her side. She looked down and saw that he had woken and was gazing around with a puzzled frown.

Had the demon spoken to him too? Specially to him? Called to him?

No!

Now Mana knew what she must do, why she was here. She moved forward, and Ko started to come with her.

'Wait,' she whispered. 'This is my stuff. It is good.'

She walked steadily forward, past Tun and Suth, past Noli and Goma, and up to the slab. The mad old eyes stared furiously at her, then fell on Okern.

The man's face changed completely. His mouth opened in a horrible grin, showing a few yellow teeth. He made a puffing sound and started to hobble round the slab.

Mana waited, standing her ground, until he stood facing her.

'No, you do not have him,' she said firmly.

'Do not have him,' whispered the cliff.

The old man poked his head forward at her and made an angry gesture towards the slab – *Put the boy there.*

'No,' said Mana again, and the cliff answered, 'No.'

The man took a tottering pace towards her, reaching out an arm to grab at Okern. Mana snatched him away. She was filled with sudden fury, fury at this fearsome old man, and all the demon men, and what they were – what they had allowed themselves to become. It had been their choice. The demon was theirs. They had chosen it.

'No!' she yelled. 'He is not yours! He is mine! He is Moonhawk!'

'Moonhawk,' shouted the cliff.

The old man staggered. It was as if the echo itself had struck him a violent buffet. He clutched at his staff with both hands, fighting for balance. His mouth gaped. A grating retch rasped through his throat. He staggered again, as if another blow had struck him, and toppled forward at Mana's feet.

She stayed where she was, staring down at him, clutching Okern to her side, until Tun came forward, bent, and rolled the old man onto his back.

'He is dead,' he announced.

'Dead,' agreed the cliff, matter-of-factly.

Moving and speaking quietly so as not to wake the echo they carried the body into the hole in the mound. They dragged out some strange stuff they found in there – old fighting sticks, horns of antelope, twisted bits of tree root, and bundles of dried grass tied into curious shapes. Almost everything had at least one skull lashed to it.

They laid the skulls aside and piled everything else into the entrance to the hole. Again setting the skulls aside they heaved up the ring of poles and the two lines beside the path and added them to the pile. They then set fire to it.

At first Mana took no part in any of this, but sat cradling Okern in her arms, touching, stroking, murmuring softly to him, as she had so often seen the Porcupine mothers doing with their babies. Slowly she realized that something had changed inside her.

Her wound was healed, the wound in her spirit that she had given herself when she had killed the demon man in the marsh. Clean spirit had grown over the place, leaving no scar. It was finding Okern that had healed her – saving him from the marshmen, mothering him and caring for him and watching him begin to grow into a life of his own, and now, finally, bringing him here and facing the old demon man, and the demon itself, and defeating them.

She had killed a man. He had been bad, bad, but he had been people.

But she had saved a man, and not just his life. If the Kin had never fought the demon men, or if the demon men had won that war, Okern would still have been born, but nameless. And he would have grown to manhood learning to be a demon man like his father, so that was what he would have become, a hunter of people, a savage killer of men. Now, perhaps, he would grow up not like that.

Mana had long had a secret fear that Okern's real father had been the very man she had killed. Now, though she would never know, she found herself hoping it might be so.

This, she thought, was what Moonhawk must have meant when she'd told her to wait.

After a while Noli came to feed Okern, so Mana passed him over and went to help the others carry the skulls and pile them up well away from the mound. They were just finishing when Noli came to give Okern back. As soon as Mana took him he fitted himself snugly against her, sighed and fell asleep.

'Noli,' she said, 'I thank. And I say this. My trouble is gone. I am well.'

'This is good,' said Noli. 'Now we do the death dance. Mana, you dance with the women.'

So Mana joined the line on one side of the pile of skulls, and stamped out the dance, and sang the long wavering wail that would free any spirits that were left in this demon-haunted valley and allow them to go wherever they were meant to by whatever First Ones had been theirs. Even at this distance their voices roused the echo in the cliff, so that it seemed to be taking part in the ritual.

By the time they'd finished it was almost nightfall. They had brought enough to eat at midday, but they had neither foraged nor hunted, and there was little left. They wouldn't take any food from this demon-infected place, let alone sleep here, so they made their way back down through the wood in the dark to a stream a little below it. There they drank, and laired for the night.

Mana slept with Okern close beside her, sheltering him with her body, warming him with her warmth, and did not dream at all.

Several more moons later the Kin was once again at Two Caves. Most of the Good Places on these northern slopes now had names of their own. Not long ago Mana had heard Ko telling Tan a wonderful story about why Snakeskin Hill was called that. It wasn't the real reason, it was just something Ko had dreamed up. Ko was always full of dreams.

By now Amola could stand, and was starting to

walk, while Okern was crawling so fast and with such determination that Mana needed to keep an eye on him all the time he wasn't asleep. He seemed to have no sense of fear or danger.

Noli and Mana were alone at the camp. Noli had stayed to soak and pound a blueroot she'd found, so that it would be ready for the Big Moon feast next night – a serious feast, because tomorrow would be Nar's last day as a child. The morning after, he would have the first man scars cut in his cheeks, and become a man, and he and Tinu could then be mates.

Mana was there to keep Noli company, something she specially needed just now because Tor had been away so long. He and Goma had gone to make their way south and see if they could find any more of the Porcupines lingering around the edges of the marsh. This was their second expedition. The first time they'd found a man and a woman, mates, and their two children, who'd somehow managed to survive.

Noli was sure there must be more. Mana didn't really understand why she said so – it was First One stuff. When Mana had confronted the old demon man at the Place that was not Spoken of, Noli said Porcupine had been there. The demon men had brought Goma and the other women to the valley to look after the old man, but the demon in the cliff had been too strong for Porcupine, because all his people were scattered in different places. But he was still around, and with Moonhawk to help him he had come back. He couldn't have done that, Mana said, if everyone had been dead except Goma and the other two women.

So now Mana was helping with the blueroot, and

Amola was also helping after her fashion, pounding a bit of rind with a stone Noli had given her. Okern had to have a stone too, of course, but he didn't care what he pounded, provided he could do it good and hard.

Noli paused in her work to regather the blueroot on the flat stone she was using as a mortar. Amola heard the break in the steady rhythm of pounding and looked up. Her lips moved. Mana could see she was trying to ask something. Noli laughed delightedly.

'Mana, Amola has words!' she cried. 'She says, *Ma?* She asks, *Mother, why do you stop?* Oh, she has words, Mana, she has words!'

This was a question the Kin had discussed endlessly from the moment Amola had been born, but more especially since she'd stopped being a wrinkled little blob of a baby and got a face of her own. Then it became easy to see that she was like Tor in some ways, with his fine bones and high cheeks, but had Noli's mouth and chin, while her skin colour was in between theirs. So would Amola be like Noli, and have words, or be like Tor, and have none, or be somewhere in between, with just a few?

Noli, after that single syllable, was certain of the answer.

Mana laughed with her, happy in her delight. Then her eye fell on Okern, who had taken his stone to the cave and was hammering away at the cliff beside it. He would hammer the whole hill away if he could, she thought. Yes, and he could do that before he could speak to me. He can never say *Ma* to me. She bowed her head, biting her lip.

'Mana, you are sad,' said Noli. 'Why is this?'

'Okern does not have words,' said Mana.

'He is clever. He is strong. He is brave. He is beautiful,' said Noli.

'Noli, this is true,' said Mana. She was in fact very proud of Okern's good looks. But she shook her head again.

'Hear me, Noli,' she said hesitantly, thinking it through as she spoke. 'Say in your heart, *Okern has words*. Now say this. *One day Okern is a small one. Then his name is Kern. He understands little. He gets big, he is a boy. Now he understands some things. Now Mana says to him, 'Kern, I am not your true mother. She is dead. She did such and such things. Your father is dead. He did such and such things.'* (Noli, I do not say, *Your mother was a demon woman. Your father was a demon man.*) *Then Mana says, 'I found you. Moonhawk took you in. Now, Kern, choose. Which are you? Are you like your father and mother? Are you like me, Moonhawk? Think, Kern. Then choose.'*

'Noli, I can never say this to him. He can never choose. He does not have words.'

Noli put down her stone, and came and squatted beside her and took her hand.

'Mana,' she said. 'Okern is people. One day he chooses. Now, see Goma. She is good, good. She says in her heart, *This is good. I do it. This is bad. I do not do it.* She does not need words for this. She is people.

'Mana, *good* is a word. *Bad* is a word. But they are more, more. They are . . . I do not know what they are, but they are people stuff.'

Mana looked at Okern. Yes, he was people, she thought. And Noli was right. She remembered the sudden rage that had surged through her at the Place that was not Spoken of, at the thought that the demon men had chosen to be what they were. That rage had come from Moonhawk, she thought. It was what had allowed her to stand up to the old demon man, and shout defiance to his face.

Yes, good or bad – whether he learnt the truth about his own parents or not – Okern would one day choose.

That was people stuff.